Artania III: Dragon Sky

Arthania III: Dragon Sky

Artania III

Dragon Sky

Laurie Woodward

Acknowledgements

This book would not have been possible without the support of several friends and family. First, I would like to thank Next Chapter, and its CEO, Miika Hannila, for taking a chance on me. It is an honor and privilege to be part of a publishing company that respects and supports its authors. I'd also like to thank my critique group of Bart Gardner, Debra Davis Hinkle, Carter Pitman, Destry Ramey, Christine Taylor, and Susan Tuttle. For close to a decade, you have helped to mold me into a better writer. Very special thanks go out to Scott Parsons who spent weeks reading the novel, making notes, and sharing ideas.

I am so grateful to my father, Tom Woodward, for his generosity in carving out time and funding our family trip to Italy. You'll never know how many exciting plot ideas came out of that vacation. Not only did I spend a glorious month with my family, but I was also able to view great art up close.

Once again, I would like to acknowledge my students both present and past. Your beautiful hearts continue to give my life meaning while inspiring me daily to see the true artist in all of us. Also, to my fellow educators and school personnel: your hard work and dedication makes me proud to call myself an educator. Your extraordinary gifts often go unsung but know that children are finding the magic inside themselves because of what you do.

Most of all to my son and daughter: Nicholas and Jessica. All your lives, you have patiently waited while I scribbled away at my notepad or bent over the computer keys. Sometimes I was so lost in the dream that you might have had to call me twice to bring me back to reality. But neither of you ever complained. I think you always understood that when I got a distant look in my eye, I was not forgetting you. I was just dreaming of fantastical worlds. But these worlds could never have taken shape without the love we share. And finally, to my mother, Claudia Stuart. So young when I was born, you hardly ever had a childhood. Yet you still endeavored to do the best you could. Like the skateboarding Gwen, you have always modeled strength for me. For this, I am eternally grateful.

For Bernice Stuart who always saw the beauty within.

Chapter 1

Alex gripped his skateboard even tighter and tried not to think of how high the ramp was. So what if it was fourteen feet straight down? As dorky as his gear looked, with elbow and knee pads, a helmet and even wrist guards, at least he was protected. All Mom's idea but he didn't care what other kids thought. In 6th grade he'd almost lost her and now he'd wear an elephant costume if it meant keeping her weak heart from worrying.

Anyhow, he'd skated in rocky caverns with slime-covered monsters in hot pursuit and lived to tell the tale. This was just Santa Barbara. Okay, it was the Volcom Games with hundreds of people watching and he'd only been skating vert for nine months. But still his life wasn't in danger.

He hoped.

He glanced at the audience below and saw his skateboarding buds, Jose, Zach, and Gwen, give him a thumbs-up. Not easy acts to follow. They'd each wowed the crowd with backside airs, fakies, and real clean kick flips. Alex raised three fingers for a quick wave wondering if his best friend had been able to make it, but Bartholomew's white suit was nowhere to be seen.

"And next we have thirteen-year-old Alexander Devinci in his first competition. Give it up for the Southern Cal Kid."

The crowd cheered.

Heart pounding, Alex stepped up to the ledge. He tried not to look down as he set the board's tail over the coping. When he saw the dizzying height, he took a deep breath and forced himself to anchor the wheels in place with his back foot. Closing his eyes, he imagined that he was safe at home standing in front of his easel, paintbrush about to create wonder.

And he was there. Ready.

Like a furious hand slapping paint on canvas he stomped his front foot and dropped over the vert wall. Wind whooshed past his face causing the few curls that had escaped the helmet to whip and tickle the nape of his neck. His eyes narrowed as his wheels rolled ever faster.

He hit the bottom of the ramp ready to scale the other side when the doubts began.

Were his feet in line with the bolts on deck? He'd fallen buko times over the summer because of bad foot placement, ripping five pair of jeans, scraping his knees and arms, and even dislocating his shoulder. Mom wasn't too thrilled about that but since he'd called Dad to take him to the hospital she only had to deal with it after the joint was back in place.

The glare of summer sun on the vertical blinded him for a moment. Blinking, Alex shifted his weight and tried to remember all the tips Gwen had given him about rolling up the transition. On the ascent, Alex tried to gauge his speed. Was he going fast enough for the backside ollie he planned to do over the rail?

"Go Alex, rip it!" Gwen cried from the crowd.

With a quick nod, Alex aimed his board at the sky. He'd lay it down just like Tony Hawk or Christian Hosoi.

"This Santa Barbara kid is holding his own," the commentator announced over the loudspeaker.

Higher Alex rolled, aiming straight for the lip. Everything was perfect.

He looked up. There, amongst the wispy clouds he saw something red shimmering. No, it was a sparkle. A glistening reflection off the underbody of a creature.

The creature opened its long snout in a plaintive wail.

Dragons over Santa Barbara? What the?

And that's when he fell.

3

Chapter 2

Bartholomew Borax III was watching the games a quarter mile away from the safety of the pier when Alex started his run. He squirted a dollop of hand sanitizer into his palm and rubbed it in. Shielding his eyes with one hand, he squinted. The two-story ramp set up on the beach next to the cement boardwalk was bordered by swaying palm trees and had a couple thousand smiling spectators crowded around. Still he could pick Alex out of a crowd from much further away. Wild curls sticking out from under a day-glow orange helmet were hard to miss.

The blonde boy wished he could stand closer for a better view but with all that sand he might get dirty. Not that *he* cared, well maybe a bit, but he knew all too well what the slightest smudge on his sleeve would do to his mother. And since she only chose shades of white for all his clothes, Bartholomew had learned long ago to avoid any places that might stain his brilliantly bleached wardrobe.

Not that he blamed her, exactly. Hygenette Borax hadn't had it easy. Raising a boy alone is challenging in the best circumstances. But having your husband drown in a mud puddle right outside your front door when you're pregnant with your only child would be enough to drive anyone over the edge.

Bartholomew often wondered how life would be different if Father were alive. He'd heard that back then they'd had real plants and grass in the yard instead of plastic ones and astro turf. Supposedly Mother used to go out to all sorts of places without her present arsenal of disinfecting wipes and hand sanitizer. She'd even strolled in parks without having to rush back to their limo and leap into the bathtub in the back. But after Bartholomew's father died, it slowly changed until eventually their house became a fortress of clean.

With her son trapped inside of it.

So, Bartholomew was forced to make up stories just so to get away. After telling Mother one of the hundred or so sneak-out lies he used, he stole out the back and rushed over to see Alex and the others compete at the beach.

Bartholomew relaxed into a sigh. *Ahh.* Two whole hours without Mother's ever watchful eyes or the constant application of germicidal spray. Two hours without a maid running a feather duster over the already hospital clean shelves or Mother crying filth when a pencil smudged his forearm. Two hours to breathe in air that smelled nothing like bleach.

Bartholomew was in the middle of a resounding cheer for Alex when the cloud took shape. He thought it was his imagination at first but as colors changed he realized that it was happening.

Again.

The visions began right after he turned eleven; strange glimpses of painted things that seemed to want something from him. He dismissed them all at first; sure, that loneliness was driving him a bit crazy. But then, in 6th grade he and Alex discovered the truth: an enchanted race existed somewhere beyond.

The peculiar visions initially terrified him and angered Alex; they'd even accused one another of infecting or hypnotizing the other. But over time they realized that these mysterious mirages were real.

And one day they stepped into a painting and ended up in a magical world where all art was alive. Wild.

In Artania he discovered something amazing. He and Alex were Deliverers, those whose art guarded sleepers everywhere from an evil race of beings. These dream-invaders, the Shadow Swine, constructing nightmares that turned humans away from true art. The Prophecy said that only Alex and Bartholomew could save Artania from these beasts and safeguard children's dreams on Earth.

The boys had battled long and hard on two journeys into that wondrous land. Because of them, Artania remained a kaleidoscopic world.

Only Gwen and Alex knew the truth. There were times when Bartholomew had almost told others but if he'd tried to explain that he'd been into another dimension where giant sculptures talked with Mona Lisa and Egyptian furniture fought monsters; people would think he was absolutely certifiable. So, he kept quiet.

Seventh grade had come and gone and now it was summer. Bartholomew was finally a teenager. Not that it made much difference.

Homeschooled again in Mother's antiseptic bubble, he had to sneak out just to do the things that normal kids did. Like watching his friends in their first skateboarding competition.

It had been months since he'd had any visions but still he knew that they could return at any time. And it looked like July 17th was the day.

When the winged beast had appeared, Bartholomew stumbled back. Mouth agape, he stared at the sky. Still he knew enough to glance at the tourists and locals ambling along the pier. It was obvious that, once again, the vision was for his eyes alone.

Or was it?

His best friend had skated beautifully up to the top of the ramp. Then Alex faltered and fell. The crowd on the beach groaned. Now Bartholomew knew that Alex had seen it too.

The dragon opened its mouth and howled. Once, twice, four times, each one louder than the last.

"And the newbie eats it," the announcer reported.

Bartholomew wanted to plug his ears as those words melded with the dragon's keening. Beating wings pulsed like helicopter blades as it dove down. The dragon left a gaping hole in the clouds, its long snout aimed at Alex who stood in the middle of the ramp gawking at the sky.

Bartholomew held his breath, hoping the creature would veer away but it only drew closer to his frozen friend.

"Alex!" he cried. But his buddy was too far away to hear.

Bartholomew raced forward. In a desperate dash he swerved around skipping children and crowds of day trippers. People on the boardwalk stared but he didn't care.

The dragon opened its mouth revealing rows of jagged teeth. Red flames shot over its forked tongue and whipped the air as if seeking prey.

When the monster tucked its wings and quickened its dive, Bartholomew tried to match its speed. If only he could get there before.... But the pounding in his chest told him it was too late; Alex would be in the belly of the beast before he could arrive.

Jostling a wheeled surrey, the laughing lovers who were trying to pedal stopped mid-chuckle. "Excuse me!" Bartholomew called over his shoulder.

The dragon was so close that Bartholomew could see the outline of each scarlet and gold scale. He looked for a clear path *Where did all these people come from?* He wondered wishing he could just brush them all away. Finally, he found an opening between a group of tightly packed lawn chairs and a picnic blanket and cut across the grass.

Faster. But the throngs were as thick as fresh clay. He quickened his pace, never taking his eyes off Alex.

Get back monster.

He pushed and shoved through the tightly packed bodies.

"Hey! Watch it!"

Fifty feet. Ducked under a sun umbrella knocking it over.

"Sorry!"

Twenty feet. He could feel the dragon's hot breath scorching the sky.

Flames licked at Alex's head. Was Alex's helmet melting?

"NO!" Bartholomew cried as he sprung into a flying leap. He thrust his fist upward hoping to knock the creature off kilter.

But his hand met only air.

"Huh?" he exhaled.

The wind cooled into nothing but a soft breeze. The keening cries silenced. And the clouds returned to white. Bartholomew lowered his arm and exchanged a glance with Alex.

The dragon had disappeared. All that was left of the beast was the faint odor of smoke as if from a distant chimney.

"You know what this means," Alex said with a heavy sigh.

Bartholomew nodded. "Task three,"

It was only a matter of time now.

Chapter 3

The hunchbacked monster ran a palm over his slime-covered face to spread gelatinous goo over his spiked hair. Then he stretched each point higher to make himself appear taller. Even though Captain Sludge had a strong frame he'd need every advantage for his meeting with Lord Sickhert.

Here, in a cavern deep beneath Artania, scores of Shadow Swine were gathered on the bank of the River of Lies. Their bodies surged and swelled as they breathed in sulfuric fumes from the bubbling river.

These soldiers began creating nightmares in the vapors, their piggish nostrils flaring with each breath of blue-grey steam. Soon horrible dreams would turn people away from creating.

"Yes, make the humans cry out in terror," Sludge said as his jackbooted feet drew closer. "Strike fear into every artist who dares sing with paint."

One thin Shadow Swine opened his yellow eyes and exchanged a quick glance with his captain. Panting, he blew more dark mist into the air.

Ghostly images floated down from Lord Sickhert's stalagmite castle. One by one the outlines of sleeping boys and girls drifted toward the hunchbacked soldiers.

One white shadow alighted in front of the lean private. With a sneering smile he said, "I'll make this boy wish he'd never seen a paint brush."

His claw-tipped nails snatched the ghost boy from the air as the captured dreamer opened his mouth in a silent scream.

"Turn paint into a drowning sea," Sludge ordered his minion. "Choke the boy with bands of color."

The private nodded. Hunched back heaving, he opened his cavernous mouth and blew. Dark smoke escaped from blood red lips in ashy wisps. Each curling twine wrapped around the boy's head and shoulders.

"Terrify him. Now!" Sludge ordered.

Like a hangman jerking his noose, the Shadow Swine pulled the dream-child beneath his dark cloak. Soon, twisting smoke erupted from the folds.

Captain Sludge smiled. He would have good news for Lord Sickhert this day.

The back of his neck usually prickled when he entered the twenty-story stalagmite, but today his boots pounded a confident march as Sludge passed through the castle's irregular doorway. His plan was so unique, so perfect, so brutal that Sickhert would surely be pleased.

His lord might even share a steaming mug of worm tea and with him. The two would stand on the balcony viewing the lava seep down the Window of Red. And *never* again would Sludge be punished in the burning Correction Chamber because of those idiot boys and their red-headed sidekick.

He strode up the twisting stair until he reached the twentieth floor. Just outside Lord Sickhert's chamber, two sentries stood watch, daring any who approached to enter their master's suite.

"Announce Captain Sludge to your lord," he said. He swished saliva around in his mouth preparing to honor Lord Sickhert.

One sentry pulled on a cone-shaped lever near the doorway and a howl reverberated throughout the castle. When a second, deeper howl answered the first, the soldier nodded to Captain Sludge.

"You may enter Sir," he said with a quick salute.

The door creaked open on ancient hinges to reveal their white-robed leader. Sludge took three steps forward and then dropped to his knees. Mouth full of sputum, he crawled toward the shining black throne. When he reached the obsidian chair, he did not raise his head. Instead he released the honorific spittle onto Lord Sickhert's maggot white feet and rubbed the foam into the chalky skin.

"You may rise," the albino monarch said cracking his long talon-like toes with a satisfied sigh.

"Thank you, my lord." Sludge stood and waited.

"What news have you of the dream draining?"

Sludge knew he couldn't lie. Sickhert had only to peer into his Lava Pool Gramarye to find the truth. And that waist-high mini-volcano was just a few feet away.

"Many humans turn away," Sludge said. "But still the Deliverers create their Knights of Painted Light making much of California immune."

"Then we assault them with more nightmares than Knights can battle," Sickhert snarled. "Overrun them with shadows of fear." His bone white eyes narrowed. "Or you know what will happen."

"Yet the soldiers craft terror," the captain spoke quickly. A chill rolled down his spine where he still bore scars from his first defeat. He'd need to be clever to avoid the Correction Chamber again. "Right now, at the River of Lies—"

"Not good enough," Lord Sickhert said, cutting him off. "Those Deliverers and their Knights have blocked too many nightmares."

"Ahh, but we craft ever terrifying visions," Sludge argued.

"Insufficient! Double your efforts. They must be trapped like rats in a maze."

"Interesting you should mention maze, Lord. For a labyrinth is just what I had in mind." Sludge suppressed a smile. He had a plan but didn't want to give away the details until it was firmly in place.

"Mount Minotaur?" Interested, the despot licked his ashen lips and leaned forward.

"Exactly. With its never-ending passageways, we can lure the Deliverers deep into the labyrinth."

"So, they spend eternity lost in the puzzle. Forever confused and searching. And our power will grow."

"Until Artania falls under your magnificent dominion, my lord."

"Proceed." Lord Sickhert smiled and nodded.

Sludge exited, no longer needing to straighten his spiked hair for height. Lord Sickhert was pleased. Right then he soared even taller than a megalosaurus-mudlark.

Chapter 4

Gwendolyn Obranovich cheered the last skater of the vert competition on in loud whoops until the crowd's excitement had waned and her voice was hoarse. With a recent braces-free grin, she turned to Jose Hamlin and Zachary Van Gromen.

"Hey, while we wait for the judge's results let's give Alex some props Gwen said. "He did finish his run, even if he fell before doing a backside."

"That was brutal; he had it down all month," Zach said shaking his head. His recently cut blonde hair barely moved from all the jell he had in it. But that was Zach, GQ Junior had been into fashion for as long as Gwen could remember.

"I know. Alex was rolling like morning waves every time." Jose smoothed and retied his long black pony tail. "But that puts me up in the standings."

Gwen stared at Jose. Mr. Zen usually was all about saving the dolphins in Japan or spreading peace.

She didn't think he had a competitive bone in his meditating body.

"Maybe so but let's not mention it now. Kay?"

"Yeah," Zach agreed. "When a skater eats it, you don't show him an instant replay on your phone." He polished his nails on his designer t-shirt. "Unless you look as good as me."

Gwen and Jose groaned before making their way through the crowd toward Alex.

Gwen was surprised to see Bartholomew leaning toward Alex as if sharing some secret when she arrived. She didn't think he'd been allowed to come. Ever since being busted for cheating in seventh grade he'd been homeschooled by his weird tutor. Poor guy was locked up in that hospital-like mansion and hardly ever got out.

"Dude!" Gwen called through the crowd. "Congrats. You finished your first compy."

Alex turned, his face nothing like Gwen anticipated. In place of the disappointment she expected, were gnarly knots of worry. He looked like he was ready to do battle or something.

"Finished, not. I missed the backside," Alex said, shaking his head.

"That was not your f–" Bartholomew's words were cut short by Alex's quick jab in his side. He choked oomph and cleared his throat. "I mean, that is to say, after all your hard work, it was unfortunate."

"It was just higher than I remembered." Alex gave Bartholomew a warning stare and both nodded.

If Jose and Zach hadn't been there Gwen would have asked if something freaky were going on. Like the year before.

"You'll nail it next time," she said.

"We all begin the competition path with scattered stones," Jose said in his Buddha voice. Then he added like he was totally full of himself. "As I did."

Gwen mouth fell open. Then she got angry. She had just readied a quick quip to knock Jose's ego down a notch or two when then the announcer's voice came over the speakers.

"The judges have tallied the results and in third place let's give it up for the amazing Brad Singh."

The crowd applauded and whooped for the skater with bleached spikes. Gwen didn't know him because he wasn't local but agreed that he had skills. After second place was announced everyone grew quiet, eyes drifting from Jose to the Brazilian champion. Gwen held her breath.

"And in first place, put your hands together for the Santa Barbara kid with technical grace and style, Jose Hamlin!"

Jose slapped Alex's hand, signaled hang loose to the crowd, and jogged up to the podium for his trophy.

"Usually Singh dominates but this kid showed us just what SB can do," The reporter's voice resounded while he shook Jose's hand. "Dude, you put it all on the line. How'd it feel out there?"

"Amazing. At first, I thought I wouldn't take any chances but then something made me want to go for air. Like the sky was calling me. So, I heeded the call."

The audience loved that. Gwen even saw a few giggling girls from their junior high scream like Jose was some freakin' rock star or something.

"And it paid off." The emcee lifted Jose's arm into the air. "Congratulations to Jose Hamlin, the official winner of this year's Volcom Games! Cham-pi-on!"

This time the crowd went absolutely nuts. Gwen was happy for her friend and all, but did he have to look so superior about it? She turned back to complain to Alex, but he was deep in conversation with Bartholomew.

She narrowed her sea green eyes. Just what were these guys up to now?

Chapter 5

Far away, in Artania, The Thinker had gathered a pair of dragons inside the Golden Grotto. Inside the great cave, the bronze statue straightened his bent form, opening and closing his steely fist.

In moments, images of Alex's competition flickered in his palm. The Santa Barbara scene began to play as the great beasts bent their scaled heads to watch Alex tumble off his skateboard before a groaning crowd. They continued observing until Bartholomew sprinted to his side and leapt into the air. Then sparks fizzled down The Thinker's bronze arm and the images dimmed.

A moment later, there was a rumbling outside of the cavern. The bronze man glanced up to see a smiling red and gold dragon enter the cave.

The Thinker curled his sculpted hand into a fist and nodded a greeting. "We appreciate your delivering the message, Flynn."

"It was as easy as blowing smoke rings," the winking beast replied blowing a single misty circle.

"But will the humans heed the call?" the blue water dragon directly opposite, mused.

"Of course, Wade, it's their destiny," Flynn replied.

"We can only hope," the water dragon said quietly.

Next to Wade, the huge female dragon's emerald green scales quavered in the firelight. "They must. I shudder to think what in heaven's name will happen if the Golden Dragon is not found. Soon. To all of us."

"Yes, Erantha we know." Flynn said with a quick bob of his horned head. "*Draco aureus* is the one who binds." He blew out a quick puff of smoke. "But still–"

"You know how few they've become!" Erantha argued, cutting him off. "Years have passed without a single sighting of golden scales!"

"Which is why I have called this Council," The Thinker said. "Every attempt to find them has failed. Time and again both knight and maiden, dragon and dragoness have come up empty handed. Many have begun this quest, but the egg still remains elusive."

"Dear Leader, is Gothia itself in danger?" the sapphire-colored Wade asked.

"Possibly, Water-dragon," The Thinker replied. "Many humans have turned away from true art. Now countless of your kind are gone. I don't even know if the Golden Dragon still exists. And you know what that means."

"The blank canvas," all three dragons whispered in unison.

"This entire land will shrink into nothingness. It will return to the Before Time," The bronze leader said.

"Are the Shadow Swine aware of this? Do they know how rare *draco aureus* has become?" Erantha asked.

The Thinker sighed, wishing he could lie. But if these three dragons were to keep Gothia safe, they needed to know the truth. "We have tried to keep it quiet, but these days Lord Sickhert's spies seem to be everywhere."

"Just yesterday, I battled a traitorous knight who laughed as my fire singed his armor," Flynn said, the red spikes at the scruff of his neck stiffening. "His last words before galloping away were how things would be different after the Change."

"The Change," The Thinker shook his head. "If the traitors only knew the horrors it would bring. But I cannot convince those who have turned to see the truth."

"Then is there no hope?" Wade asked in a voice as quiet as the waters of his home in Lambent Lake.

"Of course, you know that hope will lie in the hands of twins," The Thinker said.

"But what I'm afraid of," the green Erantha said. "Are the last two lines of *The Prophecy*."

"Me too, Earth Sister," Wade said. " 'Many will perish before they are through,' " he recited with a shudder.

" 'But our world *will* be saved,' " The Thinker said. " 'If their art is true.' The Deliverers have been suc-

21

cessful in the past. I know that *The Prophecy* will guide them now."

"Yes, with our help." Erantha bowed. The long bony plates girdling her head flowed freely like a maiden's hair in the wind. She turned toward the mouth of the cave and unfolded her green wings, then bid farewell to the Council.

As the Thinker watched her take flight, his bronze hand warmed again. New visions flickered in his palm. Wade and Flynn stepped closer and peered at the emerging scene of a Golden Dragon floundering inside a dark thundercloud.

Wade's turquoise eyes widened with fear. "What does it mean?"

"The weather is changing," The Thinker said.

Flynn flicked his forked tongue outside the cave. "Yes, I can taste storms on the horizon."

As the image of lightning bolts flashed around the struggling Golden, an involuntary shudder crept up The Thinker's spine. It seeped into his bronze form turning his bloodless veins to ice.

With no idea how to warm them again.

Chapter 6

"This is getting ridiculous," Gwen said to Alex under her breath. "He hasn't put that away since the compy."

Alex had to agree. Jose used to be so cool, but ever since winning the Volcom Games he'd changed. Now he was Mr. Ego, a trophy strutting, chest puffing braggart who gave ridiculous Zen tips to every skater he met. He even made Zachary Van Gromen look downright humble. And although Zach was a good friend, the dude was totally conceited.

Today was no different. As they walked along the pier Jose stopped every few feet to pull out a buffing cloth, hold his trophy up to the light, and shine the brass.

Of course, he only did it when the girls of summer were nearby. And then they'd ask him all about it and of course he had to tell the story, again, of how he'd beaten the famed Brazilian by meditating on the clouds. Jeez. But what was most disgusting was how he'd then show them the YouTube video on his phone, pausing at every successful aerial.

When yet another group of beach babes were done oohing and ahhing, Alex, Jose, and Gwen strolled over to the railing to watch the sailboats bobbing in the bay. Joking around, it felt like old times, for all of thirty seconds. Then Jose set the cup on the rail and snapped his dust cloth in the wind.

"Would you stop polishing that thing?" Gwen asked.

"Yeah," Alex said. "It's getting old fast."

Jose didn't even glance at Alex. Instead, he searched the constant stream of people walking by as if waiting for his entourage of paparazzi photographers to arrive. "Remember, negative self-talk does not serve. But I understand if you are having difficulty dealing with my success."

"No, we're all sick of looking at that thing," Gwen said.

Giving them a superior smile, Jose grasped the brass cup by both handles. "But mastering your-self is true power and this is a symbol of achieving dominance."

"You are kidding, right?" Gwen asked.

"If you are uncomfortable with my expertise, that is your problem."

"Give me a freaking break," Gwen retorted. "Half of what you know, I taught you."

"My excellence was achieved through meditation and focus, not through others."

"You know, some humility would rock about now," Alex said trying to bring the tension down a notch. Secretly he wanted to punch that too smug face. He had battled stuff in Artania that'd make Jose look like a friggin' wuss.

"Your jealousy does not serve you," Jose took a deep breath and exhaled as if he were a yoga teacher. "But all masters must walk their own path to enlightenment. I can only hope that you both will find yours in time. I could text you some quotes if you like."

"I'm good, but thanks," Gwen said her voice dripping with sarcasm that Jose completely missed.

"Suit yourself." Jose gave them a Buddha bow and walked away.

Alex shook his head and then, anticipating a long tirade about what an egomaniac Jose had become, turned to Gwen. But several moments passed with her just staring at the sea. The heavy feeling settling in his gut made him flash on how sad Mom had seemed before her heart attack.

"What's up, Gwen? You okay?" he asked.

Her eyes stayed fixed on the horizon. "I just hate seeing people get like that. Like mirrors are what they live for. But they never really look at the reflection." She paused and wrinkled her nose twice. "Or anyone behind them."

"Yeah I know. He went from totally cool, to full of himself."

"Why does that happen to people?" she asked.

Alex shrugged. "No clue."

He wondered if she was thinking about her mom. When had Gwen seen her last? Rochelle Obranovich had left for Europe a couple of years back and now she was some famous model or something. Gwen hardly ever talked about her except to say how she never wanted to be a girly girl like that. He wondered if Rochelle ever called. He started to ask, but when he noticed a misty look in his friend's soft green eyes, instead decided to change the subject.

"I know, let's go watch some BMX aerials. That dude from L.A.'s supposed to be filming some cool moves." He jerked his chin toward the skateboard park just south of the pier.

"Yeah, let's." Gwen's voice was distant when she turned back toward shore.

* * *

Later that night as Alex sat in front of his easel in the corner of his garage studio, he remembered Gwen's troubled expression.

"What was up with Gwen, Rembrandt?" he asked, petting his Australian Shepherd's striped head. "I never saw her so down before."

His dog flipped up one fuzzy ear and then the other as if to say, "beats me" then watched Alex tear out a piece of paper from his sketch pad and pin it to the canvas.

Leaning back, Alex closed his eyes for a few moments before outlining Gwen's slim form and elfin face. Once he had a rough pencil drawing, he set to work on the contours, shading here and erasing there, until he had a good likeness. Still it wasn't complete. Even though he posed Gwen her atop a skateboard, it didn't feel right. Something was missing.

He leaned back again and stared at the image.

"What should I change?" he asked Rembrandt who was now nestled at his feet.

The dog stared back with silver-blue eyes and then glanced at a kite hanging from the garage ceiling.

Alex followed his gaze and nodded. "Hmm... Flying. I like it."

When his mind formed the image, Alex erased the skateboard and replaced it with a few scales as smooth as polished marble. This shining patchwork grew into a curved back atop powerful reptilian legs. A moment later, a long serpent-like neck with a clump of gently curving horns extended in front of Gwen.

When wings of the lightest gossamer sprouted, Alex felt a sudden change. Sad Gwen morphed to glorious dragon rider, soaring through popcorn clouds a grin splitting her sunburned and freckled face.

Alex didn't know until much later why he added the next element. Just that at the time it seemed to balance out everything. Anyhow he'd always liked how medieval knights had rampant dragons on flags and armor. So, drawing her holding a shield with a great beast standing on its hind legs fit.

Unclipping it from the easel Alex held the sketch up for Rembrandt. "What do you think? Like it?"

Rembrandt wagged his thick grey tail and licked Alex's hand.

"*Good, young Deliverer," The Thinker said to the flickering images in his hand. "You still feel the breeze of creation. Let those scaled wings beat winds of change.*"

Although the young ones were creating, The Thinker was still uneasy. He didn't know if their sketches would carry them through the awaiting storms. A squall was building in both their worlds and they would need all their strength to make it through the tempest.

Chapter 7

"Where is he?" Gwen asked twisting around in her seat and craning her neck. "The movie's going to start any minute." Even though she wouldn't have admitted it if asked, Gwen was excited about getting a little dressed up to see the guys and Alex. Well, board shorts and a new tank from the local surf shop wasn't exactly dressed up but she was wearing something different from her usual ripped jeans and skater shoes. She'd even added a spritz of smoothing gel to her shoulder length red braids.

"Time is but an idea," Jose replied. He stood up and stretched his arms over his head before untying his long black ponytail and smoothing it for the tenth time that night. He seemed disappointed that none of the gaggle of gigglers was nearby to ask him how fame was treating him.

"Dude, you talk in riddles," the blonde Zach said. "But it would be a bummer if Alex missed the opening. "I hear there's a car chase for the books."

"Cha," Gwen nodded. She glanced around again. No curly-topped teen.

The lights dimmed and the first of the previews began. Where was Alex? "Save our seats, she told Zach. "I'm gonna see if Alex is in the lobby."

"Got it," Zach made a gun with his hand and pointed it at her with a loud tisk. This was his newest signature move, one he did about fifty times a day, double that when Jose was around.

She suppressed a groan. Man, this competition between Jose and Zach was getting out of control. Gwen would have laughed out loud if she wasn't so worried about Alex's absence.

Were those slime monsters calling him out again?

Gwen skirted past several seats and entered the decorative lobby. Even though she'd been coming here since she was little she still admired its Spanish style with balconies, stairways, and a freestanding ticket booth. But tonight, she didn't have time to appreciate the arched hallways, wrought iron lanterns, or red-tiled fountain because there across the lobby was her bud.

"Hey Alex," she called from across the room. "You are going the miss best part! Hurry—"

Her words stuck there. Instead of rushing to his seat Alex was chatting away with Lacey Zamora. Of all people! Gwen didn't think Alex would give the time of day to, much less talk with, little miss I'm-so-hot-you-could-toast-a-bagel-with-me.

Lacey wore her usual jeans so tight they looked painted on and a shiny purple top with sequins. Her brown hair was so smooth you could probably surf on it and her lips as red as a friggin' police siren.

Gwen's dad would never let her wear makeup like that. Way too much. Why not just put Day-Glo paint on and shine a black light on your face for God's sake?

What really blew Gwen away was Alex. With his devil-may-care posture and that smirk you'd think he was Zach Aphron or something. Geesh.

She thought about turning to go but Mitch Obranovich did not raise a wimp, coaching her to push her body to its limits until she could bench more than most grown women.

She squared her shoulders and marched right up to that tittering pair. "Hi," she said extending a hand. "Gwen, and you are?" she asked.

"You know perfectly well who I am, Gwendolyn Obranovich, we only had three classes together last year."

"Ahh," Gwen said twirling one red tendril that had escaped her left braid in her fingers and staring off into space as if disinterested. "Maybe I recall."

"And everyone knows you," Lacey said raising one eyebrow.

Just then two more of Lacey's pack strutted up. Coco Fontana and Michelle Peterson were both dressed in Xerox copied jeans just as body-hugging as Lacey's with equal measures of bright red lipstick.

"Ahh, girlfriends," Lacey said. "I was just reminding Gwen here, how everyone knows her."

Both her friends sniggered.

"What?" Gwen asked.

"Well you are, umm shall we say, unique." Lacey said looking Gwen up and down as if she were a big pile of dog pooh.

"Totally," one of her clones chimed in.

"And just what is that supposed to mean?" Gwen asked. She curled her hands into fists but fought the urge to raise one to that neon face.

Lacey obviously had a death wish because she didn't miss a beat before going on.

"What other chick at Las Brisas dresses like a guy?" She tilted her head back and forth as if daring anyone to disagree. "And looks like one too. Cronk."

"Hey Lacey," Alex interrupted. "Stop."

"What? You like the boy look?" Lacey asked coolly.

"No, I don't, but Gwen's not-"

"Hey!" Gwen cried, her face aghast.

"I mean, she, you dress fine, I guess. I never noticed."

"Well girls, let this be a lesson to you. If you want a guy to ignore you and treat you like one of the boys, this is what you should wear." Like a model at a car show Lacey turned her palms up at Gwen. "Come on chicas, let's find some seats." She flipped her hair and turned on her heels, her entourage tagging along behind.

Gwen raised her hands in exasperation. "Seriously?"

"I didn't mean, it, you, I-"

"Whatever." Copying Lacey's hair flip she pivoted away with a harrumph.

Chapter 8

Curling his lips, Bartholomew checked each tooth, scrubbing more until they gleamed. Next, he splashed some water on his head to tame that uncooperative cowlick that kept sticking up. When he stepped back for one final look in the mirror, he adjusted his cream-colored tie until it was as straight as a mop handle.

Satisfied that he'd pass inspection, Bartholomew raised each arm and sniffed his pits. He knew it was unnecessary; he'd just taken his third bath that day and had applied sanitizer, deodorant, and cologne. Still Mother was a bloodhound and he'd already been sent back once to bathe.

With a deep breath, Bartholomew descended the winding staircase and made his way down the long hall toward her office. He stood in the wide entryway and waited for her to acknowledge him. But all she did was sit at her Plexiglas desk and stare at the computer screen. After long moments, he cleared his throat.

No response. Thirty more seconds passed.

Bartholomew coughed, louder this time. She looked up at him coolly with diamond blue eyes that normally would cut Bartholomew to the core. But not today. Today he had something important to discuss and no broken glass glance would deter him.

"Yes?" she asked as if she didn't know a thing about their scheduled meeting. "As you can see I do not have much time for nonsense." She pointed a French-manicured nail at the computer that made her pale skin look even more translucent than usual.

"It's my education," Bartholomew began, trying to sound as grown-up as possible. "I do not believe that a tutor is enough for an eighth-grader."

"You do not know what you need. You are a child."

"Maybe, but the teachers at Las Brisas Junior High have diverse knowledge." Then under his breath but loud enough for her to hear, he added, "Not like Mr. White."

"Your tutor was educated at Oxford. He is scholar and a gentleman!"

"What does he know about the arts: sculpture or painting?"

"Nasty goops of blurred colors? Nonsense." The blue veins in Mother's forehead pulsed. "Perhaps you'll need Chemistry for better bleach formulas. But everything else? Mr. White will do."

"But at school there are other kids my age."

"I have seen enough of what being around kids your age does to you."

Although Bartholomew knew that he was wasting his breath, he tried a new tack. He was going nuts trapped in their sterile mansion. "How about history," he argued. "If I had teachers who studied the masters-"

"People like us do not hob nob with peons," Mother said cutting him off.

"But art is part of the world," he said but didn't add. *Not to mention the fact that people like me need it.*

"When will you learn that we Boraxes rise above? To the white of clean clouds." She glanced at the ceiling as if it was a painting of the pearly gates. "Where your father is."

Oh boy, now she was pulling out the your-father-is-in-Heaven-because-of-filth card. Yes, Father drowned in a mud puddle. But it wasn't the mud's fault. It was just some freak accident.

Or was it? He still wondered how a grown man could die in two inches of water. Were the Shadow Swine somehow involved?

"Well wouldn't Father want me to have a rounded education?"

"One you receive with Mr. White."

"But if I'm going to head the family business-"

"Years away. You are only thirteen."

"In some societies that would make me a man."

"Not in this one. You are a child and need protecting,"

"No, I don't."

"Oh, yes you do. Just look at what happened last year. Corrupted by those juvenile delinquents. Foul hoodlums. I will not allow that to happen again."

"I told you a thousand times, cheating was my idea. I stole the answer book all alone. My friends had nothing to do with it."

"Lies. All lies. You are just covering for them."

Even though she was right, Bartholomew denied it vehemently.

Mother fanned her face with her hand. "It's getting warm in here. And germs increase in warm environments. More and more bacteria grows. Crawling all over your skin."

"Mother, it's all right."

"They are everywhere. Can't you see them? Germs multiplying, growing, on my hands my face..." Staring off into space, Hygenette rubbed her cheeks.

"Mother, it's not real. It's just your imagination."

Looking right through him, she rose from her chair and rang the silver bell on her desk. Three maids dressed in starched white uniforms appeared at the doorway. Each held a bucket and a sponge filling the air with an antiseptic scent from the strongest disinfectant the world. Mother's own formula.

"Decontaminate this room. Now," she ordered rising from her chair.

Bartholomew tried to block her way. "But Mother–"

"I need my bath. Antiseptic soap. My bath," Mother mumbled as she swept past.

Bartholomew thought of calling after her, but her heels were already clicking away like glass tumbling into a rubbish bin.

Chapter 9

The Thinker's bronze hand flickered to reveal a moon rising over Santa Barbara's palm-lined streets. He usually enjoyed watching towns quiet into slumber as children drifted to sleep. But tonight, the uneasiness in his gut made the night darker than a Shadow Swine's heart.

Despite his noblest efforts, Lord Sickhert was still gaining power. He was destroying whole communities. From the Renaissance Nation to the Photography District his Shadow Swine sucked them into the abyss.

Alexander and Bartholomew continued to create more Knights of Painted Light, but it wasn't enough. Human children rejected art day after day. Playing mindless video games and internet surfing to nowhere.

Even though imagination had once called them to color, they no longer picked up chalk, pen, or brush.

The Shadow Swine's' nightmares had terrified all creativity away.

And in so doing, destroyed more Artanians than he cared to count.

So many lost. So many fallen. Their vibrant spirits never to seen again.

The Thinker leaned forward and peered more intently into his hand. A dark mist appeared on a dimly lit corner. The mist paused and cork-screwed up to a house he knew all too well.

"It has begun," he said squaring his shoulders.

The Thinker closed and opened his sculpted hand twice and Gwen's rooftop rose to meet him. Using his Bronze Vision, the Thinker checked to make sure the girl was sleeping before peering into Bartholomew's studio.

The sculptures arranged around the room shook off the mantle of sleep and headed for their posts throughout the city. Pterodactyl firebirds took to the skies, a multi-headed snake slithered up the spiral staircase, and sturdy centaurs loped down the street.

The Thinker breathed warm air into his palm. It passed through his skin's steely crevices and beyond Artania. When his breath fell to Earth, it breezed back the knight's helmet to reveal a noble face, chiseled chin, and high cheekbones.

"Painted Knight of Light, awake," The Thinker said.

The soldier's armor shook and rattled as he stretched his strong arms overhead. He blinked several times and glanced around the room.

"Where are you, ghost voice?" he asked.

"I am far away, in a land you will soon see. But for now, know who you are. And your purpose."

The Thinker wiggled his fingers. Electricity sizzled in his palm. Then a single bright bolt shot into the knight's head.

And he knew all.

"Where are those scum?" the sculpted one demanded.

The Thinker dropped glittering breadcrumbs to guide the knight toward Gwen's home. There, outside her second-story window, the final Shadow Swine was sliming in through the cracks, its body stretching like rubber as it snaked inside.

"Protect her at all costs. She is friend to the Deliverers," The Thinker said.

With a nod, the knight lowered his visor and began scaling the stony wall.

The Thinker looked inside Gwen's room. It wasn't good. The girl was lying face up; muscles and eyelids twitching. Two Shadow Swine stood at one side of her bed blowing dark tendrils of smoke into each ear while a third approached from the surfboard-printed drapes of her window.

Their dark slimy heads were a sharp contrast to Gwen's cheerful beach-themed room. Flaring nostrils glowed pink next to a lava lamp. Sharp teeth gnashed while Hawaiian posters invited travel. The worst were the long ratty braids dripping slime onto Gwen's floral comforter of printed hibiscus flowers.

"They do not belong there," The Thinker muttered.

Then the sculpted knight slipped his fingers under the window and wriggled inside. His armor clanged as he leapt, but all three continued to send black clouds into the poor girl's ears.

* * *

Gwen tossed and turned, each breath shallower than the last. Why couldn't she wake up?

"Come here, Tinker Bell." Mother's voice was soft and inviting from her dressing table where she sat applying long swaths of red to her pouty mouth. "Let's try a little lipstick."

As Gwen crossed the room toward her, Rochelle reached out an arm. But instead of a warm embrace she jerked Gwen close.

"Mom stop." Gwen tried to pull away, but Rochelle tightened her grasp.

Rochelle seized Gwen's face and turned it toward the lighted mirror. "So ugly. How could you be my child?"

Gwen tried to look away, but Rochelle held fast, forcing her to stare at the reflection. It was horrible. A disease-pocked face with lips paler than bone contorted in the glass. The braids she'd brushed out before bed were now a disheveled rat's nest. And her eyes had shrunken deep into her skull.

"No!" Gwen cried wrenching herself free. She began to run for the door, but it didn't get any closer. In fact, the faster she went, the further away it got, as if her feet were stretching the room with every step.

Rochelle just laughed and laughed. "You think you can escape? No one escapes the mirror."

41

Gwen turned back and was horrified to see that multiple arms had now emerged from Mom's torso. Each hand displayed a growing mirror of Gwen's twisted image.

She crouched down on all fours and covered her eyes.

"What do you want from me?" she cried pounding her fists on the floor.

The next voice was about as feminine as an ogre. "Transform. Become beauty."

Two doors appeared in front of her. The one on the left displayed her distorted face while the other had Gwen looking as perfect as Mom's air brushed photos. Gwen reached out to touch the flawless face but as soon as she did it shimmered and morphed into a crying image of Rochelle.

"Mom?"

"Don't you dare use that word with me. You are no child of mine. You are so ugly; how could any mother love you?"

* * *

The sculpted knight gripped his mace's wooden handle and stepped closer to the huffing Shadow Swine. "Get away from her!" he ordered.

The nearest Swiney didn't even turn. Not missing a beat, he blew more dark smoke toward Gwen.

"Use the light," The Thinker whispered into his palm.

With an understanding nod, the knight began to swing his mace in circles. With each pass the knobbed ball shimmered and glowed more as spikes shot multi-colored lasers at the Shadow Swine.

Now the monsters paid attention. The shortest one pulled a battle axe from his long dark cloak. Continuing to blow dark mist, he turned sideways and raised it. The silver blade shone eerie in the half light.

Then, all three Shadow Swine set upon the knight, each monster broader by half than him. Faces set in gross leers, their bulging muscles billowed beneath capes as they approached.

The Thinker was surprised at what happened next. When the shorter Swiney lifted his axe, several of the knight's colored rays tangled. Then, as if drawn by a magnetic force, these rainbows were pulled into the axe blade. At the same time, the colors wilted.

The reds went first, fading from flaming scarlet to ruddy brown in less than a second. Next amethyst shriveled like a pruning plum.

When cerulean blue turned black, The Thinker knew they were in trouble. Was there a new weapon that could suck a Knight's strength?

Then he noticed who the shorter one was. None other than Captain Sludge, whose power was said to be second only to Lord Sickhert himself.

If Sludge had designed this weapon, the knight would be hard pressed to defeat him. That Swiney had more tricks up his sleeve than Houdini in Movie Poster Land.

"Pull back!" The Thinker shouted into his hand.

But the knight dashed toward the trio. Swinging his mace and shooting lasers, he blocked a few of the tall Swiney's smoke trails.

"Okay, stop the dream draining. But be careful," The Thinker urged from his far away land.

"You think you can defeat me Knight?" Sludge said with a sneer. "Just watch."

The knight turned, giving the short Swiney just the opening he was looking for. With a tremendous kick, Sludge knocked him off his feet while his comrade shoved a jack-booted foot into the knight's chest. The sculpted one tried lifting his weapon but the tallest one yanked it from his grasp.

Turning his head helplessly from one monster to the other, the Knight's eyes implored the ceiling as if asking for The Thinker's help.

But the Thinker's powers were limited. All he could was whisper in the Knight's ear. "Resist, Sculpted One. Fight," he urged.

Eyes glinting in the moonlight, Sludge paused and looked up as if he knew The Thinker was watching helplessly.

The wriggling warrior twisted right and left. But those boots pressing upon him made it impossible to escape.

Captain Sludge raised his axe.

The bronze leader clenched his steely fists. "Close your eyes," he whispered to Bartholomew's creation.

The noble knight nodded, his face seeming to light up as the blade came down with a crash. It cleaved him in two, shooting shards of clay in all directions.

"No!" The Thinker cried.

The Deliverers glorious creation had disappeared. Leaving the shivering girl to endure more Shadow Swine nightmares.

The bronze leader shook his head sadly from side to side. "How is this possible?"

The monsters had found new powers, and for the life of him, he didn't know what they were.

Chapter 10

"And Dr. Bock says that vitamin D will help your developing bones remain strong," Dad's hands kept a perfect ten and two-o'clock on the steering wheel as he spoke. "In case you hadn't noticed you are changing. This is due to-"

"I know, Dad, I know. You don't have to give me the growing up talk *again*." Alex groaned. "Mom?" He asked looking to her up for backup.

Turning, she gave Alex a quick wink, before patting her husband on the arm. "He's thirteen, Charlie, not nine."

"I know, just saying."

"So, Mom you sure you're okay to do such a long run?" Alex asked, changing the subject to what was really on his mind.

Alex still worried a lot about her. He still couldn't shake the horror of watching her heart attack two years before. In mere seconds, she'd gone from offering cookies to clutching her chest, barely able to breathe. Then he'd clung to her, holding her in a vice grip that took three firemen to pry loose.

He still had the brown button he'd torn off in the struggle. He kept it in the top drawer of his dresser as a reminder to protect the people he cared about.

Cyndi Devinci had resumed some light activities the year before, but chest pain had sent her back to the doctor for more tests. Only recently had she been okayed to run again.

"The new medication is working great, sweetheart. Don't worry."

Alex leaned forward between the two front seats. He searched her face for signs of lying but her olive skin wasn't flushed, and she didn't once brush back her short curls nervously. After holding her gaze for several moments, he replied, "Okay, if you say so."

"Don't worry. I wouldn't let my pretty babe do anything dangerous." Dad lifted Mom's hand to his lips and kissed it several times loudly.

"Yeah, right." Alex said, trying to keep from gagging. Parents weren't supposed to be all gushy in front of their kids. "Just save the romance for later, okay?"

His parents chuckled. This was an old joke that they used to distract Alex. He had to hand it to them though, it worked.

"I hope there's parking," Dad said pulling into the lot next to beach.

Alex pointed to one spot under a palm tree and Dad slowly maneuvered the car into the lined space. Dad never did anything too quickly; whether solving an equation or parking the Jeep, every movement was careful and deliberate. Alex supposed that the reason he analyzed situations so thoroughly was because he'd inherited some of Dad's deliberateness.

"Want us to wait for you, or were you planning to skate home?" Mom asked.

"I'll cruise."

"Don't forget your–"

"I know, helmet and knee pads," Alex interrupted holding up his backpack. "Got 'em right here." With a quick salute he hopped out of the jeep. Slinging his backpack over his shoulder he tucked his skateboard under one arm and headed for Skaters Point.

Straight ahead was one of Alex's favorite places, second only to sitting in his garage studio at his easel. The Santa Barbara skate park had the best location, just south of the pier between the beachfront board-walk and grassy strips of green. Edged with tall palm trees and a wavy concrete fence it not only was a mecca for other skaters but was a hang-out for kids from Las Brisas Junior High.

Today Alex walked up just as the morning fog was burning off. Low clouds rolled out toward the grey Pacific and filtered rays cast silver light.

But just outside the skate park gate, Alex noticed something that made him pause.

It was Gwen's black backpack. Now seeing her bag there wasn't odd, but seeing her skateboard sticking halfway out was. Gwen guarded her board like a seagull guards a crust of bread, squawking at anyone that dare touch her perfectly tweaked ride.

48

He bent down for a closer look. The deck's underside was a mess. Gooey red splotches were splattered between the trucks. Tan fingerprints peppered the wheels like someone had dipped a hand in paint and poked them.

Alex gasped. *Shadow Swine after Gwen?*

But then an open tube of mascara poking out of a make-up bag caught his eye. He picked it up and saw the rhinestone initials. L. Z.

"That brat, Lacey. Acting all tough again." he said under his breath. *Well you just messed with the wrong kid.*

An angry Alex marched up toward the pod of populos blushing and giggling around a trophy polishing Jose. As usual Lacey Zamora was there with a few other chicas dressed just like her. All talking loud enough for the sailboats in the bay to hear.

He hated himself for it, but still looked her up and down. Those super short shorts were hard to miss. And since Lacey'd developed early there was plenty to see at the edge of that low-cut Roxy tank top.

"Alex," Lacey crooned when she saw him approach. "How goes it?"

"Don't act all innocent with me Lacey Zamora. I saw what you did," Alex accused.

The gathered crowd grew suddenly silent; every eye on the two of them.

"What?" she asked.

"You know."

"I really don't."

"Gwen," he said raising his voice. "You had no right to treat her that way."

"You mean like this?" Lacey pointed at someone just a few feet away.

Over there between the Zamora Barbie dolls stood someone he knew all too well. That familiar shock of red hair was unmistakable. But what really blew him away wasn't *who* shuffled from one foot to the other but *what* she was wearing.

"I think I gave her the ultimate treatment. Don't you girls?" Lacey asked. She gave the crowd a smug smile while the populos all nodded in unison.

Now Alex was used to seeing Lacey look-alikes. They were all over school. But what he saw now stopped him dead in his tracks. Gwen in a mini skirt? Gwen in a spangle top? Gwen with bright red lips and mascara?

No way.

"Movie stars would pay thousands for a makeover like that," the blonde Coco said flipping one hand toward Gwen like a model in a TV commercial.

Alex couldn't take his eyes off her; Gwen looked so weird. Each eye was lined with black as thick as the Egyptian goddess Isis. Her cheek had rosy circles that would be overdone on a clown. Her usual ginger-colored braids had been replaced with hair so straight you'd think a giant had ironed it. Plus, she teetered on high heels that obviously were a size too big.

"Gwen, wow, you, ahh," Alex sputtered. It was bad enough that the Zamora clique overdid their get-ups, but to see Gwen like this was just too much.

50

"I told you he'd notice," Lacey said.

Gwen gave Alex an expectant look as if waiting for him to say something important.

"Your skateboard's all messed up," he said.

"Yeah, I kinda rushed to change," Gwen replied glancing down at her feet.

Alex leaned in closer. Was she batting her eyelashes?

"I could wash it for you, if you want," he suggested.

Lacey elbowed the blonde-haired Coco next to her.

"Okay," Gwen said with an atypical shy smile.

"And I'll get some extra paper towels while I'm at it, to help you take that stuff off your face."

Gwen jerked back as if Alex had slapped her. All the girls started giggling. Even Jose and a couple of the dudes snickered.

"But I thought you'd like..." she began her face turning red.

"Nice job Romeo," Lacey sneered.

Now everyone was laughing hysterically while a horror-stricken Gwen rushed out the gate. Scooping up her backpack and board, she made a beeline for the nearest restroom.

Alex turned to run after her, but she disappeared so fast he knew he'd never catch up.

Lacey's voice about as sweet as those artificial packets in restaurants when she said, "You really have a way with women,"

"Shut up Lacey," Alex retorted. He tossed his board down and kicked off down the boardwalk.

51

But even a hundred miles of pavement wouldn't be long enough to escape the sad look on Gwen's face.

Chapter 11

Bartholomew ripped off his tie and headed for his special place.

Although Mother had replaced most of the estate's plants with plastic ones, one corner remained as wild and glorious as when Grandfather Borax was alive. And Bartholomew would be forever grateful. Grandfather's will had a provision requiring that the area near the glass conservatory remain untouched. Even today, lush vines, vibrant flowers, and moss-covered fountains graced every corner.

Bartholomew had first discovered the hidden space when a trap door opened and dropped him into the underground room. There, a message from Grandfather explained how he'd changed his will while designing a concealed studio under the greenhouse with enough art supplies to last years.

Minutes later, he was underground with Alex listening to his friend bring him up to speed on the latest. Ever since he'd shown Alex the secret room and how to circumvent security at the front gate, they'd often met here to catch up, make plans, and talk in private.

"And then she just rushed off," Alex said. "It's been a week and no IM, no text, no flash of red rolling by at the skate park. Nothing."

"Women." Bartholomew nodded his head knowingly.

"Yeah."

"Women," Bartholomew kept bobbing his head up and down.

"You just said that."

Bartholomew shrugged returning Alex's stare with a sheepish grin. What more could he say? He was homeschooled, and barely hung out with anyone, much less girls or the hot-tempered Gwen.

He didn't like thinking about it. It just reminded him of how out of touch he'd become these past six months. And he wasn't exactly Mr. Popular before that. Wearing a white suit to school was bad enough. Compound that with a bathtub-equipped limo to bathe in after P.E, and a mother who made visiting friends feel like a plague of frogs, it made time with other kids pretty awkward.

Except for Alex, whose shared destiny and passion for art bridged any initial gaps. The two of them had been through so much together that now he'd do just about anything for him.

"Anyhow," Bartholomew said, clearing his throat. "I keep thinking about that dragon."

"Yeah, what did it want? And why do you think it was flying over Santa Barbara in the first place?"

"I don't know, but it was terrifying."

"But even though it was mega-scary it didn't hurt me That's interesting. Do you think the Thinker sending us some sort of message?"

"Perhaps, like when we saw Zeus riding the waves," Bartholomew remembered.

Two years before at separate birthday celebrations they'd shared a vision of a white-bearded man surfing on his shield. Later, when they'd passed into the magical Artania, they'd discovered that The Thinker had sent Zeus on purpose. He wanted them to inspire the boys into creating more Knights of Painted Light.

"You may be right," Bartholomew said nodding. "Did you try painting it?"

"Drew it," Alex reached in his backpack and pulled out a rolled-up piece of paper. "I hadn't planned on making this at all. I was in the middle of sketching a pretty cool likeness of Gwen–"

"Drawing Gwen, huh?" Bartholomew interrupted. "Interesting."

"She's my friend, shut-up," Alex said making a face. "Anyhow halfway through, I thought of a dragon and it just appeared under my hand."

"It is strange how that works, isn't it? One moment you think you are creating one thing and in the next another appears. Like this sculpture."

Before Alex had a chance to unroll his sketch, Bartholomew walked over to a shelf with several small figures on display. Here, his cloth-draped sculpture was waiting to be fired in the kiln. Proud to show off his latest, he turned toward Alex.

"I was working on this guy about a week ago, when something told me to add a few elements. They seemed right, so I put them in." With a one-handed flourish, he unveiled his knight.

Alex glanced from the sculpture to Bartholomew before speaking.

"Elements? Really? What are you going for, a new style or something?"

Only now did Bartholomew glance at the sculpture. He gaped. In place of the soldier he'd masterfully sculpted, was a lumpy glob like a Frankenstein experiment gone wrong.

"What the dust bunnies?"

"You didn't do this?" Alex asked.

"No, I created a knight. He was amazing. Armor-encased with a cool mace in one hand..." Bartholomew tapped his chin several times. "I don't know what happened."

"I think I do."

Bartholomew's breath caught in his throat. "Shadow Swine?" he whispered.

"Has to be. There's no other logical explanation."

"Alex," Bartholomew gulped. "Show me your drawing."

"Sure." Alex unrolled the thick paper and gasped.

It may have been a dragon, but it was so hideous that it made the one that'd flown over the Volcom Games look like a cute puppy. And the girl riding it? Oh, my God.

"Not your work?"

"No," Alex said shaking his head over and over. "I would never make Gwen's face, so, so..."

"Repulsive? Horrible? Gruesome? Distorted? Monstrous? Warped?"

Alex held up one hand. "Okay, okay. I get it. She makes the monster in *Nightmare on Werewolf Street* look like the Easter Bunny. But what does it mean?"

Bartholomew glanced from sculpture to sketch. Their creations were supposed to be protective shields battling Shadow Swine's nightmares. Now, how were they supposed to keep their friends and family safe?

"If Swineys can undo our creations, what do we do?" he asked.

"I don't know," Alex said. "But I have a sneaking suspicion that we'll find out soon enough."

An overwhelming sense of dread crawled down Bartholomew's spine. "Alex, I'm scared," he said.

"Me too."

"I have a terrible feeling that if we don't do something soon, horrible things will happen."

Alex stared at the distorted sketch still in his hands and shook his head.

" I think Gwen might be in danger."

"What?" Alex exclaimed.

"Look at her."

Alex gaped at Gwen's cringing figure and curled a hand into a fist. Then he grabbed Bartholomew's collar. "I'm not going to let those slime-buckets hurt her. I can't."

Bartholomew knew how Alex was about protecting his friends. Heck, last time they were in Artania he'd locked them up for protection. He unclenched Alex's hand and gently pushed it away.

"Let's try to create together and see what happens. In Artania it was magic. Maybe here it will protect her," Bartholomew gave him a meaningful look. "*And our Artanian friends.*"

Alex nodded.

So, they set to creating a powerful scene. One that would keep Gwen safe. When the first draft seemed weak they covered it with primer and did it again, painting and repainting ever stronger Gwens.

Soon they were satisfied that her armor would withstand any Swiney attack. Then they added a few castles, a lake, and even a forest for good measure. By the time Alex needed to leave, there was a painted map in one corner of the studio.

"Now, we have to give her a painting. I know, you talk to her. Tell her she should keep it nearby for her own safety. She'll listen to you."

"Me?' Bartholomew said. "She thinks I'm strange. She's always calling me Mr. Clean."

"Well, so do I. You *are* kind of weird about hygiene. But she's respected you ever since she saw what you did in Artania."

Bartholomew looked away. He'd rather face a whole army of Shadow Swine than try to convince that redhead to do something she didn't want to do. He started to shake his head.

"Come on Bartholomew. She needs you."

Bartholomew sighed. Alex was right. As tough as it might be, Gwen needed the Deliverers. And since Bartholomew and Alex were the only ones who fit that bill, it was up to them.

"I'll agree, but how?"

"Go to her house. Hopefully she'll accept it," Alex said as he headed for the exit.

Chapter 12

"Thanks for the ride, Dad," Gwen said opening the Escalade's door.

"What, no kiss goodbye?" Lifting his sport sunglasses to his forehead, Mitch Obranovich gave her a playful stare.

"Someone might see," Gwen said. "Eighth grade, Dad. Remember?"

Dad puckered up his lips and smacked them in loud smooches.

Gwen giggled and rolled her eyes. "Bye Dad," she said hopping out of the SUV.

As soon as she saw the school sign, her smile faded. She checked the time on her cell phone. Okay, she had fifteen minutes to change before the warning bell. She just hoped no one saw her before then.

Gwen pulled her hood up and made a beeline for the nearest bathroom. Inside one of the stalls she hung up her backpack and wriggled out of her sweatshirt and jeans before slipping into a short skirt and tank. She couldn't do anything about the shoes; her skaters would have to do. But at least she had on some knee socks.

Satisfied that her outfit would pass Lacey Zamora's scrutinizing eyes, she pulled out a compact to check her face.

"Yuck," Gwen muttered. Nothing on her face seemed right. Her lashes were so blonde you couldn't see them. Her lips were as pale as the toilet. And her green eyes could have been the ugly tiles on the floor.

With a long sigh, she laid a long swathe of lip gloss on before lining each lid in fluorescent blue. Next, she squeezed in cheeks and brushed pink streaks up each one. *Almost passable.* She thought.

The tube of black mascara popped open with a snap that surprised her so much she almost dropped the wand. Catching it just before it tumbled out of her hand she lifted it slowly to her face and began to apply coat after coat of Midnight Black. She looked in the mirror and blinked. Weird, like tarantulas framing her eyes.

Gwen held the mirror at arm's length barely recognizing the stranger peering back her. She suddenly got a déjà vu feeling. An image from a memory, or maybe a nightmare tugged at the edge of her consciousness. What was it? She tried to summon it, but all she got was a vague feeling that this mask protected her. As if makeup would save her from something horrible.

Just then the mirror shimmered, and her image blurred. The glass rippled and seemed to melt. Unable to look away, Gwen gripped it tighter.

When her face came into focus, it looked just like it had before. And that face terrified her.

"What the–?" she gasped dropping the compact.

"You okay in there?" a familiar voice sneered.

Lacey. Oh no! Gwen scrambled to pick up her mirror and shove it in her backpack. Zipping it closed tightly, she smoothed her skirt, put on a placid smile, and opened the stall door.

"Oh my gosh," Gwen said, trying her best to imitate Lacey, "Someone must have been a total spaz. T. P.'s on the floor. Gross." She kicked at the imaginary mess on the floor and crossed her fingers behind her back.

"Probably some seventh grade cronk," Lacey said. Then she smiled. "Look at you! Love the skirt and that eye shadow. The cream!"

"Thanks, wanna borrow some?" Gwen suggested letting out the breath she'd been holding.

"Nahh, let's go to the quad and see what's up."

As they walked through the halls Gwen noticed Lacey's power. Every few steps more girls fell in line as if Lacey were leading a growing parade.

Breaking ranks, Gwen stopped to exchange compliments with Coco. She was in the middle of talking about some stupid outfit when she noticed Alex and Zach across the quad. She thought about going over to say hi.

For about three seconds.

Then she remembered how he'd humiliated her. Twice. No, better to give that jerk face the cold shoulder.

She turned away but not before he caught her eye and raised one hand to wave. *Leave me alone.* She thought.

"-so anyhow," Coco continued with mindless prattle that made Gwen want to scream. "When I saw it I just had to-." She paused when Alex and Zach approached. "Hey guys."

"Hey," Alex and Zach mumbled in unison.

"Gwen, ahem, hi," Alex sputtered.

"Hi Zach," Gwen said, ignoring Alex who was staring at her with his mouth hanging open like some stupid zombie. Man, she wished she had her skateboard right then. She'd ride out of there so fast it'd look like she was flying down San Marcos Pass.

"Haven't seen you at the Point," Zach said. "What's up with that?"

"Oh, you know, busy. Getting stuff for school."

"Yeah, me too. Went to LA for some new duds, check 'em out," Zach said jerking a thumb at his latest Hollywoodesque ensemble; rolled up jeans, a button down plaid shirt, and a dark vest covered with rampant lion patches. "But you always found time to ride before."

"I've just been into different things lately," Gwen said quietly.

"Yeah, like being a girl," Coco broke in, "finally."

Now Gwen *really* wished she had her skateboard.

Just then Lacey strutted over arm and arm with Jose as if they owned the school. For once, the pony-tailed Volcom champ wasn't brandishing his trophy. Gwen figured Lacey was his trophy here.

"Don't forget: party at my house Saturday," Lacey said passing out invitations. "Everyone who is any-one will be there." She walked right past Alex and gave Zach a card.

The warning bell toned three times and teen-aged heads turned.

"No losers allowed. No card, no entry," Lacey warned. She shot Alex a scornful look before sashay-ing away.

The crowd broke up as several kids made their way to class. Soon everyone had scattered leaving an awkward Gwen with Alex. He leaned in as if he were about to say something, but Gwen wasn't about to stay long enough to listen. He'd probably just insult her again. Before he could get a word in, she darted away.

"Hey wait for me," she cried.

As she trotted to catch up with Lacey she could feel Alex's eyes boring into the back of her head. She reached up and brushed a hand over her hair, but it did little to shake that burning stare.

Chapter 13

Captain Sludge looked over his shoulder before stepping into the lava tube tunnel. He needed to make sure no one was following. If any ambitious colonel knew what he was up to they might try and get the glory for themselves. And he had worked too hard and long to let that happen.

The torches cast long shadows across the dirt floor, fueling Sludge's imagination, a future where Artanians and Shadow Swine alike would bow to him. In one flickering flame, he saw himself waving from atop Sickhert's Stalagmite while in another he conjured up a vision of dancing with the Mud Princess on the shores of the River of Lies.

Captain Sludge quickened his pace. Oh, how he enjoyed the pounding sound his jackboots made as they echoed down the tunnel. They reminded me of how many nightmares he'd created over the millennia. And if things kept going as planned he would be able to strike terror into millions more. And forever be in Lord Sickhert's favor.

After about a mile he came to a fork in the tunnel which would have confused any other of his kind. But not Sludge. He knew exactly which route to take.

The route to greatness.

"Mount Minotaur," Sludge murmured. "A labyrinth of twists and turns. While others get lost in this maze, I find the way."

He looked down at his shining black boots and imagined every quick step was crushing Artanians into the mud.

Down that fork he found the twisting stair, its stone supports snaking their way up into the mountain. Few ventured this deep into Subterranea and the staircase was strong evidence to that fact. Twining black moss hung from the stone treads and dripped brackish water into the grotto. Everywhere dark puddles pooled making the surrounding soil soft and uneven. Yet the only footprints in the muddy ground were his.

And he liked it that way.

One more glance over his shoulder assured him that it was safe to scale the stair. His cloak blew back in a steady rhythm as he ascended. At the top, hot steam assaulted his face.

She must be asleep. Sludge thought straightening a spike on his head that had drooped in the mist.

"Halt," a gruff voice bellowed. "None may approach Lucretia's Lair."

"None but your captain, Minotaur," Sludge replied stepping up to the torch wielding guard. "Lower your fire and bow before your betters."

The bull-headed man replaced the torch in the iron sconce. He bent low at the waist and tapped each of his cow horns three times. "I did not know it was you. Forgive me, Captain," Minotaur's said his voice barely a whisper.

Sludge sneered. "Are you the mighty Minotaur, Labyrinth guardian, and devourer of human sacrifices or a sniveling human?"

"You know what I am."

"Then act like it!"

The beast pulled his shoulders back and growled.

Sludge returned his growl with a short grunt then asked how long Lucretia had been sleeping.

"The dragoness has rested five long days," Minotaur replied. "Her last raid tired her."

"Ahh, what a sight. Terrorized villagers. Thatched roofs burning. Sobbing mothers. If only I'd been there..." Sludge paused to imagine the satisfying scene. "But there is work to be done. Wake her."

"Me?" Minotaur gulped.

"Is this place not called Mount Minotaur? Do it, now!"

With another low growl the broad-shouldered creature exited through a wooden door. Within a few moments, a high-pitched wail shook the walls.

"Leave me alone. Or I'll burn your tail off!" a feminine voice whined.

Sludge rolled his eyes. It was always the same. Lucretia would go off plundering for days, returning exhausted. Then she'd curl around her jewels and sleep it off like a drunk.

"Go away! I'm sleeping!"

Minotaur shrieked. The faint scent of burning hair wafted into the room.

"I have to hand it to her, she is true to her word," Sludge muttered.

When Minotaur returned, holding his smoldering tail in one hand, he shot Sludge a dirty look before dunking it in a bucket of water. Through the steam, he growled, "She's awake. You may enter."

Inside the huge cavern the captain noticed new pearls encrusting the stalagmites on the floor and more ruby strands hanging from the ceiling. The last pillaging must have been fruitful.

Lucretia's hulking form filled up half of the room. Her dragon scales glowed orange in the firelight like jack-o-lanterns.

She heaved several angry breaths. When about five Minotaur-shaped smoke rings circled her spiked head, she flicked out a forked tongue. "Take that, you big booger!" she cried cleaving the smoke rings in half.

Sludge didn't like Lucretia. Her nasal tone grated, and her spoiled whining made him want to tell her to shut-up. But without her, his shield would not exist, so he pretended to like her.

"Good afternoon, my lovely," he crooned making his raspy voice smooth. "Don't you look beautiful today."

Lucretia smiled. She picked up one of the hand mirrors scattered around the room and gazed into it. Reaching up a taloned hand she patted each reptilian cheek as if she were applying face powder.

"I know. I am the fairest dragoness in Artania." She let out a long breath as if it were a heavy burden.

And the most conceited. Sludge thought. But aloud he agreed, flattering her with compliments about her ginger scales, ruby-red eyes, and knife sharp teeth.

When he had her purring from praise, he asked, "How is our guest?"

"Oh her, why do you want to talk about her?" Lucretia pouted. "I'm so much more interesting."

"True. But your charms cannot give us the power we need for the *Change*," Sludge reminded the dragon.

"The Change. When my cavern will become a swimming pool of jewels? When every Artanian can admire my beauty? When that dumb Council of Dragons will have to do what I say?"

"Exactly," the captain nodded. "And it is happening. Thanks to you, we are gaining power. Just last week the Shielding worked perfectly against a Knight of Painted Light. I had only to hold up my axe and all color was sucked away."

"Trapping his powers like we've trapped her, right?" Lucretia yawned. "I knew that would happen."

"I sent the defeated Knight back to his canvas. I would have loved to have seen Alexander's face the next morning. In place of his strong warrior was a terrified victim." Sludge paused, raising a hairless eyebrow at her obvious boredom. "But the power only seems to last through one dream draining. My axe needs to be recharged after each use."

"So, of course, you need me. All right, let's go get this over with," Lucretia said stretching her back in a heaving roll.

Uncurling her tail from the pile of treasure, she ducked into a doorway to her right. Sludge followed her deeper into the mountain. They turned a corner into a cavern where he immediately smelled fear in the air. He ran a tongue over his teeth to savor its delicious taste.

Next, he heard the frantic stamping of terrified hooves. Sighing with pleasure, he stepped forward to where the room widened.

There he saw the steed behind the stalagmite fence. She pawed at the dirt, as if trying to dig her way out. But there was no escape. He and Lucretia had made sure of that. The unicorn was tethered to a tree inside the enclosure.

"If only the humans knew how we use their creations against them," Sludge said.

"It is easy," Lucretia agreed.

"How did you capture her?"

"When I saw a glint of white reflected in a lake, I knew it was no typical horse. After that it was simple." The dragon flared her nostrils. "I am an amazing flyer. I can grasp bags of jewels, three men, and a unicorn all at the same time."

"Ahh, but the Labyrinth was genius."

Lucretia batted her long eyelashes and sighed. ""I know. And I suppose you want me to work my magic again?"

"If you would be so kind," Sludge replied almost choking on the sickly-sweet words. He pulled his battle axe from under his cloak.

"So be it." The dragon curled her scaled lips back and blew a long flame. Immediately sparks lit up the ground below pale hooves. The unicorn reared up and whinnied in fright.

"Labyrinth, lair. Trap the fair. Jumbling maze. Tangle the haze," Lucretia chanted. Then she said, "Hand me the axe, quickly."

Sludge passed it over and Lucretia stepped closer to the stalagmite fence. She held the axe aloft as if ready to strike.

Afraid she'd kill the creature he needed, Sludge almost told her to stop. But then Lucretia waved it in front of the horse's face and he realized that she was teasing the unicorn. *A pleasurable diversion!*

"Wave it closer," Sludge said stepping up next to Lucretia.

The dragoness jabbed the axe in front of Unicorn's face while Sludge leaned forward and bared his shark-like teeth.

"Watch out for my blade, Uni-corn," the captain taunted with cruel hiss.

The mythological horse drew back and whinnied, nostrils flaring with fright. This was glorious! Lucretia blew short flames that forced the creature back. The horned creature shrunk against the fence posts.

Lucretia began to drag the blade around the cage, digging strange designs in the soil. When the ground was covered in an intricate maze, she spat sparks into each groove. The fires blazed as she twisted the axe handle right and left.

The unicorn's nickers amplified into whinnies with each growing flame. She strained against her tether, eyes wide with terror.

Sludge smiled again.

"Labyrinth, lair. Trap the fair. Jumbling maze. Tangle the haze." Lucretia's voice rose as the blade turned red, then yellow, and white hot.

The fires twisted upward like a flaming vine. If Sludge had ever felt sympathy for another living creature, he would have felt it now as he watched the trembling unicorn gallop in circles to escape the ever-growing inferno.

Flames grew until they touched the ceiling. The panicked unicorn bolted from one fiery wall to the other. She first cantered left until a red-hot wall stopped her. Then, lifting her front hooves, she pawed at the fire. When it charred a hoof black, she twisted around in the opposite direction.

But there was no escape.

Just when it looked like the horrors were about to sear Unicorn's every resolve and destroy her, Lucretia brought the axe down. There was a blooming explosion and Sludge closed his eyes against the blinding light.

When he opened them, the fiery maze had disappeared, and the Unicorn lay in a heap. Trembling with silent sobs, Unicorn's tears dampened the surrounding ground. Smoldering cinders floated down from the charred ceiling covering her once white fur in a fine dusting of ashes.

A grinning Lucretia held the battle axe aloft until the steel's afterglow dimmed.

"Okay, here. It's ready," she said as if what she'd just done were the most boring thing in all of Artania. She handed him his axe.

"Is she dying?" Sludge asked, dreading the answer that would put a halt to all his plans.

"Oh no. It's not that easy to kill a unicorn," she said. "But this is boring. And where's my payment?" Lucretia demanded.

Sludge had almost forgotten. Lucretia always required compensation. And the payment was usually substantial. He reached into his inner cloak pocket and rifled around for the cool oval shape. When his slimy fingers closed around it, he slowly extended his hand until his clenched fist was right under Lucretia's nose.

"A jewel for a jewel," he said holding up the Hope Diamond.

"Now that's interesting," Lucretia said snatching the precious stone and rubbing it lovingly against her face.

Chapter 14

Alex stepped up to the draped easel dreading what he might find. If this one changed too, they were in real trouble. Hesitating, he took a nervous breath before reaching out to yank the fabric off. He watched it flutter to the ground before forcing himself to lift his gaze.

"No, not again," Alex groaned staring at yet another morphed painting of Gwen.

What he saw looked nothing like what he had painted the night before. The forest green eyes and crooked grin were gone, replaced by dead hollow sockets and a mouth unhinged in a horrific scream.

She no longer straddled a valiant steed but cowered on the ground. Her painted weapons and armor had disappeared leaving a defenseless girl trying to ward off the pawing stallion whose hooves now pounded into her broken and bleeding legs.

Alex pulled out his cell phone to speed dial Bartholomew.

"It's the same," he said when his friend answered. "Worse even."

"Paint over it, quickly, like the others, so it doesn't appear in Artania," Bartholomew ordered.

"I will. But this isn't working. Every piece we've created this past week has been changed overnight. We have to *do* something."

"I know."

"The only one that hasn't turned into something out of a horror flick is the painting we made together." Alex paused wondering if it had been altered by the Shadow Swine too. "I think... Have you checked?"

"It was fine last time I looked," Bartholomew replied. "But Mother has been on one of her cleaning frenzies and I haven't been able to get away for two days."

"Well you need to make sure," Alex urged. "We have to know what works and what doesn't."

"I'll look as soon as I can steal away. I believe I can manage a few studio hours this afternoon," Bartholomew said. "Can you come?"

Alex thought for a moment. He had homework and although he could try to blow it off, he knew that was futile. Along with a nose for exotic spices, his cookbook-creating Mom had an amazing ability to sniff out lies.

"It'll take a while, but I'll be there," Alex said, calculating how long his "What Happened Over my Summer Vacation," essay would take. Since he'd skip over the details of seeing a flying dragon over Santa

Barbara and just talk about the Volcom Games he could pound it out quickly. "Say an hour?"

"I will be ready," Bartholomew said in the deep voice that he used when he was trying to sound all brave and noble.

"See ya," Alex said. He hung up, pulled out his binder, and set to work.

"Done," Alex called about thirty minutes later. He waved the handwritten essay in front of Mom's face and then started to shove it in his backpack.

"Not so fast," Mom sang holding out a hand. "Show me."

"Okay," Alex agreed passing it to her. Glancing at the clock, he crossed his fingers.

"Let's see here." Mom scanned the page and was about to point out a place to correct when Alex caught her eye. She must have noticed the urgent expression on his face because her finger wavered, and her faux stern face turned to a loving one. "Oh, it's fine. You go on, have fun."

* * *

A few minutes later Alex was skateboarding along sidewalks and had just jumped a curb when he noticed a red shock of hair across the street. Almost falling, he grinded to a halt and gaped.

"Gwen?" he called barely recognizing the teetering girl opposite him.

At first Alex thought that he must have the wrong girl. That made-up Barbie clone wasn't his friend.

Someone had kidnapped her and replaced her with a cartoon replicant.

But when she raised her hand only to quickly lower it in disgust, he knew. And could hardly believe his eyes. Every time he saw Gwen, she looked stranger than before. Clothes so tight you'd think they had grown from her skin in a lab. Ridiculous heels that she could barely walk in. Hair up in some doo that only a Las Vegas grandmother would wear.

And her face? It was a mask. Like the ladies he'd seen on that seedy Hollywood street the night Mom had made a wrong turn and they'd ended up in the red-light district. When his mother read the "Hot Topless Girls," sign and realized where they were, she'd ordered Alex to cover his eyes. He'd pretended to obey while sneaking a peek through his fingers at the almost naked women standing in seductive poses beneath every light pole.

Thank God Gwen wasn't shaking her skinny booty like those ladies of the night had. Still Alex couldn't help but notice how the leering drivers slowed as they passed. Didn't Gwen realize what she looked like? How it was putting her in danger? Well angry or not, that clueless girl needed someone to set her straight.

Ignoring the loud curses that would have made a punker blush, Alex kicked off into the four lanes of moving traffic his eyes fixed on Gwen as he weaved around honking and braking cars.

"Get out of the way, you stupid kid!" a man yelled out the window of his Mercedes.

Alex shrugged unapologetically and made a bee-line for Gwen. When he popped his wheels up over the curb his horrified friend took one look at him and quickened her pace.

"Gwen, we gotta talk," he said rolling along beside her.

Instead of stopping Gwen matched his speed step for step. But that girl didn't know how to deal with high heels so every few seconds she'd twist her ankle in those ridiculous purple stilettos.

"Leave me alone," she said.

"I can't."

"Go away." After staggering yet again she let out an exasperated moan and kicked off her shoes. She grabbed them by the straps and started jogging down the sidewalk.

"What's up with you?" Alex asked, rolling faster. "I thought you were my friend."

That's when she turned on him. "Friend? Friend?" she snorted. "You talk to me about being a friend? When you have humiliated me not once but twice in front of everyone?"

"I didn't mean to embarrass you. Your looks just surprised me."

"You liked that look just fine on Lacey Zamora," Gwen retorted hotly.

"What are you talking about?"

"Don't play coy with me. Mister-chuckle-at-everything-Lacey-has-to-say."

"Whatever," Alex sighed. "But jeez Gwen have you seen your face?"

"What about it?" She turned and flashed him an angry glare.

"With all that makeup, you look like a, like a..." Alex struggled for the right words. How honest could he be?

"Like a what?" Gwen's voice softened as if expecting a compliment.

Alex considered softening the blow. But then he remembered all those morphed paintings and Gwen's bloodied and mauled body. It might be hard for her to hear but she needed to know the truth.

This all reminded of his first journey into Artania. There he'd seen a giant creature that was mostly mouth, called Mudlark Maker, gulp a beautiful cat, digest it, and then burp up a red-eyed slave of Lord Sickhert. These mindless beings did whatever the Swineys told them to.

"You look like a-a Mudlark," he finally said.

"An Artanian zombie?" she said wrinkling her nose.

"Yeah," he replied, louder this time. "Worse even. You look like that mud monster swallowed the pretty you and spit out a-a-a slag!"

Next thing he knew Alex was doubled over gasping for breath. The pain was dizzying. He clenched his gut; sure that Gwen's fist had left a permanent dent.

"You can punch me all you want. But you do!" Alex choked out while the slapping of bare feet faded down the sidewalk. Although angry he had to give it to her, even with this girly look, Gwen could pack a punch.

Chapter 15

Bartholomew peeked inside his backpack for what was probably the fifth time and sighed. Satisfied the painting was still there, he pulled out the small bottle of hand sanitizer and squirted a dollop into his palm. Patting some on his face, he removed the monogrammed handkerchief from his dress shirt pocket and dabbed the beads of sweat from his brow.

"Alex should have told me there was a gigantic hill," he muttered as he took another step up the long driveway that lead to Gwen's stucco and glass home. He hoped she wasn't watching him right then. She probably challenged everyone that approached to a race up the canyon. And he knew from experience that Gwen's challenges usually ended up with her as the winner. Like her arm-wrestling matches against half the boys in seventh grade.

Alex's words rung in his ears. *Look strong or you'll blow it.*

When teamwork had kept at least one painting intact, they decided to give it to Gwen, hoping that it would stop whatever was threatening her.

But when Alex tried giving it to her, she refused. So now it was up to Bartholomew.

Bartholomew stole a glance at the multilevel home set into the hillside and blotted more nervous sweat from his face. He knew Gwen's dad owned a bunch of *California Dreamin* gyms, but he had no idea that they were this well off. Gwen certainly didn't let on.

The scent of Eucalyptus, palm, and wild shrubs filled Bartholomew's lungs. Far off beyond the valley of oak studded chaparral, Santa Cruz Island jut out of the grey blue Pacific. If he wasn't on a nerve-wracking mission he would have stopped there and then to sketch the beautiful scene.

Bartholomew squared his shoulders and continued up the drive. When he passed the cherry red sports car in the driveway he glanced around, confused. *Where's the door?* He thought, afraid that the entry could only be reached through a superspy network of alarms.

He slowed his pace and padded quietly on the concrete, imagining that each shrub hid a microphone and motion detecting lasers. Afraid to go forward, terrified to go back, Bartholomew halted.

Sure a siren would blow at any moment.

Just when he thought a flash of light was triggering the alarms, he found the steps that lead to the entry. Heart pounding, Bartholomew tip-toed upward stopping every few feet to wipe more sweat from his forehead and the back of his neck.

Finally, he was facing a geometric wood and glass door. He was just about to ring the bell when the door swung open and a bear of a man barreled out.

"Oop," the burly man said almost bumping right into him. He stopped his leather gym bag mid-swing to survey Bartholomew.

Bartholomew straightened his tie and brushed back his hair. But he fought the urge to put on more hand sanitizer, figuring Mr. Obranovich would think it rude.

"Sorry, kid. I have my own church."

"Huh?"

"Whatever you're selling, we're not buying." He glanced at his gold watch. "And you might work on your pitch. 'Huh' doesn't cut it."

"I'm not selling anything, I'm here to…" Bartholomew cleared his throat. "See Gwen."

Muscle Man planted his fists firmly in his waist and bent over until he was face to face with Bartholomew. Keeping one hand curled into a fist, he pushed his aviator sunglasses up to the top of his shaved head and stared right into the boy's twitching eyes.

"My-daughter-does-not-date," he said.

Bartholomew gulped and bobbed his head up and down. He flapped his jaws, but nothing came out. If he wasn't stuck in that spot like a stink bug on its back, he'd have run away full speed.

"Dad, what are you doing to B-3?" a familiar voice asked. "Stop getting all blustery before you scare him to death." Gwen stood in the doorway hands on hips, a mini-me of her father. But she didn't look like Alex described; not a smidgen of makeup on today.

"Oh, that's good," Bartholomew said finally responding to Gwen's father.

Mr. Obranovich gave Bartholomew a perplexed look before turning to his daughter. "You know the rules about dating," he said.

"Dating Mr. Clean?" Gwen burst out laughing. "Yeah right. And tomorrow I'm going out with the Tidy Bowl Man."

Even though dating Gwen was the furthest thing from his mind, Bartholomew couldn't help but feel insulted. Chewing on his lower lip, he tried to think of witty come backs like the boys in books he read. But nothing came to mind.

"Oh, I remember you telling me about this kid." The man chuckled and thrust out a beefy hand. "Mitch Obranovich, damn glad to meet you."

Bartholomew was afraid the man would crush every bone in his hand, adding injury to insult; but Mother's words about being polite were hardwired in his brain, so he extended an arm. His eyebrows raised in surprise when the man's grip was firm but gentle.

"The pleasure is mine sir," he managed to say.

Mr. Obranovich glanced at his watch. "Damn, three minutes forty seconds late. Gotta go." He turned back to Gwen. "You know the drill Tinker Bell."

"Tinker Bell?" Bartholomew mouthed with a grin. Being compared to the tidy bowl man didn't sting so badly now.

"Boys stay outside. Yes Dad," Gwen replied glaring at Bartholomew.

"You heard that young man?" Mr. Obranovich demanded.

"Outside, yes sir." Bartholomew's grin faded as he stood at attention and fought a strange desire to salute.

When her Dad's Ferrari engines were revving down the hill, Gwen turned to Bartholomew.

"Okay dude, in the two years I've known you, you've never once showed up here. What's up?"

Bartholomew started to explain to a doubting Gwen how the Swineys had somehow altered recent creations. In halting words, he told her that only one had stayed the same: the painting he and Alex had created together.

He pulled it out of his backpack. "We thought this would protect you," he said, holding up the painting of Gwen surrounded by armored knights.

"You're kidding, right?"

"Of course not. I think it'll help."

"No thanks, I'm fine." Gwen held up both hands.

"Come on Gwen, you've fought them. You know what those monsters can do. And we all have had the nightmares."

He saw the blood drain from her face and *knew*. Shadow Swine had been invading her dreams. Recently.

"No, I haven't," Gwen said, obviously lying.

"Really?" Bartholomew asked. "That is not what it looks like. I hear you had, had changed."

"Do I look 'changed' Mr. Clean?"

"Well, no but-Alex said that you were acting, I don't know unGwenlike. He said you looked strange."

Gwen's nose began to twitch. Bartholomew saw some red creep into her pale cheeks; angry red, not healthy red.

"Strange?"

"Well weird, atypical." Bartholomew was not getting through.

"Now you two are talking behind my back?" Her nose twitched even more.

"It's not like that. We want to help you."

"I don't need Alex, yours, or anybody else's help."

"Just take the painting. Please?" Bartholomew tried to hand it to her again.

"No."

"But-you-I mean the dragons they help, and there's armor ..." he stammered, knowing he was making no sense.

"No way. I think it's time for you to leave."

"Come on, you have to take it. It's important. And it could help you return to-to normal."

"Normal? Normal? I'll tell you about normal. Normal is a boy seeing a dressed-up girl and telling her she's hot. That's normal. Understand jerk wad? I'm not taking anything that Alex has so much as touched, much less painted. Got it?" She slapped the painting out of his hands.

Bartholomew watched it flutter to the ground and land next to a splotch of bird poop.

"Now, leave me alone!"

He opened his mouth in protest, but the door was already slammed shut. Man, he only had one job. Give the painting to Gwen. Why couldn't he do that one simple thing?

A miserable Bartholomew picked up the limp canvas.

Just how were they going to protect Gwen now?

Chapter 16

"What!" Alex cried. "You still have it?" He gripped his cell phone tighter. It was a good thing he wasn't with Bartholomew, because if he were he probably would have strangled him. "No way!"

A few people on the esplanade stopped and stared but Alex ignored them. They could all take a flying leap for all he cared. Gwen was in real danger. He could feel it, right down in his bones. And if he didn't act soon, something horrible was going to happen to her. Just like Mom.

"And why did you wait so long to tell me?" he accused his blubbering friend on the line.

"I-uh-thought-maybe she'd-um-change her mind," Bartholomew replied. "I waited there for an hour, but when she skated past I finally gave up. I only now got home."

"You should have called earlier."

"I could not. You know how Mother is about cellular phones. Believes they corrupt your brain."

Alex thought it was weird that such a rich family wouldn't have a cell. But over their three-year friendship he'd seen plenty of Borax strangeness, so didn't argue. Instead, he said he'd think of something and hung up.

He glanced along the tiled walkway wondering what the heck he was doing at the mall. He normally avoided places like these. Only went shopping when it was time to buy school clothes and Mom was cool enough to keep him from suffering through that too often.

His Saturday routine was usually the same: paint all morning and then head straight for Skater's Point. But today something had willed him in the opposite direction.

Alex was just about to throw his board down to cruise west when a familiar voice stayed his hand.

"OMG! Did you see what she was wearing?" he overheard.

Just inside the dress shop, Lacey, Coco, and a few other populos were shuffling through the racks of clothes. Lacey had her nose so high that all Alex could see were her nostrils and chin.

Taking a step back, Alex pressed himself against the brick wall and strained to listen in on their conversation. Most of it was inane gossip about who was texting who or so and so's haircut. But the one thing that caught his attention was an upcoming party that evening.

Maybe Gwen would go. If so, then he might be able to convince her to take the painting. Or at the least having it close might protect her from whatever weird brainwashing was changing her. Wanting to hear more, he hid his skateboard behind a trash can and slipped in the side door. Alex had just sidled close enough to ask one of the girls about the party when the sound of a sliding curtain caught his attention.

He glanced up to see a slouching Gwen emerge from a dressing room.

"I don't know dudettes. Is this really me?"

"Hello? Are you a hot Las Brisas girl or a cronk? It's so you," Lacey said to a chorus of yeses.

Gwen was in a polka-dot dress so low cut you could see her sternum. Heck any lower you could have seen her belly button. Luckily it didn't show anything, Gwen still had a boyish chest. Not that Alex was looking. Much.

She turned right and left scrutinizing her image in the triple mirror. She tugged the cleavage up which just made the hem shorter, so she pulled that down. Of course, this made for lower cleavage, so she jerked on the hem again. Gwen groaned, grabbing the neckline with one hand and the bottom edge with the other to yank the material in opposite directions.

Alex couldn't help it. She looked so ridiculous. He shook his head and started to laugh.

A quintet of heads turned toward him.

"ALEX!" Gwen cried. "What are you doing here?"

"Watching you," he replied chuckling.

"Huh, why?" Gwen asked.

Even if Alex could have thought up some lie that everyone would believe, he wasn't fast enough. The dark-haired Lacey beat him to the punch.

"I know," she said pointing a star-painted fingernail at Alex. "He's stalking you."

"Yes," Coco's overly plucked eyebrows disappeared into her blonde bangs with a knowing rise. "Gwen, you have a shadow stalker. Just like in that movie, *He Watches.*"

Like a line of soldiers protecting a wounded comrade, the four girls immediately closed flanks in front of Gwen. Linking arms, they all glared at Alex.

"You just better back off, Stalker-boy," Lacey warned.

"Yeah," Coco said. "No axe murderers allowed."

"What the?" Alex exclaimed all traces of his grin gone. "I'm no stalker." He craned his neck to exchange a glance with Gwen. "Tell 'em."

"Leave me alone. Would you?" Gwen implored, her arms crossed over her chest protectively.

"You heard her," Lacey said. "So, act like a tree and leave."

"Like I've never heard that one before," Alex muttered and took a step forward. "Gwen, I have to talk to you. It's really important."

When the girls tightened their ranks, Alex tried going around them. But a bin of lace panties blocked his way. He did an about face and shuffled left. The girls retreated toward the dressing room.

"Come on Gwen, you know me."

Just then Alex felt a tap on his shoulder that made him leap out of his Vans.

"Is there a problem here?" the pretty clerk behind him asked.

"Hello? Yes," Lacey said. "This boy has been following us."

"Have not!" Alex protested.

"Uh, huh." Coco hummed, bobbing her blonde head up and down. "He is stalking our friend."

"She's lying," Alex said.

"He tried to peak at her undressing. I saw him look under the curtain," Lacey said folding her arms smugly.

"I never! I just need to talk to Gwen."

"I don't want to talk to him. Tell him to go away," Gwen said.

"I'm calling security," the clerk said.

Mom's heart! He couldn't get in trouble.

Alex shoved past the girls to escape but tripped over someone's big feet. With a surprised cry, he stumbled into Lacey knocking her backwards in the process. Arms and legs all akimbo, the arrogant brat fell into the panty bin.

A shower of satin and lace rained down on her.

"What are you waiting for? Get him!" Lacey screeched pulling a pair of purple undies off her head.

Red, pink, and blue nails clawed at air. Heart pounding, Alex's eyes darted about wildly. He dove into the nearest clothing rack in a gust of clicking and clanging hangers.

"Not so fast, Stalker Boy," Coco said lunging after him.

A heeled toe dug into the back of his leg and Alex cringed. Like a wounded dog, he began a limping crawl over the scattered skirts and blouses. Just when he felt sunlight on his face, something grabbed his hair.

"Got him!" Coco cried jerking his head back.

Her long nails dug in like needles in his scalp. She yanked and pulled. There was a sharp pain and a clump of hair fluttered next to him.

When she wrapped her fingers around another clump, Alex broke away. "Like my hair attached, thanks." He started to stand.

"Hiya!" Lacey cried leaping onto his back. Coco extended a leg and he was a pancake on the floor.

"Let me go!" Alex shouted. He pounded his fists on the floor. Tried kicking. Rose a few inches but they pushed him back down. How did such skinny girls get so strong?

"Hello, security?" the salesgirl said into her cell phone. "This is Diamond Dresses. We have a 7-4-4 going on. Hurry!"

Alex stared at the shiny carpet and saw a vision of Mom. She was sitting in a police station, her face pale and white. Her breath was coming in shorter gasps, a clenched hand over her weak heart.

If he was arrested, she'd end up back in the hospital. Or worse.

"No!" Alex cried. In a sudden burst of energy, he curved his spine, sending both girls careening back-

93

wards. Sprung for the exit, but at the door was a new blockade; mall security.

Alex groaned.

The man was at least six feet three with a stomach so large Alex thought he must be a pregnant woman in disguise. He broke off speaking into the walkie talkie clipped to his shoulder and raised both arms. "Stop!" he cried.

Like a crazed hose zigzagging over grass, Alex twisted around the confused man's legs. Wriggled past before the chubby guard realized what was happening.

Finally free, Alex tore over the concrete to retrieve his board. With a string of kicks, he was rolling down the sidewalk. Completely deaf to the outraged cries around him, he popped over curbs and wove around Saturday shoppers. He wasn't going to stop for anything.

When he reached Stearn's Wharf, he turned left and made a beeline for the skate park. Not that he planned to practice. He just a needed a safe place to think.

Skidding to a halt, he kicked his board into his hands. Alex staggered over the grass to his favorite palm tree and collapsed onto the ground. He lay there trembling, willing his breath to slow.

When he had finally calmed down enough to think, Alex sat up and leaned against the palm. After several minutes in its shade, an idea began to form in his mind. Once he'd strategized the rough points, he slipped his cell phone out of his front pocket and called Bartholomew.

"I have a plan. Find an excuse to sneak out tonight. I'll meet you at 9:00 in the usual place. Bring the painting."

Chapter 17

"Okay, let's put a little more here," Coco said brushing a mega swath of rouge on Gwen's cheeks.

Gwen barely recognized the girl facing her in the bathroom mirror. Over the past few weeks she'd gone from a skater tomboy to fashionista copycat. Weird, she had to admit. And now here it was Saturday night and instead of working out in Dad's gym or practicing fakies at Skater's Point she was in Coco Fontana's house getting ready for the biggest bash of the season.

Lacey Zamora's birthday parties were legendary. Every year since fifth grade she'd thrown an epic event that kids talked about all year. And since her birthday happened to be September 6th, kids actually looked forward to the beginning of school. The first one had a survival theme complete with a climbing wall and an animal peppered obstacle course. There'd even been a den of snakes to crawl through. Totally gross.

The year before had an 80's theme with three retro bands that were really famous back when their parents were young. Or so Gwen heard. She never went. Lacey was a queen trender and had never given Gwen the time of day. Until now.

"I don't know about this dress," Gwen said, tugging on the hem. "It's as white as B-3's suits. And too short. I can't even bend over in it."

"The invite said wear white, so we wear white. And yes, you can, girl," Coco argued. "Actually, you should. In *American Love* the heroine, Heather, wears one totally shorter than that and gets engaged. It'll get you a boyfriend in no time."

"But..." Gwen started to protest that she didn't really want a boyfriend yet thought better of it when she saw the of-course-everyone-does look on Coco's face.

There was a shave and a haircut knock at the bathroom door.

"What!" Coco cried.

"Okay, beauties," Coco's stepfather called. "Let's go."

"Just a sec, we're using the toilet for god's sakes!" Coco retorted in a snotty voice. She turned to Gwen and rolled her eyes. "Parents."

Gwen would never have spoken to her Dad like that. Mitch was all she had. She might lose her temper with kids at school, but Dad, no way. Come to think of it, she usually would have told Coco to cool it in a situation like this.

What had changed?

Later, as they pulled up to the Spanish style house with its white washed walls and red tile roof Gwen had an overwhelming desire to run away. She'd jump on her skateboard, roll off toward the beach and hit the park to do kick flips up the curving concrete. Then, when she almost touched the crescent moon dangling from the clouds, she'd be in a place where sea met sky and freedom unlocked her nervous mind.

But instead of running she thanked Mr. Sheck, put on a false smile, and followed Coco up to the iron studded double doors. Pumping techno music throbbed from the cracks around the heavy wooden frame and drifted out of upstairs windows while strange lights illuminated the palm tree shrouded landscape.

The weird glow of the stained-glass sidelights turned Coco's hand cemetery red as she pushed the doorbell.

What am I doing here? Gwen wondered as a feeling of foreboding made her shudder.

The door opened but what was there didn't make any sense. No grinning Dad or waving Mom. Not even bigheaded Lacey. Instead red glowing lips and bright green hair bobbed in space.

"Welcome to Light the Night," the clown lady with Day-Glo make-up said beckoning them in with an orange gloved hand. "Show your invite and be transformed."

"Ooo, a glow-party," Coco squealed holding up her invitation. "I saw one of these in *Epic Teenager*. Rad."

"Face paint, necklaces, and highlighters are over there." The lady, who Gwen figured was Lacey's mom, pointed and started to giggle. "And be careful in the dark, you never know what evils lurk there."

While Mrs. Zamora chortled instructions between out-of-control hyena snorts and sniggers, Gwen peered inside. In every corner, black lights lit up spinning hula hoops, a giant chessboard with kids as pieces, and tables topped with bowls of glowing liquid. A few kids were dipping brushes in the gooey detergent to make designs on the poster paper that hung on the walls. Others stood around decorating their t-shirts with markers or painting their faces.

The purple gloom was a teen zombie's dream come true. And even though Gwen had been feeling kind of like one of the undead since she'd replaced skateboarding with texting and popularity positioning, it was still full on weird.

Above a table piled high with presents, a billboard of *Happy Birthday Lacey* blinked off and on, illuminating the party girl. With a hand on one hip and head thrown back in laughter she looked like she was posing for the cover of *Teen Idol*. Jose was behind her polishing his trophy while Zach stood nearby pointing his index finger at every kid who passed by.

Gwen usually would have rolled her eyes at their silly posturing but tonight they appeared more macabre than comical. Maybe it was how the black lights made teeth glow and how phantom eyeballs sunk into skulls. Or she could just be tripping.

Her body said otherwise. Although it wasn't cold, Indian summer, goose flesh spread along her arms. She rubbed her hands together, but it didn't help; still felt like she'd been surfing for hours without a wetsuit.

"Come on," Coco urged pulling her across the room. "Hi Lacey! Happy birthday!"

"Thanks," Lacey said taking Coco's present. "And look, it's the tomboy transformed." They exchanged a conspiratorial glance that made Gwen want to step back.

"Yeah, happy birthday." Gwen held out her small gift, some scented soaps and lotion Coco had helped her pick out.

"Aww," Lacey crooned in that deadly sweet voice.

"Chica," Jose said while Zac pointed and winked.

"Dude, how goes the skating?" Gwen asked. "Anything new?"

Jose just shrugged and evaded the question while Lacey gestured toward the table with markers.

"You girls totally need some decorating," Lacey said looking them up and down. "Let me show you." With Gwen and Coco trailing she strutted over to the decorating table and scooped up three markers from the bowl. Thrusting her hip to one side, she fanned them out like a deck of cards for a magic trick. "Pick one."

Gwen grabbed Day-Glo purple while Coco chose bright pink. Big surprise there. *Not.* Coco had more pink than Barbie on Valentine's Day. Holding a marker poised, Lacey asked Coco to turn around.

"Draw big stars on my back," Coco said over her shoulder. "In *Dream Actress,* the main character magically becomes famous after painting stars on her shoes."

"Oh, like as soon as I draw these, Hollywood is going to come looking for your big butt," Lacey snickered as she began to draw multiple stars on Coco's back.

"My butt's not that big. And it worked in the movie."

Gwen was just about to tell Coco that life wasn't like in the movies when she noticed Lacey quickly whisper something in the blonde's ear. An apology? No, not Lacey-like. Coco nodded and then they both stared at her.

"Your turn girlfriend," Coco said with about as much friendliness as a teacher giving out a detention note.

The prickling at the back of her neck held Gwen back. Eying them both suspiciously she raised a hand and said, "I'm good and this is a new dress."

"Oh, no you don't. This is my birthday, so everyone celebrates. And this is washable marker. So, no excuses." Lacey crossed her arms and looked Gwen square in the face.

Gwen's resolve withered like roses in the desert and both arms went limp at her sides. She slowly turned around. "Okay, but nothing too flashy," she said, wondering why she had a strange pit in the bottom of her stomach "You don't have to worry about that," Lacey crooned. "I'll make it simple."

Coco covered her mouth and giggled. Gwen felt the outline of letters on her back.

"What are you guys writing?"

"Something to make you stick out in a crowd," Lacey said.

"I don't need that. It's your day."

"Now hold still, you're messing me up." Coco ordered.

Every tense muscle in Gwen's body told her to bolt. That she should head straight for the door, start running, and not stop until she was safe at home in the hills. But then she flashed on a memory. Or maybe a dream. It was Rochelle. Had her mother called?

Gwen knew she hadn't. The last time Rochelle called, it was to demand money from Dad. And the only reason she spoke to her daughter was that Gwen happened to answer the phone.

"Oh, hi Tinker Bell. It's Mommy. Having fun with your dollies?" she'd asked.

"I haven't played with dolls since I was six," Gwen said.

"Ouch! Hey, watch it, that's my foot!" Rochelle yelled at someone on her end. "Idiot can't do a simple pedicure. Anyhow, I'm busy, so could you put Daddy on the phone?"

No how are you's. No miss you's. No sorry I forgot your last two birthdays. Gwen had handed the phone off to Dad and headed straight for the skate park. Man, she'd skated hard that day, kicking concrete and doing 360's till the sweat soaked her t-shirt and flattened her hair against her head.

102

That was a year ago. No word since.

But still her mother's voice was in her head. Telling her to change. Telling her she was ugly. Unlovable. That no Mom would want such a child.

She shook her head to clear the cruel words. When they faded the memory of a male voice toned in her mind. For some reason, she was compelled to follow his orders. She had to do what he said.

"Transform. Become beauty."

She let Coco and Lacy write on her back. It could only help.

Chapter 18

"The answer must be here," The Thinker said rifling through the scrolls strewn over the roughhewn wooden table. Although the day was warm he felt cold prickles on his bronze arms.

"I still know not what you seek," the seventeen-year-old princess across from him grumbled. She plunked both elbows on the table, chin in hands, and sighed.

The Thinker was about to answer when footsteps padded up the stone stairs.

"You must come! It's horrible," the boy in tights and a loose tunic cried from the castle doorway.

"What is it, Squire Cederic?" The Thinker asked.

"She's scorching the clouds!" The boy stomped his leather boots as if doing so would put out the fires.

"Show us," Princess Rhea said. She lifted her long velvet gown and rose from the bench.

The Thinker and Rhea followed the young squire down the castle steps to the parapet. As soon as they reached Alnwick's stone escarpment, a wall of heat blasted them. All three jerked back instinctively.

"Look!" the young squire said pointing upward.

The Thinker could see why Cederic was so distressed. It looked as if the sky was burning. Plumes of fiery smoke mushroomed over every treetop, field, and cottage.

Thatched roofs crackled and spat red tongues at the frantic peasants in Alnwick Village. Dogs ran in every direction. Bleating calves and braying mules pawed at the earth while goats strained against their tethers.

All sought escape when there was none.

And then amongst the dark clouds a reptilian form appeared. First its long orange snout pierced the mist. Then a spiked head and jewel-encrusted throat emerged. Soon her scaled body was swooping toward them.

"Lucretia," The Thinker cursed.

"Not again," Princess Rhea said shaking her long auburn mane. "Her pillaging hath increased five-fold these last few weeks."

"If I could face her with the tip of a sword, she would think better of raiding our lands." Cederic said.

"Someday you may, young squire. But for now, we need to figure out how she is gaining such power. Because there seems to be a ripple effect on Earth."

"What dost thou mean?" Princess Rhea asked furrowing her brow.

The Thinker couldn't tell her about Sludge's victories. How he'd defeated Alex and Bartholomew's best paintings and sculptures. The Gothians had so little to hope for in recent months.

"Let us say that the Deliverers create, but not every Knight of Painted Light can withstand Sickhert's attack," he said, deciding upon a middle course.

"No, that cannot be," Rhea protested. "They should be able to stop all nightmares."

Another fireball escaped the dragon's mouth and flew towards them.

"Duck!" Cedric shouted pulling Princess Rhea down behind the stone battlements.

The Thinker extended his bronze arm over the princess to shield her body. The comet like blaze struck the tower behind them with a thunderous boom. Stone and mortar rained down, peppering them in fine dust.

"I want jewels!!" a snotty voice cried from above. "Now! Or I will burn every last cottage to the ground."

Princess Rhea glanced at The Thinker. "Do I appease?" she asked.

"No, we should fight!" Cedric argued. "If we give in, she will only demand more."

"Undoubtedly, but we have too few soldiers left to battle her," The Thinker said.

"Why did all the knights have to go on that dumb quest anyhow," Cedric grumbled. "The Golden Dragon is gone."

"I want treasure!" Lucretia screeched spitting more flames which struck two bleating goats. A little peasant girl reached for her pets, but they had already disappeared in a puff of smoke. She fell to her knees sobbing over their smoldering ashes.

"I can't take this." The princess turned to The Thinker. "Do something."

The Thinker glanced at the meager band of soldiers guarding the towers and keep. Most of the knights had gone to seek the Golden Dragon egg so there were few to guard Alnwick Castle. But even if they'd had a hundred crossbow-armed warriors, it would not have been enough to overpower Lucretia. Concession seemed to be their only choice.

With a heavy sigh The Thinker stepped up to the battlement wall. "Agreed!" he cried through cupped hands. "Just leave our people alone!"

Lifting her head in a victory roar, the dragoness swooped over them, and dove toward the grassy courtyard below. She landed in the center of the inner bailey but kept her wings poised for flight.

As their leader, the bronze man should have some sort of plan. But with more questions than answers he was just as perplexed as his companions. So, he stood silent, thinking. The princess waited long moments and then raised her hands in exasperation.

"Come Cederic, help me gather the treasure," Rhea groaned.

The fourteen-year old squire nodded and the two of them disappeared within the round tower.

The Thinker pondered over recent events. Ever since the Middle Ages dragons had raided villages, but never like this. A single dragoness terrorizing every farm, castle, and cathedral throughout Gothia? It was unheard of. He had long suspected that Lucretia was working with the Shadow Swine. But was she a traitor?

He had to know.

When Princess Rhea and Cederic emerged from the tower a few minutes later, a treasure- filled sack between them, an idea formed in The Thinker's sculpted mind. He stared after the pair plodding down the stony steps until he had a clear strategy. Then he shuffled quickly to stop them just before they reached the courtyard door.

"Wait," he said. "Just because we are giving in, does not mean that we should part ways empty handed."

"Hide some of the riches?" Cederic asked.

"Not all treasure can be held, Squire. Most is in the mind." He tapped his bronze head with a finger.

Princess Rhea's honey-colored eyes narrowed, and she nodded slowly. "Information can be more valuable than an arsenal of jewels."

"Exactly. Now follow my lead." The Thinker opened the door leading to the grassy courtyard and the waiting dragoness.

"Ahh our esteemed leader," Lucretia purred sarcastically. "Still quoting the Prophecy and how the Deliverers will save us?"

"Lucretia," The Thinker said in a voice that gave nothing away.

"Please accept these tokens, dear dragon," Princess Rhea said opening the sack that Cederic and she had carried down the castle steps.

"Of course, these jewels are nothing compared to your beauty," The Thinker said before turning to Cederic "Wouldn't you agree, young Squire?"

"Hmmm," Cederic mumbled and started to roll his eyes until The Thinker gave him a sharp look. "That umm jeweled dagger there isn't nearly as sharp as your tongue."

"I *can* flick fire with amazing accuracy," Lucretia said.

"And your scales are so much shinier than before. Did you notice that, Thinker?" Princess Rhea said, catching onto the flattery game much quicker than Cederic.

"Ahh yes, I was wondering how that could even be possible?" The Thinker asked.

"A dragon cream?" Rhea suggested.

"Yes, I know," Lucretia said with a long yawn. "My scales have always sparkled, but lately I've found ways to polish them to a finer sheen."

"Really?" The Thinker asked, feigning interest.

"Tell us, Lucretia. What is your secret?" Princess Rhea asked.

"Well, if you heat them in the caverns of Subterranea and brush vigorously at the same time, it smooths even the toughest scales."

"And you have been below recently?" The Thinker asked with as harmless an expression as he could muster.

"Well yes I did go..." Lucretia paused and narrowed her snake-like eyes. "I don't have time for this. Just give me my jewels."

Rhea and Cederic tied the bundle back up and stepped away. The dragon curled her snout in a leering smile and grasped the canvass bag in her talons. Blowing a quick flame, she ordered them to keep their distance until she was over the castle walls. Keeping her eyes trained on them all the while, Lucretia flapped her scaly wings a few times before taking off like a catapult for the skies.

The Thinker turned to Rhea. "So now we know for sure. Lucretia went below to the Shadow Swine's lair. But is she meeting with them? And if so, how does this increase their power?"

"All I know is that if we don't do something soon there will be no more villages to burn," Rhea said, shaking her head angrily.

"I for one will not let that happen, dear Princess. I pledge my honor on it," Squire Cederic made a fist and crossed an arm over his chest.

"Thank you, Squire but what we need are the Deliverers. Now, more than ever," Rhea said.

"Will they come?" Cederic asked.

"I am not sure." The Thinker glanced in his palm to check. There he saw vague outlines of Alex and Bartholomew. They seemed set on a path for Artania but exactly when wasn't clear.

But there was one thing as clear as the Lakes of Avalon. It better be soon. Or Gothia would be lost forever.

Chapter 19

The gate slammed behind him. Alex flinched and glanced over his shoulder. No glowing faces yet.

That was a relief. He couldn't be kicked out until Gwen had the painting. For some reason, he couldn't shake the feeling that without it, something horrible would happen.

He slung his backpack around and pulled out the house plans he'd downloaded earlier. According to the diagram, the box should be close to the second window. Using his cell phone as a flashlight, he set them down to memorize each detail before pressing up against the Spanish style home and shuffling toward what he thought was a metal panel.

"Yeah right," a voice came from what sounded like right in front of him.

Alex slid down, scraping his backpack against the rough stucco in the process. When a second voice joined the first, he crouched further under the queen palm, praying he wouldn't be discovered.

And counted.

But the voices drew no closer. Alex peered through the sharp fronds until he was sure the coast was clear. Taking a deep breath, he stood up and began groping along the wall. Five steps. Ten. Fifteen.

He squinted in the dim light. *Where the blueberries is it?*

These plans suck! He thought ready about to turn back and go the other way. Then he felt cool metal. Alex cupped his hand around his cellphone light and targeted in on the wall. The metal box waited like a safe ready to be cracked.

Alex opened the small grey door and examined the fuses inside, running a finger over them until he found a toggle switch labeled, *Main.* As soon as he pulled it, everything plunged into darkness. The pumping techno turned to absolute silence followed by a few surprised cries.

When Alex heard the loud curses, he hurried back through the gate. He knew he had precious seconds before someone would come check the fuses. He glanced around, expecting to find his buddy there.

No B-3.

"Bartholomew?" he whispered.

Still no reply.

Mr. Clean had better not have bailed on the mission.

"Where are you?" Alex whispered hoarsely.

Alex couldn't imagine Bartholomew running away. Even though his friend might seem wimpy to others, he'd always stepped up to the plate when there was true danger. Maybe someone had seen him.

Then Alex heard a faint moan about twenty feet away and saw something glowing blue through the murky light. He took a step closer to the figure on the ground.

"Bartholomew? Is that you?"

"Ohhh, my head," the Smurf-faced figure muttered.

Alex dashed forward to find Bartholomew lying face down over the curb. "You okay?"

"I don't know. Feel funny," Bartholomew said between long breaths. "Head spinning."

Alex tried to think. Was he really hurt? If B-3 had a concussion they would have to abort the mission.

"Look. How many fingers?" he asked holding up two.

Bartholomew sat up and said four.

"Close enough," Alex said. He wrapped an arm around Bartholomew's torso and pulled him to his feet. "Let's go," he said, half-carrying, half-dragging the boy into the side yard.

Now in complete darkness, he had to map out the steps he'd just taken to keep them from tripping over the flagstones. Even then, he bumped into the wall twice before rounding the corner to the main yard.

That's when they came face to face with the shadowy figure. "What are you boys doing here?" the flashlight wielding man demanded.

Shielding his eyes from the bright beam, Alex looked to Bartholomew.

"Umm, do you know where the bathroom is?" he blurted.

"Go back that way. There's one in the pool house," the man Alex supposed was Lacey's dad grumbled.

"Thanks sir," Alex said tugging Bartholomew toward the backyard where the party had turned into a ghostly dance of cell phone lights.

Chapter 20

Gwen clenched her fists. If she heard Lacey whine, "Hurry up Dad. This is ruining my party!" one more time, she'd scream.

In the dark house a couple of kids held up their cell phones lights making the glowing faces even more macabre. "I gotta get outside," Gwen mumbled, reaching into the pocket that didn't exist. When she realized her cell was in her jeans back at Coco's house, she began groping toward the exit.

The glass slider filtered blue crystals like distant stars. Gwen peered through the half-open door, at a back yard where faces glowed in the moonlight, two girls clung to each other beneath a palm tree, and cell phone screens danced in the darkness.

Outside rustling palm fronds and tropical leaves accompanied a chorus of how the party sucked. The breeze of a night turned cool twisted around her bare legs. Gwen shuddered and rubbed her arms, wishing she hadn't worn such a thin tee. What she wouldn't give to be snuggled against her dad's big barrel chest right then.

When she thought she heard a friendly voice, she stepped closer to the pool and called, "Zach, is that you?"

But the head that pivoted toward her like a possessed demon was not Mr. Entertainment. Not even close. The face was male, yes, but so much older that Gwen wondered why he was at a13-year-old's party. His entire chin and upper lip were covered in thick stubble and his heavy brows overshadowed his eyes. Gwen flashed on a memory of those hunchbacked monsters in Artania and stepped back.

"Another dip wad kid. This party blows," the guy sneered looking up from the screen.

In normal circumstances, Gwen would have agreed. But in that moment even Coco's inane movie quotes would have been preferable to standing face to face with someone who looked like a shadowy half-human.

She glanced away.

"Yeah, be afraid kid. Be very afraid," he said.

A yellow beam bounced past her and Gwen gave an involuntary jerk.

"Daddy fix this." Lacey's voice whined. "Now!"

"I'll take care of it Angel. Don't you worry," the voice behind the flashlight said.

The "Angel" pranced up close to Gwen. "Unbelievable," she said. "Things like this don't happen to me. I'm Lacey Zamora."

"No, you're a miserable little whiner," the older boy said.

"Shut-up creep," Lacey retorted before turning to Gwen. "So, I see you met my dumb brother."

"I'm the one that got the brains in the family. All you got was bitchiness."

"I'm telling Mom you said that."

"Go ahead. I didn't want to be here anyhow. She had to pay me to do it."

"You..." Lacey started on a nasty tirade, reminding Gwen of Mom before she left.

The brother gave back word for word. Every cruel barb meaner than the one before.

Hugging herself, Gwen slowly edged away.

Just then the entire yard was flooded with light and everyone heaved a collective sigh. Gwen squinted against the sudden brilliance but soon saw why Lacey's parties were so legendary.

The Spanish tile patio that spanned the entire length of the house had huge pots filled with trees, Greek statues, and kids lounging on wicker furniture. Off to one side was a Gazebo with a built-in barbecue, sink, and bar. Flagstone paths canopied in tropical plants led off to the side yard. The coolest of all was a huge kidney shaped swimming pool complete with a steaming Jacuzzi, rocky waterfall and eight-foot slide.

The floodlights dimmed as the black lights came to life making everyone's Day-Glo paint pop like eerie circus marquees. Coco, Jose, and a few other kids joined Lacey on the patio.

"Dog, huh?" Lacey's older brother said from be-hind Gwen.

Gwen tilted her head to one side while Coco and Lacey sniggered.

"*Total canine*," Lacey taunted.

Two girls in matching skirts pointed at Gwen's back and giggled.

"What?" Gwen demanded as three more kids pointed at the back of her t-shirt and snickered.

"Drooling dog," Lacey sneered.

Now Gwen knew. She backed up towards the gazebo.

"Dog," a few kids on that side giggled.

Gwen's face reddened. She twisted around, look-ing for an escape. But everywhere she turned were jeering kids mocked her.

Jose approached her, a scowl across his dark brow. Shaking his head.

"Not you too," Gwen gasped.

The friend she'd had since fourth grade was in on it? She sidestepped right. More glowing grins. Left. Laughing tormenters.

Fighting the urge to plug her ears, she spun round and round. Everything looked like a mad carousel blasting macabre laughter instead of music. If only she had her skateboard.

Just then she ran right into a blue faced clown.

"Bartholomew?" She blinked.

The orange painted Alex next to him held up two hands. "Gwen, I know you're mad but..."

"I can't believe... you guys too?" She backed up in horror.

"No, you have to listen," Alex advanced as he spoke.

Bartholomew waved a paper in the air. More insults? Cruel names?

Gasping, Gwen stumbled back. She tried to steady herself, but her foot caught on something. She faltered and began to tumble sideways.

Hands reached out for her.

Too late.

Choking water rushed up her nose. Gwen splashed to the surface for a gasp of air. Sputtering, she brushed long wet strings of hair out of her face and looked up.

Ghoulish clown children pointed and jeered. A few even snorted and slapped their knees. She thought they were her friends.

Stupid. How could anyone love you? You're so ugly. A nightmare voice toned in her mind.

All she could think was escape. Blinking back chlorine tears, Gwen took a deep breath, dunked under, and kicked toward the bottom of the pool.

There near the drain something warm and blue shone. Its warmth beckoned her like a sapphire beacon. She dove deeper.

Not recognizing it at first, Gwen reached out to touch the flickering light. When it suddenly grew by a third, she remembered. But it was already too late.

Bands of color shot out and wrapped around her waist, pinning her arms against her sides. Struggling,

Gwen tried to kick away, but rainbow ropes held her tight.

With no one to free her.

The drain at the bottom of the pool doubled. Then tripled. Gwen opened and closed her mouth in a muffled scream.

A yellow stripe grabbed hold of her ankle and she felt a strong tug. It pulled her down toward the ever-widening drain.

Another gurgling scream and Gwen sucked in a mouthful of water. She coughed and choked, sputtering frantic bubbles.

Her lungs burned as stars appeared in front of her eyes. The multicolored bands closed in, completely covering her. And then everything went black.

Now she was in a place without light or sound. A quiet unknown on earth pounded in her ears. But no, in the darkness her body didn't exist.

Had she died? She tried to move but couldn't feel her arms or legs.

No way! Dad would freak without her. She was his Tinker Bell!

Just as quickly as the darkness came there was light. Suddenly she found herself curled up in a ball leaned over a humming rainbow. Coughing up pool water, she spasmed. Long fizzy streams poured out of her mouth.

Gross.

Gwen blinked and tried to get her bearings. She was suspended in air atop a rainbow that stretched as far as the eye could see. Stars shone all around. But Santa Barbara, or any land for that matter, was gone.

The rainbow felt solid, but her dribble fell straight through. Gwen spat out the rest and wiped her mouth with the back of her hand. As the humming sound swelled, she thought about jumping off. But where would she land, on some freaky star?

Suddenly, a jolt propelled her forward. She hugged the rainbow as it streamed past planets, constellations, and nebula. Riding a multicolored roller coaster through space.

And now she knew for sure.

"Artania again! No freaking way," she groaned.

Chapter 21

When Bartholomew saw the rainbow flash in the pool he knew it could only be one thing. He'd seen it twice before.

The doorway between Artania and Earth had opened.

Bartholomew didn't think. He just grabbed Alex's hand and dove. Under the water the tunnel was already shrinking. They'd have to swim fast if they were going to make it. Paddling furiously, Bartholomew aimed for the opening.

When he reached the bottom, and tried to swim through the doorway, he bounced back. Some type of force field was barring their entry!

"W-w-hat?" he gurgled. He stared at Alex who was trying to break through the same invisible wall.

This wasn't right. He and Alex were the Deliverers. Not Gwen. She may have helped last time they'd journeyed into Artania, but she still wasn't an artist. It didn't make sense.

The doorway continued to shrink. Now it could barely fit the two of them. What to do? Bartholomew punched but the force field held him back. Alex's karate kick had the same result.

Then Alex pointed at the painting of Gwen and the knights still held in in his grasp. With immediate understanding, Bartholomew pressed it toward the force field.

There was a slight vibration. A shimmering. Then the rainbow quivered in undulating waves.

Bartholomew reached out a tentative hand. The force field was gone! Kicking wildly, he dove for the opening.

Suddenly he was atop a rainbow; the same one he'd ridden two years in a row. The pool was gone, and a warm breeze was picking up speed. A crescent moon and twinkling stars shone in the inky sky. It was all so beautiful.

He blinked. Where was Alex?

"Dammit! Let go of my shoe!" he heard from above.

Overhead Alex dangled upside down, one foot caught in the nearly closed doorway. His hair dripped onto the rainbow as he struggled to get free.

"Use your hands," Bartholomew said.

Alex nodded. Bending at the waist he reached his fingers into the wedge between his foot and the hole. Once he had both hands in, Alex forced the doorway apart and fell onto the rainbow next to Bartholomew.

Minus one tennis shoe.

He didn't have time to talk about it because the next thing he knew they were jetting through space.

Wind whipped their hair as galaxies blurred past. While watching this stream of stars Bartholomew wondered where they would go this time. Would there be pyramids with Egyptian gods? Or a Renaissance town helping Leonardo de Vinci find his daughter? Perhaps they'd go to one of the lands he'd heard mentioned on previous journeys like the Photography District or the Paleolithic Territory.

Shivering from both excitement and fear, he glanced at Alex. Although they would have powers in Artania, he knew that many dangers lie ahead. For both of them.

Alex always made him feel braver. Something about the way he put his own feelings aside as he faced whatever they met. Oh, sure Alex flinched at terrifying monsters like anyone, but whenever his friends faced danger he'd clench his jaw to tackle whatever might come.

He was so glad to have him by his side.

The rainbow suddenly halted, and Bartholomew tensed, knowing what was next. Sure enough, two seconds later the rainbow disappeared.

And they were falling through the blackness of space.

In a blink the sky grew bright and a midday sun appeared. Cotton clouds and paper geese whooshed past. After what seemed like an eternity, they splashed down in the middle of a lake.

Still holding the painting, Bartholomew kicked to the surface and starting treading water. His best friend's lost tennis shoe bobbed next to him on the surface. "Alex? Where are you?" he called.

Quiet.

Throat tight, Bartholomew glanced around and turned a full circle. The ripples on the water had calmed. No bubbles fizzed at the surface.

"Alex?" Bartholomew was about to dive down when his best friend popped up next to his floating shoe. He flipped the water out of his hair and spat.

"Are you okay?"

"Fine," Alex replied grabbing his shoe and slipping in on under water. "Where are we?"

Bartholomew squinted at the painted landscape. Mountain peaks jut chins at the cloud peppered sky their hill feet rolling toward the lake. Of course, these weren't a literal landscape. Because Artania was created by art, it all looked a little more like a movie set than a remote wilderness. Even though he'd seen it before, Bartholomew had to blink at the breathtaking view where paint, clay, and collage melded together into a single cohesive land.

Bartholomew's free hand glided back and forth as he scissor-kicked. "Nothing looks familiar. And there's no sign of anyone. Or Gwen. That's strange."

The lake's fingers stretched about two miles away from them reflecting the clouds above but not a single house, hut, or road graced the landscape.

"Maybe she's on shore. Let's head there," Alex turned toward the nearest bank and began lifting his arms in a choppy crawl stroke. Noticing how his hands slapped the water, Bartholomew considered inviting Alex over once this was over to practice in their pool. He immediately shook his head. *Even if Mother did say yes, she'd probably order the pool drained as soon as he left.*

Alex's pulling ahead roused Bartholomew from his daydream to the task at hand. He looked at the painting still clasped in one hand. Miraculously it had survived the splash down intact. Thinking it might work more magic, Bartholomew rolled it up and tucked it inside the neck of his t-shirt. He then began following Alex with the smooth even strokes coaches had taught him over the years.

Swimming was his sport and he was actually pretty good, which made sense, since it was the only one Mother allowed. Hygenette liked the idea of her baby exercising and getting clean at the same time. If the chlorine was strong enough to kill Ebola, he could swim daily bleaching his blonde hair nearly platinum.

Bartholomew felt a ripple from Alex's direction. Wow, his friend was kicking hard over there. He was about to stop and give him a few tips about streamlining when a great wave splashed over his head.

For a moment, he couldn't breathe. Sputtering, he bicycled his legs and had just caught his breath when he noticed another wall of water gathering strength and rolling toward them.

"Look out!" he shouted, pointing.

Alex turned toward the oncoming wave. "What the?"

Both boys were beginning to dunk under when the watery wall stopped mid-roll. A scaly head emerged from the waves revealing two blinking sapphire eyes.

Flapping the fins on either side of its face, the reptilian creature tilted its head to the side. "Deliverers?" it whispered in a voice as quiet as the lake they paddled in.

Alex dove in front of Bartholomew and splashed the creature. "Stay back," he warned.

"Why, is there danger afoot?" the blue dragon asked.

"Well...yeah...uhhh..." Alex looked to Bartholomew.

"I think it's all right. I don't think it means to hurt us."

The blue dragon drew its head back and said in the softest of voices, "Wade hurt the Deliverers? Never."

Bartholomew felt a cramp starting in his right foot. "Mr. Wade, do you mind if we go to shore?"

"Of course," Wade said lifting his long neck out of the water in a rolling nod.

A few moments later, Bartholomew was next to Alex on a large grey boulder. He combed his hair back with his fingers while Alex shook his out like a wet dog. Then they sunned themselves on the huge rock and started asking questions.

"I know little except that The Thinker did not anticipate your landing here. He expected you to be delivered at Princess Rhea's castle as it was the last one attacked. Still the doorway between worlds connects where it does. As you must have noticed on previous journeys."

Artanians seemed to assume that he and Alex understood a lot more than they did. As if just because they were Deliverers they knew everything about this painted land. Well, Artanians might be born with complete awareness, but Bartholomew had no idea who this princess was or where they were.

"Okay, let's back up," Alex said, with his usual tactical approach. "Tell us where and who you are and what we need to do to help."

"Oh, do forgive me. I thought...but of course. I am Wade, the Water Dragon, and we are in the Northern reaches in Gothia. This is my home, Lambent Lake. And problems? Sadly, our land has many."

"Yes, but I'm talking about the Soothsayer Stone. You know it?" Alex asked patiently.

"Their battle will be long with 7 evils to undo. But our world will be saved if their art is true," Wade recited solemnly.

"You got it. Now B-3 and I have undone two evils. And the Thinker told us there'd be seven in all. So, it only follows that we're here for our third mission."

"Ahh, that which endangers our land."

Nodding Alex and Bartholomew waited with expectant faces. A few moments passed but Wade said nothing more.

"Mr. Wade? Do you know?" Bartholomew asked, crossing his fingers that another kidnapping wouldn't be involved.

"The Golden Dragons filled the sky,
Uniting Gothia in creation ties,
But one by one the great ones died,
As we search both low and high,

For a hatchlings birthing cry," Wade said as the flippers behind his jaw flapped sadly.

Shrugging, Bartholomew exchanged a bewildered look with Alex. He'd read that dragons often spoke in riddles but solving them wasn't really his thing. And Alex was good at math, not puzzles. He shrugged and was about to ask what the riddle meant when he heard a helicopter-like sound.

Bartholomew looked up to find an oil painted dragon swooping towards them whose green and brown scales shone like dewy autumn leaves. While he couldn't help but imagine sculpting that lovely form, her sheer size was so terrifying that he found himself ducking for cover.

"Water Brother. You have found them!" she called down.

"Stay back," Alex called shielding Bartholomew with his body.

"I'm not going to land on you for Heaven's sakes," the dragon said in a motherly voice. Flapping her leathery wings, she glided past, landing on a grassy knoll some twenty feet away.

"Erantha, I am glad you have come. Confusion surrounds the Deliverers."

"The Thinker told me as much. Somehow the doorways crossed, separating the younglings."

"Well we do have two," Wade said, resting a heavy forepaw on Bartholomew's shoulder.

The added weight thrust Bartholomew forward, knocking him to his knees. He barked his shin on a boulder and gave an involuntary yelp before rolling over onto his bottom to rub his sore leg.

"You okay, bud?" Alex asked, shooting Wade a dirty look.

"And now you've hurt the little darling," Erantha clucked her tongue and shook a single claw at Wade.

Wade blinked his sapphire eyes with a wounded look. "I was trying to be friendly."

"I know, little brother. So, don't pout. We have work to do. We are at least half a day's flight from Rhea's castle and heaven knows they need us." She lowered her head until it touched the ground. After several moments poised in that position, Erantha raised her hairless brows at Bartholomew. "Well, what are you waiting for silly boy?"

"Dude, I think she's inviting you for a ride," Alex said.

"In the sky? Seriously? What if she drops me?" Bartholomew gulped. He was not a fan of heights.

"Oh heavens. I've been soaring over Gothia for over a millennium. I think I can manage carrying one small boy."

"I'm not small! I'm five feet three," Bartholomew protested indignantly.

"Don't get your tighty whities all in a twist, B-3," Alex said.

"Shut-up," Bartholomew said making a face.

Chuckling, Alex stepped up to Wade who had lowered his head and swung a leg over his long neck.

Bartholomew pulled his bottle of hand sanitizer out of his pocket. The bottle was full of pool water. Dust bunnies! He still squirted a comforting dollop before approaching Erantha.

Taking a tentative step forward he surveyed her massive body. She was approximately thirty feet long and covered with bright green scales except for her wings, which were polished chestnut. Her snout was rounder and more feminine than Wade's and her emerald eyes shone in the sunlight. But the conical spikes down the center of her neck looked more like a something out of a torture chamber than a comfy seat.

"Where do I go?" Bartholomew asked imagining how painful those spikes would be to sit on.

"At the base of my neck, of course," Erantha replied flicking her wings.

"O-kay." Chewing on his lower lip, Bartholomew closed one eye and kicked his leg up. But as he wasn't exactly a seasoned knight, his foot bounced off her neck sending him reeling backwards. "Sorry," he muttered as he got up to brush the dust off the seat of his pants.

Fighting the urge to apply more hand sanitizer, Bartholomew avoided Alex's gaze. He knew Alex would be wearing a teasing smirk and the red was already creeping up his cheeks.

He studied that thorny neck deciding he'd grab a hold of one of her spikes and try a little hop. It almost worked too. He had just got his leg over when he started to slip again.

Clucking, Erantha wriggled her neck as undulating waves sent him bumping like a cowboy atop a bucking stegosaurus over her spikes. He bounced down until he finally landed between her wings rubbing his bottom.

Ouch.

"There you go B-3," Alex said chuckling again.

Bartholomew started to retort, but Erantha began flapping her wings, cutting him off. As soon as they were airborne, he grabbed hold of a spike and held on for dear life.

Chapter 22

When the freaky ground rose to meet her, Gwen used her skateboarding skills to tuck into a roll. It softened her landing, but she still scraped her knee on some gravel. With an angry tug on the hem of her short skirt, she brushed it off.

Why the heck did she let Coco talk her into wearing this stupid outfit?

She was in what might be called a forest, if she were at the Santa Barbara Art Museum. Painted oak and ash trees sprouted from play dough soil. Construction paper shrubs swished in the breeze. Her empty stomach growled but the fuzzy cloth berries on the wire brambles didn't look very tempting.

She heard a rustling and a hedgehog with sculpted metal fur waddled by.

It didn't freak her out though; she'd seen this arty land before. Everything may have looked weird, but life here was pretty much like on earth. Artanians ate, slept, sweat, and even pooped. And they were mostly friendly. Except for those jerk Shadow Swine things. Gwen hated them. Not only did they hurt her friends, but they got inside her dreams.

Although she now was perfectly dry, her ears fizzed with pool water. Tilting her head to one side, she hopped up and down clearing one ear and then the other. Then she waited for Alex and Bartholomew to follow her like last time. She should be hearing a booming crash any second now.

Gwen wriggled her nose. Where were her buddies? Last time they'd landed right after she did. Glancing around, she tapped her foot.

One thousand-one... One thousand two- ... One thousand nine...

No Alex or Bartholomew. Her nose twitched.

She was alone.

Taking a deep breath, Gwen squared her shoulders. "Never let it be said that Mitch Obranovich raised a wimp."

Since the leaf covered footpath lead in two equally confusing directions, she chose one at random and set off.

Along the path, she saw a painted deer that reared up before flicking its white tail and darting into the underbrush.

"Hey, I won't hurt you," she called after the timid creature. Gwen started to follow but then thought better of it in case Alex and Bartholomew turned up.

After thirty minutes of trudging along she felt like she hadn't moved at all. Just trees and more trees.

Where were those doofuses anyhow? They were supposed to travel to this weird place, not her.

She plopped down on a stump and plunked her chin in her hands.

A few minutes later, a feminine voice came from the trees. "Please hasten your pace, I'd like to reach the inn before nightfall."

The next voice was even closer.

"Forgive me Princess, but this armor weighs a dragon's stone. How does Sir Gawain wear it into battle?"

"He is more than a head taller and half a tail heavier than you, Squire." The female's reply was louder yet.

Straight ahead.

Gwen's gut tightened, imagining yellow-eyed monsters with long clawed fingers. She leapt behind the stump and crouched into combat stance, every muscle tensed.

There was a rustling in the trees and then something bumped into her back. But they were in front of her. Weren't they?

Gwen tumbled forward, tripping over the tree stump and grabbing whoever was behind her in the process. Leaves stabbed her eyes and a hand slapped her face. She cried out as legs and feet jumbled.

With a ferocious punch into something hard, she tore free of the shrubbery. A tree branch scratched her face. Gwen pivoted and raised her fists.

"Stay back or you'll get this!" she cried shaking clenched hands. She leaned back on one leg and glared at the painted pair on the ground.

A boy about her size in tarnished armor and a teen-aged girl in a long dress blinked up at her. The skinny knight was trying to pull a sword out of its sheath at his hip. But since it was under him, he just bounced up and down in irritating creaks that made Gwen want to plug her ears.

Finally, the girl next to him gave him a strong shove, rolling him over far enough to expose the sheath. He leapt up and waved the rusty sword in an awkward circle. "Threaten my princess? 'Not, Photo!"

Gwen raised her eyebrows. "I'm supposed to be afraid of that? Yeah right."

"It may not be Dragon steel, but *Hornet* could fell you nonetheless!"

"Doubt it," Gwen said.

The painted girl placed a hand on the boy's shoulder while scrutinizing Gwen. This princess didn't look like the ones in fairy tales Gwen had read. Instead of Barbie doll slim, she had a strong build. So much, Gwen thought she should be the one wearing the armor instead of the wiry boy next to her. The girl's long reddish-brown hair wasn't done up in some fancy style either. Instead it flowed freely and even had a few tangled knots bobbing over her broad shoulders.

Gwen liked her immediately.

"Movie Poster, why have you come to our lands? You know it is forbidden. We must stay within our own countries," the princess said.

"Poster? I'm no poster," Gwen said.

"Photography District?" the boy asked adjusting his crooked helmet with the missing visor.

Gwen shook her head and thought a moment. Then she remembered something Alex had told her the year before.

"Oh, I know what you're talking about. I look different. Yeah, my buds explained it." Gwen paused wondering if she should trust this pair with the truth. On her last trip here, she'd discovered that some Artanians were traitors. A rare few even kidnapped their own kind with intentions of handing them over to those gross monsters.

"You must be made of film. The realism of your face is too great," the painted princess said eying her suspiciously.

Gwen crossed her arms across her chest. "I'm not saying a word until you tell me who *you* are, and *your* story."

"How dare you demand action from Princess Rhea!" The boy's over-sized armor shook and clanged as he jabbed his rusty sword toward Gwen.

"Bring it on pipsqueak."

The boy took a creaking step closer.

"Well, what are you waiting for?" Gwen smirked.

"Stay your hand, squire," the princess said. She turned toward Gwen. "Forgive our manners. I am

Princess Rhea of Castle Alnwick. And this young man with dragon fire in his eyes is Squire Cederic."

"Gwen, of Santa Barbara."

They both waited, expectant looks on their faces. Gwen knew they wanted her story, but she couldn't help but draw this out just a little. That squire looked so funny with his armor all askew, she smiled inwardly.

"Is that in the Photography District?" Cederic finally asked tilting his head to one side. His helmet teetered as he clapped an awkward hand to right it.

Gwen cleared her throat to keep from laughing. "Umm, no. Actually, I'm from Earth."

Gasping, Cederic and took a step back.

"But you are not one of the Deliverers. You shouldn't be here," Rhea said.

"Cha! That's what I said last time your rainbow dumped me here. But obviously, someone or something thinks differently. So here I am."

"We need the true art of the Deliverers, not some human serving girl."

"Hello, I'm a skater and an eighth grader. So, shut your rusty helmet!"

"And what would a nearly naked wisp of girl do to me?" Cederic demanded.

"Kick your squeaky rear for starters!"

"I would welcome such a challenge if it didn't dishonor me."

"What, 'cause I'm a girl? I've beat bigger guys than you, Tin Man."

"Please, cease this. We have more pressing matters to deal with. Gothia hangs in the balance. There is no time for petty quarrels," Princess Rhea said.

Immediately abashed, Cederic's shoulders slumped. Feeling just like he looked, Gwen stared at her white sneakers.

"The quest. I nearly forgot. Forgive me princess," Cederic said, bowing his head.

"Yes, we did not leave Alnwick Castle for naught," the sturdy girl turned to Gwen. "We are journeying to the south in search of the Golden Dragon Egg. Some say it is no more. But that cannot be. Its scales must keep blazing overhead for Gothia to continue."

"Don't tell me. Or your land will shrink. And everyone with it. Right?"

"You do have knowledge of our lands," Rhea said.

"Yep, been here before. Mona Lisa kidnapping. Renaissance Nation in peril. Whole bit."

"I did hear tales of another human helping the Deliverers a while back," Squire Cederic said.

"So, you are she, and can be trusted. But where are the Deliverers?" Rhea asked.

"Your guess is as good as mine. Last time we all landed together."

Rhea stroked her chin thoughtfully. "Powers have been shifting. Hmm."

"Princess, perhaps we should bring her along. A nearly naked girl in this part of the forest would not be safe."

Gwen wrinkled her nose. Blushing, she tugged at her skirt again.

139

Rhea looked her up and down with an appraising stare. "Yes, I agree. But she cannot travel as such. She will need vestments. However, I'm afraid she's quite a bit smaller than I am."

"She's about my size. And I do have a spare tunic and trousers. If we dress her as a boy and top her head with a felt cap, she could be your page."

A few minutes later Gwen had her hair tucked into a cap and was slogging along wearing loose forest green pants and a big linen shirt called a tunic. Cederic had given her an old belt to hold it all together but it didn't help much. She still had yank the trousers up in the back every time they fell.

Groaning, she was in the middle of tugging them when she heard the ground begin to rumble.

Chapter 23

"I told you. I don't know where it is. No one knows. So, stop asking," Lucretia whined with an angry flick of her tail.

"We must find it before the Deliverers. If allowed to hatch–"

"I know. I know. Gothia stands and you lose power. But this is boring. Wouldn't you rather speak of something else? Like my beauty?"

Sludge curled his claw-tipped hands into fists so tightly they cut into skin. He was getting sick of complimenting Lucretia every three minutes.

Still he didn't reach the rank of captain for his stupidity. He knew how much he needed this alliance. Only Lucretia had access to the trapped Unicorn that gave his axe powers to defeat the Knights of Painted Light.

Twisting his lips into a faux grin, he said, "I *am* enchanted *every time* you blow smoke rings and your smooth spikes are wonderful to gaze upon.

You know, I would much rather spend hours talking about how the jewels encrusted in your neck sparkle or how your long lashes set off your red eyes. But sadly, I am but a servant. I must do Lord Sickhert's bidding."

"My eyes *are* as red as death, aren't they?"

"Terrifying," Sludge said pretending to shudder.

Lucretia giggled. "I know."

"Now," Sludge paused, hoping he'd complimented her enough to get back to business. "Where was the Golden mother last seen?"

"Oh, I'm not sure, maybe the Plains of Bramear. The flatlands have many sinkholes perfect for a dragon's nest. Or so I've heard. Of course, they're nothing in comparison to my glorious cave." Lucretia waved a claw at the mounds of jewels and fine silks surrounding them.

"Yes, yes, of course. But that might be the place to start," Sludge said rubbing his slimy chin thought-fully. Then more to himself than her, he continued. "I cannot allow a single egg to hatch. I have to find the Golden before those idiot boys."

"Then go and stop boring me," Lucretia gave a long yawn before raising her head in a screech. "Minotaur! Get in here!"

The bull-headed man immediately appeared from a side tunnel. He bowed his head and said, "Yes, what is your bidding?"

"-your bidding, what?" Lucretia snarled.

"Your bidding, your *majesty*," Minotaur replied with sarcasm that completely escaped Lucretia. That dragon was so vain she never noticed Minotaur's veiled mockery. She was no queen that's for sure.

"Show our guest out, I'm going to take a nap. And you had better be quiet while I sleep, or I'll singe off the rest of your tail!"

Minotaur glanced down at the burned stub and tucked it behind him. Meanwhile, Lucretia curled around a large pile of gems and with a smoky sigh, dropped her head onto her jeweled pillow. She immediately began snoring away, dual smoke rings billowing out her nostrils with every other breath.

Sludge followed Minotaur through a growing smoke ring to the exit tunnel. When he reached the end, he turned to the bull-headed creature.

In a low voice he asked, "Do you love being a slave?"

"What? I don't understand–"

"You hate it. It's written all over your face."

"So, what if I do? It will never change." Minotaur shook his head sadly.

"Do you really believe that? Perhaps I misjudged your strengths."

Minotaur narrowed his eyes suspiciously. "What would you have me do?"

"Simply be my eyes and ears and report Lucretia's movements," he whispered.

Minotaur raised his furry brows and for a moment Sludge wondered if he'd misjudged the creature. He started preparing a speech about how this would all be in Lucretia's best interests when the bull-headed man leaned in closer. Minotaur tapped an index finger to his right ear.

"My sight and hearing are excellent, Captain."

"Pray that they are, or slavery will forever be your fate," Sludge said before exiting the cavern.

Chapter 24

When Alex leaned left, the castle come into view. Cool. During this long ride, he'd learned how to adjust his body to match the dragon's movements. If Wade went up, Alex bent forward but if the dragon were descending, Alex tilted back. This way, he didn't slide up and down the water dragon's slippery neck.

It was all a lot like skateboarding. Alex figured that with practice he might even be able to stand up while they were flying. Unlike poor Bartholomew who was clutching Erantha's spikes as if his life depended on it.

Wade swooped over the castle walls and slowed into a gentle landing on the grassy inner courtyard. Alex patted the blue dragon's back and dismounted with a quick hop.

"Prin-cess Rhea! Yoo-hoo," Erantha called from above. Lifting her head, she flapped her earth-colored wings and hovered over the castle. Her emerald eyes skimmed over the round towers, stone walls and inner keep. When no one answered, she landed next to Wade.

But Bartholomew didn't move an inch.

"You can let go now, B-3," Alex said. He grinned at his buddy who still had a vice grip on her spiny neck.

"Oh, okay," Bartholomew said. Puffing out his cheeks that were still streaked with dayglow blue, he leaned over. But he forgot to unwrap his legs and barely moved. Goof.

"Hurry up."

His friend nodded. Then, with a body as stiff he as a sword, he slanted left. Inch by slow inch he slid sideways taking nearly a minute to finally fall to the ground with a soft thud. Then he just laid there, his legs sticking up like a bowlegged cowboy.

"Pretty graceful Richie." Alex shook his head and chuckled.

A blushing Bartholomew scrambled to his feet.

Just then Alex heard a door slam open. When he turned toward it, he saw an old man emerging from the castle keep. Dressed in a faded black tunic with a red dragon in the center, the soldier squinted at them and adjusted his hooded cape. Then, with shaky hands, he pulled his sword from its sheath.

"Halt, who goes there?" he called in a quavery voice that reminded Alex of Dad's right after Mom's heart attack.

"Fear not, Sir Donald. It's us: Erantha and Wade," the blue dragon called.

Keeping his trembling sword held high, the elderly knight shuffled across the lawn. He leaned forward until he was nose to nose with Wade. Alex figured he must be nearly blind because only now did he seem to be able to see the water dragon.

"So, it is. And what you be doing 'ere at Alnwick Castle?"

"We seek a human girl and Princess Rhea," Erantha replied for her brother.

"I 'ave not seen humans in a millennium. And the princess aren't 'ere."

No Gwen? Alex's throat tightened.

"But where is she?" Erantha asked.

"Donnow. She 'ant been seen oh, on three days now," the elderly knight replied.

"And how fares the king?" Wade asked.

"King Gerald is sicklier than ever. His mind been a' wandering."

"Oh, phooey and fiddlesticks." Erantha turned her emerald head toward Alex. "This might be a bit of a challenge, manling. Although the king has some knowledge, he is quite ill. It is Rhea who has studied the ancient writings the most. Her understanding of the Golden Dragon would have been invaluable."

Alex felt a shadow of foreboding twist in his gut. "But you said Gwen would be here," he accused.

"No one knows where your ally landed. Even the Thinker's Bronze Vision was clouded," Erantha replied.

"I do pray that she is safe. There have been terrible happenings of late," Wade said with a shudder.

Alex stared at him. "What do you mean?"

"Now don't you fret, young Deliverer. I'm, sure she is fine. Right Wade?" Erantha gave her brother a warning stare that didn't escape Alex.

"If she landed *outside* of Gothia," Wade said under his breath.

Erantha opened her reptilian mouth as if to say something but then snapped it shut. "Sir Donald, these manlings are all tuckered out. If it please your king, take them inside for rest and refreshment, I need to have a little chat with my brother." She turned her scaly lips up into a half smile.

"Of course," Sir Donald nodded and pointed his sword with his shaky hand. "Just this way."

"I wouldn't mind cleaning up a bit," Bartholomew said glancing down at his grass stained pants.

Alex eyed Erantha. There was something she wasn't telling them. What was Wade talking about? He considered probing further but had the sneaking suspicion that it wouldn't do any good. Erantha would just say something motherly and smile.

"Alex?" Bartholomew asked searching his face.

"Okay," he agreed, deciding to grill Sir Donald with questions.

He quickly discovered several things. First, this castle was in the exact center of Gothia and that gave it some sort of mystical power. Also, the princess they sought, Rhea, had only recently become its mistress. When the king grew ill, her two older brothers set off on a quest, the same one, it seemed, that he and Bartholomew had been brought here for.

"Young, Manling," the dragoness called just before Sir Donald lead them inside. "Wade and I must fly. But you are in good hands here. Do not fret."

With a flick of her emerald wings Erantha took flight with Wade just seconds behind.

Alex watched them shrink in the painted sky and then followed the elderly knight inside the castle.

Chapter 25

The ground shuddered again. A chill filled the air as if an invisible snowstorm had fallen. The teetering pine overhead threatened. Shivering, Gwen watched looming branches quiver and lean toward her.

Then a white hole appeared next to them.

"The Blank Canvas?" Princess Rhea grabbed Gwen's arm. "No!"

But the sinking tree told them that it was.

"Princess, we must go!" Squire Cederic cried.

The bleached pit grew, swallowing ferns and shrubs in its wake. Another tree wobbled ready to topple over. Menacing limbs stretched towards them.

Gwen felt her pulse both in her chest and under Rhea's grip. Twigs scratched her face as sweat beaded on her upper lip. Any other time she would have punched and kicked.

But how do you battle a valley of nothing?

Rhea's breath. She heard it in short, gasping bursts. She felt it too. Hot and sticky on her neck. *Get away! Run!*

Gwen tore free of her grip and leaped off the trail. She ran blindly. Pebbles shot out from under her feet. Branches slapped her arms.

She looked back. And then she was on her knees. Trousers torn. Blood dripping from one knee. Gwen rolled over and clutched her ankle; tried to stand but lurched forward. Scraped off more skin.

But the cry she heard was not her own.

"The tree. I'm trapped!"

More rumbling. Another cry.

"Rhea?" Gwen called. "You okay?"

The only reply was the rolling sound of more forest sinking into the white. Dragging one leg behind her, Gwen limped back toward the anguished voices.

Just yards from that white abyss, a huge pine tree covered the princess. Now on the verge of being sucked into the growing chasm, she pressed against the trunk. But it did not move. And that skinny squire who was wrestling with it probably couldn't lift a branch, much less a full-grown pine.

"You left us," Cederic accused when Gwen approached.

Gwen started to retort but the squire turned back to Rhea. "I will free you. Worry not, Princess. All is well." His voice quavered as he pulled.

Princess Rhea shook her head. "You and I both know it isn't."

Gwen gasped. Only one arm and Rhea's head were free. The rest of her body was entombed in a bark-covered coffin. The pain must have been excruciating. Her tormented face was screwed up in such agony, Gwen had to look away.

A wheezing Cederic pulled out his sword and wedged it under the tree trunk. He pressed down, but the tree didn't budge. He grasped the hilt in both hands and leaned forward. As Cederic put all his weight onto it, Gwen thought she saw some movement.

But it was just the blade bending.

"It's no use. Save yourself, go!" Rhea said.

"I cannot leave you."

Just then Gwen remembered something Dad had taught her. It just might work.

"Hey Rust Bucket, put that sword down and grab Rhea's wrist. When I say go, pull with all your might," Gwen ordered jogging toward him. She swung one leg over the tree, straddling it. "Are you ready?"

"I trust you not. You abandoned us."

"Give me a break. In case you hadn't noticed, that hole is getting closer and what you're doing is not working. So, get your clangy rear in gear and grab her wrist!"

Gwen thought he would keep arguing but instead he shot her a dirty look and bent over. With a quick apology to Rhea for any pain he might cause, he took hold of her wrist and gave Gwen a curt nod.

Taking a deep breath, Gwen wrapped both arms around the tree. She closed her eyes and visualized the steps Dad had taught her. *Bend the knees. Let your legs do the lifting. Protect your back.*

Gwen tried to straighten, but her legs were locked in place. *You are the bear.* She thought. Remembering Dad's words, she tensed her muscles again, but this tree must weigh a thousand pounds. Even with Dad and all his gym rats helping, she doubted she could lift it.

Her shoulders sagging, Gwen started to loosen her grip. But then she heard her father's voice. *You are an Obranovich. A strong Russian bear. Now stand!*

"Hurry human. The white approaches!" Cederic gasped as another tree toppled just yards away.

Gwen grunted, glaring at the huge tree. She tightened into a grizzly grasp Dad would have been proud of.

Just then the ground heaved and rolled, nearly knocking her over. Gwen stared horrified as the white pit engulfed another patch of green.

Only five feet away.

"Hurry, please!" Cederic implored his eyes wider than that crazy hole.

"I'm trying," Gwen said managing to straighten her legs just an inch. A few branches lifted off the ground.

Rhea's hand quivered in Cederic's. Her cheeks glistened with silent tears.

Gwen closed her eyes again. Her back ached as she strained more than she thought possible. There was a rustling sound. She blinked at the rising branches.

"Now!" she ordered between labored breaths.

153

She didn't have to tell Cederic twice. He yanked hard and Rhea began to slip out from under the pine.

Sweat trickled into her eyes. Her straining legs twitched but she refused to relent. Gwen leaned back. It felt like her shoulders were being pulled from their sockets.

"Hurry! I can't hold it much longer!"

There was a whooshing sound and dust swirled in front of her eyes. Gwen sputtered. Lurched forward.

But the tree didn't crash when she let go. "W-what?" she muttered as it tilted up like a teeter-totter.

"Get off, human!" the now freed Rhea called from below.

The pine tree rose higher taking the straddling Gwen with it.

"Whoa!" she said, extending her arms for balance.

"Jump human, jump!" the princess cried.

Remembering a surf lesson, she'd taken the summer before, Gwen pressed her hands against the tree. Stood. Counted to three.

Then she leapt.

And tried to avoid the bone white abyss.

Chapter 26

Bartholomew wished he had a clean napkin. It was hard enough to watch Gothians eat meat with their bare hands. But that greasy communal towel hanging over the edge of their dining table was so filthy he wouldn't touch it if King Gerald ordered him to.

He reached into his pocket for his hand sanitizer and slowly pulled it out. Quietly he unscrewed the lid trying to keep the now watery lotion from sloshing noisily. He didn't want to make the wrong impression. This was a dinner with the king after all. Keeping his hands under the table, he secretly rubbed a dollop into his palm and sighed.

With Alex and the sickly King Gerald on his left, Sir Donald directly across, and several stewards and courtiers seated around the table, prying eyes were everywhere. Not that they were looking at him. The king's hacking cough kept everyone's attention.

Bartholomew had just discovered that Gerald's illness began when the first golden dragon disappeared. It started with general malaise and a small cough, and at first everyone thought it was just a cold. But as fewer goldens flew over Gothia, he spent more time in bed. Soon he grew so weak that he was sleeping more than not. And two days after the last dragon vanished, he contracted a fever which seemed to affect his mind as well as his body.

King Gerald made Bartholomew's mother seem almost normal. But while cleanliness was his mother's middle name, the king could have been called Lord Grubby. His tarnished crown sat askew over ratty hair while his fur mantle hung in tatters around his shoulders as he used his long-yellowed fingernails to tear it up bit by bit.

"Prince Ulmer? Kelvin My boys?" The king's head pivoted from Alex to Bartholomew, his rheumy eyes seeming to recognize them.

Bartholomew felt sorry for King Gerald. But he could relate; sometimes he imagined Grandfather was still alive teasing Mother by shaking the dust from his long purple waistcoat.

"Sire, the young princes are off on a quest. Remember? They've been gone two years now." Sir Donald said gently.

"My queen went off somewhere. I can't seem to remember. Was it to the northern lands? Or perhaps a ship over the channel. My lady, where are you?"

Bartholomew gave Sir Donald a questioning glance and the elderly knight shook his head. "Heaven," he silently mouthed.

Bartholomew pitied the poor man even more. His wife dead, his children off on what could be a futile quest, and he didn't even know where he was.

"So, you haven't heard of human girl anywhere near Castle Alnwick?" Alex asked, changing the subject.

Everyone looked to the king, but the man suddenly seemed very interested in a fly that was buzzing over his trencher of pork and turnips. His wild eyes followed it in circles until it landed on the edge of the bread bowl. He reached out a hand as if to caress the insect but when it buzzed away he pushed away from the table and followed it across the vast dining room.

"My friend, come back. Your king orders it!" he called stumbling about the room.

Sir Donald and a couple of servants leapt up and rushed over to the wandering king. The old knight grasped his elbow and tried to bring him back to the table.

"My dragon. The golden. Where's it gone?" King Gerald muttered. He shrugged off the knight's grasp and began ambling in circles.

The servants must have been used to this because in a matter of seconds there were four stewards surrounding him. The tallest one whispered a few words in the king's ear before guiding him out of the room.

"Whoa, awkward," Alex said.

"I know. So sad." In that moment, Bartholomew understood how his mother must feel, losing her husband while pregnant, then raising a boy alone.

157

He stared off into space wondering why his father had died in such a freak accident.

Sir Donald sat back down at the long table apologizing.

"So, Castle Alnwick is in the exact center of Gothia?" Alex said, returning to the earlier question.

"Yes. Special 'tis. The greatest kings of this medieval land have long pilgrimed 'ere to seek the Golden Dragon knowledge. But that was long ago, when they filled our skies with gilded wings and color reigned from border to border." Sir Donald shook his ancient head. "Before Lucretia started scorching the skies."

"Lucretia?" Alex asked.

"An evil fire dragon bent on power."

"Is she a traitor?" Bartholomew asked remembering defectors they'd fought on their last journey.

"No one knows for sure," one of the stewards who'd just returned from helping King Gerald to bed replied. "But there have been rumors."

Sir Donald lowered his gravelly voice. "They say she may be in league with them. That's how she's able to raid time and again without painted skies dropping her to earth."

"How do you fight her? By sending out knights?" Bartholomew asked.

"She could not be defeated if Saint George himself were to attempt the slaying," Sir Donald replied.

"No, we appease her desires," the steward continued.

"How?" Alex asked.

"All dragons are drawn to treasure, but Lucretia, in particular, craves gold and jewels. We give her what we can and hope that the Creation Magic will provide more," Sir Donald said.

"Although it has been sparse of late. Are you humans creating?" a lady with long blonde hair at the end of the table asked.

Bartholomew and Alex explained how the paintings and sculptures they'd recently made had been altered overnight. How the only painting that had survived was one they made together, which was now rolled up in one corner of the room.

"I know not of your lands," Sir Donald said. "But this does sound ominous. The White approaches."

Bartholomew knew what the knight was talking about. Supposedly if he and Alex didn't fulfill the Prophecy, each Artanian land would shrink into whiteness like a blank canvas. One by one every country would become no more.

"Well we're not going to let that happen. Are we bud?" Alex said with his usual confidence.

"No, of course not," Bartholomew agreed. Then he leaned over the king's empty chair and said to Alex under his breath. "But how?"

Alex glanced around and then said, "So, these uh, ancient scrolls. Could you show them to us?"

Bartholomew nodded. Maybe there'd be answers there.

"Gladly Deliverer," the steward said grabbing a candle and rising from the table.

Alex and Bartholomew followed him up the spiraling steps. By now the moon had risen and soft light filtered in through the arrow slit windows. Still, with only a single candle to guide them, he had to be careful not to trip on the narrow stone stairs.

The trio was eerily silent as they made their way up the tower. Footsteps scratched and whispered up the stairwell giving Bartholomew a moment to think.

Where was Gwen? And why were they separated?

When they reached the library, Bartholomew saw several scrolls strewn about on a roughhewn table. Some were half unrolled or even flattened by stones in the corners. Several others appeared to have been untouched.

The steward lit a candle on center of the table and handed to Bartholomew. "Now I will take my leave. May you find what you seek, Deliverers," he said with a bow.

When the steward exited, Bartholomew brought his candle closer and noticed that although the writing was Latin, he seemed to understand every word.

"Isn't this interesting Alex?" Bartholomew said pointing at the center of the scroll.

"It's all chicken scratch to me," Alex said shaking his head.

"It's Latin, you know that dead language they talked about in English class last year?"

"I remember. Roots and prefixes and scientific stuff. Boring."

"It says that Alnwick was the first castle to appear in Gothia. It is exactly in the center. You can't read this?"

"No."

"Strange. Mr. White taught me a little, but this is clearer than English to me. It should be for you too." A chill slithered down Bartholomew's spine. Like two halves of a circle, their powers usually complemented each other.

"I understood Leonardo's backwards Italian during our last trip. Why can't I read this?"

"I don't know. But something's different this time." Bartholomew shuddered. "And I do not like it."

"Me neither."

With a nod, Bartholomew sat down to try and figure out what the dust bunnies was going on.

Chapter 27

Fingers grasping tree roots, Gwen's feet dangled over the hole's ever-growing edge. The howling wind whipped at her stretched arms, its roar gouging her ears. Gritting her teeth, she tried to break free, but an icy tug pulled back, trapping her in invisible quicksand.

Cold prickles crept up her legs.

"No!" She clawed at soil and roots but sunk deeper into the abyss. One fingernail bent back and tore off. When she cried out, dirt filled her mouth. Gwen kicked wildly but the stinging frost only creeped further.

Her muscles cramped and spasmed. She wriggled her torso, but this only made her slip further into the white.

Until she was barely hanging on.

For some reason, an image of Dad and Rochelle laughing about some little kid thing she'd said came to mind. She'd only been six and couldn't recall the comment, only that they'd all started cracking up right after.

Gwen started to giggle. Her torso spasmed.

Then the ground under one hand gave way. And the nervous laughter became a sob. Just four fingers and a tiny tree root were all that was left between her and a gnarly drop into the glacial pit.

The frost moved up her body freezing muscle after muscle. She tried to lift her other arm, but it was glued to her side. She was numb from the shoulders down.

Just about the time it reached her clinging fingers, she heard a loud shout and the shuffling of feet. And then she was being dragged face down in the moss. She felt strong arms around her back and kind voices asking her if she was all right.

Gwen rolled over to see Cederic and Rhea's concerned faces.

"Are you well, human?" the princess asked.

Gwen sat up and spat some dirt from her mouth. "I think so. Thanks."

"Then let us hasten from this place," Rhea said offering Gwen a hand up.

"Before *they* come," Cederic added with a furtive glance.

Gwen didn't dare ask who *they* were. That white hole was bad enough. She just took Rhea's hand and stood.

"Quietly now. We must be as dragons and fly." Rhea said trotting down the path.

"Yes, your grace," Cederic said matching her pace. Keeping silent, Gwen jogged after them.

Once they were safely away from the white pit, Cederic and Rhea explained how the Shadow Swine often crawled from these holes, taking Artanians below, never to be seen again. They might be out of immediate danger, but still had to be very careful.

"There have been rumors of traitors in our midst. I don't think it wise to let on that humans are in Gothia," Cederic said, appraising Gwen.

"I agree. Remember that you are a boy, a page serving Cederic and I." Rhea cautioned as they walked and sighed.

Gwen gave them a thumbs-up. *No problem there. According Alex, I look like one anyhow.*

* * *

About an hour later they passed a few stone houses with thatched roofs and shuffled into a small village to stop at a timber-framed building. Here, a creaking wooden sign with a painted spider hung from the arched doorway. Above them, smoke curled from the chimney and a girl leaned out a window to pour a pot of something foul smelling into the street.

Gwen hopped away from the splatter and wrinkled her nose. Chamber pot. "Yuck, painted pee," she muttered under her breath.

"Welcome to the Spider Arms," the black widow painted on the sign overhead hissed.

Gwen thrust out an arm to shield the princess. "Watch out!"

Rhea threw her head back and laughed. "Watch out for Beatrice? Why she is known far and wide as the friendliest sign in the realm."

Gwen blinked and twitched her nose again.

The black widow waved one of her eight legs and opened and closed her fangs in mocking bites. "Ooo, I am so frightening. Beware Photo," she teased.

"Ha. Ha. Whatever," Gwen said following Cederic and Rhea into the inn.

The room was empty except for three heavily cloaked men playing dice around a low table. They barely glanced her way when Gwen entered, although she did notice that one of them pulled his hood down to cover his face. It gave her an uneasy feeling, but since she'd already overreacted to spider Beatrice, she didn't say anything.

"Welcome Princess! We are honored by your presence," a fat man wearing a brown apron over his tunic said with a long bow. "Girl, the best seats for our guests."

A painted girl not much older than Gwen scurried up to them and curtsied. "Just a moment your Grace, while I clean the boards." She dashed over to the largest rectangular table and wiped the crumbs off with her tattered rag. Then she dragged a tall wooden chair over to the head of it and wiped it down too. When she'd finished dusting the benches, she waved them over.

"Just this way," the chubby innkeeper said leading them to the table. He pulled out the large chair for

Princess Rhea and waited for her to sit before gently pushing it in.

"Thank you, Thomas," Rhea said.

Gwen sat on the bench across from Cederic. Behind him a whole pig roasted on a spit in the huge fireplace, but it didn't make her mouth water. She had already been thinking of going vegetarian, but after seeing that thing was convinced. Blackened eye pits. Gross times two!

She hadn't eaten since, when? Way before Lacey's party. Yeah, she'd had a little panini for lunch but that was how long ago? Time was all mixed up. When she'd leapt in the swimming pool it had been night, but the forest adventure was during the day.

Thomas went through a door that Gwen guessed lead to the kitchen and quickly returned carrying a pewter plate with an assortment of carrots, turnips, and radishes.

When she smelled vinegar, Gwen realized that they were pickles. Not her favorite, but beggars can't be choosers. And anything was better than that staring pig. As soon as the princess began, she grabbed a carrot and began munching away. Not bad.

The serving girl arrived with a tray of earthenware mugs and a pitcher. "Cider, the best we 'ave." As she poured them each a cup, her face began to shimmer and ripple. Then as if a rainstorm had taken over her body, her painted form began to melt. Starting with her shoulders, everything went from smooth canvas to rough cloth. In a matter of seconds, she looked

166

completely different, transforming into something sewn.

Gwen blinked but didn't start. She'd seen this last time in Artania. Alex had explained that if multiple creations of the same person were created, the Artanian could morph from paintings to sculptures to embroidered tapestries. Trippy.

With a curtsey, the doll-like girl bowed exited as Thomas asked, "So, why have you graced our humble inn?"

"We seek what every Gothian does," Rhea replied.

"Ahh, the golden dragons. Many have passed through these doors on that same quest. If only they had found them."

"We will. Our hearts are true," Cederic said.

"I pray that you speak truth. For all of Gothia's sake." Thomas raised a cup of ale. "To the true quest."

"To the quest," Rhea and Cederic chimed in, clinking their mugs to his.

There were all silent for a few moments. Gwen fidgeted, wondering if they were thinking what she was. That it was a real long shot. After seeing that white pit, she doubted this land stood much of a chance.

"Where go thee from here, Princess?" Thomas asked, breaking the silence.

"I have studied the scrolls much these past few months and the last place the Goldens were seen was the Plains of Bramear. They contain underground caverns a dragon could nest in. We will head south and then search every one until the egg is ours."

"I pray for your success. The Blank Canvas grows," Thomas said.

"As we are well aware," Cederic said. "The white nearly swallowed my lady." He went on to explain how it had knocked down a tree trapping the princess. "But for this page, I know not what would have happened."

"I raise a cup to you, Boy," Thomas said, lifting his mug again.

"It was nothing," Gwen said looking away. Then she noticed that the dice players in the corner had suddenly grown very quiet. Their dice were still and all three seemed to have their heads tilted as if they were listening in.

A shiver went up and down Gwen's spine. Who were these guys? Something about them reminded her of the gangsters back in Santa Barbara. People she'd learned long ago to avoid. Gwen was about to mention it when a group of loud minstrels tumbled in with a rowdy song.

"I sing thee a tune of my maiden fair. My lady love with the golden hair," A man sang while plucking what looked like a small guitar. Behind him two men dressed in green and yellow shirts and pointed slippers juggled a few balls.

Distracted by the jugglers and music, Gwen forgot all about the hooded men in the corner. She found the tune so catchy that she started singing along. But when the princess gave her a warning look, she clamped her mouth shut.

Oops, supposed to be a boy.

She glanced back at the dice players, but they had disappeared. Gwen tilted her head to one side. Odd. But she was relieved. They gave her the willies.

"We hear that Princess Rhea graces this place. It is for her we play!" the man with the guitar cried while another minstrel blew through a wooden flute.

"You honor me," Rhea said with a slight bow of her head. "Come forth and show us your talents!"

For the next couple of hours these traveling musicians played, did flips and cartwheels, and juggled flaming sticks. Gwen watched mesmerized until all the roast pheasant and bread pudding were gone.

"...and my love was no more," The player sang. He lifted his little guitar in the air with a flourish and twirled on one foot.

Gwen started to yawn.

"Ahh but you all must be weary," Thomas said apologizing. "I will show you to your quarters." He picked up the iron candleholder on the table and led them all upstairs.

And Gwen fell into bed.

Chapter 28

Alex woke with a start. Was that Mom screaming? He blinked and for a few terrifying moments didn't know where he was. But when he saw the candle nearly burned to the quick, it came back to him. *Artania. Castle Alnwick. The quest for the Golden Dragon.*

A few hours earlier when he couldn't decipher the Latin manuscripts, he'd asked Bartholomew to read them aloud before sitting back to listen to tales of dragons, knights, and battles galore.

Bartholomew told of brave kings who'd sacrificed themselves for their kingdoms and how the Golden Dragon became the symbol for Gothia. That their shimmering scales were the true art that held this land together. He then read how Rhea's family came to Castle Alnwick, at the exact center of this land, to guard the Gothian scrolls.

But nothing explained why Gwen was nowhere to be found.

After several hours both their heads were bobbing, and Alex's lids had grown heavy. Stifling a yawn, he set his elbows on the table and rested his chin on his fists.

"Let's give it a rest. I'm wiped and don't see any clues here."

"We must be missing something," Bartholomew replied looking over another scroll.

"Well, we're not gonna find it if we're too sleepy to think." Alex stood and motioned to Bartholomew who begrudgingly agreed to quit for the night.

Even though the moon had long set by that time, Alex still spent the next few hours tossing and turning. He kept thinking that he'd missed something in what Bartholomew had read. But his scattered dreams had no answers. Just vague images of a terrified Gwen running over a pockmarked landscape.

Since he was wide awake already, Alex decided he might as well get up. Using the nearly burned out candle to light the fresh one on the bedside table, he shoved it in the holder. Then he grabbed the robe that Sir Donald had loaned him and stepped into the long hallway.

He almost woke Bartholomew who was in the next chamber but then thought. *Why should we both be tired and cranky in the morning?*

Wind howled through the arrow slit windows and ruffled his hair. He pulled the robe tighter around his waist. He had no idea where he was going, but something guided him forward.

Alex had learned long ago to trust his instincts. So, when a course of action felt right he followed it.

And it often worked. In his last two journeys into Artania, Alex had been able to come up with effective strategies. Well, mostly. Except when he got paranoid and started worrying about whether his friends were safe or not. That had sucked in the end.

Apart from the flickering light from his candle, the hallway was pitch black. But Alex wasn't afraid of the dark. Sometimes the dark brought dreams of new creations. When he reached the end of the hall, he decided to go back up to the library. Maybe he'd understand those manuscripts now.

The scrolls were strewn about from hours of reading, the words just as undecipherable as before. Then Alex noticed a fresh pot of ink and a quill pen that hadn't been there earlier with a blank scroll lay waiting beside them.

Almost in a daze Alex picked up the quill and dipped it in the ink. And he began to draw. Outlines at first. A few details emerged. An odd shape. A circle or two. A squiggly line.

Faster he went. Quill submerging. Ink splashing. Feather flying. More features took shape. His hand blurred over the parchment.

When it was done, Alex leaned back and stared.

He'd drawn a 3-D map with Castle Alnwick in the center, banners flying. Lambent Lake rippled in the upper right-hand corner, its surrounding peaks jutting up. Alex reached out a tentative hand and felt a sharp prick.

"Ow," he said sucking on his bleeding finger. He surveyed the weird map, tracing a hand over where they'd splashed down to end at his present location.

While the mountains and forest they'd flown over were clear, all other details were blurry. Alex blinked and squinted but it didn't help. He passed the candlestick over the map but couldn't make out the fuzzy contours.

He started to pick up the quill again, but something stayed his hand. He knew he was done.

For now.

Chapter 29

Gwen tossed and turned, trapped in the dream.

"Ugly!" Mom hissed, shaking a jar of face powder at her.

Gwen raised her hands over her head as yellow dust rained down.

"More. You need more…"

The powder piled at her feet, over her legs, and up her torso. It covered her neck and chin. Granules pooled in her eyes and mouth shrouding her face.

Gwen tried to cry out but instead sucked in powder as rough as coarse sand. It scratched her throat and raked her eyes. Suffocating, she sputtered and choked.

With a gasp, Gwen threw back the covers and blinked fearful eyes around the room. She barely had time to realize that she'd been dreaming when she noticed the shadowy movement.

A hooded figure too tall to be Cederic and too thin for the innkeeper was hunched over the sleeping Princess Rhea's bed. As he leaned closer, his cloak seemed to change color; one moment black as death, the next tombstone grey. The filtered moonlight dug dreadful patterns into the fabric conjuring up corpse images.

His creeping form made Gwen shiver. He looked familiar but for the life of her, she couldn't place him. She was about to call out, when she realized she shouldn't give herself away just yet.

Instead she watched.

The hooded man pushed back both sleeves and bared his arms. They were strong but pale and terribly scarred, whether from burns or cuts it was too dark to see.

The princess's breath was smooth and even. Gwen suddenly realized that Rhea had no idea there was a stranger hovering over her.

Then she heard a hissing sound like a sword being pulled from a sheath. A glint of metal shone in the moonlight. His knife wielding hand hung suspended on invisible threads.

Gwen leapt. And she was on him. Straddling his back. Tugging on his broad shoulders.

He twisted to one side, reached around to grab her. Gwen ducked, pulled on his cloak.

"Be the viper. Grab the arm for a take down," Dad had said while teaching wrestling moves.

I'm a snake. Gwen thought wrapping a leg around his knee. She thrust a hand in the crook of his elbow.

"Get off!" the hooded man cried jerking his arm free.

A cobra. Gwen tried to hold on, but when the stranger leaned back she fell to the floor. He turned on her, dagger extended.

"Your quest stops here, Photo," he sneered. His hood fell back to reveal a long scar on his left cheek.

She scrambled backwards on all fours, but the hooded man slid forward and thrust. Gwen rolled away and the wooden floor caught the blade. A nightcapped figure appeared in the doorway just as the scarred man pulled the dagger out.

"What's this?" Cederic cried dashing into the room.

Gwen didn't wait for Scarface to strike but somersaulted toward Rhea's bed. The princess was already standing on the mattress candlestick in hand. She hurled it at the stranger's head. Missed.

Cederic shouted a curse and charged, punching with both his fists. Scarface rolled right and Cederic's fist connected with his side. The cloaked man doubled over, but only for a moment. With the young squire now on his knees, he loosened a tremendous kick knocking the boy flat on his back.

The stranger turned back toward Rhea. "Now for you."

Gwen wasn't sure what happened next, only that one moment a hooded man was thrusting a dagger toward the princess and the next he was wrapped in a blanket.

Hands flailed and waved as if in a ghost costume and the knife fell to the wooden floor with a clang. Gwen kicked it away.

176

"Quick, get some cord while he's off guard!" Rhea cried.

Gwen snatched up the rope belt on the floor and flung it at Rhea who immediately tried to wrap it around his arms. But the stranger struggled to escape, and she couldn't get it round.

Princess Rhea coiled the cord and tossed it again.

It landed on his shoulder.

While Scarface lumbered back and forth, and Rhea danced about, Gwen tried to reach for the dangling rope. She swiped but missed twice, her grasp falling short. Would this guy hold still? Clenching her jaw, she focused on the swing's intervals until she finally grabbed it.

"Got it, pull!" she cried.

Holding opposite ends, she and Rhea stepped apart until the stranger's arms were firmly pinned to his sides.

On the floor, Cederic moaned clutching his gut as candlelight flickered from the hallway. The innkeeper appeared at the door, his long nightshirt riding up so high an embarrassed Gwen looked away.

"Your grace, what is afoot?" Thomas asked swaying sleepily.

Keeping her eyes averted, Gwen said, "This guy tried to kill Rhea."

"Verily? In my inn?"

"Seems so."

"But why?" Thomas took a step closer making his nightshirt fall over his knees. Thankfully. Then he waved his candle back and forth in front of the blanket-covered stranger.

Cederic held his gut as he got to his feet. "I do not know, but plan on finding out."

"He murmured that our quest stops here, as he struck," Princess Rhea said.

Cederic clenched his teeth. "Which means but one thing."

Rhea nodded. "Traitor."

"Sickhert's allies in my inn? It's never been so before."

Rhea sighed. "These are dark times. The Blank Canvas grows."

Would that white hole appear here like in the forest? Gwen felt something at her feet and shuddered. But a glance told her it was just a little cartoon mouse scurrying across the floor. *Get a grip.* She thought.

Thomas stroked his chin then turned toward the doorway, "He should be questioned. Bring him downstairs."

Chapter 30

"Get up," the voice whispered. Bartholomew didn't want his dream of twisting clay into amazing shapes with Father and Grandfather to stop. He squeezed his eyes tighter.

"Come on, wake up!" Alex said nudging his shoulder.

With a long yawn, Bartholomew opened one eye.

"Look, and tell me if I'm crazy," Alex said snapping a piece of yellowed paper in his face.

Bartholomew squinted at the parchment. "Okay, hand it to me."

Alex placed the vellum on his lap. "Isn't it full on weird?"

When Bartholomew stared down at what looked like an ancient map, he immediately recognized Alex's handwriting. Funny, for an artist he had the worst penmanship. But Bartholomew had learned a long time ago to decipher it.

"Here we are," Alex said pointing at a castle drawn in the center. "And there's where we landed at Lambent Lake.

"I see, but Alex you're a better artist than this. Most of the map is all blurry."

"I know. That's why it's so weird. I thought I was drawing other places, but when I finished, this is what I got."

"Why didn't you fix them then?"

"As soon as I set the quill down all the fuzzy places I'd drawn disappeared from my mind."

"Do you think it was the ale you drank at dinner?" Bartholomew asked.

"No, I didn't even finish one mug. Didn't like the taste."

Bartholomew chewed on his lower lip. "Perhaps it's related to all that morphed art back home."

"Yeah, maybe. Hey B-3, where'd you put that one we made together? The powerful one that didn't change?"

The two of them had had many conversations about how this painting and Gwen were linked. Since they agreed that its safety and hers were intertwined, Bartholomew had vowed to keep it close always.

Bartholomew pointed at the rolled-up canvas in the corner. "I don't know how it survived our trip into Artania, being in the pool and all."

Alex scampered over to the painting, scooped it up, and in two strides was back at the canopied bed unrolling and flattening the canvas. He glanced down and gasped. "No way!"

Bartholomew's jaw dropped. Gwen and the armored knights they'd painted back in Santa Barbara had disappeared. In their place were several new elements. In one corner were two figures splashing into Lambent Lake with Castle Alnwick on the opposite side. In an open doorway stood a shadowy figure that looked a lot like Sir Donald.

But the image at the bottom really freaked him out. There a flickering candle illuminated a partially rolled parchment exactly like he and Alex had made the night before. Every tiny detail mirrored what really happened.

Crazy.

But it was unlike the morphed mutations back in Santa Barbara. No monstrous creatures or tortured faces filled the page. If anything, these changes were beautiful.

"What is going on?" Bartholomew asked.

Placing his map next to the painting, Alex ticked off each parallel part. "Alnwick, both drawings, Wade's home, identical. From lake to forest to castle every detail is the same.

"What do you think it means?"

Alex glanced from map to painting and back again. Then he got that aha smirk Bartholomew knew all too well. "They are like mirrors."

"I can see that." Bartholomew shrugged, wondering where his friend was going with this.

"Don't you notice anything special about them?"

"Umm, well they all are all places we have been."

"Yep. See? We splashed down in the lake here," he began, pointing at the top corner of the map. "Then we flew over the forest there. And finally landed at Alnwick Castle here," he finished with a flourish of his hand.

"Ahh, like a puzzle with missing pieces."

"Yep, but still the question is. What do we do with it? The other times we were here Apollo took us to where we needed to go. Now it's all riddles and confusion."

"Well, the missing dragon eggs are causing problems here in Gothia," Bartholomew suggested.

"And no one knows where they are,"

"This map surely won't help."

"There you have it!" Alex said slapping Bartholomew on the shoulder.

"I do?"

"Of course. The map will only show us places we've looked already that DON'T have the egg. The fuzzy places are those we still need to search. And you know what that means."

Bartholomew grinned. "Yep. We've got some exploring to do."

Chapter 31

When the three of them finally got the stranger into the chair after a lot grunting, groaning and shoving, Gwen began wrapping a long rope around him.

"You think yourselves bright," the muffled voice sneered from under the blanket. "But you know nothing."

"What knowledge have you?" Rhea took a step forward, but Gwen shook her head and glanced toward the bindings she was trying to fasten round the stranger.

She pulled one end and tied three sturdy knots. With the stranger lashed securely to the chair, she yanked up the back of the fabric. Both hood and blanket fell back to reveal a scarred face.

Gwen gasped. It was the same man who'd been playing dice in the corner when they'd arrived.

"Le Savage!" Thomas cried. "You were banished. You cannot be here."

183

"Yet here I sit." Le Savage sneered making the scar on his cheek twist and wrinkle in hideous shapes.

"Who is he?" Gwen asked.

"Roger Le Savage is an outlaw. A robber and thief. Sent to the north long ago by King Gerald himself. And told never to return."

"So, that's why he pulled his hood down when he was with his buds earlier. He wanted to hide his face," Gwen said.

"Of course, I should have noticed how suspicious they were when we arrived. With the princess in my care, it is my duty to be aware of such things." Squire Cederic shook his head.

"You have acted bravely, young squire. Do not berate yourself," Rhea said.

But Gwen could tell by Cederic's expression that he was full on beating himself up. She felt pretty stupid herself. She'd noticed that those guys were acting strangely but hadn't said a word. Of course, everything about this art world was a trip down a half pipe. So, telling normal from weird wasn't always clear.

"Disclose your purpose. Why were you after the princess?" Cederic demanded.

"I will tell nothing to a weak child." Roger Le Savage narrowed his snaky eyes and curled a scornful lip.

The squire shot him a sharp look. "Put me astride a horse in the tourney and I will show you what this child can do."

"Fall off and break your arse, I'm sure."

Cederic lifted a fist and stepped closer. "What? Why you overgrown–"

"–Go whimper to your horse-faced mother," Roger interrupted.

"My mum aren't–"

"Ugly as a braying mule."

"Hush your mouth!"

Roger widened his eyes mockingly. "Eee aww. Eee aww."

At this Cederic lost it. Screaming in fury he rushed at Le Savage and got him by the throat.

"Cederic no!" Gwen cried when the squire started choking Roger Le Savage.

But Cederic only squeezed tighter. Gwen came up behind him and tried to pry his hands loose, but Le Savage must have been waiting for this. He butted Cederic with his head knocking them both back.

While they were tangled up on the floor, he jerked his body to the side and the chair teetered over with a deafening crack. The wood splintered as the bindings Gwen had worked so hard at, fell away. Before they knew it, Roger La Savage was on his feet.

Cederic reached for an ankle but instead got a handful of blanket as Roger hopped past. With a bellow, Gwen rose to all fours. Shunting her arms, she aimed an elbow at the man's shins. But he was out of reach and she fell flat on her face.

La Savage leapt onto the table and vaulted over a barrel onto the floor. In three strides, he was in the doorway lifting the latch. With a quick kick, he forced open the door.

And the scar-faced outlaw disappeared into the
night.

Chapter 32

Captain Sludge emerged at the roots of the gnarled oak in Dread Woods. He glanced right and left before tapping the ground near the hole with his battle axe. As soon as the opening leading to his Subterranean home closed, he circled the ancient tree.

"Where is La Savage? I told him just after midnight," he grumbled.

The quarter-moon was just rising over the twisted pines and half-dead oaks. Spider webs clung to the cracked bark while moss draped the denuded branches like scores of burial shrouds.

To him this place was beautiful. A nightmare scene perfect for dream invasions. The scattered piles of ghost wood atop a cemetery of leaves made him think of two children whose dreams had been hard to twist. Perhaps if he sent them this image with a few cackling witches in pursuit, they'd be terrified enough to turn away from art.

Several minutes passed with Sludge lost in dream draining plots before the distant howl of a wolf brought him back to the present. The sickle moon was now a high blade cutting the tree tops. He frowned and circled the gnarled oak once more.

Just as he returned to his original spot Sludge heard a rustling off the left. Widening his stance, he lifted his axe. Ready to fight any unsuspecting Gothian.

"-I weren't saying that, it's only that if we'd been there perhaps-" a voice whispered from the underbrush.

"Shh. I told you this discussion was to cease. So, shut your mealy mouth unless you'd like a scar matching mine on it," a second voice rasped.

La Savage. Sludge thought. *Finally.* He lowered his weapon and leaned his hunched back against the tree.

Within moments a trio of hooded men came into view. In the front was the scarred La Savage, sword slung over his back. His cohorts trailed behind, longbows in hand.

"So, you finally decided to show up," Sludge said.

"I arrive when it suits me, Swiney," Roger La Savage replied.

"We had an agreement."

"I have not forgotten. But it did not include my rushing into a nightmare place just to appease you."

Sludge wanted to retort that Roger had just better rush if he knew what was good for him. He'd love to see that smug smile wiped off the outlaw's face.

Sludge always dealt with his type the same way. And enjoyed their look of terror when he threw them into Mudlark Maker's mouth. He could almost hear Roger's cries as the beast's stomach acid morphed him into a mindless slave.

But he bit his forked tongue and said, "Tell of the princess. Is she gone?"

Lip curling slightly, La Savage stared past Sludge. The captain thought he noticed an uncomfortable shrug from the cocky outlaw. The other two exchanged a glance and one kicked at the dirt with his leather boot.

"Well?" Sludge asked when La Savage hadn't replied after long moments.

"Let us say that there were some unexpected guests in her room. A young page–"

"A page? But I thought Rhea just had the one squire, that ridiculous Cederic."

"As did I. And this one guards her bedchamber."

Sludge narrowed his mud brown eyes, unbelieving. There was something La Savage was holding back. "A mere child stop you?"

"It was not just any child, but one as strong as the Sword of Bramear. He leapt atop my back and held fast. Then the imp blinded me."

"You told me that you were powerful and stealthy. Able to cut down the princess in the dead of night. But it seems that you are as weak as a maiden in–"

"I was ill-informed. You lead me to believe that Rhea would be alone."

That's when Sludge noticed the empty sheath at Roger's hip. "Where is the dagger I gave you?" he demanded.

"Dropped it. I suppose the innkeeper has it."

"But that had powers to kill the princess! I told you to safeguard it! You must get it back. Quickly!"

"Do not order me around, Swiney."

"Idiot. Rhea has dragon wisdom. And that was the only weapon powerful enough to kill her. Stupid lackey!"

"Shut that bulbous mouth or I will knock you on your slimy arse," La Savage growled.

Sludge felt heat rise in his cheeks. "No one talks to me like that. I am the most powerful dream drainer in all Subterranea. Second only to Lord Sickhert himself!"

"Think I care about your underground domain? With all its tunnels and dark caverns? I will speak as I see fit."

Now Sludge's anger turned his brown cheeks red. He felt his face dry and crinkle like charred meat in a lava oven.

"Don't you dare disrespect me." Glowering, Sludge took a single step closer. "If you know what's best for you."

"Ha! George, Roderic, help me show this," he paused and said the next word with a sneer, "*Captain* how respectful we can be."

La Savage pulled a sword from the sheath on his back and the other two fletched arrows on their long bows. Before Sludge could say River of Lies all three outlaws had sharp tips pointed at him.

He drew his battle-axe from under his long cloak. "Stand back, Gothian scum."

"Now we're scum?" La Savage sneered with a quick thrust of his sword.

Sludge didn't even flinch. He refused to show any fear. Raising his axe higher, he rolled his shoulders and flexed his hunched back. "Yeah you're scum. And weak."

"We'll show you the real meaning of weakness," The outlaw to his left said pulling the bowstring back further.

"Too busy showing off to realize how easily I could defeat you." He grinded the ground with his jackboot and glared at them with yellow eyes.

"Ha! We are three and you but one," La Savage said.

"And which of the three will I drop first?" Sludge swung his axe in a circle and pointed it at George. "You?" He repeated the action with Roderic. "Or you?"

The bowmen both stared at Roger La Savage as if waiting for instructions. The leader raised a single eyebrow. Then he threw his head back and began to laugh.

"I had you there, did I not, Shadow Swine?" He lowered his blade and the other two relaxed their bows.

The last thing Sludge felt like doing was laughing. But he didn't get to where he was by being stupid. He needed this outlaw for his schemes. So, he curled his bulbous lips back over his serrated teeth and croaked out a guffaw.

Laughing heartily La Savage pat Sludge on the back several times.

And Sludge let him. All the while dreaming of the day he would throw that cocky criminal into Mudlark Maker's mouth.

Chapter 33

Gwen made a sour face at the plate of dark bread topped with salted fish. She wasn't hungry to begin with and fish usually weirded her out. Her dad liked to tease her about this. Every time he fixed it, he'd describe the guts and eyes in gross detail until she ran from the kitchen covering her mouth. If after a half an hour she still hadn't returned he'd laughingly offer her his special almond milk, banana, and peanut butter protein shake.

She wished she had one of his shakes right then instead of the weird breakfast Princess Rhea and Cedric were munching on. It might give her the energy she needed to figure out what the frigg was going on.

After Roger La Savage had escaped everyone went back to bed for a few hours. If you could call it that. Between imagining shadowy villains in every corner and Rhea's loud tossing and turning, Gwen maybe got about three and a half minutes of sleep.

Now she was cranky, bleary eyed, and had to watch a painted princess and a sculpted squire eat fish and rye bread. Gross. Why these Artanians needed to eat anyhow was beyond her. It made no sense that a sculpture or a sketch would need food.

As if anything in this freaky place did.

The dagger Roger had dropped rested in the center of the table, its jeweled handle a sharp contrast to the roughhewn wood. Gwen looked at the strange markings carved into its handle and leaned forward to picked it up. The yellow topaz gem in the center gleamed in the morning light making prismatic shapes on the wall.

"It is an odd blade, is it not?" Rhea asked.

"Cha! Check out the patterns," Gwen said tilting the handle back and forth to make more yellow designs. The patterns changed like a kaleidoscope with the slightest movement.

Blinking, Princess Rhea slowly set her tankard of ale down. "Hand it to me."

Gwen did so, and Rhea began examining the foot-long weapon. She ran her strong hand over the blade stopping at each etching or jewel. Holding it over her head Rhea played with the prism effects Gwen had discovered. Even more shapes appeared on the walls. She brought the dagger closer to her face and did a quick intake of breath.

"What is it, my lady?" Squire Cederic asked.

"Do you see the oval shape in the center? The one surrounding the topaz?" She held the dagger up, so he could see.

194

Cederic rose from the bench to get a better look. When he leaned in the squire gasped. "Can it be?"

"It must be so. Still the question remains–"

"–as to why it was in an outlaw's hands?"

"I know not, but it is a bad omen," Rhea said.

Gwen listened to their words bounce off each other like a tennis ball volleying in a medieval match. After several more lobs, she cleared her throat. "Dudes, could you explain what the frick you're talking about?"

"Ahh, of course. A *photo*," Cederic winked here as if sharing some huge secret. "–would not know the Gothian symbols."

Gwen rolled her eyes. She knew she was supposed to keep the fact that she was human a secret, but he didn't have to act all gothic-spy. She waited for the princess's explanation.

"It is the Golden Eye," Rhea said pointing at the center of the handle. "The most important symbol in the Gothian coat of arms. In the beginning this symbol was everywhere. It represents the dragon we seek, that which holds our land together."

"Okay, then why is it on a dagger?" Gwen asked.

"The Golden Eye comforts our people," Rhea said.

"But over time it has disappeared," Cederic added.

"Every time the Blank Canvas pulled parts of our land into the nothing, Golden Eyes vanished," Rhea began.

"Until they became as rare as the Golden Dragon herself," Cederic said, finishing her thought.

Gwen wrinkled her nose. Okay, so they were on a quest to find this dragon, or one of its eggs anyhow. But no one seemed to know where to go. And where were Alex and Bartholomew? Even if she was full on ticked at Alex for making fun of her new look, she still wished he was there.

She didn't want to admit it, but Alex gave her strength. When he was around she felt braver. Not that she was a wuss, but something about him made skateboard falls and even Mom's silence a lot easier.

The Innkeeper Thomas came in with an empty tray. While stooping to pick up the breakfast dishes he froze, dropping the tray. Wood thud against wood as it hit the floor.

"Sightgiver," he gasped staring at the dagger.

"Impossible," Rhea said turning the handle over in her hands. "It has not been seen since the time of the great knights."

"The dagger of legend? Guiding the Deliverers of old?" Cederic asked.

"This could not be such a blade. It was in an outlaw's hand," Rhea argued.

Gwen wriggled her nose again. "Maybe Scarface got it from those nasty Swiney things," she suggested.

"Perhaps. But I shudder to think what would happen if the dark ones had that kind of power," Rhea said.

"We need the true art. Now more than ever." Cederic shook his head.

"As has been foretold on the Soothsayer Stone. But, where are they?" Rhea asked.

Gwen grinded her teeth and glanced at the door as if expecting her buds to come in at any minute. Then a horrifying thought came to mind. What if they never followed her? They could still be at Lacey's party laughing it up. She gulped.

"I don't have a clue. But I sure as dog doo don't think sitting around here is doing us any good."

"I agree. We must continue with the quest. Deliverers or not."

Rhea nodded. "Yes, and it is time we were off. Prepare our bundles Squire Cederic. We have some distance to travel."

"I anticipated such a need. All is prepared," Cederic said pointing to the bundles at his feet.

Just then a piercing screech that shook the inn's walls filled the air.

Rhea stood up dropping the dagger.

"Where is the princess?" a nasally voice screamed. "Bring her to me!"

Thomas dashed to the lattice window. "It's Lucretia! Out the back. Quickly!"

"No."

"Hurry, Princess! Before she finds you," Thomas implored.

"But my people. I cannot let them suffer in my name," Rhea protested.

"There's nothing you can do. She'll destroy the village whether she finds you here or not," Thomas said opening the doorway to the kitchen.

Gwen and Cederic exchanged a glance. Gwen picked up the dagger and tucked it in her rope belt and then without a word grabbed the princess by the elbow and started pulling her toward the exit.

"No."

"If you go to her, the quest is lost. Please, your Grace," Cederic begged tugging on her other arm.

"Absolutely not!" Rhea cried digging her feet into the floor.

Gwen hated what she did next. But she had no choice. She drew her free hand back and punched the princess square in the jaw. Rhea's head slumped over, and Gwen slung her over her back. Bracing her legs for a jog she told Cederic to grab the packs.

And the two of them ran.

Chapter 34

"You're slower than a herd of snails in peanut butter. Get a move on B-3," Alex said, curling and uncurling his fists.

"I am going as fast as I can. It's not like I hike through a forest daily."

That was an understatement. With his neat freak mom, Bartholomew barely stepped outside, much less into a forest. Most of the plants on his property were plastic. If it weren't for that area around his conservatory, Bartholomew never would be around real ones.

Alex glanced back to see his friend putting on hand sanitizer. Again. Shaking his head, he started to rag on him. But then he remembered the button that he'd torn off when Mom had her heart attack. He kept it safe in a drawer, pulling it out when he was feeling low.

Alex got it. He had his button and B-3 had his lotion. All good.

He trudged ahead a few more yards and then stopped dead in his tracks.

"I am fine. You don't have to stop and wait for–" Bartholomew's voice trailed off into silence.

The both stood staring for several moments as Alex's heart pounded in his chest.

"What is it?" Bartholomew asked his voice barely a whisper.

Laboring to slow his shallow breaths, Alex muttered, "Hell, if I know."

Bartholomew reached a tentative hand toward it.

"Don't!" Alex cried pulling him back. "You don't know what that is."

"Actually, I believe I do," Bartholomew said chewing on one lip thoughtfully. "The Blank Canvas."

Alex glanced from the white pit in front of him to B-3 and back again. He nodded slowly.

"Of course. Gothia's shrinking just like Sir Donald said. But I never imagined it would be so…"

"Empty?" Bartholomew said.

"Yeah." Alex shuddered.

The gaping hole in front of them was cold. But not a cold like winter. More like death, like the lifeless snake Alex'd found when he was five. Its silent body had chilled him more than any nightmare and he'd flung it as far away as his kindergarten arms could muster.

"Alex, let's go. There aren't any answers here."

Holding one arm out to protect Bartholomew, Alex backed away from the white chasm. When he felt like they were safely out of range he said, "Come on. The village is due west."

"Which way is that?" Bartholomew asked.

Shielding his eyes with one hand he pointed at the sun, now low in the sky. "Well, the sun sets in the west so if we veer toward it we should be all right."

"You're the navigator. Not me."

It was true. Alex's family loved nature hikes and Mom had taught him how to use the sun and a compass to navigate directions way back when they were living in Colorado. If not for this feeling of foreboding, this forest would have been just as peaceful as Rocky Mountain. Painted oak and ash trees swayed gently in the afternoon breeze. Purple and white flowers with multi-colored clay mushrooms sprouted from the leaf carpeted ground. Two red squirrels, pointed ears perked, scampered past and up a tree.

But still that whiteness left a cold shadow everywhere.

They had only walked a few hundred yards when Bartholomew raised his nose. "Smell that?"

Alex sniffed. Frowned. "Smells like smoke."

"Forest fire?" B-3 glanced right and left.

Suddenly a hot wind blew back Alex's hair. He blinked. Ashy smoke billowed as the air grew thick.

Alex coughed and sputtered. "Let's get out of here." Hoping B-3 was right behind, he broke into a run. Ducking under branches and scraping past bushes. Why the heck painted things weren't softer was beyond him.

A grating screech stopped him dead in his tracks. He held out an arm for Bartholomew. But he wasn't there.

"Where is she? Bring her to me!" a shrill voice cried from above.

A huge fire breathing dragon swooped over the canopy, flames reflecting off her orange underbody. Whooshing wings bent back tree tops rippling Alex's t-shirt.

And Bartholomew had not emerged from the smoky underbrush. Her long tail whipped back and forth, a snake ready to strike.

Where are you?

Alex turned to head back just as a gasping Bartholomew grabbed his arm.

"Okay?"

"Yeah, I couldn't see in the–"

Three little peasant girls trailing a shouting man cut B-3's words short. "'ere lassies! Where she aren't able to find you," he cried tugging on their hands.

Alex had a flash of Jose's little sisters and immediately went into protector mode. "This way," he called waving.

The painted man paused narrowing his eyes suspiciously. But Bartholomew's lip-biting grin must have put him at ease because it was only a second before he ran toward them.

"In here," Alex ordered pointing at a hollow inside a tree.

Bartholomew stepped up closer and said under his breath, "Be careful until you know they can be trusted."

Alex gave him an imperceptible nod as the little girls burrowed inside. Overhead, the dragon spit fire, and screeched again.

Alex turned to the man. "What's going on?"

"She's after the princess. But she aren't about to get her, now is she?"

"Who?" Bartholomew asked.

"Lucretia, of course. What are you? A foolish photo?" the aproned man said with a guffaw.

"I happen to be a sculptor. A Deliverer," Bartholomew retorted, forgetting his own advice.

"Bartholomew. What happened to *be careful*?"

"Oh. Sorry."

"Is it true? Are you the Deliverers? I be Thomas, by the way. Innkeeper of the Spider Arms," The man brushed back a few wisps of his balding hair. He extended his chubby hand to B-3 who shook it twice.

"Umm, yeah, here to find some dragon egg. If we are *careful*." Alex raised his eyebrows at Bartholomew.

The Richie coughed and suddenly seemed interested in a leaf that had clung to his shirt. Alex shook his head and asked Thomas what was happening.

"Somehow that vain Lucretia got wind of Princess Rhea's location and came looking for 'er," Thomas said.

"I don't believe that dragon wants Gothia saved," the tallest girl said.

"No, all she wants is to look at herself wearing all the jewels she steals," the middle sister added.

"I am soo bootiful," the smallest piped in. All three sisters giggled until the dragon's shadow silenced them. Lucretia's screech filled the air and the middle girl plugged her ears while the smallest clung to her sister's waist.

"Don't you fret, lassies. You got Thomas to look after you."

"Your daughters?" Alex asked.

"Me serving girl and her sisters. Orphans, they is. That witch of a dragon scorched their home leaving them parentless, goin' on a year now. They live in the back of my inn."

"Give up the princess right now!" the dragon screamed in the most nasal voice Alex had ever heard.

"I must stop her. Can you Deliverers watch over my girls while I try to talk to her?" Thomas asked.

Alex was about to agree when he glanced at Bartholomew brushing some dust off his pants. When dirt always distracted B-3, he'd stop whatever he was doing. So annoying. Alex wished he could stop the dragon that easily.

Could I?

"Hey Thomas, you say this dragon is really conceited?"

"Never seen another more vain. I've heard told that she polishes her scales before every raid. And you can see the jewels in 'er neck. Sometimes she even forces villagers to tell 'er how beautiful she is. Crazy dragon."

"So, if anything messed up her looks, she'd get pretty upset?"

"I know not the aim of your words. But I suppose she would."

"Hold on. I have an idea." Alex motioned Bartholomew closer and whispered in his ear.

His buddy raised an eyebrow and nodded. "We will need some lumber, rope, and iron."

"And if they have pigs, that would be even better," Alex added with a grin.

Bartholomew cocked his head to one side, confused. When he got it, he chuckled. "Oh, that'll be disgusting. Good thinking, Alex."

"Lassies, stay hidden here. I will return as soon as I show these two the way," Thomas said brushing the smallest girl's cheek with the back of his hand.

The three of them jogged to the edge of the forest where the innkeeper pointed across a wheat field toward some smoldering huts. "That's the smith's. And there's the wheelwright's. Most of what you need will be in there." Meanwhile he explained how Princess Rhea, along with her squire and page, had arrived at his inn the night before. That she'd been attacked in the middle of the night by the outlaw Roger La Savage, but the fast thinking page had saved her.

But he'd seen no trace of a human girl.

"Thanks, Thomas. We'll take it from here." As the innkeeper returned to the forest, Alex surveyed the path they'd need to take. Using the wheat stalks as cover they could get to the blacksmith's unnoticed. Then, if they timed it just when Lucretia was turning for another pass, they could steal over to the wright's. But pig pens were way down at the other end.

They'd have to be quick.

"Okay, here's how it'll go..." Alex started assigning roles.

"No, I'll go there. You do...th-that," Bartholomew argued with a shudder.

Alex's head pounded. B-3 needed to use his skills where needed. Taking a deep breath, he patiently explained his logic.

"But..."

Alex fixed him with an angry glare and Bartholomew clamped his mouth shut. He'd do his part, but he wasn't going to like it.

While the dragon swooped overhead, Alex rasped, "Go!"

Scrambling under two fallen logs, they crept through rolling wheat and behind woodpiles to reach the first hut unseen. As soon as Lucretia turned south for another pass, they split up. Alex dashed over to the stacks of lumber while B-3 rolled the wooden wheelbarrow down the street.

Alex called inside the blacksmith's shop, relieved to find no answer. Stuck a head through the doorway just to be sure. Since no burly smith wielding a hot iron waited for him, he slipped inside where luckily the brick forge still had hot embers.

He began to gather the wood and iron and had just got a good pile at his feet when he heard the dragon screech overhead. He was ready.

But where was Bartholomew?

Chapter 35

Cederic jerked his arm toward a small stream. "Here we stop. I pray this little brook will revive my lady."

With a curt nod, Gwen bent her legs and lowered Rhea up against a tree. Her gut was in knots. The princess still hadn't woken from that sock in the jaw. Had she hit her too hard?

Cederic pulled out a rag from his pack and dipped it in the stream. Wringing it out, he knelt next to Princess Rhea and swabbed her face.

She didn't move.

Gwen put her ear up to the Princess's mouth. She was breathing all right.

"Princess, wake up," she whispered gently.

Nothing.

"You needn't have hit her so hard," Cederic accused.

"We had to get her away from there. You saw. She wouldn't listen," Gwen protested. She rushed down to the brook and filled her hands with water. Careful not to spill, she made her way back to Rhea and splashed her face.

Breath held, she waited for some sign. But long moments passed without the slightest stir.

Glowering at her, Cederic returned to the stream and soaked his rag again. Without a word, he twisted it over Rhea's head, wringing every drop from the cloth.

Still nothing.

What have you done?

The brook's gurgling babble jeered.

Dog.

The populos pointing at her t-shirt splashed through her mind. Taunts burbled in her ears. Every ripple cutting like acid. *Give up.*

"No, she *will* wake up." Gwen dashed back and scooped up another desperate handful. Hoping for some freaking sign that she was coming out of it. She poured it on the princess's face.

Same result.

Gwen shook her head and set her shoulders, repeating the splashing sequence three times. Four. Seven. Twelve.

But the princess never moved.

Exhausted, Gwen stopped. Breath heaving, she glanced down at Rhea's brave face. All traces of nobility were gone. Her long auburn hair was plastered against her head and her skin was as pale as paper.

"Please don't die, my Lady. Gothia needs you." Cederic knelt by her side and swabbed her face with a rag. "*I* need you."

Gwen rubbed the hilt of the dagger still tucked in her belt. God, she wished she were back in Santa Barbara. There you could call 911 and the paramedics would take care of everything.

But here she was powerless. Like during Nightmare Mother's attack. Gwen hugged herself and began to rock back and forth.

A few moments later she heard a deep voice. "It is because death fills her mind."

Gwen froze. Turned. Her jaw dropped.

Behind a boulder stood a bright green creature. Covered in leaves, every square inch looked like a weird tree complete with trunk legs and branchy arms.

"What?" she managed to croak.

"Princess Rhea cannot awake because of the death images." Green Man closed his eyes and the lids fluttered. "She sees fire and ruin. Smells burning homes. Hears crying children. And blames herself."

"Her grace wanted to comply to Lucretia's demands, but this *Photo* would have none of it." Cederic shot Gwen another dirty look as he swabbed the princess's forehead.

"It wouldn't have helped. That dragon would have kidnapped her or worse," Gwen protested.

"The Photo speaks rightly. Lucretia is brutal. And the princess's knowledge of the Golden Dragon is important for the quest. Her part will be needed for some time."

"Can you help her?" Gwen implored searching the creature's face for some hope. Although his cat eyes glowed, she saw something kind there, sort of like a cool teacher or Alex before he turned into a jerk.

"I am not sure."

"You are the Green Man, are you not? Do you not help the spring to come?" Cederic asked, standing up.

"We do symbolize rebirth and life returning. Yes, I may be able to bring her back from shadow." Green Man's arms stretched towards Rhea as vines sprouted from the tips of each finger. These wrapped around the princess several times until only her face showed, and she looked like she was inside a spinach cocoon.

"You're not hurting her?" Gwen asked.

The Green Man did not answer but smiled gently as he tilted his head back. Sunrays lit up his face like beach glass as he began to whisper in a strange language.

The princess moaned. But then was silent again.

Green Man continued to murmur some sort of a chant while Rhea's cocoon glimmered as if emeralds were burning beneath each leaf. Gwen noticed that they brightened and dimmed with her every breath.

The Green Man chanted louder. In moments, his body blazed in light and he was a full-on viney inferno. But as Gwen squinted against the painful brilliance, she thought the princess's head moved just a little.

"I think she's waking up," she whispered.

Suddenly, the entire forest ignited in radiant stars and a hum like a thousand vibrating suns filled the air. Then the green turned supernova.

Gwen squeezed her eyes shut.

A balloon-like sound popped and there was a flash on the back of her eyelids. Next, a sweet floral smell wafted her way.

When the light faded, Gwen ventured a peek and saw the vines roll back into Green Man's fingertips.

Princess Rhea sat blinking in front of him. "Where art I?"

Chapter 36

From behind the wall, Bartholomew picked up the overturned wheelbarrow.

Again.

He pointed it at the cottage. *One-two-three!* The dragon turned, and he leaned into a run, praying it'd stay upright this time.

"Don't tip over. Don't tip over," He muttered, bumping over the dirt path. He glanced skyward. A shadow fell over the huts behind him.

At the last cottage, Bartholomew kicked open the door. He backed through the entry, pulling the barrow inside only seconds before Lucretia unleashed another deafening screech.

"Close the door, before she sees us!" a man in the corner cried.

The man had his arms stretched protectively over a thin woman and three small children. All five clung together, eyes wide with fear. Bartholomew stood gaping while the father ordered him to shut the door again.

"Now quiet, lest she breathe fire our way," the man said placing a finger to his lips.

Bartholomew nodded and surveyed the pitiful family. All were dressed in brown woolen clothing and the little kids' faces were streaked with dirt. His mother would have fainted about now if she'd seen them. Not only did all five have on muddy boots and stained clothes but a piglet was lying right next to them rooting into the dirt floor.

For a moment, a wave of revulsion passed over Bartholomew and he nearly forgot his task. He reached into his pocket for his hand sanitizer and applied a few drops to his hands. It didn't help.

"Who are you, Photo? And how did you traverse the forbidden?" the painted father asked narrowing his eyes.

That's when Bartholomew remembered himself. *Do your job.*

"I don't have time to explain right now. But if you want to save your family, I need to fill this barrel with..." he choked on the words, "... pig poop."

The father gave him a quizzical look but didn't hesitate to answer. "The stable is just through that doorway. Take all you like."

"Thank you." Bartholomew rolled the barrel through the doorway.

Here two sows and a snorting hog lolled in the muck. Snuffling, they gave Bartholomew a lazy look.

Do pigs attack? He wondered.

Bartholomew wanted to turn right around and run. But he fought it, forcing himself to take a tentative step inside the stable.

"Okay, Piggy stay back. I just need some of your, umm droppings." He swallowed back some bile. "And there's plenty of that."

He wished he had nose plugs. The stench! Bartholomew shuddered and glanced around. Although a wooden pitchfork hung on the clay wall across the room, there wasn't a shovel in sight.

He hesitated. To get to that pitchfork he'd have to slosh through slippery manure. And even though it looked kind of like a painting, it was real.

But Father slipped and drowned in a puddle smaller than this. He chewed on his lower lip. Did not move.

Then he remembered the terrified eyes of those kids and took a cautious step forward. His foot sunk into the muck. He lifted it and heard a disgusting sucking sound. Curling his hands into fists, he cringed. Another step. Tiptoe this time.

"Don't fall." Trying to stay up on his toes, he sidled toward the far wall. But with every step. pooh squished up inside his shoes.

Bluck.

One of the pigs oinked. Bartholomew froze, eyes as big as its flaring snout.

"S-stay back," he stammered. Forgetting to stay on tiptoe his feet sunk into the sludge.

Bartholomew raised both hands to keep from teetering over. He was still only halfway across the room.

215

Was it his destiny to hit his head like Father and drown? The thought made him want to bolt. But then he remembered Alex's encouraging words. "You can do it B-3," his buddy had told him time and again.

Could he?

"Yes," Bartholomew said with determination.

In three strides, he had the pitchfork in his hands. And in a few sloshing leaps he was back at his wheelbarrow. Of course, shoveling watery pooh with a big fork isn't exactly efficient. Most ended up slipping through the tines. He tried speeding up but after five minutes he'd barely covered the bottom of the barrow.

"Bring me the princess!" the dragoness screeched overhead.

Bartholomew looked out the window. A hole appeared in the dark cloud overhead. Lucretia emerged from the blackness, nostrils puffing smoke, beating wings over thatched roofs.

She swooped down and opened her mouth, revealing rows of sharp teeth. Just like the dragon during the X Games, red sparks shot out and flared. A jagged flash bolted earthward.

Then the hut next door burst into flames.

The time was now.

Holding his breath, Bartholomew thrust his arms into the muck. Sludge dripped down his arms as he tossed a handful into the barrel. Ugh! His chest tightened and spasmed.

He grabbed more. Started a toss. Warm rivulets rolled toward his head.

Too late Bartholomew clamped his mouth shut. Got a mouthful. Gagging and spitting, he fought the urge to reach for his hand sanitizer.

By now the cottage next door was engulfed. Rippling heat rolled toward him as steam began rising from the dung pile.

The smell made him retch. If he could fill the bucket without vomiting it'd be a miracle.

Hot tongues licked at the walls. He had to go faster. Bartholomew scooped up another armful. Still not enough. The pigs snuffled and squealed, kicking up dung.

Blisters appeared on the plaster. The plaintive wails of the little children in the other room filled the air. Bartholomew cringed trying not to imagine what would happen to those painted faces if he wasn't successful. The dragon had to be stopped.

Setting his jaw in grim determination, he clawed at the muck.

Finally, after what seemed like hours his wheelbarrow was full. Lucretia discharged another furious shriek.

Ignoring the creature's cries, Bartholomew yanked the barrow out the back door and began rolling it down the dirt path. The wheelbarrow seemed extra wobbly as it bumped over the uneven ground, even harder to keep upright than before.

When it became nearly impossible to push, Bartholomew stopped. Holy dust bunnies! There was a six-inch crack in the axle and the wooden wheel was hanging from splinters. When did that happen?

His heart pounded. If he didn't get to Alex soon this whole village would be up in flames.

Lifting as gently as possible, he tried pulling backwards. Which went okay for about seven seconds. Then he heard wings beating and glanced up. No Lucretia yet, but he forgot to watch where he was going. Hit a rock. The barrow lurched.

Fighting to right it, Bartholomew clutched the handles. It teetered.

"No!" he cried trying to keep his reeling load level.

The barrow sunk into a pothole and the handles slipped away. He only let go for a second. But it was enough. Tipping over, it spilled all that poop.

He stared at the pile in the road. *What now?*

Chapter 37

When Bartholomew threw open the blacksmith door empty-handed, a stunned Alex demanded, "Where's the dung?"

"It spilled. Back there." Bartholomew jerked his hand toward the road.

Trying to think fast, Alex tapped his chin once before pointing to a stack of lumber piled high in the center of the room. "Help me move this."

Once it was all dumped near the road, he picked up an armful of iron and tossed it into the forge.

"If it stays hot, we might be okay."

Bartholomew held up crossed his fingers and nodded.

Soon fiery embers were atop the anvil and Alex's arms were flying. Without a word, Bartholomew joined him mirroring his every move. The Creation Magic was freaky that way.

Alex tongs gripping hot metal. Fastened more pieces together. Returned to the forge again for more.

Faster they went. Molding, shaping, forming.

A few seconds later they stepped outside and began to mold the wood.

Overhead, Lucretia looked like she was frozen mid-air. Of course, she wasn't. They were just speeding up. The Creation Magic accelerated every movement until they were faster than the speed of light.

Suspending even a dragon's cry.

In three seconds, it was done, and a wooden catapult sat in the road. To Alex it looked like a giant seesaw. But while seesaws were gentle rides, this trebuchet could launch projectiles at 150 miles per hour.

They aimed it at Lucretia. They'd only get one chance.

Alex cranked back the arm until the bucket was horizontal. "Okay, I'll make sure the aim is right, you fill it," he said.

Groaning, Bartholomew glanced at the pile of dung in the road.

"Hurry!"

All around cottages were going up in flames. Making a disgusted face, Bartholomew thrust his hands back into the poop and scooped. Soon armfuls of dung were in the catapult's bucket.

Alex rotated the trebuchet just a smidgen to adjust the aim. The restraining rope vibrated against the bucket's weight.

The dragon turned.

"Ready?" Alex asked placing a hand on the release lever.

His buddy nodded.

Bartholomew came up next to him shielding his eyes with one hand. "One, two, – now!"

Alex pulled back the lever and the arm blasted upward hitting the crossbar with such force the impact shook the ground. Pig dung shot towards the approaching dragon.

He crossed his fingers. And eyes. And toes.

Time stretched. The brown missile zeroed in on Lucretia as puffs of smoke emerged slowly from her nostrils. Her leathery wings undulated, each flap of in slow motion. Frame by frame her taloned feet clawed at clouds.

She opened her mouth wider and was just about to release another fireball when, splat! Goo plastered her face. Brown balls stuck to her spikes and slimy strands dripped down her jeweled neck. Even her long lashes were caked in dark gunk.

Alex almost felt sorry for her.

"Ewww!" she shrieked in a voice loud enough to knock down a forest.

Bartholomew turned toward the blacksmith's shop. "Run!"

Alex started to follow, but then the amazing happened. Lucretia turned away. With a snotty wail, she disappeared behind a cotton cloud.

"Yes!" he cheered giving Bartholomew a high five.

A few painted, sewn, and sculpted heads poked out of doorways, scanning the skies. Slowly, the villagers emerged from their huts.

"Come on, help us!" Alex called as he dipped a wooden bucket into a trough and tossed it on a flaming cottage.

Next, he and Bartholomew organized a bucket brigade. He ordered Gothians into two lines, to pass pails of water from the well to the flaming buildings. The boys tossed bucketful after bucketful until every cinder was extinguished.

Finally, the two boys faced each other. Alex raised his eyebrows and looked Bartholomew up and down.

B-3's hair stuck up in wild directions and his face was streaked with ash. Pig dung had hardened on his sleeves while cartoony stink waves wafted up around him.

"Nice look," he said, chuckling.

Bartholomew winked and took a bow.

And they both cracked up.

Chapter 38

"Get it off! Get it off!" Lucretia whined.

Sludge dropped the towel in the bucket. "I think it's gone."

"It's all over my beautiful scales. Look!"

Stepping back, Captain Sludge pretended to survey her long neck. He rolled his eyes. Even though he had been wiping her down for hours, he couldn't convince her that she was clean. He clenched his jagged teeth and wrung the towel out again.

"Now, explain to me how this happened," he asked sponging her shoulder.

"My lovely scales!" Lucretia cried, ignoring his question.

"They're fine," Sludge said.

"No, they aren't. I can feel the yuck. Get it off."

Twisting the towel for the ninety-seventh time, Sludge flicked his wrist and snapped her wing.

"Oww!" Lucretia screeched.

"Sorry," Sludge said flatly.

"Be careful! My scales must shine."

"Now that you mention it, this towel is scuffing them." Sludge paused for an effect.

"What?"

"It'll probably take weeks to get them back to their original luster. But if you think they're still dirty I'll keep going." For emphàsis, the captain began scouring one wing roughly.

"Well, perhaps I am pooh free. You may stop."

How dare you talk to me like that? Clenching his claw-tipped hands into fists, Sludge threw the towel into the bucket and took deep breaths through flaring nostrils. When he'd calmed down enough to arrange his face into a friendly mask, he repeated his question.

"Now how did you get covered in pig dung?"

"I don't know what happened. It was so strange. I was scorching the village, demanding they hand over Princess Rhea like you asked. Things were going splendidly. Those peasants were running in all directions while glorious plumes of smoke and fire shot into the air. My orange scales glowed beautifully amidst the flames. Each like a fiery ember–"

"The attack?" Sludge asked cutting her off.

Lucretia glared at him but continued. "Well, one minute I hear the thrum of a catapult and the next I'm covered in eww."

"But Midshire has no catapult. Or soldiers to direct it. Where did it come from?"

Lucretia shrugged.

224

Sludge rubbed his chin, musing. Had Alexander and Bartholomew returned? No one knew what forces brought them into Artania. That bronze Thinker was tricky.

"Well, I'll just have to be trickier," Sludge said.

"Hmm?" Lucretia asked.

Sludge shook his head. "Nothing for you to trouble your pretty face over."

"I'm still beautiful, aren't I?"

"Of course. The loveliest dragon ever."

"I know." She glanced around her cavern and then unleashed a piercing shriek. "Minotaur! Get in here now!"

In seconds her bull-headed servant skidded into the room, his tail tucked well behind him. "Yes, your majesty?"

"Where are my mirrors? I can't find a one!"

"Forgive me, Dragoness but I took them into my lair for cleaning. They'd all gotten so fogged from your breath you would barely be able to gaze upon your *lovely* reflection," he said his voice dripping with sarcasm that Lucretia completely missed.

"Bring me one now or I'll burn your tail to a crisp."

Sludge didn't think such a bulky creature could move that fast. But in three seconds Minotaur was back, mirror in hand.

Lucretia snatched it from his grasp and began gazing at herself. "Oh no! My jewels are dull. Minotaur, remove them and get me new ones from the pile."

Minotaur grabbed a couple of sacks from niches on the wall and stepped up to the dragon. Placing one

225

bag at his feet, he began plucking out the score of rubies, diamonds, and emeralds embedded between her scales. Then he headed over to the mountain of treasure with the empty one.

Following Minotaur over to the pile of jewels, Sludge leaned in and asked under his breath, "Have the Deliverers arrived?"

"Perhaps," Minotaur replied turning his back to Lucretia and pretending to polish a few stones.

"What do you know?" Sludge asked keeping his voice low.

"There have been rumors of strange visitors at Castle Alnwick. Photos with odd clothing," Minotaur whispered.

"Alone?" Sludge mouthed.

Minotaur shook his head. "I hear the Council of Dragons carried them over the castle walls."

"What are you two muttering about over there?" Lucretia asked.

Sludge gave Minotaur a warning glare and replied, "Why, which jewel best matches your burnt orange scales of course."

"Well find one quickly. I need my gems."

Minotaur picked up a few random jewels and rushed back to Lucretia's side.

"I am off. There is work to be done," Sludge said.

"Fine, fine. I will summon you if need be," Lucretia said with a lazy wave of her hand.

Sludge grimaced. If he got out of that cave without punching that conceited mouth it'd be a miracle.

He stepped into the tunnel and rubbed his chin. Were the Deliverers in Artania? The signs were there, but he had to know. As soon as he returned home he'd head straight for the River of Lies to breathe in their sulfuric fumes. Dream draining would tell him the truth.

If humans were dreaming, all was as it should be. But if Earth time was frozen, trouble was ahead.

Frozen time meant one thing. Alex and Bartholomew had passed through the doorway and joined the Gothian quest.

And he had better be prepared.

Chapter 39

"Princess, you're woken!" Cederic cried kneeling at her side.

"What? Where am I?" she asked blinking slowly. Rhea's gaze passed over the trees and the little brook with its muddy bank. When she saw Gwen, her head tilted to one side.

Gwen looked away. Ashamed.

"Half a day's march from Midshire," Cederic replied.

Princess Rhea leapt up, raising her arms in protest. "It cannot be! I must save my people! Take me back!"

"No, it is too dangerous," Cederic said.

"Cha," Gwen added under her breath.

"You can and will. As is so ordered by Princess Rhea of the Gothian Realm," she said throwing her shoulders back.

"No, we can't." What Gwen wouldn't give to be back in Dad's gym right then. She'd be lifting weights instead of arguing with a reckless princess.

"I am your sovereign. You must obey."

The Green Man stepped in front of Rhea and held up one hand. "Returning you to Midshire would help no one and place you directly in harm's way. We cannot have that."

"Green Man, what are you doing here?" Rhea asked.

"I sensed I was needed."

Princess Rhea rubbed her jaw and twisted it back and forth. "For that matter, what are all of us doing here? I remember not what happened."

Cederic shot Gwen a dirty look.

Knots of guilt tightened in Gwen's stomach. What could she say? She'd done what she thought was right. But it sucked hurting Rhea and she really admired this princess. Even though her dad was sick with some crazy fever and her bros were off on the quest, she was totally noble.

"It was me. I did it. When you refused to leave, I knocked you out."

"With much more power than was needed, if you asked me." Shooting another dirty look, Cederic dabbed Rhea's bruised chin with his wet rag.

Gwen glanced at the smeared footprints she'd left on the bank, muddy reflections of Mom's nightmare words. *You are so ugly.*

Right then she felt more so than in any nightmare. It made her wonder. *Had she driven Mom away?*

Gwen rubbed the hilt of the dagger still tucked in her belt.

The Green Man let out a long sigh and came up beside her. A single leaf sprouted from a fingertip and flicked her nose.

"Hey!" she said.

"We have no time for self-recrimination. The quest awaits."

"But Midshire–" Rhea began.

"Is safe for now," the Green Man said cutting her off.

"How can you know this?" Princess Rhea asked.

"The trees of course."

Gwen did not even want to ask. Artania was freaky enough without talking trees sending messages. She crossed her arms and listened.

"Ahh, the Sylvan Signals." Rhea nodded.

"So, which way now?" Cedric asked.

"Toward the Plains of Bramear, as was decided," Rhea replied.

The Green Man nodded. "There are but two paths to the Plains. And each is wrought with danger. If we head southeast, we must pass through the ghostly Dread Woods. But if we go directly south, Mount Minotaur blocks our way."

"With a labyrinth we could wander in for years." Cederic added tapping his chin. "both present challenges for protecting the princess."

"I do not require the safeguarding you think, squire," Rhea said putting her hands on her hips. "I have been known to wield a sword."

"Still a sword would provide little protection from the ghosts of Dread Woods."

Each time someone said *Dread Woods* Gwen felt a strange coldness at her side. She reached down to the dagger tucked in her belt. It was ice cold.

"Yes," The Green Man said. "I have heard that those wraiths can drive any Artanian mad. Be they painted or sculpted."

Cederic paced back and forth. "We could lose our way in either place."

"I, for one, would prefer to keep nightmares at bay. Having Father's mind touched by these times is burden enough," Rhea said.

Wintery fingers gripped Gwen's hip, an icy hand digging into her side. With immense will Gwen grasped the freezing *Sightgiver* and held it up.

The blade was glowing blue.

Cederic, Rhea, and Green Man gaped at the dagger.

"*Sightgiver* speaks," the princess said.

Gwen thought for a moment, then asked, "Which way are these scary woods?"

The Green Man pointed past the stream. Gwen aimed the dagger in the same direction. It glowed even more and became so cold she could barely hold it.

"Try directing it at Mount Minotaur," Cederic suggested, jerking a thumb over his shoulder.

Gwen pointed the dagger past him and her hand immediately warmed. But now the topaz jewel in the handle shone golden yellow.

"It is decided. Mount Minotaur it is." The Green Man nodded and with a wave of his woody arm, led them forward.

Chapter 40

At the edge of a meadow, Bartholomew held the map up to the sun hoping that its fading light would make those blurry places come into focus.

"Would you stop looking at that? You know it won't make any difference. Places don't look clear until we've been there." Alex sounded exasperated.

"I know. It's just there's no one to show us the way. And it's a little-."

Alex interrupted. "Irritating, annoying, frustrating?"

"I was going to say unsettling. Last two times we had Apollo to guide us,"

"Well we don't know, and we don't have Gwen either. But I'm at least trying to do something about it."

"What?"

"You could at least pretend to keep an eye out. Or do I have to do everything, as usual?"

"Well, what do you want me to do? You're this Indiana Jones trail blazer. Not me. Just tell me."

"That's the point. I always have to tell you." Alex sighed.

"Hey," Bartholomew began, hurt. "I just waded through pig poop, helped build a catapult, and was part of a fire brigade. I'm doing the best I can!"

"Maybe your best isn't–" Approaching voices stopped him mid-sentence.

Bartholomew's eyes widened. "Who is that?"

"Dunno. Better hide, just in case." Alex whispered, casting a furtive glance over his shoulder.

Bartholomew looked around. Open fields lay on either side of them and they couldn't return to the copse of trees behind. That's where the voices were. The only way was straight ahead. Into that spooky forest.

What horrors waited behind each ghostly oak?

"Come on B-3," Alex whispered jogging forward.

"Alex. I don't want to go in there." He froze, sensing something evil in that place.

"Hurry!" Alex rasped. He darted between two trees and branches with skeleton arms closed behind him.

"Alex no!" But it was too late. His friend had already disappeared behind mossy webs.

The voices behind grew louder. Deep guffaws blustered. Definitely men. Maybe they were friendly?

He stood motionless, chewing on his lower lip. But then Bartholomew remembered what the innkeeper had said about outlaws at his inn. Disfigured, murdering, scary outlaws.

A scent like decaying logs wafted his way. He stared into the misty woods where bare branches crisscrossed in macabre shapes. Dead pine needles hung down, sharp points poised to pierce skin. Creeping vines with hangman's noose tendrils twisted up trees.

All telling him to stay back.

"...and this time no little page will get between my steel and the Princess's throat," a deep voice snarled.

Bartholomew gulped and ran right into the forest.

Almost immediately he skidded to a halt and stared blinking. It was as if he'd stepped into a dream.

Now Artania always had a slight dreamy feel. But this was different. In one step the light faded, shades of grey replaced all color, and a strange mist rose from the ground.

It was like a vampire movie from long ago. All black and white with spider webs dripping from the trees. Bartholomew expected a caped man to appear any second and say, "Welcome to Castle Dracula," as he bared his fangs.

A wolf howled in the distance, freezing Bartholomew's heart.

"Alex?" he called into the darkening woods. "Where are you?"

No answer. Just another distant howl.

Clenching his fists Bartholomew took a step forward. Wet leaves carpeted his shoes and ankles. He could feel their dampness soaking into his trousers. Another step. Drenched socks.

"Al-ex. Don't be like that. Come on out."

He heard a fluttering sound and looked up. Two huge bats flickered through the trees. Swooping toward him. He ducked, stumbled over a log. Stopped.

"I'll try harder. Just come on out," he called aiming for a dry patch ahead.

He tried slogging through the wet leaves, but the pile deepened, slowing his every step. Soon the leaves were up to his knees. And they were morphing; liquefying into a slushy goo. A goo he was sinking into.

"Quicksand," he gasped.

He tried to lift his legs but only sunk deeper. The mud rose around his hips. Toward his chest.

"Alex!"

Still no answer.

It covered his arms, pinning them to his sides. A viscous pulp pressing against his throat. Choking him.

Bartholomew was trapped.

He had a single thought before he sank below. *Drowning, just like father.*

Chapter 41

A cool wind whistled through Gwen's linen tunic. Shivering, she faced the looming mountain and rubbed a shoulder. A piney smell that would have been a comfort back in California filled the air.

But here it only seemed strange.

In front of her, Green Man pointed at a distant trail cut into the mountain. "The entrance to the Labyrinth lies up that path."

"More distance?" Cederic asked mopping his brow with the back of his hand.

"A bit of incline will be but variety," Princess Rhea said.

Gwen noticed the kind smile Rhea gave Cederic. She wasn't beautiful like in Disney movies or model thin like Rochelle. But Gwen really admired her strength. It inspired confidence.

Gwen realized that this was what a real leader should do. Not act like Lacey who used fear and humiliation to be popular.

When they reached the mouth of a cave, Green Man halted. "This is where we must part."

"No. We need your counsel," Cederic protested.

"Where you are destined, I cannot follow. My leaves need the open air. Without sky, I shrivel to winter."

Cedric shot a glance at the shadowy entrance.

"Trust in your training, Squire. You are a knight, and we have *Sightgiver*," Rhea said pointing at the dagger tucked in Gwen's belt.

Gwen placed a cautious hand on the hilt. It was warm.

"We have no torches," Cederic pointed out.

Gwen nodded. The idea of going through a maze of dark caverns wasn't exactly her idea of fun. She wished that Alex and Bartholomew were there to whip up one of their magical art thingy's and light the way. But she had no idea if those two were even in Artania much less nearby.

"Sightgiver will lead you," The Green Man said.

Gwen tilted her head, not understanding at first. Then she remembered how the dagger had glimmered when they pointed it at Mt. Minotaur. She pulled it from her rope belt and held it up.

The topaz jewel in the center gave off a yellow glow.

With a hard swallow, Gwen moved toward the entrance. "Okay then, let's get going."

After Rhea nodded a noble farewell to the Green Man, Cederic moved in front of her and offered her his hand. "Come, Your Grace."

Taking it, she lifted her skirts and stepped over the boulder at the entry.

As soon as they entered the cavern, a veil of darkness shrouded them. Gwen held up the dagger, so a pinhole of faint light could illuminate spots here and there.

The air was heavy and full of damp odors from mossy rocks and dripping stalactites. She wrinkled her nose. "This is going to be one friggin long journey."

"What say you, human?"

"Nothing," Gwen replied heading toward the back of the cave where they faced a narrow tunnel.

Gwen wasn't weird about enclosed spaces or anything. But the dark? Even at Disneyland she avoided rides that plunged you into blackness, making excuses like the lines were too long. And leaving the openness of a large cavern for that narrow tunnel walls gave her pause.

"All well?" Rhea asked when Gwen took one step and stopped.

Overhead, stalagmites huddled into lifeless formations like ghostly sentinels in some weird House of Horrors attraction. Gwen shuddered.

"Sure," Gwen replied doing her best to sound brave. Wielding her strange light, she took another tentative step forward.

"The floor is rubble littered. Do take care, Princess," Cederic warned.

"*Princess-cess*," echoed through the cavern.

All three of them halted. Cederic and Gwen exchanged a glance.

"Would you both please stop fretting," Rhea said
breaking the silence. "I am not a fragile dove with
clipped wings. I too had a knight's training along
with my brothers."

"That may be, but you have never traversed the
labyrinths of Mount Minotaur," Cederic replied with
a sniff.

"*-inotaur, inotaur, -taur,*" bounced through the
tunnels in eerie repetitions, turning Gwen's blood
cold.

Her next steps were heavy enough to drown out
the unnerving echoes.

After what seemed like hours of treading over the
rocky floor, they came to place where the passageways smoothed into black cylinders. Here the walls
looked more like cut glass than chomped stone.

It made the walking easier. But there was one
problem.

Five exits.

Gwen stifled a gasp as the trio halted again.

"Which one?" she asked.

"*Sightgiver* should know. Try it, human," Rhea
suggested.

Gwen waved the dagger in front of each tunnel,
observing the hilt for signs of change. At the third
channel, the topaz jewel seemed to glow more, but
she tried all five again just to be sure.

"I guess this is the way," she said.

They entered the tunnel but within a few yards were another five exits.

Exasperated, Gwen sighed. "Seriously?"

"We are in Minotaur's Labyrinth. Many have entered while few have departed," Cederic said.

"A maze? No way."

"But they did not have *Sightgiver*," Rhea soothed.

"Fine, I'll try again. If I can put up with Coco applying eyeshadow for a freaking hour I suppose I can keep holding this magic knife."

"Now there's the spirit. Which way now?" Rhea asked.

Gwen repeated her dagger waving trick until the hilt glowed. Then they entered that tunnel only to find quintuplet exits a few feet ahead. She did this so many times she couldn't count. Twisting and turning channels only led to more forks. It all started to make her dizzy.

Then as they were treading down one long curving tube the dagger began to dim. Gwen banged it against her hand thinking it was like a flashlight with dying batteries. It did spark just a bit at this, so she continued forward.

Until they came to solid wall.

And the light went out.

Chapter 42

Why can't Bartholomew just follow orders? Alex clenched his jaw and trudged further into the woods.

Every time B-3 started getting it together, his stupid phobias would kick in. All nerves. Doubting what to do. It was so frustrating!

They had a job to complete. The least B-3 could do was pretend to be working on it.

Alex knew from experience that the rainbow bridge wouldn't appear until they found the dragon egg. The Prophecy said there were seven evils to undo. In their last visits that rainbow home had appeared only after they'd completed them. Not a second before.

Home. It seemed so far away. Like a dream.

For the first time in a while, Alex started to worry about mom. What if these crazy events were somehow tied to her heart attack? Maybe the Swineys had caused it. That evil Sludge had threatened to invade her dreams before.

The dark forest loomed. Grotesque branches twisted like malformed creatures while dead brambles wielded knifed thorns. A few boulders leaned against each other for support.

One of them seemed to grow. Alex blinked.

"What?" He stared.

The stone shimmered with a ghostly light. As Alex gaped, it stretched, morphing into an arch. Immediately, a coffin-shaped trench appeared in front of it.

A grave?

Heart quickening, he took a step back. A weeping willow's ground-sweeping branches brushed over his shoulders. He gasped and flinched, shrinking back from the sharp leaves.

Then he heard a strange moaning. Not a howl or a scream, but a pained wail, as if some poor woman were sobbing.

"A-lex," the disembodied voice cried. "H-elp me..."

"M-m-mom?" Alex called.

"Freeee meee."

"But, where are you?"

A wispy shape ascended from the dark pit. Alex covered his mouth when he realized that it was Mom.

The horror was paper white with skin sagging on its skull. Mom's usual dancing eyes now stared blankly from hollow sockets. Then her mouth twisted into a silent scream that constricted around Alex's heart.

"Help meee," she implored extending a thin arm his way.

Alex gasped, stepped back. "It can't be."

"Saaave me," the keening voice begged.

Alex backed further up. This couldn't be real. Mom was frozen in time back in Santa Barbara, probably experimenting with one of her recipes. She couldn't be in Artania. It didn't make any sense.

"It huuurts. Help meee." Ghost Mom clutched her chest.

"You're not real. You're not real," Alex said squeezing his eyes shut.

A cold hand touched his face.

Alex turned and ran. Sharp branches scraped his face and arms, but he barely noticed. He had to get away from that thing. The thing that wasn't Mom.

But as he raced there she was. Right in front of him. He skidded to a halt. How did she get there? She'd been behind him.

He veered right. She popped up from another freshly dug gravesite.

"Saaave meee."

"Get away. You're not real!"

Alex swerved left. This time the ghost placed icy hands on his shoulders. Stopping him dead in his tracks.

"Aleeex, my heart. pleaase..."

Alex tried to wrench free, but the cold fingers clamped down.

"Let me go!" He jerked to the side and then noticed something strange. If anything could as stranger as a Mom-ghost grabbing him.

For just a moment the spirit disappeared. He could see the gnarled forest beyond.

Slowly Alex opened and closed his eyes. It appeared again.

Alex tapped his chin a few times in quick succession. *When I told it to let go, I moved left.* He decided to give it a try.

The ghost vanished again. But reappeared as soon as he stood upright.

At least it wasn't holding onto him anymore. He jerked left again and stayed sideways. The mist and the gravesites were gone.

Then he heard a garbled mumbling behind. Trying to maintain his sideways stance, Alex turned.

Bartholomew was kneeling in the center of a pile of leaves, clutching his throat, mouth opening and closing like a beached fish.

"Bartholomew?" Alex called, confused.

The only reply was another gurgle.

That's when Alex realized that this place was the forest Thomas had said most Artanians avoid. It gave people waking nightmares. And Bartholomew was having one right now.

Keeping his head tilted to one side Alex made his way over to his friend.

"Bartholomew this isn't real. It's just a hallucination."

No response. Just a vacant stare.

"Wake up!" Alex forgot to keep his head tilted and the ghost appeared again.

"Saaave mee."

"No!" Alex slanted his head. But this time the ghost stayed. Had the forest figured out his trick?

The white apparition moaned.

Alex jerked right. No change. The ghost loomed nearer.

"Not...real," Alex said fighting to see beyond this crazy hallucination.

Remembering that his friend had been just inches away, Alex reached through the misty ghost. He felt something solid just beyond it.

"Huh?" came B-3's confused voice.

"Bartholomew– you're hallucinating."

It took all he had to say these words. He tried closing his eyes. She appeared on the back of his lids.

"Pleaaase, helllp me." Her cavernous mouth opened into a long scream.

If only he could plug his ears. Alex stumbled. Almost fell. Swallowed hard. "It's...not...real. Just... a nightmare."

Exact copies of the Mom ghost appeared all around him. Fluttering specters. As if a murder of albino crows had surrounded him.

"We... gotta get out of here." Blinded by spectral light, Alex grabbed his best friend and began to run.

And run.

245

Chapter 43

Gwen gulped. It was so dark. Darker than any place she'd ever been.

Although she wouldn't admit it if you asked, the dark weirded her out. She'd had a lava lamp in her room as long as she could remember. Its pink glow warmed that cold hole Mom had left in her heart.

"Try it again," Cederic said.

Gwen banged on the dagger's handle. Nothing.

"Perhaps more firmly," Princess Rhea suggested.

Gwen grasped the dagger's hilt and recoiled. "Ow," she said blowing warm air on her hand.

"What is it?" Rhea asked.

"It's turned to ice," Gwen said shoving the frozen dagger deeper into her rope belt.

Cederic jumped in. "Then warm it. Fists that fly so freely, surely can draw sparks from *Sightgiver*."

Gwen clenched those fists. She was getting sick of Cederic ragging about that punch every five freaking minutes. Mouth tight, she said, "I didn't see you doing anything when that dragon attacked."

"I have always stayed by her side, as duty bound. And I did not run from the White like you!"

"Seriously? You are working *me*, Mister-let-La Savage-escape? I saved your rear. Some thanks, Rust Bucket."

"Why should I thank you for getting us lost? Because of you, *Sightgiver* no longer burns!"

"You get it to work then!" Ignoring the frosty bite, Gwen grasped the dagger and threw it in his direction. It hit the floor with a clang.

Heaving a sigh, the princess said, "Cederic?"

Rhea's patient voice made Gwen feel stupid. She hated losing her temper. But she couldn't see jack. And that squire was getting under her skin.

She heard him drop to the ground and grope around. "I have it," he cried.

"Ooo look at it light up. Wow."

"At least it's in knightly hands."

"That can barely wield a sword."

"Be quiet or feel just how well I can–"

"Cederic, stop,"

"But Princess she–"

"DO AS I COMMAND," Rhea's voice was full of royal authority.

"Yes, your highness. Forgive my impudence."

"Forgiven. Now, let us backtrack. Perhaps *Sight-giver* will glow anew in fresh hands. Hand it here, Squire."

There was a rustling sound, but the dagger stayed as black as death.

Gwen crossed her arms across her chest. She didn't want to move. The darkness was too deep. And that stupid tin man was no protection from God knows what lurked in the black.

"I shall stay on this side and feel my way along. Cederic, you will follow behind me. Gwen, please keep to my left on the opposite wall, thus, keeping us from tripping over each other."

"Yes, your Grace," Cederic said. A scuffling sound told Gwen that the pair was moving.

"Friend of the Deliverers, are you coming?" Rhea asked, her voice already some ten feet away.

Still angry, Gwen muttered a yes. She waited another minute to calm her breath. Then she placed her hand on the wall and began to grope along, shuffling forward toe-heel, toe-heel.

"Make haste human." Cederic's voice was dim.

Rhea's was just as low. "Yes, Gwen, this way."

Gwen stopped and cocked an ear. "What? I can barely hear you."

"Veer right." Rhea sounded even more distant.

How had they gotten so far ahead? It made no sense. It'd only been a few minutes. "Princess? Squire?" she called.

"Over here," a wan voice replied as swishing feet murmured and echoed.

Gwen moved toward what she thought was Rhea, called out again. This time the reply was barely audible. She came to a fork and repeated her call. Louder this time.

"Cederic!"

The faintest of whispers wafted her way. How could that be? She should be getting closer. Medusa nightmares flashed in her mind.

"Rhea! Where are you?" she cried unsure of which way to turn.

Then she heard crunching feet and heaved a sigh. *There they are.*

"I'm coming!" she called, groping toward the sound.

When shadows were flickering on the walls, Gwen wondered if the dark was playing tricks on her eyes. She blinked twice and rubbed them.

Had *Sightgiver* started glowing again?

The tunnel brightened as the silhouette of a hulking form slanted toward her.

"Rhea?" She halted.

No regal form came into focus. Instead a phantom shape rippled against the wall.

The shadow took form. Now a horned head emerged atop the hulking figure.

This was no princess.

She backed up. One step. Two. Seven. Soon her spine was pressed into another dead end. Sharp rocks boring into her back.

A torch wielding arm rounded the corner. In the firelight, red eyes blazed below silvery horns.

The bull opened its mouth in a snarl as brutish arms lifted a black net. The shroud covered Gwen's face. Plunging her back into darkness.

Gwen screamed and screamed.

Chapter 44

The Thinker sensed the wrongness before he gazed into his steely palm. The shadows in the lines only confirmed it. The Deliverers were lost. On a path of darkness and despair.

As was their young friend. The skateboarding girl with ginger hair. She too was beyond his vision.

This could mean only one thing. All three were in Sickhert's realm. Whether they had gone below to Subterranea or were trapped within a traitor's lair, he could not tell.

It was time to call the Council of Dragons.

He raised his fist to the sky. Soon sparks crackled down his bronze arm and flew from his fingertips. Multiple lightning bolts sizzled overhead in glowworm shapes.

It took only moments before the beating of scaled wings filled the air. The Thinker glanced up to see Erantha's forest green body shadow the hills. Next to her Flynn's scarlet scales shone in the sun while trailing behind Wade dipped in and out of clouds, his sea blue body melding with the sky.

The Thinker stood aside for the dragons to enter the Golden Grotto. As soon as Erantha had curled her tail into a coil, he welcomed them all.

"Thank you for your haste, as it is needed," he began. "I need you to find the Deliverers."

Wade tilted his blue head. "But we already have."

"Brother and I carried the little lambs to Castle Alnwick ourselves. Sir Donald was going to prepare them for the quest," Erantha added with a nod.

The Thinker sighed. "They were there. But since have journeyed towards the Plains of Bramear."

"There are but two paths from Alnwick to the Plains," Flynn said. "And even *my* breath wouldn't make them less treacherous."

"That is why I called you. I last tracked them near Dread Woods but now my Bronze Vision is blurred."

"Then we will seek them there," the red-scaled Flynn said.

"I-I have heard tales of that forest. They say it drives you mad. Nightmares live in the trees."

"Now, little brother, you yourself carried Alexander Devinci and swam with Bartholomew. You've seen the manlings' faces and called yourself friend. Could you shy away from helping them now?" Erantha scolded with a cluck of her forked tongue.

Wade hung his blue head in shame. "I didn't mean... it's just that..."

"We know Water Dragon," The Thinker said. "Even the strongest of minds have been unable to withstand the madness of those trees. Many brethren have entered never to be seen again."

"D-do you suppose they just wander forever?" Wade's voice was softer than lapping waves.

"Or become Mudlarks for Lord Sickhert."

"Flynn, just because there's a few stories about lost Artanians fighting us with zombie eyes doesn't mean that everyone who enters Dread Woods becomes one of those mindless slaves," Erantha said.

"I would never." Narrowing his eyes, Flynn blew out an angry puff of smoke.

"My hope is that none of you has to discover it, one way or another. I called you so that you might search from the skies. I need you to look for signs of the Deliverers and their red-headed companion."

"Easy." Flynn lifted his crimson head.

"I have never flown so far south."

"You do have wings, Wade? Or are you not a dragon?" Flynn accused.

The scalloped fins on either side of Wade's face drooped as he hung his head. He flicked his forked tongue once and gazed off into the distance.

"Hush Flynn. Not everyone lives under a volcano facing fire. Some dragons have quieter lives." Erantha's emerald eyes softened as she glanced at her little brother. "That's what makes each of us unique."

Wade smiled but Flynn huffed another puff of smoke.

"I will not lie to you, Water Dragon. Danger may lie ahead. But you are needed. And the alternative..." The Thinker shuddered.

"I know. The Blank Canvas. They say the white grows," Wade said.

The Thinker nodded. One forest had completely disappeared; replaced by an empty abyss. Many of the Green Men had been lost, making it more difficult for spring to burst forth from the land. It seemed as if autumn had held its grip on Gothia for so long.

"I will try. I just hope my wings are strong enough."

"Baa," Flynn guffawed. "We are dragons. We were created for flight. Come, brother. My flames will lead the way." He twisted his massive body around and exited the cavern, Erantha and Wade right behind.

"May the strength of the Goldens guide you!" The Thinker called as the trio took flight. He watched them disappear and then glanced back into his palm.

Shadows. Only shadows.

Chapter 45

Alex glanced ahead. The edge of Dread Woods had to somewhere.

Half-carrying, half-dragging Bartholomew, he had just made it to a thinner part of the forest when B-3 dug his heels in.

They both jerked backwards and toppled over, legs akimbo. Before Alex could untangle himself, a swimming foot connected with his stomach.

Rolling away, Alex clutched his gut. "Bartholomew, I keep telling you, it's not real. Just a hallucination!"

Bartholomew's head wobbled but he didn't respond. Staring into space, he seized his throat again, opening and closing his mouth with short gasps. At the same time, another Mom-ghost appeared between them, its twisted mouth screaming.

"Heelp meee."

Alex curled his hands into fists and forced himself to pass through the wraith to shake his friend.

"Bartholomew, you're not drowning. It's not like your Dad. It's a dream."

B-3 sputtered, reached upward.

Twilight was creeping in and long shadows would soon cover everything. And now multiple ghouls were erupting from cemetery pits. Alex had to get out of there.

Or go insane.

"Bartholomew, come on!"

It was no use. His friend was trapped in the dream. Alex shook his head.

"*True art. Make it true, Alex.*" Bartholomew had told him when all hope seemed lost. And Alex had remembered. He'd looked deep inside himself and found that wonderful place of creation. It had saved them both.

Alex's eyes darted back and forth and up and down. Nothing. Then his gaze rested on some hanging vines. They just might work.

He took a step toward them, but the ghost-mom popped up, blocking his way. "Saa-ve me-e," she moaned.

"Get out of my way. I have work to do," Alex said dodging her grasp.

He yanked one down. Another. Skirting the spook's outstretched arms, he removed a few more. Next, he laid them side by side. Closing his eyes, Alex envisioned the rope. It would be brilliant white to shine like a beacon, and beckon Bartholomew from his nightmare.

He laid one over the other and began intertwining the greenery. When he had a nice braid, Alex wove in more vines.

Alex tried to work faster but without Bartholomew's help he couldn't even approach their usual light speed. Still he moved his fingers as quickly as he could and in a minute the lifeline was almost done.

Then he felt a tug.

"You can-no-t..." The shade yanked his weaving from his hands.

"What the-" Alex gasped trying to grab a hold of his unfinished rope.

The wraith began floating upward. Alex swiped at his weaving. Missed. Leapt again.

This time he managed to grasp a few threads in his fingers. He got a better grip and tugged. "Give it back."

Suspended over him, Mom-ghost wailed, "You wi-ll sta-yy. Forev-er."

"Nope. Not gonna happen." Alex yanked, and the rope slipped from the shade's hands.

Knowing he only had precious seconds, Alex piled leaves into a circle shape. These he attached to his weaving. When it looked done, he ran a hand over the piece for the creation magic to do its work. And waited.

Nothing. Still vines and leaves.

Was there something about this place that blocked energies?

Alex ran his hand over the vines again. "Come on. Come on. Change."

Then there was shimmering, and the creation morphed. In place of vines and leaves, was a life preserver attached to a long white rope.

Alex immediately tossed the ring to his dazed friend. "Grab it B-3!"

Barely seeming to comprehend, Bartholomew blinked slowly. But then he reached out a shaking hand.

"You will drow-n, boy. Dro-own," the spirit keened.

"You will not, B-3, there's a lifesaver. Put it around your head."

"Noo. You are tra-aaped. In mu-ud."

"Don't listen B-3. The ring is right in front of you. I'll pull you out."

Bartholomew started to lift his hands, but the ghost stepped between him and the lifeline. With a wail, she bent to snatch it away.

"Oh, no you don't." Alex tried to shove her backwards. Hands passed right through.

The ghost turned its glare toward Alex. Now it looked nothing like Mom. Rather it resembled some possessed demon with red eyes rolling back in its the skull. Its rotting skin cracked while yellowed teeth grew into fangs. Hissing, it raised a bony arm.

Leaning back, Alex snapped the hand end of rope and waited. Ripples snaked up, generating a shock wave that drove the creature back three feet. "Grab it. Quick," he urged Bartholomew.

As soon as B-3 had his shoulders through, Alex tugged but the shrieking ghost lunged and scratched Alex's face. "No-oo!"

He cringed as long red streaks stung his skin. Still he pulled, glad B-3 wasn't any heavier. Now the specter leapt up on his back and began whispering in his ear. Horrors of mom suffering in a hospital. Her face pale and wan. Machines stopping. Her heart slowing.

Alex tried to ignore it. But the image of Mom was too much. His hands went limp and he covered his face.

Horrible nightmares filled his vision. The unthinkable flashed on the back of his lids. Alex stifled a scream.

Just then he heard a voice. "Back off hag. That's my friend."

Alex uncovered his face. Bartholomew stood behind the ghost, life line in one hand. He circled the rope over his head like a cowboy with a lasso. When he let go the ring flew right at her head. She recoiled but didn't fall.

Bartholomew tossed it again. This time the life preserver hit her square in the gut sending her flying backwards into the trees.

"Grab hold, Alex. I think if the two of us hold creation, we can escape."

Alex did so and immediately the visions faded. He could still make out a faint outline thrashing about in the trees. But now it had so little substance that the leaves barely moved.

"Okay, one problem solved. Thanks bud. But now the question is–"

Nodding, B-3 finished his thought. "-where the dust bunnies do we go?"

Chapter 46

From the banks of the River of Lies, Sludge took a deep breath. A sharp acidic scent wafted through his piggish nostrils, filling his lungs with sulfuric fumes.

He waited in the warm mist. One moment. Two. Ten. A full minute passed. Nothing appeared. Then he knew the truth. There were no dreams to twist.

That meant one thing. The Deliverers were in Artania and time was frozen on Earth.

Why hadn't he sensed their arrival? He usually could smell humans from miles off. And the opening doorway should have shook all Subterranea, letting them know that dream draining was futile.

He glanced around. Other Shadow Swine were lined up and down the steaming river acting as if they were hard at work. To look at them you'd think that the idiot Deliverers were still in Santa Barbara.

"Private, come here," he called.

The short underling marched up and saluted. "Sir."

"Describe your dream draining."

"Lord Sickhert sent the dream to me. It from-from a-a boy who used to always color. Now all he do is fiddle on phone. I make nightmare melting crayons."

"The dream moves? It's not frozen?"

"No sir. Why?"

"Your job is to follow orders without question. Is that clear, Private?"

The quivering minion nodded quickly.

Captain Sludge repeated the queries with several more Shadow Swine. The answer was always the same. Lord Sickhert had sent dreams that each was turning into a horrible nightmare.

His Lord must know the Deliverers were in Artania. That Lava Pool Gramarye supposedly told all. What game was he playing?

Sludge toyed with the idea of confronting Sickhert. He'd march up that long stairway of the stalagmite castle and demand to know what was going on. But you didn't demand of Lord Sickhert. He'd throw you in his torture chamber and spray you with boiling water until your skin peeled off in long sheets.

Sludge rubbed his strong chin and muttered to himself. "He is hiding something, something he wants kept secret. But why?"

It didn't make sense to keep the troops ignorant. They were needed to battle those idiot boys and foil any attempts to find the Golden Dragon. For the life of him Sludge couldn't see the logic in Lord Sickhert's actions.

"Unless he actually believes the dreams are happening."

There was only one place he could go for answers. Sludge hadn't visited her in many years but every time he saw her, the Crone spoke truth. The only problem was that the price was usually substantial.

He followed the River of Lies upstream to Swallow Hole Swamp where the young ones hatched and grew. Her shack stood beyond it against a rocky wall.

The dwelling was unique in Subterranea. Whereas other Shadow Swine lived inside stony walls, the Crone alone dwelled among wood. The shack appeared small and dilapidated from the outside, but Captain Sludge had discovered long ago that this was an illusion.

Inside those cabin walls were untold rooms that held a single boiling pot, each unique. Some cauldrons looked ready for a witch's brew whereas others were forged into perfect ovals like dinosaur eggs. A few were warped and twisted as if twenty Mudlark elephants had stomped on the cooling iron. Once he had even seen an exact replica of Sickhert's Stalagmite.

But when they boiled he was always reminded of Mudlark Maker's smacking lips. And while that creature's stomach held morphing acids that turned Artanians into slaves, these kettles each held answers.

Most Shadow Swine shied away from the Crone. But from the time Sludge could wade through the waters of Swallow Hole Swamp they'd exchanged shrewd glances. Even before that, as a pupa, he'd watched her from the waters. As soon as he morphed into a nymph, he braved the swamp's shore to seek answers from the wizened woman.

Of course, each reply came with a heavy price. The hardest one was his height. He would have been just as tall as any other Shadow Swine had she not given him the knowledge. She helped mold his natural intelligence to a cunning brain, inventing nightmares like no other.

So, he gave her a few inches of his height. And now spiked his hair to reach his underlings' shoulders. But it was all worth it. It made him the most powerful Shadow Swine of them all. Save Lord Sickhert of course.

Today he wondered what price she'd ask. Now that he was an adult, he could offer no more height. But there were other things that cost just as much.

He glanced back at Swallow Hole Swamp. There he'd crawled over pupae and nymph alike to gain notice. Even before he'd bowed before Lord Sickhert on the banks of the River of Lies, he'd practiced dream draining on his peers.

Not that they liked it much. But he didn't care.

"Idiots. All of them. If they'd had half a brain they would have killed me before I morphed to nymph," he muttered shaking his head.

"I see you have learned great compassion in your years away," a woman's shaky voice criticized.

He turned toward the sound. The Crone had appeared on her rickety porch and now sat rocking in a chair that hadn't been there before. Not that it

264

surprised Sludge. The Crone did many mysterious things.

"You always did speak of things no Shadow Swine could understand."

The dwarfed woman gave him a snaggletoothed grin as she rocked. "One must empathize to dream drain. Or have I taught you nothing, Pupae?"

He hated when she called him that. Anyone else would have gotten a slap across the face for such impudence. But, for some reason, he never grew angry with this wrinkled witch.

"Funny you should mention, as dream draining is why I have come," he said.

"You finally noticed. I was wondering how long it would take you."

"You knew?"

She leaned her tiny body forward and planted her clawed feet on the ground. "Of course."

"But Lord Sickhert–"

"Lord Sickhert does not see everything in that Lava Pool Gramarye. My cauldrons, on the other hand." She raised a hairless eyebrow.

"But why?"

"For that answer, I need payment."

Sludge pursed his lips. "What now? Tell me."

"What weapon do you have under your cloak?"

Sludge blanched. "My axe? But, I need this to battle the Knights."

"Answers require payment."

Captain Sludge reached under his coat and pulled out his battle axe. The handle fit his palm perfectly and the steel blade shone in the lava glow. With the unicorn power, it had helped him defeat many Knights of Painted Light in recent months.

How could he give it up?

"One year without this weapon, and your question is answered." She held out her hands.

He stared. So much could happen in a year. Those idiot boys' art could block scores of nightmares in a year.

Still it wasn't forever. Sludge gave a curt nod and placed his axe in her arms.

Leading him inside, The Crone hung his axe on a bracket that was such a perfect fit it seemed to be waiting for his weapon. He glanced back longingly at the shining blade before turning the corner.

At the end of a long hallway a round door opened by itself. Inside, was a dragon-shaped cauldron on the fire. The boiling brew popped as the stunted woman waddled up to a three-legged stool beside it.

Stepping up on the stool, she grasped the long ladle hanging from the ceiling and dipped it in the brew. As the Crone stirred, misty images of the Minotaur, Lucretia, and the unicorn appeared overhead.

Sludge stepped closer. "What does it mean?"

"There are consequences for trapping a unicorn. Even for our kind."

"I don't know what you're talking about," Sludge lied.

"I'd expect that sort of a response from Stench or Bile, but I thought you were brighter than those mud-for-brains."

The Captain's face blanched. She knew. He opened his bulbous lips to speak but clamped them shut again. He couldn't argue.

"It gives me power. Power I can use to defeat any Knight of Painted Light." He paused and gave her an earnest look. "Oh, the nightmares I've made. If you could have seen them–"

"Pshaw. Your dream draining excelled before you used the unicorn. Look into the brew." She beckoned him nearer with a tilt of her head.

Sludge leaned over the oddly shaped cauldron and gazed into the simmering potion. A sick sweet smell filled his piggish nostrils. The concoction bubbled and swelled in peaks and valleys. But he didn't see anything special. He turned toward the Crone and shrugged.

A pewter mug had appeared in her hand. She dipped the cup in the cauldron and held it out for him.

"Drink, and you will know."

This was new. In times past, he only had to gaze into the brew and be transformed. He hesitated. The tiny woman pushed the mug toward him. With a shaking hand, he reached for it, downing it in a single gulp.

And fainted dead away.

Chapter 47

The ghost in the distance wailed. Bartholomew's pulse quickened, and he glanced at Alex padding behind.

"Go!" Alex cried.

Dropping his head Bartholomew scurried toward a lighter copse of trees. The woods' edge must be there.

He hoped.

Then the trees thinned, and he could see a heather carpeted meadow ahead. It seemed to whisper *safety. No more nightmares.*

Imagining a landing on soft grass, he gave Alex a thumbs-up and leapt. But bounced right back, slamming straight into him. They tumbled over arms and legs akimbo until they were in a tangled heap.

"What the?" Alex unraveled his limbs from Bartholomew's and rolled away.

Brushing some leaves off his pants, Bartholomew stood. He took two steps toward the tree line and reached out a shaking hand. An invisible wall that felt like cool glass vibrated slightly under his touch. "Alex?"

His friend approached and extended a single finger. It was blocked too. "I think it's some sort of force field."

The ghost's howls drew closer.

Bartholomew glanced over his shoulder and shuddered. Night was falling and the last thing he wanted was to be stuck in this spooky place after dark. "We're trapped?" he croaked out.

"Now don't freak out. We'll–"

"The nightmares, they're closing in."

"They're not real."

Bartholomew pointed at the scratch on Alex's face. "And what do you call that?"

Alex reached a hand up to his cheek. "Yeah, well."

"We have to get out of here!" Bartholomew said trying to keep the panic from his voice.

"Okay, let's think. Maybe it's localized. Let's check and see if there's a break somewhere."

Swallowing hard, Bartholomew tramped behind Alex who was staying as close to the tree line as the foliage would allow. After a few yards, they tested the barrier. It was solid.

"No!"

"Keep trying," Alex said quietly. Bartholomew knew that voice. It was the one Alex used to soothe panicky people.

They trekked further along but everywhere the invisible wall stopped them. They went backwards. No dice. Bartholomew tested the barrier with his foot. Blocked! Thrust out a hip. A shoulder. One time, he bent down and charged like a bull.

All he got was a bump on the head.

They were trapped, and it was getting darker by the minute. If horrific visions appeared during the day, Bartholomew shuddered to think what sort of nightmares attacked at night.

"Damn wall!" Alex cried punching it with his fist.

Staring at the ground, Bartholomew rubbed his upper arms. "It's hopeless."

"Stop."

"We're never getting out of here." Bartholomew shook his head.

"Well, if we can't go down, let's try up."

Bartholomew glanced at the trees twisting into the canopy overhead. By now the moon was rising and a few stars were twinkling in the sky. Maybe Alex could climb up there but he sure as sanitizer couldn't.

"Umm..." he hemmed.

"Fine, I'll do it." Alex rolled his eyes and started scrambling up the nearest oak's trunk. When he'd scaled about ten feet, the trunk split into two. He clambered up the right fork toward the treetops.

It just might work.

"Go Alex," Bartholomew urged.

At that moment, he felt a breeze waft through his hair. He turned but the forest floor was still. Then he noticed that wind was blowing from one place, and downward, as if a giant hairdryer had just been turned on over the trees.

He cocked his head to one side. Now a lot of things were strange in Artania. But Bartholomew had realized a long time ago that wind was wind, even here. It did not blow straight down.

"Alex did–" A sound, like hundreds of paper fans, cut his words short.

He glanced up. A winged shadow passed over his friend. A creature was swooping towards Alex. Bartholomew's blood turned to ice.

No! Not her!

Chapter 48

Growling, Sludge rubbed his slimy temple. His vision was blurred, and he had a headache to end all headaches. Like a jackhammer pounding inside his skull.

The Crone's brew was potent.

But now he knew. Those idiot boys had been in Artania for days and were somewhere near Dread Woods. Damnit! If he didn't act soon, they'd reach the Plains of Bramear before him.

The rising steam from the River of Lies blew back his cloak. He looked down at the fabric flapping in the breeze and curled his long fingers around the lapel. Digging his blade-like nails in, he said, "The Golden may still exist. And if they find one...."

For a moment, he considered letting Lord Sickhert in on his newfound knowledge. But if Sickhert knew where the boys were, he'd take over and Sludge's chance of glory would be gone. No, it was best to issue orders now, before anyone else discovered that the Deliverers were in Artania.

His head throbbed with every step, but he still strode forcefully toward the Shadow Swine lined up along the steaming river bank. As soon as he reached the first one, he gave him a hard shove.

"S-sir?" the thin private stammered.

"Find Stench and Bile and bring them to me. I have jobs for them."

After giving his lieutenants orders, it was time to march up the long staircase to chew out the outlaw La Savage and his band. He found them wandering Dread Woods, hypnotic expressions on their faces. Roger La Savage was swiping at some invisible foe while his companions, Roderick and George, were cowering on the ground.

Sludge admired how these illusions completely altered any sense of reality and wished he had time to study them for his own schemes. But right then he needed to snap these guys out of it.

"Idiots. You'd think they'd know better than to wander in Dread Woods." Rolling his eyes, Captain Sludge waved his arm like a flag twice hand in front of La Savage. The outlaw leapt back and raised a fist.

"Back beast!" he cried.

"Don't be stupid La Savage. It's me."

Roger La Savage pursed his lips making the scar on his cheek pucker and fold. Then he cocked his head to one side. "Sludge?"

"None other. Now let's wake up your companions and get out of here." He repeated the waving motion in front of the other two and they all began trudging toward the forest edge. Sludge could tell that the outlaws still had questions but at least had enough sense to keep their mouths shut. Even idiots knew that noise could draw more nightmares their way.

A few minutes later, the Captain stepped past the forest periphery onto open ground. He had only gone a few paces when he heard a loud oomph. He turned to see La Savage on his rear.

"Get up fool," Sludge said.

Shaking his head, the outlaw leapt up and tried to step past the last tree, but an invisible wall stopped him. He slapped it. "What trickery is this?"

"None that a Shadow Swine set, I assure you."

"Is we trapped Roger?" Roderick's basset hound jowls juddered as he spoke.

"Looks like Sludge is playing tricks on us. He thought a dupe would be funny. Or motivate us to find the Princess faster."

George shook his pin head back and forth with a tisk tisk.

"Idiots! Dread Woods acts on its own. Lord Sickhert might send a few nightmares here and there but this forest has its own power, separate from Subterranea."

"Then we truly are trapped because of you Sludge? If I ever get out of here." La Savage raised a fist toward the captain.

"I didn't say it was immune to Shadow Swine influence, only that it had independent forces."

"Then get us out of here." La Savage said. "Now."

274

Growling at the impudence, Sludge glared at Roger and lifted a hairless eyebrow. "Now? You dare speak that way to me?"

The outlaw crossed his arms and scowled back in what might have been a long staring contest if Roderick hadn't intervened. "Come on Roger, make peace before anoder monster grabs me."

La Savage glanced back to Sludge and gave a little bow. "Could you get us out of here, please?"

Reminding himself to slap that insolent Artanian later, Sludge reached under his cloak for his battle axe but then realized he'd given it to the Crone.

He considered a moment. Would the dirk strapped to his ankle work? Only one way to find out. He pulled it from its sheath and made a rectangular shape in front of La Savage. The air vibrated and there was an electric sound.

"Try now," he told the outlaw.

With a doubtful look, La Savage took a tentative step forward. And passed through easily.

"Pinhead, you're next."

Groping like a blind man, George shuffled up to the forest edge and thrust an arm through. When he realized that worked, he squeezed his peanut face into a stupid grin and joined his leader on the other side of the force field.

"Come on Roderick, haven't got all day," La Savage said.

With a war whoop, Roderick lurched forward careening left and right as he made his way toward the break in the field. Just as he reached the opening, he teetered right.

"Wait idiot, stop!" Sludge warned.

But Roderick hit the opening sideways. Part of his body passed through fine but then the sizzling force field popped, suspending him in place. Now he was trapped, half in and half out of the barrier.

His basset hound face stretched and distorted. "Heelp maee…"

With a long sigh, Sludge raised his dirk again and made a rectangle around the warped outlaw. Nothing. He jabbed at the force field. His hand bounced off. He tried scratching at the surface, but the invisible wall held fast.

"Oh well, he should have listened." Sludge shrugged and turned away.

"Nooo pleeeese…" Roderick slurred.

George grimaced and apologized while La Savage turned away.

Sludge led the pair up the hill and then pointed at the mountain peak above. "The Deliverers are somewhere between here and there. They must be stopped at all costs. But if you fail me, beware. Roderick trapped in Dread Woods will be a sail on Lambent Lake in comparison to what I will do to you. Understand?"

La Savage narrowed his eyes and Sludge thought he might retort with some snide remark. But instead he grabbed George by the scruff of the neck and headed up the path.

As soon as they were out of sight, Sludge dropped down a hole in the ground to traverse the long tunnel to Lucretia's Lair.

Chapter 49

A familiar voice called from the treetops. "Young ones, worry not. We have come."

"Erantha?" Alex said.

With a motherly yes, Erantha swooped down and grabbed Alex in her talons. The next thing he knew, he was on the other side of the barrier.

"Your turn, B-3," he said, grinning. "Just climb up and Erantha will get you."

Bartholomew shook his head and Alex's smile faded "Come on Bartholomew."

"I can't." The Richie shook his head adamantly.

"Of course, you can. It's easy," Alex coaxed. He was annoyed but knew full on that yelling would not get results. He'd just fold up and quit. That Hygenette was so critical that B-3 cringed if you looked at him sideways.

"Youngling, all you have to do is find the footholds and pull yourself upwards," Erantha said bobbing her great head.

Alex noticed how her scales shone like emeralds in the moonlight. It made him think of the mission. How beautiful it must have been when all those Golden Dragons filled the sky. About how ugly King Gerald's illness and the burned villages were. The terror of Mom's heart attack. Why did disease and destruction have to exist? He shook his head.

"Like this?" Bartholomew asked placing an awkward foot sideways.

"Well, straighten out a little. You need to face the trunk."

Bartholomew pivoted around slipping off in the process. He hopped a few times on one foot but at least didn't fall.

"Now try again."

This time Bartholomew stepped up and got a handhold on the branch. It was looking good.

For all of four seconds.

This time he did fall, landing with an oomph.

Alex looked to Erantha. The dragoness let out a long sigh and then turned her mouth upward. She blew a few small puffs of smoke that drifted upwards and snagged on the rising crescent moon like cottony fibers. Then the fibrous puffs stretched into wisps and swung back and forth.

Suddenly a flame like a comet shooting across the sky streaked past. Alex stumbled back while Bartholomew's jaw dropped open.

Erantha blew three more puffs of smoke. Another flame shot overhead. Now Alex could make out a dragon's head, red scales glimmering in the firelight.

It passed by the moon, with a second, more familiar shape following behind.

"Wade!" Alex called.

The fins on either side of Wade's his neck flapped a hello. Meanwhile the huge dragon in front of him swooped down for a landing. The water dragon followed, alighting a few feet further on.

"You called?" the red dragon asked Erantha.

"What runs smoother than any rhyme? Can easily fall, but cannot climb?"

"Water, of course," the fire-red dragon replied.

"Correct but also The Deliverer of Dread Woods." Erantha said with a tilt of her reptilian head.

"A Deliverer that can't climb? Bah!"

"Now Flynn, just because the boy has slippery hands doesn't mean we should insult him."

"Hmm. In my day a Deliverer could scale a castle wall and then create an army of clay."

"Regardless, he needs to reach the skies. But his feet stay on the ground."

"No wonder we're needed."

Alex cringed and avoided looking B-3's way. His friend's face was probably as red as this dragon's scales.

"I'm sorry," Bartholomew stammered. "It's just–I–"

When Flynn opened his mouth to reply, Erantha flicked him with her tail. Instead of a retort, he sputtered a few sparks. Then he glared at the female.

"Just ignore my brother. Living next to a volcano has singed a few of his manners. Now Wade, I need you to swoop down and scoop up the youngling while Flynn and I keep watch from the skies."

Wade's face fins quivered when he replied. "Me? Landing in Dread Woods?"

"Yes, you. Flynn and I will be right behind you. Now go." Erantha gave him a shove with her graceful snout.

Slumping his blue shoulders, the water dragon trudged a few feet away. With a backwards glance, he flapped his iridescent wings and took to flight, his siblings right behind. He circled over the forest three times before diving straight for Bartholomew.

Alex had to hand it to him. B-3 didn't so much as flinch when the giant creature grabbed him in his talons and flapped upwards. Just waved and gave them a sheepish smile.

The next thing Alex knew Bartholomew was standing next to him squirting hand sanitizer into his hand.

"See, it's never hopeless," Alex said giving him a punch in the arm.

Bartholomew rubbed the hand sanitizer in before turning to the blue dragon for a thank you.

"It was nothing," The water dragon said shyly.

"So where are we anyhow?" Alex glanced around. In the shadow of the forest it looked like they were next to an open field. Round tuffets with grassy tops rolled off in the distance. And he could make out some clumps of flowers in the pale moonlight.

"Between dread and hope, lies a slippery slope," Flynn said while Wade and Erantha bobbed their heads in agreement.

Alex raised his eyebrows waiting for an explanation.

When none came, Bartholomew pulled the parchment out of the burlap sack slung over his shoulder. Suggesting it was time to look at the map again, he smoothed it out on a boulder and bent down for a closer look. "It's too dark," he said squinting.

"Step aside," Flynn said. He took a deep breath and exhaled a long slow flame.

Now Alex could see Dread Woods clearly on the map, its spooky trees and ghosts protruding from the parchment. Man, he was glad to be out of there. Next to the forest was a pale field on top of a mountain. Beyond the hill everything was still blurry.

"Well, at least a couple more things have come into focus," Bartholomew said brightly.

"Yeah, and we know the Plains of Bramear were supposed to be beyond Dread Woods, but this is a mountain, not a flat plain."

"I hope we didn't end up on the wrong side. Erantha?"

"Didn't you hear what Flynn said? Between dread and hope lies a slippery slope." she said.

Riddles. Dragons were known for riddles. Alex supposed they were so used to speaking in them they didn't realize how confusing it was to kids like him. He shrugged.

"Dread and hope," Wade repeated waving his fins at the forest and then the mountaintop in the opposite direction.

"Oh, I get it," Bartholomew said. "Dread Woods is the dread, and hope is us finding the Golden Dragon like in the Prophecy."

"Oh yeah, 'Hope will lie in the hands of twins.' That's us. So, I guess that means we head toward the top of the mountain."

"That's what we just said, silly goose," Erantha smiled gently at them before lining up behind her brother.

"Yeah right," Alex said to B-3 under his breath. "As clear as mud."

His friend covered his grin with a hand and fell in line as the five of them set off in single file. Flynn was first, next Erantha and Wade, then Alex with Bartholomew at the rear.

At first Alex thought the moonlit hike with three huge dragons was cool. The view of their curving backs, spiked necks, and swishing tails was so mesmerizing that he started to plan out a painting he'd create when he got home. But as they trudged further and further on, these thoughts were replaced with how to keep up with the dragons' long strides.

Hours later, Alex could hear Bartholomew yawning loudly behind him but it barely registered. He rubbed his eyes. Was he walking or sleeping? Either way, there must be bricks tied to his feet since every step was heavier than the last. In a haze, he took another scuffling step and tripped over a tree root.

Alex extended his arms, tumbling into Wade who in turn fell against Erantha who bumped into Flynn.

"Whoa—hh!!" The red dragon blew out an angry flame. "Watch where you're going!"

Bartholomew grabbed Alex's arm and dug his fingers in.

"Now Flynn, these younglings are tired. I think it's time we stopped to rest."

"In my day, Deliverers would have foregone sleep for the quest," Flynn growled.

"I know a place," Wade said before his brother could argue more. "It's just a little hole, not much of a cave. But the Deliverers would be protected until sunrise."

"Wonderful idea Wade," Erantha said. "Lead on."

After a few minutes, they reached an embankment where Wade flapped his fins at a hollow depression. It was only about three feet high, more a hole in the ground than a cave. Still it looked dry and warm.

Bartholomew halted and raised his eyebrows at the opening.

"Go on now youngling. Get some rest," Erantha coaxed.

Mumbling about dirt and messes Bartholomew crawled inside, Alex right behind. The dirt walls smelled a little musty but at least they were out of the chill air. B-3 scooted into a corner, rubbed some hand sanitizer over his face, and covered his head with his sack.

"Nite, B-3," Alex said worming to the opposite side.

Almost as soon as he'd settled in his own corner, Alex felt his eyes grow heavy. The day's events floated by in a fog. Leaving the smoldering village. Trudging into Dread Woods. Erantha's talons on his shoulders as she lifted him skyward.

By the time he'd wrapped his heavy coat around his shoulders and snuggled up into a ball, they were drooping. The last thing he remembered before drifting off was Erantha shushing Flynn and warm dragon's breath blowing into the cave.

Chapter 50

Gwen glared at the Minotaur, hoping the solid gaze would keep him from slapping her. His raised hand came closer. Sweat beaded on her forehead but she raised her chin and tried not to flinch. While desperately searching for something to distract him, a shriek came from the other room.

"Booger! Get in here!"

That nasal whine was worse than Lacey's birthday tantrum. And just as annoying. Gwen would know that voice anywhere.

Lucretia.

Holding his tail, the monster dashed out of the room.

Now with her hood off, Gwen had a chance to look around. She was in a little cave with rocky walls and four doorways. The Minotaur had exited to her right, so it must be the dragon's chamber. Two other doors were heavy and looked like they might lead back into labyrinth. Gwen guessed that the last one with a piece of fabric hanging down was the Minotaur's bedroom. If bull-headed monsters slept.

The cave had a fireplace with a heavy kettle on a dirty spit. There were chunks of old meat hanging on the iron skewer and Gwen shuddered to think where they might have come from. There were no pictures on the wall. Only a single tapestry with strange symbols hung above the stone fireplace. If her feet weren't bound to the chair legs, Gwen would have stepped up for a closer look.

The Minotaur had tied her to a wooden chair facing a tall table with a messy bunch of pewter mugs and crockery. She had just started to scoot her chair toward a bent fork just out of reach, when approaching footsteps stopped her.

"I told you to keep an eye out," a gravelly voice began.

"I have been," Minotaur replied with a growl. "But in case you haven't noticed, my mistress keeps me occupied.

"You still could have found a way to tell me that Princess Rhea had–" the creature paused mid-sentence and gasped. "You!"

Gwen felt the blood drain from her face. Of all the creatures she might face, this one she dreaded the most.

"How did *she* get here?" Captain Sludge demanded.

"She?" The Minotaur replied with a puzzled look.

"Yes, *she*." Sludge jerked a claw-tipped thumb toward Gwen.

"But that's a boy. Rhea's page," Minotaur said, confused.

"Do I have to strip her to prove it to you?"

Gwen gulped and shrunk back into her chair.

The Minotaur's eye's narrowed as he stepped closer. He began to survey Gwen from head to toe. His hand extended toward her tunic.

Gwen spoke quickly. "Okay, okay, I'm a girl. You don't have to check."

"I do not understand," Minotaur said drawing back.

"She is friend to the Deliverers. Idiot. Don't you know anything?"

"The girl of legend? Who helped keep the Renaissance Nation safe?"

"I wouldn't put it like that. But yes, she foiled my plans for Mona Lisa." Captain Sludge rubbed a slimy hand over his chin. "But this time..."

"Yes?" Minotaur asked.

"This time she will foil their plans."

"Bait." Minotaur bobbed his bull head up and down.

"A little worm on a hook." Sludge twisted his clawed thumb into a hooked shape before patting the chortling Minotaur on the back.

While Gwen shivered.

Chapter 51

"Achoo! Oops, sorry." Wincing, Bartholomew sat up.

Inside the burrow, Alex wiped his face with a corner of his t-shirt. "No problem, I love waking up to sneeze spray. It goes great with the kink I have in my neck from using my jacket as a pillow."

"Ahh, you younglings have woken. Come let us make haste," the green Erantha said from the mouth of the cave.

Wiping his nose the best he could with a dirty handkerchief, Bartholomew brushed his hair back with his hand, and crawled out behind Alex. Although the sun was rising over the mountain peak above, its long rays of light did little to brighten Dread Woods behind them. Holy dust bunnies was Bartholomew happy to be out of there.

He squirmed in his stiff and dirty clothes. What he wouldn't give for a bath right then. As if expecting one to appear on the mountainside, he glanced around and saw trickling stream about one hundred yards above them. It looked so clean and inviting.

"Okay, let's go," Alex said.

"Ummm," Bartholomew began, glancing lovingly towards the stream.

"What?" Alex asked, irritated.

"I need to go up there for a bit of umm, morning stuff. You know?"

"No, I don't. You have some dried jerky in your knapsack. Eat that."

"That's not what I mean. It's..." He sighed.

"I think the youngling needs to make water. Am I right?" Erantha asked.

"Oh, why didn't you say you had to go? Come to think of it so do I. Where's a tree?" Alex glanced around.

"I'll be right back," Bartholomew said as he trotted toward the stream. Then to himself, "I'll bathe quickly, and they'll never know the difference."

Once Bartholomew had followed the stream until it curved out of sight, he slipped off his shirt and gently shook out the dust. Laying it flat on a boulder he stepped out of his shoes and tucked the sox in. With a final glance to make sure the coast was clear, he did his business before slipping out of his pants and silk boxers.

Bartholomew shivered in the cool morning air. Dipping in a tentative toe he sprung back. Brrr it was cold! He almost threw his clothes back on, until he got a whiff of his armpits. Whoa. Worse than that pig dung.

He jumped.

The water was a like ice and goosebumps popped up on all over his body. Although his skin prickled, he let out a long sigh. To finally be clean.

Splashing his face, Bartholomew knelt in the waist high water and gargled. Now for the tough part. He counted to three and dunked under, rubbing his chest and under his arms. His hair flowed freely in the swirling currents. It felt great.

Alex's muffled voice called from down the hill. "Bartholomew, hurry up!"

Remembering himself, Bartholomew leapt out of the water landing on the rocky bank.

He was just reaching for his clothes when a pair of wide eyes met his. Gasping, Bartholomew staggered back and toppled into the stream with a splash. His hands shot between his legs as he dropped to his knees.

"Bartholomew, what are you doing?" Alex asked from behind him. "Oh. Hello."

The painted girl in a long gown cocked her head quizzically.

"Is that how you address a princess?" the boy next to her said.

"Sorry, didn't know. Your majesty." Alex gave a little bow.

"She's a princess not a queen. *Your grace.*"

While they were talking, Bartholomew looked around for a place to dress. Not even a shrub skirted this stream.

"Okay. Hello, your grace."

"Greetings. Who are thee, Photo, and what purpose have you in traversing Mount Minotaur?"

If I can just get to my clothes without standing up. Bartholomew thought.

"You first," Alex said crossing his arms.

The long-haired princess opened her mouth in reply but the boy in rusty armor would have none of it. "Don't answer these Photos princess. They could be traitors."

"Cederic, I do not think a Photography District traitor would enter Gothia just to strip off his garments and bathe in our streams."

Looking down to make sure his hands were covering the most embarrassing part of his anatomy, Bartholomew scooted a little further away. Even though he was absolutely freezing he could feel his cheeks turn red.

The amber-eyed painting turned back to Alex. "I am Princess Rhea of Castle Alnwick, and this cautious one is Cederic, my squire. Does that satisfy thee?"

"Hey, we heard about you. We were at your castle," Bartholomew blurted out. Forgetting himself, he started to stand but the breeze on his bare chest reminded him to where he was. He looked down, embarrassed.

"Yeah," Alex added. "We've been shadowing you for a couple of days. First at Alnwick, then in the village. Sorry about your Dad by the way."

Rhea, who appeared to be around sixteen, passed a hand over her long brown hair. She stroked it and got a sad look in her eyes but did not speak.

"You still have not answered, Photo," Cederic said thrusting his fists into his hips.

"You think it's okay, B-3?" Alex asked.

Bartholomew considered for a moment and said between shivers, "I think they are who they say they are."

Alex nodded and gave the pair a sober look. "We're not Photos. We're human."

"The Deliverers?" Princess Rhea gasped.

"That's us." Alex quickly explained how they'd splashed down in Artania, met dragons who took them to Castle Alnwick, made a morphing map, and then a pig-dung-hurling-catapult to repel Lucretia.

"You peppered that vain dragon with manure? Ha! I would have given all the jewels in my crown to see that."

"Yeah, my bud has been known to take on a monster or two, when he has clothes on, that is."

Bartholomew gave them both a sheepish smile.

"So, that overzealous maiden needn't have knocked you unconscious," Cederic grumbled.

"Maiden? You mean girl? What girl?" Alex asked.

"Your friend, Gwen. We've been traveling with her," Rhea said.

Bartholomew was confused. "But the innkeeper said there were only boys with you."

"We disguised her, as a page," Cederic explained.

293

"What? Is Gwen okay? Is she still mad at me? Where is she?" Alex kept lobbing questions at Rhea until she finally held up a hand for silence.

As soon as Alex quieted, the royals explained how Gwen had saved Rhea from the White Canvas before joining forces with them. She'd been great luck for the princess ever since, foiling Roger La Savage's attack at the Spider Arms and helping them after fleeing from Lucretia. But then they'd wandered through the Labyrinth.

"...that, alas, is where we parted ways. One moment we were three, the next she was gone." Princess Rhea shook her head sadly.

"If she'd just curbed her temper we might have stayed together." Cederic curled his hands into fists.

Bartholomew knew just what Cederic was talking about. When that girl got angry, there was no talking to her. "Then how did you escape that Labyrinth? I've read that it is a near impossible maze of twists and turns," he asked.

"I am not quite sure. At first, the dagger, *Sight-giver's* light illuminated our path. Later it dimmed to complete darkness. That was when we lost young Gwen. But as we groped along there was a sliver of light ahead. We followed it and ended up just over there." Rhea pointed to a tunnel in the side of the mountain.

"Glad of it too. I've heard tales of Minotaur and I, for one, desire not to become his next meal," Cederic said.

A loud shuffling made them all turn.

"Young Ones we have miles to go. What in heaven's name–" Pausing mid-sentence, Erantha bowed her great dragon head. "Your Grace, you are here. But why?"

"It seems that the Quest has fallen on my shoulders," Rhea replied.

"Your brothers?" Erantha asked.

"No word for many months now. As next in line, Gothia's fate rests with me."

"Not anymore, Dear. *Hope will lie in the hands of twins*," Erantha said.

"*Born on the cusp of the second millennium.* Yes." Rhea looked at Alex and Bartholomew in turn. "Tell us your plan, Deliverers."

Bartholomew and Alex exchanged a glance. Between shivers, Bartholomew shrugged.

Ever the confident one, Alex said, "We were going to the Plains of Bramear to find the Goldens."

Bartholomew nodded in agreement. Then he shook it. "You're forgetting something, or rather, *someone,* Alex."

"Oh, no I haven't. I said, that *was* the plan. Now of course we have to–"

"I know, I know. Go into the Labyrinth, face the terrifying Minotaur and rescue Gwen. But first..." The shivering Bartholomew raised his eyebrows.

"First what?" Alex asked, his eyes twinkling. "Haven't we waited long enough for you? Come on B-3, hop out."

"I-I can't." Bartholomew quivered.

"Why?"

"Y-you kn-kn-know." Bartholomew's teeth were chattering so badly by now he barely got the words out.

"No," Alex teased his eyes wide and innocent.

"You g-guys go ahead. I- I'll c-catch up."

"I don't know if we should separate. I might lose you."

"Alex!"

Chuckling, Alex beckoned the remaining members of their party to follow him around the bend.

And, a slippery popsicle boy leapt into his clothes.

296

Chapter 52

Alex's playful chuckles ceased abruptly when he reached the Labyrinth's shadowy opening. Replaced by images of a terrified Gwen. Wandering alone in that dark space. Hands groping blindly. Horrified eyes seeing nothing but a black shroud.

Clenching his jaw, he asked, "Ready?"

The princess shook her painted head. "I cannot. The Labyrinth is full of too many twists and turns. Only good fortune helped Cederic and I escape."

"Come on," Alex implored giving Rhea a meaningful look.

"You heard the princess. She will not venture back into that maze," Cederic said.

Bartholomew trotted up with his usual puppy-like gait. "Then you and I will go."

Alex peered inside the gloomy cavern. "How, B-3? We'll get lost in the dark."

Bartholomew brushed his still damp hair back with his hand. "I read in the myth, 'Theseus and the

Minotaur' that Ariadne gave Theseus a long thread, so he wouldn't get lost. We could braid a super long rope. Light? I'm not sure."

"You will need neither where you are going," a voice hissed from behind them.

Alex didn't need to turn around. He'd know that voice anywhere. "Sludge," he spat pivoting on one heel.

The Shadow Swine leader raised a hairless brow and with a smug smile said, "Human."

Alex almost slapped that smile right off his face. But sensing he needed information, held back.

"What are you doing here?" Bartholomew demanded. Alex was surprised to hear no fear in his voice. But they had faced Sludge before and Bartholomew knew what to expect. He could prepare himself.

It's the unknown that is terrifying.

When Alex took a step closer, Rhea warned him back. "Be careful, that Swiney is dangerous."

"Don't worry Princess. He and I know each other well, don't we Sludge?" Alex said glaring into the monster's yellow eyes.

"I am acquainted with many you hold dear, Human," The Swiney paused and licked his bulbous lips. "Closely acquainted."

"What do you mean closely? Who are you talking about? If you've been invading Mom's dreams, I'll–"

"Oh, that is not the human to whom I refer. This female is closer than that. Much closer."

"Gwen? Where is she?" Glaring, Bartholomew took a step toward Sludge.

"Safe, for now. But if ever you want to see your precious side-kick again, you will give up this ridiculous quest."

"If you hurt her, I swear to God." Alex curled his hands into fists.

"Ha! You are in no position to threaten me, stupid human. You will return to Alnwick. Then maybe, just maybe, you'll see your precious Gwen again."

Alex felt his blood boil. This kidnapper giving him orders? Yeah right. "You've just made a huge mistake, Sludge."

Sludge leaned in closer and grabbed Alex by the collar. As he spoke spittle peppered Alex's face. "You are the one who makes mistakes! Idiot. But know this. I have eyes everywhere. And they will be watching. If I hear you've crossed me, you'll never see her again." With a snap of his cloak he strode away.

There was a long silence. No one looked each other's way.

Alex breathed heavily trying to calm the fury boiling inside. If Sludge held Gwen at some hidden place, how could they rescue her? She could be anywhere; down in Subterranea surrounded by Swineys or deep inside the Labyrinth. For all he knew she was trapped in Dread Woods as nightmare after nightmare filled her mind.

Alex rubbed his temple. "Maybe we should do like he asks and head back to–"

Bartholomew shook him. "No, that is not an option. I don't care if every rock and tree is watching, we will not bend to Sludge. We must be true. Remember?"

"But he has Gwen."

"I know, but true art is on *our* side. We defeated him before and we'll defeat him again."

Alex wanted to believe. Maybe they had beat Sludge's army before but then they'd had the gods help. Now all they had was some crazy map with fuzzy images and comrades that were just as clueless as they were.

"We don't even know where to look. Our map doesn't show where she is," Alex argued.

Bartholomew shoved Alex back. "Of course. The map. That's it!"

Chapter 53

Bartholomew dashed over to the knapsack and pulled out two rolls of canvas: the map that Alex'd made at Castle Alnwick and the painting the two of them had created back home. He set them side by side on the grass and smoothed them out. "Check it out, Alex. They've changed again."

Alex bent down on one knee for a closer look and shook his head. "No way."

Whereas before they'd morphed into mirror images with Gwen gone, now their friend was back in the center of the painting. Her feet and hands were tied to some wooden chair and she appeared to be in a cave-like room. All the Gothian places they'd visited were in order like a comic strip. Splash down in Lambent Lake. Flying over mountains atop dragons. Alnwick Castle. The burning village. Even Dread Woods was there.

"That's us, Alex," Bartholomew said pointing at the last panel that looked like two teenaged boys bent over tiny pieces of paper.

"I see. And look there seems to be empty spaces waiting to be filled."

"Perhaps they'll appear after we visit them."

"Looks like that's the pattern. Weird how the map only shows the places we've been while the painting shows Gwen changing." Alex said.

"You made the map here, but we created the painting together. That could be a clue." Bartholomew smiled wondering how soon Alex would catch on.

"Still doesn't help us," Alex said.

"Doesn't it?" Bartholomew asked with a smirk.

Palms up, his friend shrugged.

"Just because places haven't appeared doesn't mean we can't find them. If we use true art. And a little information."

"Huh?"

Bartholomew was really enjoying this. For once, Alex was the confused one. "Erantha, Rhea, Wade, can you all come here?" he asked.

When they had done so, Bartholomew pointed at the painting of Gwen. "Does this place look familiar to any of you?"

Rhea and Cederic shook their heads. Erantha's green eyes blinked blankly at the map but Wade's gaze was long and uncomfortable. He leaned forward for a closer look then back, his neck fins flapping slowly.

"It does look like a place I visited, long ago. But it can't be," Wade said.

"Where, Little Brother?" Erantha asked.

Wade blushed under his blue scales making his cheeks turn violet. His fins flapped awkwardly. "I-I was young and thought she was so pretty that if I went there she might accompany me on a midnight stroll or a swim in Lambent Lake. Maybe enjoy a fish dinner together. You know, dragonesses are so few today, I thought the rumors might not be true."

"*Who* are you talking about?" Erantha said.

"Her." Wade said simply.

Erantha shook her scaled head. "No, you didn't try to court *her*?"

Wade flicked his blue tail nervously and looked away.

Watching this confusing exchange made Bartholomew's neck sore from turning back and forth. Just as he was about to break into the conversation and ask, Alex blurted out. "Would you mind explaining to the rest of us what the heck you are talking about?"

"Sorry, Youngling. But it looks like my brother had a little crush on a dragon we all know too well."

"Lucretia? Yuck!" Bartholomew exclaimed.

"Cha," Alex added. "What could you possibly see in her?"

"I was lonely. We dragons are so few now. Anyhow it was futile. She let me bring her some jewels and then threw me out saying she was too beautiful to fall in love with a slimy salamander like me." A tear grew in one of Wade's blue eyes and his head drooped.

Bartholomew felt sorry for the water dragon. At the same time, he couldn't help but wonder what the washcloths he was thinking. Lucretia was beyond evil. He was glad he didn't have to deal with mean girls like that. Not that he had many opportunities to meet any, being homeschooled and trapped inside a fortress of clean.

"This place looks like her home?" Alex asked, pointing at the picture of Gwen.

"The walls look like the same stone. The room is too small for a dragon of course. But it could be–"

"The Minotaur," Erantha finished.

"Isn't *this* Mount Minotaur?" Bartholomew asked tilting his head toward the mountain.

"And if it is," Alex continued.

"Gwen could be inside," Bartholomew completed the thought. His heart quickened. "Can you lead us to her cave, Wade?"

The water dragon shook his head. "She moved the entrance. I tried to visit her one last time, hoping she'd just been in a bad mood or something. But when I got there, the entrance was walled up, gone."

"Then we'll just have to make a new one, won't we?"

"With true art," Alex nodded, finally catching on to Bartholomew's plan.

And the two set to grinding colored stones into paint.

Chapter 54

Alex leaned back and nodded at their painting. The opening leading straight to Gwen was nearly done. Just a dab more stone black. But would it create a real tunnel or just fade into a blur as soon as they finished?

Before setting to work, they'd decided to split up. Didn't want Cederic's clanging armor and the dragons rumbling tiptoes to give them away. The others would guard the Labyrinth exit while he and Bartholomew stole inside Lucretia's lair.

"A bit more black here," Bartholomew said, pointing to a light spot on the canvas.

Alex carefully dipped the scrubby brush in the paint and cupped his hand under it to keep from messing up everything they'd done. Just as he was extending his arm, Alex felt cold steel press into his back.

"Weren't you told to leave?" a surly voice said from behind.

Alex refused to stop now. Gwen needed him. It was his stupid mouth that got her here in the first place. Trying to keep his shaking hand steady, he dabbed at that light spot. "I like it here," he said not daring to look back.

"So, you need some encouragement," the sword-wielder said, driving the steel blade deeper, piercing skin.

Alex gasped, stifled a cry. Blinking back involuntary tears, he leaned forward to steal a glance at the man behind him.

This guy looked like Robin Hood, if the outlaw was in a scary movie. He wore knee high leather boots and a hooded jerkin with lots of folds for hidden weapons. A long scar divided his face into two puckered sections. Spooky. Next to him was a thinner man dressed similarly except for the fletched arrow aimed straight at the wide-eyed Bartholomew.

"Stand, both of you," Scar-face ordered.

Heart racing, Alex tried to think.

"What are you waiting for, an arrow through your friend's throat?"

What he really needed was the creation magic. Why wasn't it working?

The archer pulled his bowstring back farther.

Alex closed his eyes and forced his breath to slow. Then he saw it. Simple really. Jerking his chin from the painting to the mountain, Alex gave Bartholomew a secret wink. "I think we better do as he says."

The outlaw relaxed the pressure on the sword allowing Alex to stand. With a quick nod, B-3 slung the knapsack over one shoulder, dropped the canvas on the ground, and placed a foot on top.

Alex crossed his fingers. And waited.

There was a loud rumbling in the distance as the mountain began to groan and creak. Alex glanced up to see loamy spray exploding from the summit. It rained down, peppering the four of them in earthy droplets.

"Earth-quake?" the thinner outlaw stammered.

"No George. Never in Gothia. This is Deliverer trickery. Calm yourself." Scarface said punctuating each word with his sword.

Boulders rolled down the hillside like a theme park avalanche ride.

"I think it's working!" Bartholomew cried.

Then the ground under them buckled and Alex dropped to all fours. Knowing he'd only have one chance, he waited until the rolling earth threw the outlaw off balance. Then Alex head-butt his gut and Scarface fell over with an oomph.

Meanwhile, B-3 stuck a foot behind the other guy and shouted, "Look out!" making the archer turn and trip over his leg. Skinny tumbled backwards, arrows flying from their quiver, as Bartholomew cried. "Run Alex!"

Alex didn't have to be told twice but scuttled over the undulating ground toward the growing crack in the mountain. The snaking fissure widened until it was about six inches across. But then it stopped growing. Unsure if it was large enough to wedge into, Alex turned sideways and crammed his head and shoulder inside.

But there he met solid rock. "No!" he groaned pressing against the rocky face.

B-3 came up behind and tried to push him inside. "Hurry Alex! They're coming."

"I can't. It's solid."

"Got you!" Scarface cried reaching a hand toward B-3.

"Bartholomew, the painting! Pass it here!"

When B-3 shoved the crumpled canvas his way, Alex pressed it against the wall. The ground rumbled again, louder this time.

The stones parted.

Alex nearly fell over but caught himself just in time. Then he ran headlong into the darkness.

Chapter 55

Bartholomew kept his voice low in case the outlaws were nearby. "Alex? Where are you?"

His words echoed back like whispering snakes, but his friend did not reply. Assuming Alex was just out of earshot, Bartholomew put one hand on the wall and groped forward. Holy bleach buckets, it was dark, and getting darker with each step. Dread Woods shone like the Borax mansion compared to this pitch blackness.

A crunching sound made him pause. Bartholomew cocked an ear. "Hello?"

He waited five seconds. Ten. Whatever it was, stopped. Chewing on his lower lip, Bartholomew continued forward.

Even though they'd only been friends for two years, it felt like a lifetime. He could hardly recall a time when Alex hadn't been there, guiding and encouraging him. Alex advised how to deal with Mother's constant cleaning frenzies, Mr. White's ever-watchful eyes, or how to kick Shadow Swine butts.

Not that they'd hit it off right away. In fact, Bartholomew had mistrusted Alex at first. He remembered that first day they'd met. He'd just snuck out for the first time and was feeling as free as an uncaged eagle.

Until he crashed headlong into Alex.

Then they'd both experienced the same vision: a lightning flash of color with brightly painted Artanians. The vision was freaky enough but when Bartholomew saw his dirty hands, true panic set in. He knew his mother would go into a cleaning frenzy if she saw them. So, Alex took him home and let him wash up. But when a second vision appeared, a nasty argument ensued, and it was months before the two boys spoke again. And that was only because they'd ended up in the same class. It took more mystical glimpses of Artania and a few sad events to finally become friends.

And now Bartholomew would do just about anything for Alex.

Alex, where are you? He could not have gotten that far ahead. They were right next to each other only minutes ago. Bartholomew adjusted the knapsack and continued feeling his way along the rough surface. Then his hand caught on a sharp rock.

"Ow!" he hissed, recoiling from the razor-sharp rock. *That stings.* He opened and closed his hand as long scratches started bleeding on his palm.

Ever his mother's son, Bartholomew applied a dollop of watery hand sanitizer. But here is where they differed. Mother would be moaning and rushing off to a doctor about now, whereas Bartholomew took control and imagined the cuts healing.

A couple of years back, an Artanian goddess had explained that as a creator, he had healing powers. Here he could close wounds or knit bone. Sadly, it only worked inward; the powers couldn't heal sick or hurt Artanians.

He'd done it before, mending a broken arm, but then Alex had been by his side. He didn't know if he could repair these cuts alone. Still he needed his hands to feel his way forward. And right now, it hurt too much to be of much use.

Alex's voice filled his mind. *Come on B-3, try.*

Bartholomew slowed his breathing and tried to envision a healthy hand. Breathe in, bleeding stops. Breathe out, skin scabs over. Breathe in, scab shrinks. Breathe out, and his palm was healed.

He opened and closed his mended hand.

Brazened by this success, Bartholomew cast his arms forward, fumbling for the wall. But he must have stepped into the middle of a large cavern because he couldn't feel anything but air.

Bartholomew stumbled over a rock. He twirled and floundered, barely getting his balance before tripping over a second one. He fell to his knees and new scrapes cut into skin.

Wincing with pain, he crawled forward, groping toward what he thought was the wall. When he

sensed something solid in front of him, Bartholomew
leaned back on his haunches and extended his arms.

Moss inside a cavern? That was strange. He patted
the fuzzy wall.

Then it moved. And growled.

That wasn't moss. It was fur. And Bartholomew
knew exactly what it was attached to.

"Holy dust bunnies. The Minotaur." Bartholomew
groaned.

Chapter 56

"Bartholomew?" Alex whispered into the darkness. "You there?"

Nothing but silence.

Alex stopped to think. If it worked right, his painting was carving a new entrance toward where Gwen was being held. So, if he kept groping along the wall with it outstretched, he should eventually reach her.

That was the plan, anyhow.

He held out the canvas, took a few steps forward, and then cocked an ear. It was too quiet. He should hear Bartholomew's stumbling feet by now.

Alex considered going back in case the outlaw had grabbed him, but it was so freakin' dark that he couldn't tell which way that was. Man, he wished he had a light.

Keep going Alex.

He repeated this step-stop- cock-an-ear sequence. His ears met silence as deep as his care for his friends. He did it again. Three times. Seven.

After about fifteen minutes, Alex heard something in the distance and slowed his pace. He listened. Voices? Yes, definitely. One deep and grumbly and another full on mad.

"Leave Mr. Clean alone!" an angry female cried.

Gwen! And only one person could be called Mr. Clean. How the heck did Bartholomew get captured? Alex shook his head. Now he had to figure out how to rescue them both.

He tiptoed forward until some sort of wavering light in the distance made shadowy shapes on the wall. With the added light, he could also make out the elements on his painting. It had changed in the last few minutes. Gwen was still tied to a chair but now he could make out more details from where she was being held. This room had four exits: three wooden and a fourth of cloth.

Alex ran his finger over the painting's tunnel which seemed to stop just short of the cloth doorway. If his new opening led to an empty room, he'd be able to steal inside unnoticed. But if the Creation Magic carved a doorway to the Minotaur, he was screwed.

"It's okay, Gwen. I'm, fine-ow-ow-" Bartholomew squeaked out.

"Be quiet, human scum. Or I'll gag as well as tie you," a deep voice that Alex figured must be the Minotaur snarled.

Alex cringed, almost feeling the cords cut his own skin. *I'm coming B-3.* Taking a deep breath, he moved a few feet closer.

As he rounded a corner he could see that the tunnel opened into a small room where a couple of candles flickered atop a strange maze-shaped table. Beside this, lie a large wooden bed with crumpled furs hanging half onto the stone floor. That bull-headed monster had either risen quickly or was lazy.

A fabric doorway hung on the opposite side of the room just like in his painting. But no creature drew it back. Maybe he could sneak inside unnoticed. His heart raced as he made his way toward the bedroom. But then he felt something strange beside him. Rock.

Was it his imagination or were the walls closing in?

He tried pressing the painting against the stony ceiling, but instead of growing, it pushed back.

"What the?" he gasped as the tunnel contracted, squeezing around him like a boa constrictor.

Then the distant doorway began to shrink. Shriveling with every step.

"No way!" Alex cried making a mad dash for the bedroom. Abandoning all caution, he plunged forward. One wall scratched his arm and he recoiled, bumped his head. Didn't stop to check his brow but hunched over stumbling forward. Sharp stones raked his t-shirt forcing him to his knees.

Please stay open. He prayed, scuttling on all fours like a beetle. Dodging the hungry rocks, he struggled to keep the mountain from swallowing him. Then the rocky overhang sank down, blocking his view of the room ahead.

Boulders pressed from all sides. Wriggling through the ever-smaller tunnel, Alex dropped to his belly. Dirt filled his mouth and nose, choking him. His heart pounded as visions of being buried alive flashed in his mind.

With a burst of speed, Alex extended his arms and dove headfirst. Rolled over on his back. Sputtering, he slithered through the last bit of empty space. He pulled his feet through.

Then the doorway hissed closed.

* * *

Rat farts. Alex thought with an inward groan. His clean escape was gone and now the only way out would be through the Labyrinth. Or past that evil Lucretia.

Clenching his jaw, Alex ducked behind the huge bed. In the adjoining room, Gwen was still giving the Minotaur an earful. *You go girl.* He thought with a wry grin.

Not that he was surprised. That girl was no wuss. In fact, she was tougher than most guys he knew.

Alex leaned against the bed's wooden frame and waited. After several minutes of Gwen trading barbs with the Minotaur he heard a loud roar and retreating footsteps. Alex immediately stole to the doorway and peaked through a gap in the fabric. He could see a red-faced Gwen wrinkling her nose and the back of Bartholomew's head but no sign of the Minotaur. While the coast was clear, he hurried into the room.

"Alex!" Bartholomew gasped.

Putting a finger to his lips Alex rolled up his painting and shoved it inside the knapsack at Bartholomew's feet. Slinging it over his friend's shoulder, he began working on the knots. "Do you know how to get out of here?"

"Our tunnel, of course," Bartholomew whispered.

"It closed up, almost making me Mount Minotaur's lunch in the process," Alex explained.

Gwen shook her head and then replied in a low voice. "He put a hood over my head when he brought me here."

Alex looked to Bartholomew who shrugged. "Same here."

He glanced at around the room. "Which door did the Minotaur use?"

Gwen and Bartholomew pointed at the center one.

Alex scratched an eyebrow, thinking. "Did he say if he was going outside or deeper into the Labyrinth?"

Both of his friends shook their heads.

"Whatever way we go, we better go soon, Alex. He could return any second." Seeming to remember something, Gwen punched Alex in the arm. "I shouldn't even be talking to you, Dummy."

"Can we talk about my intelligence later?"

Gwen crossed her arms over her chest. "You humiliated me."

"I'm sorry. It wasn't on purpose. But right now, we need to choose the right door."

"In front of everyone."

"I wouldn't call Lacey and her Populos everyone. And I didn't mean to-"

317

"You called me a-a- you know!"

"We have to get out of here. Now," Bartholomew whispered.

Alex turned to him. "Is that middle one the only exit Minotaur has used?"

"I've only been here a few minutes. I don't know."

"Gwen?"

She just glared at him.

"Please. He could come back any second."

"No, whenever the dragon screeches he goes through the other one. Jerkface." She curled a lip.

Ignoring Gwen's insult, Alex stepped over to the far door. "Then it follows that we should go this way. The dragon probably has an exit to the outside."

Just then he saw the other door handle begin turning.

"Go, now!" Alex pushed his friends in front of him. He started to follow but a roar and clacking hooves stopped him.

He stood frozen, mouth agape as the bull-headed creature lumbered toward him. Then, as if waking, Alex leaped through the opening and slammed the door closed.

The handle twisted back and forth while Alex fought to keep it shut. When a crack opened, Alex rammed his shoulder into the wood. It latched closed.

Bartholomew turned gawking.

"Just go!" Alex cried, searching for something to jam against the door.

"Where's a friggin chair when you need one?" he gritted, struggling to keep the Minotaur inside.

Planting his feet firmly, he leaned back, pressing his spine against the trembling wood.

Thud! Thud! Fists pounded into the door.! Soon the wood would begin splintering and he'd be facing a man-eating monster.

Not about to wait around for that fun fate, Alex ran.

Right into the dragon's lair.

Chapter 57

Gwen skidded to a halt just short of the great lizard. Holding out an arm to keep Mr. Clean from tripping on its tail, she pointed at the dragon's sleeping face. Bartholomew nodded and mouthed a thank you before taking a few steps backwards.

They were inside of a great cavern next to the Halloween-orange Lucretia whose hulking form filled up half of the room. The snoring dragon's tail was curled around a huge pile of red, gold, and turquoise gems. With each breath, smoke rings escaped her nostrils and circled her spiked head.

Like something out of a fairy tale, mounds of treasure were everywhere. Pearl encrusted stalagmites grew from the floor and strands of ruby necklaces hung from the ceiling. In some weird way, the dragon reminded Gwen of Lacey and she started to chuckle at the idea of that spoiled Populo hugging jewels and snoring smoke. But then an angry growl brought her back to reality.

"Stop!" the Minotaur bellowed.

Gwen turned to see a panicked Alex running towards them, legs all akimbo. "What are you waiting for?" he cried waving them forward.

Seriously? Did he have to ask? Gwen shook her head and gestured at the mounds of jewels on all sides. "A direction, Brainiac."

She looked to Bartholomew who shrugged and then back at Alex who kept hopping from one leg to the other like he had to pee or something. Jeesh. Neither one seemed to have a clue.

Then Lucretia snorted and flicked out a forked tongue. "Who's that?" she yawned, her long eyelashes twitching.

Gwen stopped thinking, just grabbed Alex in one hand and Mr. Clean in the other. Like a draft horse she pulled them past the sleepy dragon's face, around its body, and over another pile of jewels. As soon as they reached a mound large enough to hide behind, the three of them ducked down.

"How dare you wake me up at this ungodly hour?" Lucretia screeched.

The cavern lit up like a beach bonfire and there was a deep yowl followed by a smell like burned hair. Then Gwen saw smoke rising from where they'd just escaped.

She rubbed a hand over her head as fear as sharp as diamonds scored her throat. Waving her friends on, she scrambled forward.

She clambered over emeralds, dug through rubies, and brushed past pearls. You'd think being in a room

321

with all those riches would tempt a thirteen-year-old girl. But for some reason Gwen didn't even consider grabbing a handful.

She had too much to think about. Like where the freak was the exit? And how the Hades could they find it without being burnt to a crisp?

"I said, why did you wake me up at this crazy hour? You know I need my beauty sleep!" Lucretia wailed.

"It wasn't me. It was the humans."

"What! You let them escape?"

Alex grabbed Gwen's shoulder. "We gotta get out of here fast."

"Cha!" Gwen shook her head. Alex sure could state the obvious. "That's what I'm trying to do."

"There! I see a light." Bartholomew pointed.

The three of them raced toward it. But then the ground rumbled, and jewels began to rain down on their heads. Gwen didn't need to turn around. She knew why.

"Oh, dog doodies!" she cried pumping her arms.

Hot flames shot over their heads. Instinctively Gwen ducked and darted ahead of Alex.

Smoke filled her lungs making her cough and sputter. Her eyes tearing, she struggled to continue forward. "Where's that dumb exit anyhow?"

More rubble rained down. The cavern filled with dust and smoke. Gwen felt like she was inside an oven during an earthquake. But this one was as big as a school and rattled with roars, squawks, and thundering crashes.

322

Off to her right Gwen saw some rays of light through the fog. "Guys, over here."

As soon as she reached the exit, sweet air filled her lungs. But she sure as surf didn't have time to enjoy it. A flash of fire followed by a crazed shriek filled the air.

"You brats get back here. Or I'll burn you to a crisp!"

Gwen glanced over her shoulder and saw Alex and Bartholomew careening toward her, the dragon's gnashing teeth at their feet. She backed up. One step. Two. Started on three.

"Gwen. Look ou–" was all she heard.

Before falling into the abyss.

Chapter 58

When Alex saw Gwen's red hair disappear over the edge of the cliff, he didn't think. Just leapt. And immediately regretted it, because the next thing he knew he was rolling head over heels down a mountainside. His tumbling body banged against the ground as grime filled his mouth. Again.

Rocks scraping his skin, Alex tried to reach for something to break his fall. Only got more cuts. This might have slowed his descent but now he was sliding sideways. He blinked. It wasn't good. Another sharp drop-off waited just below a ledge down to his left.

The shelf was only about ten feet wide. That was bad enough. It also appeared to be the only thing before a sheer drop off. If he didn't land there, he'd become boy pudding.

His aim had to be perfect.

Alex lurched to the side in a desperate attempt to change course. But the mountain had other ideas. It put him on a collision course with the rocky gorge below.

Alex could feel the inevitable plummet through air. Then the collision and the ultimate crush of his organs and crunching bones. Alex Pudding.

And he imagined Mom. Forever wondering where he was. Forever searching. Her heart growing weaker by the day.

"No!" Alex cried clawing at the ground. He dug his nails in, bent three backwards. Ignoring the pain, he burrowed his hands deeper into gravel. Clutching this soil, he turned his body 90 degrees. Maybe it'd work.

But now he was head first.

"Ahh!" He slid downward like a kid diving into a pool. More gravel scraped his chin and chest. Alex struggled to protect his face but only extended his arms halfway up before smashing into a boulder.

Alex blinked through the stars swimming before his eyes. He'd made it. Although dazed, he got up and peered at the canyon below.

Where was Gwen? He couldn't see that shock of red hair anywhere. Alex shuddered. If she'd rolled downhill like he had and missed the ledge she could have...

"Don't think like that." He shook his head. Still she could be lost or hurt. He needed to get down there fast. Alex glanced up. B-3 didn't exactly love heights so Alex doubted he'd follow a crazy jump off a cliff. Knowing Bartholomew, he'd probably try to find a safe path down.

Alex was on his own.

"Get back here!" Lucretia screeched from over the ridge. Alex saw orange wings and shoulders appear over the rise. He scanned the flat ledge. Nowhere to hide. Not even weeds grew on this rocky outcropping.

Her great horned head turned right and left before homing in on him. Alex rifled through his pockets. No weapons. He dropped to his knees and rummaged under the boulder. Nothing to fight her off with.

Alex's hands were shaking but he forced himself to stand. Lucretia tucked in her wings and dove. Alex's gut tightened.

Beating wings pulsed as she drew closer. Jagged flames licked the air.

"No, I refuse to be a sitting duck," Alex said through gritted teeth. Knowing his best hope was to be a moving target; Alex clenched his jaw and started zigzagging from side to side.

Breathing fire, Lucretia scorched the hillside only yards above the ledge.

Alex peered up. The red eyes in that reptilian face narrowed as she lowered her chin into a dive. Then like a fletched arrow, her long snout drew a bead on Alex who was still crisscrossing the ledge.

Lucretia sucked in a deep breath and Alex's heart froze. She opened her mouth and there was a flash. Flames started to whip his face and hair.

Covering his head Alex halted. Running was no good. She'd put fiery walls in every direction. It was only a matter of time before one turned him into Alex toast.

He only had one choice. Alex stepped up to the edge. The heat was unbearable now. He could smell burning hair and embers singeing his neck.

Alex closed his eyes, extended a toe.

"Back off shrew!" a familiar voice warned.

"Bartholomew?" Alex blinked.

There astride a hovering Erantha sat his best friend, the crimson Flynn gliding at their side. Baby face screwed up in rage, B-3 shook an angry fist.

Lucretia screeched and unleashed another fireball but this time Erantha and Flynn returned the shot with their own red-hot spears. All three flames collided right over Alex in a thunderous crack. He dove for cover, sliding behind the boulder just as they flared into a conflagration.

"You!" Lucretia screamed as sparks rained down like fireworks over the sea.

"Yes us, vixen," Bartholomew said curling one lip in a sneer.

Vixen? Almost laughing, Alex brushed a few embers out his hair. Even full on ticked, Bartholomew wasn't very scary.

Flynn fluttered a few feet closer. "And it's three against one, so why don't you go back to your cave and play with your jewels."

Seeming to know when she was beaten, Lucretia hissed and flew back over the rise. Bartholomew did a fist pump and cheered. When the hovering Flynn landed next to him with an earth-shaking thud, Alex had to hold out his arms for balance.

"Did you see where Gwen went?" Bartholomew asked from above.

Alex's relief at avoiding becoming barbecue-boy was short-lived. Shoulders tensing, he shook his head.

"We shall find her, youngling. Don't you fret," Erantha soothed.

Alex wasn't afraid of that. He knew they'd eventually find her. What turned his hands to ice was the condition she'd be in when they finally did.

Chapter 59

Gwen moaned. Everything hurt. Her head, neck, back, legs. Even those toenails she'd painted silver to match Lacey's, ached.

Moments ago, she'd been rolling down a mountain like a vert skater who'd lost his board. Of course, this drop wasn't over smooth lumber but a gnarly tumble over boulders and gravel. Even though years of skateboarding had taught her how to fall, she'd still scraped every square inch of bare skin and probably bruised the rest.

If bruises were all they were.

Slowly she opened her eyes squinting in the dim light. "Okay, Gwen. Assess injuries," she recited the words Dad had drilled into her since she was little.

Hunching her shoulders, she started to sit up but a sharp pain in her thigh laid her back down. Swallowing hard she tried to roll onto her side, winced in pain. Something was cutting into her leg. She rose on one elbow and glanced down to see a huge stalagmite atop her right thigh. It must have come loose in the fall and was now trapping her under its weight.

Gwen lay back banging her head against the soft floor.

Daylight streamed in, its long rays lighting up the walls of the tunnel-like opening overhead. She seemed to be in some sort of sinkhole about thirty feet underground. Stalagmites grew from the floor and there was a turquoise pond off to her left.

The rest of the ground was carpeted in soft green. It ran from one end of the sinkhole to the other, up under her, covering everything in a thick layer that felt like moss.

So that's what saved me, Gwen thought running her fingers over the soft peat.

Now she needed to save herself.

Inch by inch she forced her throbbing torso up until she was sitting upright. Bending her free knee for balance, she started examining the stalagmite. It was twice as long as her body and about as wide as her waist. Her leg was wedged under the formation's widest part. She could see blood pooling under her torn leggings and knew enough anatomy to realize that the calcite tube was acting like a huge bandage.

So how could she move it without bleeding out? Remembering what she'd heard about leg injuries, Gwen decided to begin with slowing the blood flow. She'd have to work around the stalagmite, first applying pressure with her hand to her upper thigh. Gwen felt around until the pulsing femoral artery was under her palm.

She pressed down and watched. The seeping blood did slow but she sure as snot couldn't stay like this indefinitely. She was alone and heck if she knew whether help was on the way or Alex and Mr. Clean had been captured by that fire-breathing dragon.

She'd need a lot more pressure than just her hand. But she remembered from her first aid class that tourniquets should only be used in severe cases by trained rescuers. She knew the basics. Dad made sure of that. But she'd never been taught how to properly apply a tourniquet. Gwen read that there were all sorts of dangers from applying it too loosely and then bleeding to death or too tightly and destroying tissue. Then you'd end up having to amputate. Not her idea of fun. Other risks included using the wrong materials that could cut into skin or putting it in the wrong place.

Still, what choice did she have? If she was ever going to get out of here, she first had to free her leg. And for that she needed to stop the blood flow.

"I'll leave it on just long enough to get this stupid rock thing off." Gwen said aloud, surprised how weak her voice sounded.

Vowing to move fast; Gwen untied the rope belt from around her waist. Holding it in her teeth, she ripped a handful of moss from the ground and laid it across her upper thigh just above the stalagmite.

"You're okay. You can do this," Gwen said seizing the rope.

Gwen's nose twitched wildly. For a moment she wavered, remembering all the horror stories Dad had shared. If she didn't strap it tightly enough she'd bleed to death in the process.

With barely an inch of space under her, it was going to be Hella hard to ease the cord between her leg and the ground. She brought it closer, poised to wind it under. Hesitated. What was she thinking?

If she didn't get on right, she'd lose her leg. With a dry swallow, Gwen bunched up the rope ready to fling it across the cavern.

Gwen grit her teeth. "No. Do it. Now," she said arching her back before she could change her mind.

When she lifted her butt, Gwen gasped in pain. Held her breath. Didn't stop but kept threading the rope through the mud. After agonizing seconds, the rope was finally all the way under, so she yanked the opposite end to even out the line.

Barely breathing, she twined one end over the other and cinched it tight. An immediate dizziness overcame her. She started panting, making it worse, as nausea joined her vertigo.

Lightheaded, Gwen leaned forward and rest her head on her free knee. "Huh. Huh. Huh." She gasped, feeling like she was about to throw up any second.

Black spots and silvery snakes streamed in front of her eyes. She gagged on some rising vomit.

Swallowing the bitter bile, Gwen curled her clammy hands into fists and tightened the rope. More stars clouded her vision and she retched.

Sour stomach acid surged up her throat. Gwen leaned to the side spewing acrid liquid in a long stream. It kept coming up until it felt like her gut was the thing being cinched in a tourniquet.

Several dry heaves later, when she was finally able to breathe again, she spat out the remaining chunks.

With an empty stomach and the rope as tight as she dared, it was time to work on that stony trap. Taking a deep breath, Gwen reached out both hands and tried to roll the stalagmite off her leg.

But it wouldn't budge. She wedged her fingers under the column and strained. Nothing. She glanced around. Maybe if she had a stick to use as a crowbar she could work herself loose.

Just soft freaking moss! Gwen punched at the ground and her fist left a depression. She stared at the small pit nose twitching angrily.

So, this was her fate? To die in some sinkhole?

You were such an ugly baby. Ugly. Mom's words came back.

What did it matter? Mom wouldn't even notice if she were gone. Probably be relieved.

Memories mocked like strobe lights. Alex calling her a slag. Looking at her phone a thousand times on her birthday knowing Mom had forgot, again. *Dog* on her t-shirt. Populos pointing and jeering.

Then the nightmares flashed in her mind. Mirrors reflected ugliness as Mom covered her in face powder. This piled at her feet, over her legs, and up her torso, covering her neck and chin. Granules pooled in her eyes and mouth like handfuls of sand.

Gwen had tried to cry out, but it scratched her throat and raked her eyes. Suffocating, she sputtered and choked, drowning in a dust she could barely dig free from.

She'd woken clawing at air.

Gwen almost slapped herself when she thought of it. Dig? It was so simple. If you can't move the stalagmite, move your body.

Gwen twisted her fist in the depression, then, opening her fingers, scooped up a handful of soft peat. She lifted her eyebrows; this was as easy as shell combing on East Beach. She thrust her hand into the soil again; hollowing out a nice sized hole.

Clawing at the soil with both hands, she flung armfuls that splashed in the pond like a hope fountain. Then she felt a slight movement under her leg.

"Yes!" she cried digging more feverishly. Once she had a nice cavity on the left she chiseled into the peat on her right. When both holes were deep enough, she tried tunneling from one to the other.

Her trapped leg dropped two inches.

Was it enough? Gwen placed both hands at her sides for leverage and tried to slide out from under the stalagmite.

Still stuck.

But I moved. Gwen thought, her heart quickening. She stabbed at the soil more feverishly, deepening the hollow beneath her.

Suddenly, Gwen felt a strange coolness in her body. More flashing shapes swam before her eyes as her head lolled forward. Through her blurry vision she could see that the tourniquet had come loose when she'd dropped into the newly dug crevice.

Why is red stuff spurting into the air? She wondered staring at the small fountain of blood gushing from her leg. Her woozy brain didn't register it at first until the queasiness returned and a shaking Gwen realized what was happening.

She slapped a hand over the streaming wound. It was immediately drenched in blood.

Fighting the nausea that threatened to take over, her thoughts clouded as Mom's words returned. *Ugly child.*

But then she heard another voice. Dad's. *Slow your breathing, Tinker Bell. There's plenty of air.* Dad had coached when she'd almost quit during that marathon run.

Gwen took a deep breath. Held it two seconds. Blew it out. Imagined Dad next to her rubbing her back.

She opened and closed her other fist. Mud squeezed between her fingers. Cool and comforting peat dripped down her arm.

And she knew what to do.

She slopped a handful of the mossy mud onto her thigh and pressed. Blood still soaked in but at least it wasn't a freaky fountain. She spooned up another handful and repeated the process. Slower still. Now she just needed something to hold the bandage in place. Where was that friggin rope?

She groped around in the muck but felt nothing. She tried to tear at her tunic, but she had no finger-nails to cut the rough woolen fabric. And as soon as she released pressure, the wound began seeping

335

again. She clapped her hands over it and felt hot tears roll down her cheeks.

It was no use. She couldn't do it.

"Mama?" a small voice called from behind her.

Gwen glanced back. Between her tears she saw a shimmering creature, no bigger than Alex's dog, Rembrandt. It was covered in yellow scales with eyes as soft as a gentle lion.

The Golden Dragon!

"No, I'm not your mother. But if you help me, I'll try to help you find her."

The glorious creature cocked its head to one side and shook out its wings. "O-kay. What I do?"

Chapter 60

"You have returned!" Princess Rhea called from her lookout with Cedric at the Labyrinth exit.

Alex barely lifted his chin as his mount dove down to land on the grass in front of Rhea. Without a word, he slid off Flynn's back. Eyes downcast, he shuffled towards the princess and her squire.

"But where is fiery Gwendolyn?" Rhea asked.

"I wish I knew." Avoiding her gaze, Alex shoved his hands in his pockets, only glancing up when he heard Erantha's flapping wings. With dull eyes he watched a lip-chewing B-3 cling to her neck as she landed next to Flynn. Even when Bartholomew tumbled off and landed with a thud, Alex didn't so much as smirk.

Bartholomew brushed off his slacks and applied some hand sanitizer. As he walked up he explained how Gwen had fallen off the cliff during their escape from Lucretia's lair. "But I'm sure she's okay. That girl is super tough."

"Enough to withstand a fall from Mount Minotaur?" Squire Cederic mused.

Alex cringed imagining a broken Gwen somewhere below.

"Perhaps the young human fell into one of the sinkholes on the Plains. Many are boggy and soft," the gentle Erantha replied.

Alex looked up from his shoes. "Is that true, or are you just saying that to make me feel better?"

"Everyone knows that the Plains of Bramear is a marshland of deep pits," Cederic said with a scoff. "That is why we avoid them; one false step and you are either sinking in peat or falling into an abyss.

"But why have you not looked?" Rhea asked.

"We have. We flew high and low, but the female was nowhere to be found," Flynn said with a flick of his red tail.

"Then she must have fallen in a sinkhole, of which there are scores," Rhea said. "Still it gives us hope for brave Gwendolyn."

Alex blinked. Gwen was somewhere down there, in a pit. Alone. She needed him, and he was standing around talking. He started tapping one foot, glanced from the nodding Bartholomew to Rhea and the dragons. "What are we waiting for?" he blurted. "Let's go find her! Where's that map and painting?"

Bartholomew set the knapsack still slung over his shoulder onto the ground and pulled out the mystical drawings. Now they had morphed again. The tunnel they had painted was gone from Mount Minotaur, as was the view inside. The plains below had come into a hazy focus, scores of sinkholes peppering both map and painting.

Gwen had not appeared in either one.

But Alex could see dragons and a few small figures hunched in front of a mountain doorway. "There we are," he said pointing.

"And there's the Plains of Bramear. At least we can see them, and the pictures are sort of clear. I suppose we could search one sinkhole at a time," Bartholomew suggested.

Alex started to count some of the holes. "Forty-five, fifty," he mumbled. "That would take forever! Gwen might be really hurt or…" he couldn't finish the thought.

Bartholomew rubbed more hand sanitizer in. "Well, do you have a better plan?"

"I don't know. It's not like I have my cell and can text her."

"Smoke?" Cederic suggested.

"If she's underground she wouldn't see the signal," Bartholomew said.

"Even my long flames, so powerful and bright would not be seen," Flynn added blowing a short flare for emphasis.

"We could try calling to her," Erantha said. She shook her dinosaur-like head. "But no, the sound would only echo in confusing directions."

Princess Rhea folded her hands in front of her wide belt and began to sing.

"Our world was born from the magic of two,
The smiling twins whose creations grew.
They painted walls with ideas anew,
Until the dark day we came to rue.
When one jealous hand used mud to undo,

And the life of many too soon was through." Here she
paused and whispered, "But not that of Gwendolyn,"
before returning to the song.

"But listen to this prophecy with open ears,
To know what happens every 2,000 years.
The Shadow Swine will make you live in fear,
Bringing death to those whom you hold so dear,
For they will open the doorway so wide
That none of you will find a place to hide.
And the Creators will stop
As their dreams are drained,
Before 12 moons wax and wane.
But hope will lie in the hands of twins
Born near the cusp of the second millennium."

With this line, the blue dragon, Wade fluttered to
a landing next to them shaking his head sadly. He
hadn't found Gwen in his search either.

Wade settled down next to his sister and Rhea
continued singing in her clear, sweet voice.

"On the eleventh year of their lives
They will join together like single forged knives.
Their battle will be long with 7 evils to undo.
Scattered around will be 7 clues.

And many will perish before they are through... And many will perish before they are Through."

When she repeated this line, Cederic and the Dragons joined in. "But our world will be saved if their art is true. Yes, our world will be saved if their art is true."

As his new friends finished the last line Alex flashed upon memories of Gwen. Skateboarding the Point. Hanging out in the quad. Splashing each other with salt water in Santa Barbara Bay. And helping to save Mona Lisa and little Pico in the Renaissance Nation.

So many flashes like a strobe in his mind. Or a signal light.

Signal light? Yes! It would be true and could be seen.

"I got it!" Alex turned to Bartholomew and punched him in the arm. Then he began to outline his plan.

Chapter 61

In Subterranea, an angry Captain Sludge slapped the first private he saw in line. "Pay attention idiot!" he barked.

"Yes-sir," the quivering Shadow Swine replied from his place near the River of Lies.

"And that goes for the rest of you! You will follow my orders to the letter. It just might save your sorry lives on the Plains of Bramear."

"But why we have to go there?" a thin lieutenant next to him asked.

Sludge turned on his heel and loosened a vicious kick, knocking the impertinent minion on his cocky butt. "Because I order it! How dare you question me!" he cursed, kicking him until viscous sweat poured down either side of his face.

The whimpering lieutenant crawled back into line.

Heaving, the out of breath captain stood over the stupid lackey and shook his head. "You all know why Gothia is important!" Captain Sludge said pointing at the rows of soldiers in front of him. "Look around! The Blank Canvas is growing. There are scores more of you than ever before and new pupae hatch in Swallow Hole Swamp daily. The Golden Dragon flies no more!"

"But might they return?" another lieutenant asked tentatively.

Sludge wondered whether the time was now to reveal the truth. Even Lord Sickhert didn't know that the Deliverers were in Artania. He considered a moment, weighing the pros and cons. Finally, after long seconds he decided that his army should be armed with knowledge.

"While that dragonless sky gives us inroads of power, victory is not guaranteed. The Deliverers are here. Seeking the Golden Dragon."

A collective gasp followed by an anxious buzz filled the cavern. The nervous humming grew louder as soldiers mumbled to each other and themselves.

"Silence!" Sludge roared with a stomp of his jack-booted foot. Glaring at them, he waited for the huge cave to become as quiet as Lord Sickhert's breath before continuing. "They may be here, but we have allies above. Traitors ready to thwart their quest. The Goldens will not come back."

With these words Sludge divided his army into squadrons and led them up the long stair toward the Plains.

Chapter 62

Bartholomew leaned in to listen to Alex's plan, and immediately envisioned it. That's the way it worked for them; when one had an idea the other pictured it as clearly as if it were already made.

Before he'd moved to Santa Barbara the only friends Bartholomew had were the creations he'd sculpted or sketched. He had never hung out with a buddy to watch a movie and gorge junk food or bike around the neighborhood jumping curbs and doing wheelies. But when he met his fellow Deliverer all of that changed. Not only did Alex stand up for him against fist-threatening bullies, but he also stood by Bartholomew's side against scores of slimy and grotesque creatures. They were comrades, working for a common goal.

Once again, he considered explaining it all to Alex. How much this friendship meant to him. How he'd do just about anything for him. But he knew what his response would be. Yeah right, Richie. I'll send you a love note when we get home.

"Well, what do you think?" Alex asked, keeping his voice low.

Swallowing the rising lump in his throat, Bartholomew rubbed some hand sanitizer in. "It could work. I remember in *Historical Mirror Making* that glass in Gothic times had two parts: a metal back and a glass surface. So, if we could find some silica and bits of metal, as well as something to act as a mold..." Bartholomew ticked off each item with a finger as he spoke.

"Plus, a good fire and some tools to smooth it out." Alex glanced around.

Bartholomew followed his gaze past the gathered company of Rhea, Cederic and dragons standing on a mountain ridge to the sinkhole pocked Plains below. Somewhere down there Gwen was waiting for them, perhaps injured.

Their new friends shuffled around, Erantha blinking her emerald green eyes while Wade's neck fins flapped in the late morning breeze. Flynn blew out a fiery sigh as Rhea brushed back the stray strands of hair that had fallen across her face. Off to the side, Squire Cederic adjusted that rusty helmet that always seemed to be askew.

Bartholomew shaded his eyes against the harsh sun casting rays on the strange rock formation to his right. "What are those?" he asked lifting his chin toward the circle of rectangular rocks protruding from the ground.

"They are the stone circles of old, cairns to the Scotts," Rhea explained.

"A place of worship long ago," Cederic said righting his helmet again.

Alex nodded slowly three times and said, "You know, they are the right shape."

"Perhaps, but we can't have empty spaces around a mold," Bartholomew argued. "The liquid will spill out,"

"No problem," Alex turned to Erantha and Wade and asked them to fill in all the gaps with rocks. While the dragons set to work rolling boulders with their snouts, the boys discussed where to find everything else.

"What is silica, anyhow?" Alex asked.

"You know those glass crystals Jose's mother likes to collect? The ones he says have good energy?"

"Seen them. But not here." Alex sighed. "Can't exactly go to Mystic Path to buy them, can we?"

"What'd you say you need?" Flynn asked.

When Bartholomew explained, the red dragon lifted a scaly eyebrow. "Oh those. I have piles of them in my lair."

"Go get them," Alex said, nearly jumping out of his shoes.

Flynn just flicked his long tail.

"Now. Hurry!" Alex urged.

Flynn bared his dual rows of serrated teeth. "I do not take orders from children."

"I'm not a child. I'm a teenager! Anyhow we don't–"

"–Flynn, it would help tremendously," Bartholomew cut Alex off before he really ticked off the dragon. Flynn had a temper as bad as Gwen's. "Would you mind?" He crossed his fingers hoping he wouldn't fly off in a huff.

Flynn glared at Alex. "In my day, Deliverers had manners. They spoke to a dragon with respect."

Alex tapped his foot. "But–"

"Please," Bartholomew said, giving Alex a quick nudge.

Flynn looked from Bartholomew to Alex but didn't reply.

"Heavens, Brother, we don't have time for nonsense. So, stop blowing smoke and go get them," Erantha scolded.

With two more angry puffs Flynn flapped his leathery wings and took off. When his fading form shrunk in the sky, Bartholomew chided Alex for his outburst. "Alex. What were you thinking? You can't argue with a dragon."

"I don't care. Gwen's in trouble. Maybe hurt or worse."

"I know, but still." Bartholomew sighed and changed the subject to finding some metal.

He was midsentence when a clanking sound made him turn. Cederic was pacing back and forth, his armor clanging with every step.

"That's easy," Alex tilted his head toward the squire.

Bartholomew stared at Cederic and nodded along with Alex.

347

"What say you, Deliverers? Why hath your gaze fallen on me?" Cedric asked.

"Umm, Squire Cedric, we really need something from you," Bartholomew began.

Alex added, "Yeah, it'd really help Gwen."

"I am a knight in training. I am duty bound to save damsels in distress."

"Cool, then give us your armor."

Cedric's face blanched. "What?!"

"So, we can melt it down for the mirror," Bartholomew added.

Cedric stuttered and stepped back. He started arguing about how precious his helmet and breastplate were, that they had been forged for a great knight and how honored he was to wear them. Shaking his head, he backed up two more steps.

"Fulfill your duty, squire," Princess Rhea said.

Halting, Cedric opened and closed his mouth in protest. But Rhea thrust her fists into her hips and gave him a commanding stare. Hanging his head, Cedric muttered a yes before removing his armor piece by piece and setting it in the center of the stone cairn.

Cedric was still grumbling when Flynn returned; a barrel of quartz crystals in his claws. Swallowing hard, Bartholomew put on a polite face before asking the dragon if he could melt down the armor and crystals for the mirror.

The dragon balked, his crocodilian jaw dropping to the ground and for a minute Bartholomew was afraid he'd say no. But when Flynn began to protest, his sister shook a warning talon, and with a low growl, he made his way over to the stone circle.

Meanwhile Alex and Bartholomew ran their hands over Cederic's sword to create a cold layer which would protect the blade when it smoothed the metal and glass surface. When Flynn's fiery breath heated Cederic's armor, they stood poised waiting for the metal to glow red hot.

As soon as the surface was bubbling Bartholomew lifted a hand for Flynn to stop. In two seconds the molten steel had quieted enough for Alex to run the sword over its surface and smooth the irregularities and ripples.

When it hardened, Bartholomew and Alex grabbed handfuls of crystals and threw them onto the smooth metal disc. Flynn blew fire again and the Creation Magic began. Time sped up as the boys took turns stirring the smelting glass.

Bartholomew breathed out cool air, and the rising steam dissipated.

The sculpture shimmered and the ground shook before morphing into mirror some fifteen feet in diameter. The surface was irregular like most glass during the Middle Ages but that didn't bother Bartholomew. This one wasn't designed to check for specks of dirt but to reflect the sun's rays.

And hopefully attract Gwen's attention.

"Okay, Wade & Erantha. Your turn. Get it upright," Alex said.

Erantha wrapped a giant tail around the glass while Wade nuzzled it from below pressing his nose under the great mirror until it was facing the sun.

"Now slowly rotate it," Bartholomew said.

Alex looked worried. "Are you sure B-3?"

"Well when I read *Military Messages of the Past—*" Bartholomew began.

"Light reading?" Alex interrupted with a wry grin.

Bartholomew hit him with the back of his hand. "It said you have to aim your mirror with precision."

"Of course, it did," Alex said shaking his head.

"And that the angle of incidence should be equal to the angle of reflectance. Also, it's necessary to make an adjustable aiming site like two sticks or fingers in the shape of a V. This makes the aim for accurate."

"But that's for a little signal mirror. Ours is huge," Alex argued.

"I was just getting to that. I will make a V with my arms for light to pass through. Like the sight on a gun."

"And I'll correct the aim. Got it."

While Bartholomew got his body into a V-shape Alex stepped behind Erantha and Wade. "Pivot slowly and carefully. We want every sinkhole to see the light," he said, directing them to fine-tune the angle.

The huge mirror tilted right as the sun reflected down into the valley below. The rays passed from sinkhole to sinkhole until half the Plains of Bramear had been etched in light. Each dark cave's illumination was like a bright quill sketching light on

Bartholomew's heart. Gwen *would* see this. They *would* find her.

The dragons swiveled the massive mirror in the opposite direction and the white ink lit up the rest of the valley. Not a single sinkhole remained in darkness.

"Yes!" A smiling Alex kicked a foot and released a joyful cloud of dust.

The little cloud rolled over the grassy bluff toward Wade. The dragon wriggled his nose, still pressed beneath the glass. Sniffed. "Ah-ah-ah choo!" Wade sneezed.

The force launched the mirror into the air. Erantha tried to hold on with her tail but the slick glass slipped from her grip. It bounced once and started rolling toward the cliff. Faster and faster it spun heading straight for a huge boulder.

Bartholomew had just launched into a run when the mirror hit, shattering it into a thousand pieces.

Chapter 63

"Here go," the baby dragon said, ripping a long strip off Gwen's tunic with her teeth.

Gwen cringed when the quick jerk opened her wound again but clamped her jaw shut and waited for the baby Golden to pass her the piece of fabric. Next, she scooped up some fresh moss and placed it on her wound, wrapped the cloth around her thigh, and secured it tightly.

Whoa. Gwen gasped as she knotted the fabric, fighting the urge to cry out. She didn't want to frighten the newborn.

The Golden had just hatched after all. A moment before, the baby'd explained how she'd recently woken to a warming sensation surrounding her egg. Everything'd felt so cramped; she had to peck at the shell with her egg tooth, breaking through just in time to see Gwen's fall.

Leaning sideways, Gwen bent her good knee, and forced herself to stand. It hella-hurt but she wasn't going to find a way out of this the cave sitting on her butt. She took a few halting steps, stopped.

The baby dragon blinked her wide topaz eyes. "You 'kay?"

Holding her breath, Gwen nodded.

Just then she noticed a flash of light overhead. "Did you see–" Her words were cut short by what looked like sparkling droplets raining down. One splashed in the pond next to her. Then another.

She was confused at first. Silver dripping on the pond? She held out a hand to capture some of the glittering mist. Dry. Artania was freaky but she usually got wet when it rained.

Crash! A piece of glass shattered next to the Golden.

Gwen extended her arms and leapt. "Look out!" she cried covering the baby's body with her own.

Eyes squeezed shut, she remained splayed out in a protective blanket, listening to her pounding heart, the soft breath of the baby dragon, and the crackle of dripping glass.

After long moments, the glass rain stopped.

Gwen glanced up at the tunnel-like opening overhead. The sky was clear.

Patting the baby's spiked head, Gwen rolled to one side and forced herself to stand. Lightheaded, she glanced down to make sure her leg hadn't started bleeding again. That's when she noticed that the cavern floor was spangled in shards of mirrored glass. Strange.

Shadow Swine? Attacking her here?

Gwen bent down and picked up a six-inch sliver. Cocking her head to one side, she gazed at the stranger in the glass. Once again, Mom's words came back to haunt her. *You're so ugly.*

Gwen gripped the sharp shard tighter. It began to cut into her hand. *Ugly. I can't believe you're my kid.*

"What you name?" the baby dragon said.

The words barely registered on the edge of her consciousness. She couldn't look away from those hollow eyes. Diarrhea green. Not bright gems like supermodel Rochelle's. Pale brow. Freckled face, peeling nose. Frizzy red hair.

"What *my* name?"

Look at you. You make me sick. Put some makeup on for god's sakes.

"Girl who not mamma? Why you not talk?" The little dragon sniffed. "You not my fwiend?"

Gwen shook her head. Friends. Did Rochelle even have any friends? Buds who showed you how to grind your board on a curb or fought minotaurs and dragons for you? Bros who kept coming back even when you told them to get lost? Friends who didn't care what the frick your reflection in the mirror looked like?

The baby dragon hung her gilded head and swayed back and forth. A single amber tear rolled down her round cheek and fell on the soft moss. "I not have fwiend."

Gwen tore her gaze from the reflection and curled her free hand into a fist. "Yes, you do, little goldie."

"I do?"

"Me, and I'm here for you." Gwen knew these words were as much for her as for the dragon.

And that's when she realized. These mirrors could not have come from Swineys. Not their style. Her buds had sent them! Of course, Mr. Clean and Alex were trying to signal her.

Not the safest way to get her attention. But those dudes didn't always have a clue. And they were up there somewhere looking for her.

Gwen tilted the glass shard back and forth wondering how to catch one of the long rays that shone into the sinkhole. Not easy since the opening was straight down, and the only tunnel of light was in the center of the cavern.

In the frickin' middle of the pond.

"You just stay here, okay?" Gwen said hobbling toward the edge of the pond. She tried again. Couldn't get a glimmer. She put a tentative boot into water. Freezing.

Gwen waded out in the ankle-deep water until she was directly under a shaft of light. Holding the shard overhead she rocked it right and left as flashes bobbed up the cavern wall. Keeping her eye trained on a single bead of light, Gwen angled her hand. The light beam rose like a bright balloon and flew over the opening.

"If they don't see this, they really are clueless," Gwen said to the dragon who just cocked her head like a sea turtle.

She sure was cute.

Shivering, Gwen kept her arm overhead until it started to cramp. Switched hands. Cracked her neck and repeated. One minute passed. Two.

"Why you stand in water?" the Golden asked.

"I'm trying to get help. To protect you. You're pretty precious, you know." Gwen switched hands again.

"I am?"

"Yep. To lots of people." Gwen blinked. Was that a glimmer off to her right? Or had she done it? She lowered her arm and counted to ten.

There it was again. A definite flash.

Gwen tried covering and uncovering the glass with her free hand three times.

They signaled back!

She repeated her signal and three flashes responded. Gwen's heart skipped a beat.

A sudden wind blew her hair into her face. When she went to brush it out of her eyes she saw Mr. Clean clinging for dear life astride Erantha.

"Down here!" she cried. "In this one!" Gwen limped out of the pond and rushed to the baby dragon's side.

Erantha hovered overhead and with a fluttering of wings landed in the middle of the pond, splashing Gwen with cold water.

Bartholomew started to lift a leg to get off but slipped backwards into the water instead. He came up sputtering with a lopsided grin.

"Guess you couldn't wait to take a bath. Huh, Mr. Clean?" a giggling Gwen teased.

"Of course," Bartholomew replied, nonplussed. "I am a Borax."

They both started laughing. Man, it felt good.

Chapter 64

Alex was astride Wade when he saw the dark mass oozing up from the ground. He thought he knew what it was but still leaned over and squinted to be sure.

Shadow Swine. Hundreds of them. Spilling onto the Plains of Bramear like a spring bubbling mud.

He full-on hated them.

Mind racing, he scanned the skies for Erantha and Bartholomew. He hadn't seen them since they'd split up to search the sinkholes for Gwen. Twenty minutes at least. Although he and Wade had flown over the entire southern section there had been no sign of that red-head anywhere.

Why the frick did he kick up dirt in the first place? Stu-pid. Clumsy moves were Bartholomew's M.O., not his. He usually was more in control than that. That signal mirror could have been their only chance to find Gwen.

The pit in his stomach grew, clawing his insides. If Gwen was hurt and those Swiney's found her before he did...

And then what the hell would he do? They were just a ragtag group of a few dragons, a princess, and a squire in his underwear. No match for a Shadow Swine army. Their weapons consisted of a dagger, a sword, and what? His shoe laces?

What a joke.

"Wade, look," Alex said pointing.

The water dragon flapped his neck fins and bobbed his head.

"We have to do something!"

"You are the Deliverer. Have you not amazing powers?"

"Yeah, and they're working great right now," Alex muttered. He gripped the dragon's neck tighter and clenched his jaw. "Where the heck is Gwen?!"

"I see no signals from below." Wade paused. "She is your true friend?"

"Since sixth grade." Alex swallowed and said in a quieter voice. "She's pretty awesome."

Without replying, Wade lifted one wing and flapped it a few times. His great body tilted to the side turning back toward Mount Minotaur.

"Where are you going?" Alex demanded.

"We must not be seen," he replied, his body dipping up and down like waves.

Alex peered at the plains filling with Shadow Swine and couldn't argue. He let out a frustrated sigh and settled into his seat at the base of Wade's long neck. This was going to take longer than he'd planned if it worked at all.

Suddenly, a flash of green from one of the sinkholes near the cliffs sparked on the fringes of his vision. Right next to the streaming Shadow Swine.

Alex squinted. "Wade! Look, over there," he said pointing. "I think that's Erantha. And she's coming up right in the middle of the Swineys!"

Wade didn't reply but dipped his head and dove. Alex started to slide backwards, fumbled for the dragon's neck, nearly tumbling to the valley below. Wrapping his arms around the slippery scales, he held on as the water dragon surged forward. Eyes on their green friend, the wind whipped his hair back. Yes, it was Erantha and she was surrounded.

The rasping army droned a chorus to the rhythm of pounding war drums. A guttural refrain that made death metal sound like a lullaby in comparison.

The ever-browner land blurred past. Flapping furiously, Wade drew closer to the group of sinkholes near Erantha.

"Hurry!"

Wade locked his wings and tilted into a dive, plunging downward in a crazy descent. Alex clung desperately to the dragon's neck while images of striking battle axes filled his mind. They fed his cries as he screamed Erantha's name into the cacophony.

When the ground rose to greet them, Wade leveled out and thousands of slimy heads turned skyward. A collective roar pulsed while they dove toward the sinkhole.

Below them, Erantha paused at the earth's surface. Wade hovered just over her while she blinked at the deluge all around.

"Go back!" Alex cried as an arrow sailed past.

Erantha ducked back into the hole. Then another whizzed through the air. Four more.

Wings straining, Wade followed mere inches behind her rippling tail.

Alex tried to peer into the cavern but couldn't see past his mount's huge body. Then he heard Erantha splash down in some sort of pond as Wade slowed his descent with a few powerful strokes. The water dragon hung suspended for a moment then followed in a deafening splash that soaked Alex to the skin.

Bellows and howls echoed down the sinkhole's walls while Alex wiped his face. He brushed his hair back with one hand and hopped off Wade's back.

"You guys okay?" he asked, concerned. He glanced toward the Earth dragon expecting to see B-3 astride her. But no rider sat at the base of her neck.

Alex's eyes scanned the circular cavern. Fell upon a trio of figures in the shadows. Half-hopping, half-running Alex sloshed through the water toward them. When he reached Gwen, he didn't care but pulled her into a bear hug swinging her around until she begged him to stop.

"Alex, you're hurting me," Gwen said, pointing to her bandaged leg. When he set her down, she explained how she'd been wounded during the fall.

"Sorry. But how—did—" he paused when he noticed the creature at her side. "Who's this?"

"I call her Goldie," Gwen said with grin.

"Kind of babyish name for a dragon, don't you think?"

"Why, what name would you pick?" Gwen thrust her fists into her hips. "Lacey?"

"No."

"Yeah, you probably would. I bet your planning on naming your first kid Lacey. Then you'd be reminded of her beauty all the time."

"Lacey's not beautiful, kind of ugly."

"Well you sure as surf do stare enough."

Interrupting, Bartholomew stepped between them. "Guys, guys. In case you hadn't noticed, we have, umm, company."

As if on cue, an arrow landed in the ground next to them with a thwomp. Both Alex and Gwen jumped back.

"We gotta get out of here." Alex mind raced as he turned toward the adult dragons. "Can you carry all of us?"

"Too much weight," Erantha replied. "Besides, our scales are not as strong as they look. Arrows can pierce our skin as easily as yours."

Alex looked to the little dragon. "Is there another way out of here?"

Goldie blinked her amber eyes while Gwen patted her head. "She just hatched. Doesn't know anything but this place."

"Erantha? Wade?" Bartholomew asked.

The huge reptiles shook their heads.

Alex stroked his chin. "Gwen you're injured so our first task is keeping you and Goldie safe. Come over here behind these stalagmites. They'll offer you some protection."

Before Gwen could argue, Alex began pacing from one end of the vertical cavern to another. "You know, if there are tons of these sinkholes around the plains they are probably connected somehow."

Following his lead, Bartholomew bent down to look at rocky crags and tap on the stone walls. Of course, Mr. Clean applied hand sanitizer as soon as his hand got dusty even though the arrows kept whizzing into the sinkhole. Alex shook his head.

The angry howls grew louder but after several minutes they'd still found nothing. Leaning up against the wall, Alex clenched his fists. "I guess we'll have to chance it. I'll ride Wade and try to draw them away. We'll come back later for you guys."

Wade's blue face blanched to sky. "I don't want to fly past those Shadow Swine."

"Even at top speed I doubt you could escape unscathed," Erantha nodded.

"I suppose B-3 and I can try to make some weapons."

"Alex, do you hear that? There are thousands of them. Even if we had catapults and giant crossbows we would be no match for them.

"Then what the frick do you suggest? Wait here like sitting ducks in an arcade game?"

"Why evewyone angwy?" Goldie asked.

"It's okay," Gwen said. "We're just looking for a way out of here."

"Where watew comes in. It must fwow out. While neither bweath nor air flows in you mouth," The baby dragon recited while waving her tail back and forth like a kitten.

With an understanding bob of her head, Erantha smiled down at Goldie "Of course, little one."

"I should have remembered that," Wade added.

"Would somebody explain what's going on? You dragons are talking in riddles," Gwen said raising her arms in exasperation.

Bartholomew shrugged. "That's their culture."

"Watch, humans." Dipping his sinuous head into the pool, Wade slipped below the water. Alex was surprised that he could disappear in such a small pond. You'd think half of him would be sticking out.

After a few moments, the waters quieted. Not even a ripple passed over the surface. Alex exchanged a confused glance with B-3.

"Where did he–" Alex's words were cut short by a head.

"Where water comes in, it must flow out," the dripping dragon said with a grin.

Alex gaped until Erantha tapped him on the shoulder with her long green tail. "Neither breath nor air flows in your mouth." She took a deep breath, held it and dipped her head into the pond. When she came back up she wrapped her tail around Goldie and the two of them submerged beneath the surface.

"I get it. We have to swim for it. Ready Alex?"

"Wade and Gwen first. I'll take up the rear."

Wade bent down and let the injured Gwen slide onto his neck before following his sister. Bartholomew strapped his knapsack on tightly and dove after.

Another arrow whizzed past.

You thought you had us to rights, huh? "Think again Slime buckets!" Alex cried cannonballing into the water.

Chapter 65

Bartholomew emerged from the freezing water with a gasp and threw his head back. He'd never been so cold. Even when they lived in Philadelphia, where there were heavy snows he'd stayed indoors, warm, cozy and, as Mother put it, "safe from filth."

Ice floes bobbed all over the surface of the shadowy pond. One bumped his shoulder and he pushed it out of the way as he waded to shore a few yards away.

He barely had time to glance around before Alex popped up sputtering and shivering. "Brrr. Full on brrr," he said.

Bartholomew nodded and turned back to inspect his surroundings. This cavern was about ten times as large as the one they'd just left and at least that many times as cold. Snowy chunks floated in the pond and the smooth walls were encased in blue-green frost. Icy stalactites hung from the twenty-foot-high ceiling in groups like gossamer curtains.

Beautiful if it weren't so freezing.

Erantha and Wade huddled together, Gwen and the baby Golden between them. Beyond them, in a niche in the wall, he saw what looked like a human form. Titling his head to one side, Bartholomew pointed toward the shadowy figure.

Alex's gaze followed the line of his hand. "Woah. Am I in the middle of a dizzying 360, or is that a mansicle?" Alex asked.

Dripping, Bartholomew stepped up for a closer look and almost fell over. Alex was right. It was a popsicle man, but he wasn't alone. At least fifty knights were suspended in ice, each encased in his own slot as if some great ice ray had frozen them mid-step. Many were dressed in full battle armor, swords or shields raised, staring with unblinking eyes.

Bartholomew reached out toward the nearest knight and noticed his fingertips whiten. Then every finger blanched. Confused, he tilted his hand back and forth. Cold needles shot up his arm and both limbs. Then a sweet coolness rushed through his veins bringing peaceful thoughts and Grandfather Borax's words.

We come here to be true. From well before I was born on down to your Father. Remember that Bartholomew.

Bartholomew nodded at the invisible Grandfather as the delightful cold caressed him.

"B-3 step back!" Alex cried.

His friend's words didn't register at first. Instead he smiled at his late grandfather, with that old-fashioned waist coat and wild Einstein hair. "I have remembered, Grandfather. I have been true," he whispered.

"Young one, away!" Erantha's voice came from a distance.

Bartholomew blinked. Why were people calling him? He leaned back and forth.

His legs wouldn't budge.

Hands grabbed his shoulders. Tugged. "Bartholomew move!" Alex yelled pulling him back.

"W-what?" Bartholomew muttered staggering back from the frozen knight.

"That wall was turning you into a popsicle," Alex said.

Rubbing his chilled arms, Bartholomew stared down at his frost covered hands. "Ugh."

"Cha. But why would Artania have a place that froze people?" Alex asked.

Gwen limped up to them. "I think I know. Look. Over there, past the pond," she said pointing with her chin.

On the opposite side of the cavern were hundreds of shining objects that Bartholomew thought were metal drums. At first. But a second glance made him gasp. "We've found the Golden –"

"–dragon nest!" Alex cried completing his thought.

Behind a series of boulders were huge eggs piled up in clusters of twenty or thirty. Stony stalactites instead of icicles hung down, enclosing the precious clutches in a rocky nest. Compared to where they were standing that corner was cozy and dry.

Scattered light rays reflected off their shells, dancing up the icy walls. Bartholomew smiled. They were hypnotically beautiful. And for some reason they made him think of his father. Something he seldom did.

He recalled listening in on a conversation between Grandfather Borax and Mother about Father. "*Hygenette, my son would have wanted his paintbrushes to go to the boy. Give them to him.*"

"*Absolutely not! He used them THAT day. Who knows? They could be what caused him to trip. One was found in his pocket. Maybe he was fiddling with the filthy thing instead of watching where he was going. Leaving me alone.*" A sob caught in Mother's throat before she rushed off to bathe.

That was the first time he'd realized that, like him, Father was an artist. Drawn to scenes as beautiful as this one.

"So, Goldie, do you know anything about this place?" Gwen asked when the baby dragon came up to her side.

"No." She looked around sadly. "But maybe my Mommy here?"

Bartholomew knew just how the little dragon felt and was about to say something sympathetic when Erantha bent down and nuzzled the baby with her snout.

"Don't worry, we'll take care of you little one."

"Yes, we will," Gwen chimed in.

"Hey, Erantha, what do you know about Goldens anyhow?" Bartholomew asked.

"It has been so long since they filled our skies that even the stories have faded away. But, I do remember that their hatchlings were said to be unique. For example, my family hatched near our intended home; Wade near Lambeth Lake, Flynn inside Cinder Cone Hill. I was a wyrmling in an earthy cave near Alnwick Castle. We emerged when Mother sang the creation song. But the Goldens? I wish I knew."

"Then, how should we-" Bartholomew paused, still staring at the brilliant golden eggs. "You know, help them hatch?"

"We emerge when it is our time. And no sooner," Wade said.

"I wait in quiet, hou-rs and years.

For a time lacking feaw.

When land is healed.

By sculpted stone.

And evil life tuwns to bone," The baby dragon recited flicking her glossy tail.

Gwen stroked the baby's head while Erantha's emerald eyes crinkled in the corners. *More riddles?* Bartholomew groaned inwardly.

"Just what is that supposed to mean?" Alex asked with an exasperated sigh.

"I'm assuming she's telling us how eggs hatch," Bartholomew began, thinking about each line. "It makes sense that they'd wait for a time without fear. But sculpted stone healing land? I really don't know."

"Well cha! You guys are sculptors. Aren't' you?" Gwen asked.

Bartholomew nodded. "And this land definitely has some sickness. That growing white."

"Maybe we're supposed to create something to wake them up," Alex suggested.

Bartholomew shrugged. Then, from far off came a rumbling and the walls began to shake. Next, a few icy stalactites loosened from overhead and splashed into the pond. Everyone stared at the growing circles on the water.

"Sickhert's army," Erantha said, breaking the silence.

"Looking for us." Bartholomew nodded. "Who will soon discover that we're not in that cavern—"

"—and will start looking for us and might come here. Wherever that is," Alex said completing the thought.

Remembering the map, Bartholomew wriggled out of the backpack straps and pulled out both the paintings. He shook them out and set them on the ground side by side. "Interesting," he mused.

"Did they change again?" Alex asked stepping closer.

Bartholomew nodded. Now the map included finer details of the Plains of Bramear. The painting, on the other hand, had morphed to include a panel of all of them inside their present cavern. Just like before, their Gothian adventures were laid out like a comic strip. Starting with the splash into Lambent Lake each square represented a place they'd been. Only now the painting included their escape from Mount

Minotaur and the landing inside the sinkhole Gwen had fallen into.

"Could we make another doorway with it?" Bartholomew asked.

"Well I don't think we can use the existing one unless we want to turn into kidsicles," Alex said chuckling at his own pun.

This led to a long debate about the freezing spell and whether it was localized or not. They all agreed that someone had made a booby trap to keep the Golden Dragons safe and stop any approaching Artanians or Swineys. But whether the spell would extend into a new doorway, was anyone's guess.

Bartholomew chewed on his lower lip. Hoping they could make it work.

Hoping their art was true.

Chapter 66

Sludge thought back over the past few minutes. How had two dragons disappeared into thin air? His soldiers had searched every square inch of the sinkhole yet there was no sign of them. Maybe they'd never been there at all and it was a mirage to trick him.

That red-headed brat had escaped along with Bartholomew. That he knew for sure. Somehow the other Deliverer got inside Lucretia's lair and freed them.

At least she had Alexander to rights, terrified on a ledge. For a while. Until those meddling dragons rescued him, or so she said.

He glanced around. They could not have gone far.

He examined the sinkhole one last time, thinking that there must be some sort of passageway between the caverns that allowed the dragons to escape. Striding over to the nearest one, he peered inside. It appeared empty. He paced to another, paused. Nothing but sunrays and green moss.

His lieutenants halted their marching squadrons to watch him, shuffling their jackbooted feet. Sludge growled.

"Don't just stand there! Look. Search these caverns and shafts. Don't leave a single stone unturned until you find them!"

Chapter 67

Gwen wanted to shout, *No freakin way. I'm coming with you!* But she'd already argued until her voice was hoarse and all that got her was silence. Not that she cared what Alex thought anyhow.

Well, maybe a little.

"Ready?" Alex asked putting the final touches on the moss and stick figures.

He and Mr. Clean had just spent a few minutes sculpting copies of themselves and tying them to the dragons' backs. Erantha and Wade would then be decoys to lead Sludge's army away.

The earth dragon exchanged a look with her brother and nodded.

"Go!"

The dragons dipped their heads into the lake and snaked under the water.

Meanwhile, Bartholomew rubbed in some of that hand sanitizer that never seemed to run out and secured a knapsack to his back. With an awkward wave, he joined Alex at the wall just beyond the frozen knights.

Alex extended the painting he and Bartholomew had just altered toward the icy wall. With a creak and a groan, it parted to reveal a blue-green tunnel that was so smooth it looked like someone had poured hot water in the center of an ice cube. Gwen was expecting it but still her nose wriggled in surprise as Alex darted inside the new exit, Bartholomew right behind.

"I hope this works," she said limping over to the eggs and Goldie where it was warm. Once there, she leaned up against a boulder to rest her throbbing leg. She gave the little dragon a half-smile. "Now I guess we wait."

A few minutes later she noticed a dripping sound. Then more, like rain on a roof. Gwen glanced up, but the icicles weren't melting. And when she looked at the lake, the surface was smooth.

Drip-drip. Hish.

Gwen cocked an ear. The sound seemed to be coming from the new exit. Were her buds returning already? She couldn't tell from where she was.

"I'll be right back. You stay here." Gwen told the little dragon.

She barely took a step before the hatchling started quivering. The golden eyes grew wide as it extended both wings. Even though the light was dim, it was easy to see its veins pulsing through the paper-thin skin.

376

"Hey, it's okay." Cupping Goldie's face in gentle hands, Gwen whispered comforting words until the baby stopped shaking. When it finally folded its wings back Gwen guided it back behind a boulder to curl up around some eggs.

Gwen gave the baby a final pat and backed away, waving. At the boulder, she lifted her injured leg and had just begun to slide it backwards when her foot hit something hard. She pushed again. Solid.

Turning Gwen came face to face with an armored knight, still covered in frost. Gasping, she tumbled over the rock and fell on her butt.

"Hello," he said.

"Stay back," she ordered holding up her fists.

"Huh?"

Keeping her fists up, Gwen tried to stand. But with her bad leg only got off the ground a few inches before plopping back on her rear again.

Lifting his visor, the knight leaned over her. "What ails you, young squire? Need you assistance?"

Gwen narrowed her eyes. He was an oil painting and not very tall, maybe five feet eight or nine. The armor covering him from head to toe was shinier and thicker than Squire Cederic's, as if designed for a king.

"I said stay back." With one fist raised she leaned against the boulder and hoisted herself up.

"I mean you no harm. And, where am I?"

Even though she knew that knights had set out on a quest to find the Goldens, he could be a traitor, like Roger La Savage. Still, there was something in his

377

blue eyes that made him familiar. And trustworthy. She answered slowly. "You're inside a cave. Don't you remember?"

"I recall my brother and I on the quest. Tales of Goldens on the Plains of Bramear led us to explore some vertical shafts. Then we chanced upon a hidden opening in a hillock. After that, I recall little."

"You've been frozen, by some sort of spell. Don't know how long."

The knight touched his dripping armor with a gauntlet covered hand. "No. You jest."

"Yeah. There seems to be some sort of protective magic around the eggs. If anyone comes near, it's freezer time."

"Which eggs? The Goldens? You hath found them?"

Gwen jerked a thumb toward the shining clusters behind her.

"Thank the stars, our land is saved."

"Not quite," Gwen said, finally deciding to trust him. "We've got a few problems. I'm Gwen by the way."

"Prince Kelvin, son of Gerald, brother to Ulmer and Rhea." The knight bowed.

"Oh, that's why you look familiar. You're Princess Rhea's brother. You look like her. She's a cool girl, brave too. Taking off on a quest with just a skinny squire to help her."

"Was she frozen too? I thought she was at home." Kelvin flinched causing his visor to fall back down.

"No, she–" Gwen's words were cut short when a taller, thinner knight approached.

"Brother, why hath my memory been erased? Is this some miniature warlock casting spells upon us?"

"No Ulmer," Prince Kelvin barely had time to explain the freezing magic before several more creaking and dripping knights approached.

Gwen glanced past them at the thawing ice. Every slot that had contained a frozen knight was now melting. Long rivulets trickled down the wall gathering into streams that flowed into the pond. She was about to ask the Kelvin another question when some water lapping at her feet forced her to take a step back.

Goldie popped up from behind the rock nearly knocking Gwen over. "Wook!"

Gwen blinked, confused at first. But when she realized that the baby dragon was pointing a tail at the rising waters, she gasped. "The eggs!"

"Get them to higher ground," Kelvin ordered scooping up the nearest one.

Heart pounding, Gwen limped over a boulder and put her arms around an egg. Leaning back, she hefted it onto the rocky ledge and rolled it as far back as it would go. No easy task since they were as large as the exercise balls in Dad's gym and lots heavier. Meanwhile, Ulmer and the other knights lined up along the wall to pass the Golden Eggs along, so she and Kelvin could boost them higher up the cavern wall.

Ignoring her throbbing leg, Gwen reached for another and hoisted it onto the ledge. When that niche filled, she hobbled down the wall where more rocky hollows waited.

The baby dragon crawled up on top of some boulders and shook out her scales like a dog after a bath. Gwen wished she could smile at it but seeing the knee-deep pond splashing the beautiful spheres in muddy water just made her nose twitch nervously.

"Thank the stars these walls have so many ridges," Kelvin said picking up another.

Cha!" Gwen agreed straining to lift what felt like her five-hundredth egg. She rolled her shoulders, wondering how much longer she could keep it up. Even Dad would be having trouble about now.

Prince Kelvin glanced over his shoulder at the side of the cavern that was quickly becoming a waterfall. "It grows worse," he said.

Ulmer's hazel eyes were wide as he replied. "Yes, our exit is now halfway submerged."

"We must leave." His brother nodded.

"But the eggs–" Gwen couldn't finish the thought.

"We secure the final three and go." Kelvin said.

Clenching her jaw against the pain, Gwen willed herself to go faster. She was in the middle of rolling the last one into a recess when she heard crackling followed by a high-pitched creak. She turned to see a shifting wall of ice behind her.

Ulmer scooped up Goldie in his arms and turned toward the exit. The baby dragon began to wail. "My famiwy gonna die!"

"Not if I have anything to do with it," Gwen cried as her boots sloshed in the rising flood.

The ice soon turned to slush, dissolving into waterfall walls. Then half the glacial mass cleaved off and fell into the pond with a crash. Scattering mini icebergs throughout the pool.

Gwen didn't think but immediately began wading through the icy floodwaters toward the exit. In three steps, it was waist high. In five, her feet barely touched the bottom.

"Hold Goldie up high. It's deep! And getting deeper," she cried over her shoulder as a bobbing ice floe knocked her off balance.

Gwen fell backward. And went under. Flailing her arms, she struggled blindly toward the surface where her head bumped against an icy ceiling. She kicked right and left searching for an opening. When she found a break between two icy sheets, she lifted her chin and sucked in a quick breath. But then a wave swelled over, forcing her below.

Rotating her arms in a crazy swim, she tried to find up. Where was it? Goldie wailed behind her as more icicles crashed into the ever-growing pond. She bicycled her legs but stayed under.

Then she thought she saw a glimmer overhead. Shot toward it. Just before surfacing, an icicle hit her shoulder, rolling her head over heels.

Toward the entrance that had frozen every knight.

She leveled out and a tingling prickled up her spine, whether from cold or the trapping spell she couldn't tell.

The waters rushed again. Taking her with them.

Her lungs ached. She'd need to breathe soon, or...
No! I won't go there. Gwen thought kicking her good
leg wildly.

Aiming for the exit, she recalled being tossed by
her first big wave when Dad took her boogie board-
ing at Rincon. She'd been a lot littler then and had
followed his advice, holding her breath while letting
the wave carry her to shore. He'd given her a big high
five that day.

This was just a pond, not the Pacific. *You can do
it.* She thought. *No freezing spell will turn you into a
girlsicle.*

Chest spasming, she angled upward until her feet
hit solid ground. Hopping on one foot, she lifted
her head to suck in a mouthful of freezing slush.
Coughing and sputtering, she bobbed again. Spat
twice before finally inhaling fresh air.

"This way. Come on!" she called over her shoulder.

Within seconds Ulmer and Kelvin arrived, the
hatchling suspended above their shoulders followed
by rows of armored knights. When everyone had
gathered in the passageway, the limping Gwen led
them ever upward toward the light.

Just as they reached a brightly lit shaft with steps
carved into the stone, she heard a loud rumbling.
Gwen glanced back. Stalactites began to fall from the
ceiling.

"Run!" she cried leaping onto the first step.

Everyone lurched forward staggering en masse.
Pebbles and dirt fell from the ceiling. There were

shouts and cries as their dripping troop scrambled up the stair.

They almost reached the sunlight when the tunnel closed.

Chapter 68

"Get down," Alex rasped. Grabbing his friend's collar, Alex dropped to his belly, pulling B-3 with him.

Through the thick reeds of the marshy grassland he could see wooden pikes sweeping to and fro. The marching Shadow Swine were just yards away.

"There are so many," Bartholomew whispered in his ear.

Alex nodded. When they emerged from the passageway moments before he'd expected to see a few Swineys, but nothing like this. Across the plains and all around the grassy tuft that hid their new tunnel, trooped hundreds, if not thousands, of the hunch-backed monsters.

The slime-faced army was in battle gear with long army cloaks over combat trousers tucked in jackboots. Many had battle axes raised in the air, carried clubs swinging from gorilla-like arms, or held bows aloft ready to unleash arrows. Alex had battled this formidable army before and knew he couldn't face them unarmed.

"What do we do?" Bartholomew asked.

Alex clenched his jaw, unsure. He hadn't planned on meeting such a horde. He thought that the decoys strapped to Erantha and Wade's backs would look enough like thirteen-year-old boys to lure what few Swineys there might be away. Meanwhile, he'd come up with some sort of true art and save everyone.

In theory.

But the reality was another story. If even half of the Shadow Swine chased after the dragons, that'd leave hundreds for him to contend with.

Not very good odds.

"Just wait," he whispered.

A moment later Erantha's shining head rose from the sinkhole. Although fifty yards away, he could still see the fear in her emerald eyes. Poor thing. Wings flapping furiously, her shoulders topped the rise. Scaling the rim, she climbed ever higher, Wade just inches behind.

A war whoop split the air. The pig-nosed monsters thumped their chests unleashing their arrows to the thrum of bow strings.

Alex held his breath as singing arrows sailed toward the dragons.

One bounced off Erantha's chest while Wade's underbelly reflected the second as easily a mirror.

"Yes!" Alex exhaled, slapping B-3 on the back. Applying the mud to their skin had hardened over their scales like armor.

385

The dragons soared higher while marching boots drummed an angry rhythm. Excited pikes clicked together as many of the nearby Shadow Swine turned to pursue the flying pair. Gothia just might have a chance. Ready to work on the next phase, Alex turned to Bartholomew.

But then he heard that hated voice. "Stop idiots! Those are stick figures. Are you blind?"

Alex exchanged a horrified glance with Bartholomew. He thought the dummies straddling the spiked necks had looked real. Man. Why hadn't they used the Creation Magic when they had a chance?

"We better do something, fast."

"We need some weapons."

"Or at least a better place to hide than this clump of cotton grass." He glanced around. Not easy in a flat valley with heather and reeds as the only cover. There were sinkholes but the nearest one was fifty yards away and Swineys were searching it.

"Maybe we should go back," B-3 suggested.

Alex nodded but when they turned, the tunnel was gone.

"Plan B?" Bartholomew squeaked out.

Alex was in the middle of a soothing lie when something behind Captain Sludge turned his blood to ice. He squinted. "No!"

Bartholomew followed his worried gaze to where Gwen was limping out of a cave cut into the mountain face.

He almost leapt up and ran to her, but Bartholomew held him back. "Wait. She's hidden, see? Behind that rocky outcropping. And most of the Shadow are facing inward pursuing the dragons."

"For now," Alex whispered, rubbing his forehead. "But that could change in a microsecond."

Or less, he thought as a sound like a thousand rusty car doors creaking open came from the cliff face.

"What?" A confused Alex said.

The hobbling Gwen didn't even turn but kept approaching. Then there was a glint of something shiny.

Bartholomew tilted his head to the side. "Cederic?"

But the shining knight behind Gwen was no skinny teenager. This guy's broad shoulders and powerful gait said, *ready to kick butt*. When he reached Gwen's side, he raised his sword in the air and cried in a strong voice, "For the Goldens and glory!"

The Swineys turned.

An army of steel clad knights emerged from the cavern; maces, shields, and swords held high. "For Goldens and glory!"

"It's a trap! To arms!" Captain Sludge roared.

For a moment, all was silence, as if time had stopped. Hundreds of eyes glared at each other, unblinking.

In the next, there was a horrible bellow followed by pounding feet loping across the valley. Then came the crash and clang of metal as swords met axes and pikes met chain mail.

"What the?" Alex said.

"It's the frozen knights!" Bartholomew cried.

Sure enough, all those knight-pops had thawed out and were now emerging from the cavern. Halberds waving, some wielding war hammers, but most swinging long swords, these armored men slashed at the oncoming army.

The shining knight who'd led the cry jogged to meet a snarling Swiney. Stronger than any Mudlark, he leaned back on one leg and aimed his sword. In a single thrust the monster disintegrated to ash.

Alex was about to give a triumphant whoop when a loud screech pierced the air. He looked up to see Lucretia, the Minotaur in her talons. Her red eyes narrowed as she sloped ever closer. Then, swooping down toward the knights, a long orange blaze flared off her tongue.

As she blew, hot flames licked at armor, shooting sparks that sizzled in the marshy grass. One knight with a dragon rampant shield stumbled backward, steam rising off his helmet.

The second time she dove, the knight raised his shield. But it wasn't necessary. On this pass, she flew past him and dropped the Minotaur.

Just feet from Gwen.

Upon landing, the bull-headed creature bore down on Gwen and growled. "You!" he cried stretching a burly arm toward her.

That reckless redhead aimed a kick, but her bad leg threw her off balance and she stumbled back against a boulder.

"Gwen!" Alex cried springing from his hiding place.

"Alex, no," Bartholomew rasped behind him.

But the boy ignored his friend and dashed forward. He didn't care that Sludge stood in his path but bolted straight for the open-jawed captain, veering right at the last second. Slimy arms swiped, too late.

Eyes on the panting Gwen, Alex sloshed through mounds of chickweed. Ran past a fist-shaking Swiney and over tufts of grass. He was just yards from Minotaur when his feet hit moss.

And it was slippery. Too slippery.

Teetering, Alex thrust out his arms. Still he slid, skating sideways over the slick grass. Directly toward the bull-headed creature. He lurched left, hoping to escape collision, but tumbled over instead.

Right between the monster's legs.

"Huh?" Minotaur grunted looking down at the boy under him.

This was oddly familiar. But this time he wasn't being chased by a gaggle of girls, diving toward a chubby mall cop. This time he had landed under an ugly beast with legs as thick as trees.

Alex started to wriggle away but the monster clamped both legs. Trapping him in a vice-like grip. Squirming, he punched and pounded on the creature's cloven feet, but Minotaur just laughed before slapping the back of his head.

"Leave him alone!" Gwen cried limping forward.

"Gwen no–" Alex said, too late.

Reaching out huge arms, Minotaur shoved. Gwen fell back. And a second later, she struck her head on the boulder with a horrible crack.

Gwen crumpled into a motionless heap.

"You jerk!" Alex screeched flailing his arms about wildly. Hot blood pumped through his veins as he tried elbowing knees, grabbing the bull-man's fur, and head butting its calves.

Never loosening his crushing grip, Minotaur bent over. Alex started to open his mouth to bite a leg as the monster drew its arm back. A dark shadow fell across his face.

He blinked. The slap snapped his head back like a tree in a hurricane. Alex's body suddenly went numb and limp.

He lay there blinking at the snarling enemy. Opening and closing his mouth in silent protest.

Why couldn't he move?

Chapter 69

Bartholomew was bending down to mold some of the mud into some sort of weapon when he saw his friend's head recoil. Bartholomew was afraid that Minotaur had used enough force to snap Alex's neck. And now that his friend lay there unmoving, he was sure of it.

Bartholomew stood to run towards them. Even took a deep breath and lifted a leg. But then he noticed his mud-caked hands and Mother's words came back to haunt him. *You can't.*

All around knights were thrusting swords and whirling cudgels against the approaching Swineys. And some were doing a pretty good job of it. He tried to tell himself that they'd be better off without him. He'd just make things worse.

As if that were possible.

He lowered his arms ready to duck back down. But then he glanced over at Alex. His friend was as still as stone. Pale face, mouth opening and closing in desperate gasps.

As bile rose in his throat, Bartholomew remembered Alex helping him time and again. Making him laugh at his ridiculousness. Like when he said, *"Don't get your tighty whities all in a twist, B-3."*

Bartholomew wriggled inside his stained slacks. Come to think of it they were a little twisted. With a wry grin he adjusted his fly, curled his empty hand into a fist. "I *can*. I am a Borax. Like my father before me and his father before him. And we Boraxes create *true* art."

Turning his focus inward, Bartholomew envisioned a powerful club like the battling knights carried. Next, he scooped up a handful of mud and began pressing, twisting, and pulling. As the Creation Magic accelerated time and everything around him blurred, he molded his weapon into shape. Finally, he added texture by brushing his fingers lightly over the surface.

The sound of metal meeting metal tolled discordant in his ears. Biting his lower lip Bartholomew fought the urge to reach in his pocket for hand sanitizer. With a deep breath, he raised his bludgeon and rushed forward. "I'm coming Alex!"

Everywhere knights clashed with Shadow Swine, sparring in pairs and trios. Mud flew up beneath their scuffling jackboots and over armored shoes. The smell of hot sweat and fear filled the air.

Planning a path that avoided the warring troops, Bartholomew tried to make his way toward Alex. He turned left and almost collided with a huge Swiney who swiped at him with a battle axe. He sidestepped this attack only to find slimy arms reaching for him.

The monsters seemed to be everywhere.

Then he came face to face with a red-eyed stallion, its matted fur and twisted face mocking everything that was right and good.

Bartholomew immediately recognized this creature for what it was; a Shadow Swine slave. At one time, this steed had been a wondrous painting, galloping over the plains. Until a beast called Mudlark Maker got a hold of it. Then, as Bartholomew had seen before, this monster altered it forever. Two years ago, he'd watched Mudlark Maker swallow and regurgitate Ramses's pet cat, turning the sweet feline into a mindless zombie that did its master's bidding.

The misshapen horse rose on hind legs and pawed at the air. Bartholomew ducked just as the hoof passed his left ear. He darted to the right and then glanced around, confused. Where was the cliff face?

"Dust bunnies!" he groaned realizing he was going the wrong way. Twisting on his heels, Bartholomew veered left, vaulting over a fallen Shadow Swine.

Harsh shouts climbed as the dark creatures kicked booted feet at him. Breath in ever shorter gasps, the boy wove in and out of the fray, dodging a sword's blade here, clamoring past a long pike there. Long beads of sweat rolled down either side of his face as he skidded and slid through swerving monsters.

When a wall of three Swineys approached, Bartholomew swung his club. Missed. Swung again, cracking two skulls. The third Shadow Swine blinked unbelieving, before jabbing with his dagger. It sliced Bartholomew's t-shirt leaving a long scratch in his side.

Gaping at the thread of blood, Bartholomew barely had time to dive at the monster before it swiped again. Twisting around, he heard a screech overhead, felt his heels burning. He turned to see hot flames licking at his feet.

The Swiney used this moment to thrust, piercing Bartholomew's arm. The boy cried out and parried with a hammer blow. The creature teetered but didn't fall.

Now with it dazed, Bartholomew sprinted toward the cliffs. More flames grazed his back and his head suddenly felt very hot. He patted at what he feared was blazing hair. Some cinders singed the nape of his neck but the rest of him was unscathed. Zigzagging to avoid Lucretia's hot blasts, he quickened his pace.

Bartholomew was just twenty feet from Alex when two dark figures slid down the hillside landing directly in his path.

He halted.

The outlaw they'd escaped at Mount Minotaur sneered making that horrible scar on his face twist like a macabre rope. "You!" he spat.

The thin bowman behind him fletched an arrow. Grinning as cruelly as Con when he threatened to pulverize Bartholomew, the man raised his longbow and aimed it at the boy's chest.

Bartholomew lifted his bludgeon like a shield, but another string of fire sent him reeling back. Although he stumbled over sparks, the bowman kept his arrow trained on him.

Swallowing hard, Bartholomew scanned the scene. Lucretia crowed from overhead shooting more flames at the knights. Gwen lay in a crumpled heap while Alex hung motionless in Minotaur's grasp, burly hands wrapped around his throat.

His best friend implored with fading eyes.

Bartholomew gaped. Everywhere he turned there was disaster. If he rushed forward an arrow would pierce his chest. Backwards meant a wall of flame. Sideways wouldn't work. Swineys were approaching his flanks.

Was there no one to help him?

Just then he saw a golden flash from the cavern opening behind Gwen. The baby dragon poked her nose out and looked around with large sad eyes.

"No!" Bartholomew cried rushing forward.

Bartholomew thought he'd been stung by a bee at first. But then glanced down and saw the arrow sticking out of his chest. He dropped to his knees. Everything swirled around him in a foggy daze.

His breath slowed as a dark curtain fell across his eyes.

Chapter 70

Captain Sludge rubbed his hands together, grinning at the surrounding scene. He flicked a forked tongue past serrated teeth. The air tasted of death and suffering. "Delicious," he said.

He had those idiot humans now. One paralyzed. Another fallen, a beautiful arrow in his chest. And that stupid red-head unconscious, perhaps never to waken.

Meanwhile his army was winning.

"Soon all of Gothia will be mine. Mine!" Sludge chuckled as he watched his minions drop knight after knight.

A few yards away Stench and one of them had faced off, exchanging battle axe and broadsword blows. They thrust and parried but neither one seemed able to gain to upper hand.

Sludge scratched his slimy face with claw-tipped fingernails, thinking. Then, smirking, he strolled over to a dueling pair. Raising a cocky eyebrow, he got behind the knight.

This is too easy, he thought. *Like that glorious time when Kandart smeared water and ash over the first cave painting, birthing our race.*

Exchanging a secret glance with Private Stench, he raised one finger. Stench bent his knees and choked up on the axe handle. Two. The private leaned back. Hoisted the axe over his right shoulder.

At three, he unleashed a tremendous kick, hurling the knight forward. Stench pushed off the ball of his back foot and twisted his hips. Swung.

And the knight was on the ground, as quiet as death.

"That good, sir," Stench said, bowing his head.

Sludge grunted. "You should have dropped him sooner. Have I taught you nothing?"

"Sorry, sir."

"Let's finish this. It's time I was in Swallow Hole Swamp bathing with a Mud Princess."

He turned. And the pair made their way toward Bartholomew.

Chapter 71

Kneeling, Bartholomew looked down at the wooden arrow protruding from his chest, confused. The three feathers at the end were stiff and tattered. He tried to think, but everything was so foggy. *How did that get there?* He wondered as he ran a hand down the shaft.

His hand recoiled as painful shock waves surged throughout his torso. He began to pant, and stars swam in front of his eyes. Bartholomew swayed, nearly teetering over.

Then Sludge approached with another Swiney. Grinning.

Bartholomew's eyes darted back and forth, seeking escape. The Shadow Swine kept advancing. The mountain loomed behind him while Roger La Savage and the bowman blocked his right. He was surrounded. Even if had any strength, there was nowhere to run.

It's over. We've lost.

A single tear pooled in the corner of his eye. Rolled down his cheek. Memories of Alex and Gwen swam with the stars. A teasing Gwen challenging him to arm wrestle. Alex sculpting proud animals out of mud with him.

All those memories will soon be gone. He thought and before sending a silent prayer safeguarding Alex and Gwen.

A wracking sob escaped his throat. The arrow dipped, it's sharp blade cutting deeper into his chest. Pain rippled throughout his body. He grew faint.

The fog thickened. His lids began to close. He dropped his head to let the blackness take him.

He was barely conscious when words from a for-gotten place inside came to mind. Then, as if some-one were whispering in his ear, he heard a voice. Opened his eyes and blinked.

You can create whatever you want. He recalled the goddess Isis saying. *Imagine strength and you are muscled.*

Sludge drew closer, his upheld dagger glinting in the afternoon sun.

Imagine strength. *I am strong.*

Two more steps.

I can heal myself.

Slowly he lifted his head. Gazed at the surrounding scene. His backpack lay on the ground near La Sav-age and his bowman. The rolled-up sketches bulged under the fabric.

The paintings. Both had been so powerful. Dual art that had guided them throughout this long journey.

The one they'd created at home had survived a swimming pool, Dread Woods, and Mount Minotaur while the map morphed with every new step.

"Get up," he muttered, "before Sludge stops you."

Bartholomew stood on shaky legs and backed away from the approaching captain of the Shadow Swine. Clenching his jaw, he met Sludge's gaze with a look of steel.

Never wavering, Bartholomew reached up and yanked the arrow from his chest. Flesh ripped, and blood trickled from his chest. Sludge's jaw dropped open and he halted.

Quietly, the wooden shaft fell to the ground. Bartholomew looked at the gaping wound under his collarbone. But for some reason, he wasn't horrified, or afraid.

He had the Creation Magic.

See it healed. Believe.

He breathed in. *You are a Deliverer, a creator of wonder.* He imagined arteries and veins knitting together. He exhaled, and the wound closed.

Now he knew what he must do.

Chapter 72

Helpless to act under the Minotaur's choking hands, Alex watched the scene of the arrow piercing Bartholomew's chest in horror. *B-3!* He thought, bitter bile rising in his throat. Choking, he tried to spit, but couldn't get it out.

His body wouldn't move.

Am I dead?

But dead boys don't feel a monster's hands on their throat, do they?

He tried to think. What happened? He recalled the slap and then what? Frozen.

Unlike B-3, Alex wasn't a real book type. But he'd skated long enough to know that if you can't move after a fall, your neck might be broken. He knew one skater who was grinding rails and swerved to avoid a cat that ran in front of him. The dude'd flown, landing on his head. Ended up in a wheelchair.

It looked like he was headed for a similar fate.

"Take my prize, Human. I show you!" The Minotaur squeezed tighter.

Alex's face turned red, then purple. He gasped for air but there was none. His windpipe was cut off with no rescue in sight, his own paralysis rendering him helpless.

Gwen lay crumpled by the cavern, B-3 kneeled nearby with a fatal wound. Outlaws stood poised with bows raised on one side while looming Shadow Swine approached from the other. The knights were far across the valley clashing that slimy horde. While they fought bravely, they were no match for the Shadow Swine's army.

Hot tears rimmed his eyes.

Then he thought he saw the slightest movement from Bartholomew. His friend raised his head. Glanced around. Then, was he mistaken or was Mr. Clean getting up? Alex blinked.

B-3 was okay! But then he reached to remove the arrow.

No! Alex thought, straining to shout. But his mouth was as frozen as the rest of him. Nothing came out.

Don't do it! The steel end is stanching the wound. You'll bleed out dummy!

But when the arrow dropped to the ground, B-3 did not look weaker. Instead he seemed to be gaining strength. Was Alex dreaming or had Mr. Clean grown Mr. Obranovich-sized muscles in a few seconds?

Hunching his back, Bartholomew stood and raised his club raised overhead. In a single swipe, he dropped both La Savage and the skinny bowman. Then he turned and shoved Captain Sludge out of the way before dashing toward the Minotaur.

"Get away from my friend, you filthy fur guy."

Filthy fur guy? That's the best he can do? Alex thought with a tiny chuckle.

The growling Minotaur obviously didn't think it was funny. Its eyes turned red as it squeezed Alex's throat even more. Claws dug into skin as it stomped its cloven feet.

Then Alex heard the crack of his trachea crumbling.

He opened and closed his mouth, but no air passed into his lungs. He suddenly felt so tired. Rest would be so wonderful right now. Alex could almost hear a distant lullaby as he closed his eyes.

"No, Alex! Remember. We can create any state just by seeing it. Imagine air and our lungs are full. Imagine life and it courses through our veins."

Bartholomew's words didn't register at first. The shade of sleep was too overwhelming.

"Alex, breathe!" B-3 raised his club and swung.

Alex felt a jolt and the Minotaur's huge hands loosened ever slightly around his throat. With Bartholomew's words in his ears, the healing magic passed over him in a delicious wave. He imagined sweet air filling his lungs and bones knitting together cell by cell. As he visualized every torn and broken part cured, his body tingled like thousands of little feathers tickling his skin.

He wiggled a finger.

More feeling returned to his body. Now he could bend his legs and arms. He felt his heart pumping blood, filling every vein and capillary with nutrient rich life. Even though the Minotaur was still squeezing his throat, Alex had no trouble breathing.

"True art, Alex. That's what we made. That's what we need now," Bartholomew said.

They'd made true art? Alex tried to recall something that felt true recently. But for the life of him he couldn't think of a single thing. Catapults, mirrors, and maps were cool but not exactly heartfelt. Nothing like a painting of Mom or a papyrus scroll to rescue pharaohs.

Ever since they'd landed in Artania it had been just action-reaction. Nothing from deep inside.

Alex closed his eyes and looked inward. Seeking the true art B-3 had mentioned. When he finally saw it, he almost laughed.

In that moment there was a lurch and the huge hands relaxed. Alex didn't waste any time but wriggled out from between the Minotaur's furry legs. While Bartholomew kept it occupied, he crab-crawled away.

Bartholomew didn't give Minotaur time to comprehend what was happening before swinging again. The bull-headed beast again stumbled back. Then, as soon as Alex was on all fours behind it, B-3 whacked the creature in the chest. It tumbled over Alex's back landing with a crash and Minotaur rose no more.

Chapter 73

"Are you all right?" Bartholomew asked holding out a hand to help Alex to his feet.

"Yeah." Alex rubbed his neck and glanced at the cave entrance where Gwen was just beginning to stir beneath licks from the baby dragon.

Bartholomew sighed. "I know, I feel terrible too."

"I didn't know how to be there for her. If I'd just figured it out sooner–"

"–we might not have gone through all of this? You know as well as I do, that our destinies were laid out a long time ago. Before we were even born."

"That's why I'm so ticked at myself," Alex said shaking his head. "The true art was right in front of me all along. And it was so obvious."

"The true art is all of us,"

"There for each other, I know," Alex said, bending down to scoop some soil into a pile. He didn't need to say anything else. Bartholomew knew exactly what they were about to make.

The Creation Magic would do everything else.

Bartholomew dug his club into the ground tossing up soil for Alex to pile into two mounds, a large one which topped both of their heads, and a smaller girl-sized lump of clay. Then they began shaping the earth while mirror images flashed in their minds. As their sculptures grew, the boys worked as one; molding, forming, and hewing.

And in a dragon's breath both were complete. But did not move.

Bartholomew stood next to the sculptures, confused. Usually their creations came to life the instant they were complete. He tried running a hand over the larger one, but nothing happened. He looked at Alex and shrugged.

A few yards away, Gwen stroked the baby's scales as a roaring Captain Sludge loped toward her, dagger raised. Bartholomew was about to race her aid, when the sound of beating wings stopped him.

Erantha and Wade hovered overhead, Princess Rhea and Squire Cederic replacing the stick boys atop their scaly necks. The Earth dragon lifted her snout and unleashed a keening wail. The captain halted and took several steps backwards, seemingly unsure of what to do.

Alex gave them a thumbs-up before glancing back at the huge statues. "Why aren't they moving?" he asked.

Then Rhea hurled something at them. "Try that," she called down as *Sightgiver* landed at their feet.

Bartholomew plucked the jeweled dagger out of the soil and turned back toward the sculptures as the vain Lucretia soared from over the mountain. He gripped the dagger handle tightly, unable to peel his eyes away.

"Noo!" the dragoness shrieked. She reared her orange head and butted Erantha before turning on Wade.

Wings fluttering, the water dragon's blue eyes widened. Lucretia screeched as a fiery ribbon twined toward Wade. Bartholomew cringed, sure that Cederic and the gentle dragon would soon be burnt to the bone. The flare was mere inches from his new friends when Flynn spat a wide flame to block it.

"Yes!" Alex cried with a fist pump before making his way over to Gwen.

Hoping all of this worked before the Shadow Swine could make their way across the plains, Bartholomew touched the dagger to the smaller sculpture. The topaz eye in the center began to glow, shedding gentle light over the form.

The sculptures began to move.

Lucretia jet above Wade, opened her great talons, and dug them into his blue neck right in front of Squire Cederic. Wings tucked in, Wade whipped his tail and began to falter. Crying out, Cederic pulled *Hornet* from it sheath and jabbed at Lucretia's clawed feet. Each strike bounced off her scaled skin.

"Brother!" Erantha jet from the clouds, her powerful legs outstretched. At the moment she kicked, Flynn blew another angry stream that singed the

407

bratty dragon's long eyelashes. Releasing Wade, Lucretia yelped and retreated over the cliffs.

Captain Sludge shook an angry fist, resuming his advance on Gwen.

"Stay back!" Flynn bellowed blowing a wall of flame in front of the Swiney. The captain turned right and left and then halted.

Propped under his arm, Alex guided the limping Gwen to the dual sculptures in front of Bartholomew.

"Hey, is that–?" Gwen began.

"You riding a dragon? Of course," Bartholomew replied before turning to the recently formed girl and her steed.

He brushed the blade over both sculptures. The newly-hewn dragon and girl quivered until every grain of sand and leaf transformed to rippling life.

Now there were two Gwens, one of clay and one of flesh.

"The change is nearly here," the clay girl said from atop her huge mount. The statue lifted her face to the sun and the dragon followed suit, slowly raising its snout to the sky. Both began to shimmer like glitter suspended in water. Within moments they went from crumbling clay to shining gold and silver.

The real Gwen shuffled over to her sculpted twin. "This is me? This is how I look? So strong?" she asked pointing at the newly formed sculpture's face.

"And more. Hello," Alex said as Bartholomew nodded from his side.

Her shining twin smiled and beckoned her to climb up. "You are the true art. You symbolize all that is strong. Show your true face and be known to all."

Nose twitching in that funny rabbit way, Gwen hung back, arms crossed.

"What are you waiting for? Go on," Alex said to the usually bold skater girl.

"Yeah Gwen. It was made for you," Bartholomew said, but didn't add that her friendship had inspired it. She hated gushing language as much as Alex and would probably punch him in the arm if he started in.

Squaring her shoulders, Gwen grabbed a hold of the long neck and swung a leg over to mount the dragon directly behind her doppelganger. Meanwhile the sculpted Gwen started morphing from silver and gold to skin. Soon she was a mirror image of her real counterpart.

Gwen's voice was hushed. "I'm not ugly at all.,"

"Cha! That's what I've been trying to tell you." Alex said.

Gwen shook her head in amazement then gave her counterpart a big hug. The entire valley seemed to grow silent in a single moment. The swords, shields, and battleaxes ceased clanging. The muddy army left off their guttural cries. Rhea's brothers stopped shouting orders to the other knights.

Even the beating of dragons' wings overhead became a hushed breeze.

Then when the silence was as wide as the Plains of Bramear, a single beam formed in the center of Gwen and the sculpture's chests. Another joined it. Then a third. Soon hundreds of silvery rays were spouting into the air.

With one great flap of its enormous wings, the sculpted dragon took to the skies. Gwen whooped as the glimmering beams shot in all directions, growing until the entire valley was aglow.

To Artanians, these lightning bolts were living beauty, but to the Shadow Swine, they meant death. The muddy creatures scattered to escape, hopping, dodging and darting. A spark hit one and he melted into a puddle of mud. Another scurried for a sinkhole, but his feet turned to slush as he ran.

Everywhere silvery rays struck the fleeing creatures. At the same time, the freed knights smote others crumbling them into heaps of dust. Overhead Rhea and Cederic cheered from atop dragon backs while Flynn continued to shoot flames at the remaining Mudlarks and Swineys.

Soon Sludge was left alone in the center of the valley.

"Bahhh! You idiots haven't seen the last of me!" Captain Sludge bellowed, dropping into the nearest sinkhole.

And a great cheer burst from the valley.

Chapter 74

As the dragon beneath her alighted in front of the cavern, Gwen felt a strange warmth grow in her chest. It passed over and through her unlike anything she'd ever known. And in that moment every wound was healed.

"Thank you," she said to her doppelganger as she dismounted.

"You know, you are thanking yourself. Not me," the sculpted one said.

"Huh?" Gwen asked.

"She is you, don't you see?" Bartholomew began.

"She has all your strength, dork," Alex continued.

"Hey, who're you calling a dork?"

"You. You thought acting like Lacey and her crew was somehow better than who you really were. But you already rocked. You didn't need their stupid make-overs."

Fighting back the tears that threatened to overtake her, she said, "But I'm not beautiful like them, or..."

411

"Your mother?" Alex asked.

Unable to speak, Gwen nodded.

"I've always thought you beautiful," Bartholomew said.

"In the true sense. That's why our sculpture of you atop the dragon could defeat the Swineys. It showed your true face, like your friends see it. Strong, capable, talented." Alex paused for a moment and exchanged a meaningful glance with Gwen. "If your Mom doesn't get that, well I'm sorry, it's her loss. Because I think you're amazing."

A single tear rolled down Gwen's cheek. "You do?"

"Hello? Why do you think I was trying to give you that painting, or traveled all over Gothia looking for you?" He shook his head. "Clueless."

"Shut-up," Gwen said. She started slapping him with the back of her hand, but it turned into a hug. She buried her face in his shoulder sobbing.

After long moments, Bartholomew cleared his throat. "Ahem, we have company."

Gwen pulled away. All around were the friends she'd made on this long tiring journey. Princess Rhea was embracing her brothers while Cederic beamed at her side. The three kind dragons were waving their tails while little Goldie looked on confused from Gwen's sculpted twin to her.

Just then the huge sculpted dragon spread her wings and flapped them once. A great wind rustled over the gathered company. As Gwen watched, her doppelganger started to dissolve and meld into the dragon's flesh. In a single spark, she was gone.

In the next moment, the dragon took to the blue skies once more. It circled the Plains of Bramear once, twice, three times. As wispy clouds trailed behind and turned a golden hue, the earth began to shudder. Everyone held out arms or tails for balance.

Gwen felt a sprinkling of dust in her hair before a few unearthed pebbles and rocks began rolling down the cliff face. The mountain groaned, and she looked up.

A single crack appeared above the collapsed cavern. Hair thin at first, it soon widened, branching into forked vines that were big enough for two kids to fit through. A few yards from the mountain top, it suddenly stopped and everything from the clouds down began to pulse.

Gwen held her breath. The sculpted dragon glided down to hover in front of the open fissure and began humming a melody so sweet that even butterflies were suspended mid-air. The mountain answered in its own seraphic chorus.

A moment later, thousands of round golden eyes appeared.

"My famiwy!" Goldie cried unfurling her little wings. In an awkward launch she fluttered over to meet the curious faces now peeking from the fissure.

One, about half as tall as her, tottered out, blinking.

"Hi!" Goldie said, rubbing noses with him.

He wagged his tail and unleashed a lilting purr. The others stumbled out until, soon, scores of hatchlings emerged. Then they all lifted their voices in song and began to flutter their wings. Like a choir of angels, they took to flight.

Gwen shook her head in amazement as the skies turned from blue to gold.

Chapter 75

Lost in thought, Alex emerged from the wooden tub and grabbed the linen towel draped over the bench. He heaved a long sigh. He'd been so busy since splashing into Lambent Lake with everything from meeting the dragons to seeing crazy King Gerald, this was the first time he'd slowed down enough to reflect. Between battles with a Minotaur and his own freaky hallucinations in Dread Woods, he'd barely thought of home.

Home. Painting with Rembrandt's furry face in his lap. Mom recovering, even running again. Dad quoting Dr. Bock's parenting books all the time. It was annoying, but Dad took it so seriously Alex had to chuckle like the last time Dad had driven Jose, Zach, and Gwen to the skate park....

Smiling, Alex rubbed his damp hair, and slipped into the hose, tunic, and jacket the stewards had laid out for him. The short-pleated skirt that came next seemed girly and he was considering whether it'd be okay to skip it when Bartholomew rushed in.

"You ready yet? It's started!" B-3 asked waving the blue cape that went past his knees at the door. His outfit matched Alex's but the silk shoes and fur-trimmed cloak he'd pinned with a broach made it look more like something out of a King Arthur cartoon.

Alex snapped him in the butt with the towel and grinned. "Well if somebody hadn't used up all the hot water, I would be. How long were you in the bath anyhow? Two hours? Three?"

"Forty minutes, tops." Bartholomew dipped his fingers in the pewter bowl of rosewater on the bench and flicked some at Alex. "Come on. Let's go!"

Wiping the sweet-smelling droplets from his face, Alex chuckled. After looking at Bartholomew, he finally decided that if his bud could wear a skirt and not look too wussy, he was safe. He slipped into the pleated skirt and the two of them made their way down the stone stair in the octagonal tower toward the inner baily.

Castle Alnwick was quite a different place than when he and Bartholomew first arrived. All the cobwebs had been swept away and long tapered candles in iron sconces lit every dark passageway. The old moldy rushes that had carpeted the bottom floor were gone, replaced with freshly cut herbs and reeds. Festoons of primrose, violet, and lavender draped the halls, their sweet smell filling the formerly dank air.

"Ready?" Alex asked Bartholomew who gave an excited nod.

When they stepped into the sunlight, a great cry rose from the gathered crowd. In a courtyard full of pavilions, trumpeting banners, and ladies with tall wimples atop their heads, people clapped and cheered.

Princess Rhea who was standing next to her father on his throne, waved at them from the dais near the wall at the opposite end of the inner baily. Her brothers, who flanked her on both sides, raised their shining swords before sitting on their thrones.

Alex looked over at B-3 whose mouth was hanging open so wide he could have caught a ball from one of the jugglers in it. "Trying to catch flies?" he teased pointing at Bartholomew's gaping mouth.

His friend clamped it shut while Alex distracted everyone with a three-fingered hello.

"Thanks," Bartholomew said under his breath before marching forward to greet the guests.

"There you are!" Gwen cried rushing up to them, baby Goldie on her heels. "What took you so long?"

"With a bathtub available, you seriously have to ask?" Alex asked.

"Mr. Clean, living up to his name. Got it."

That was when Alex noticed Gwen's clothing. Instead of a long gown with hair in a coned wimple like most of the ladies surrounding them, she wore new tights and a knee length tunic that had a rampant lion on the chest.

"You're still dressed like a boy," he pointed out.

"Cha! I want to have some fun here, not worry about tripping over a stupid dress. You think I want to look like those giggling populos over there?" Gwen jerked a thumb at a couple of teen girls who were lifting their skirts just to walk.

Alex considered. "Back home you did."

"And where did that get me?" Gwen asked stroking Goldie's shimmering scales.

"Here," Bartholomew swept an arm toward the fete. "In Artania."

The three of them glanced around at their sculpted and painted friends. Everywhere acrobats, jugglers, and fire-eaters entertained the crowd. Stalls with dancing bears and monkeys competed with burly wrestlers while armored swordsmen demonstrated their skills in roped off areas.

"Come on. It's a party, and it may be another year before I can attend one." Bartholomew heaved a great sigh. "With Mother..." he trailed off and there was an uncomfortable silence.

Alex opened and closed his mouth trying to think of something to say. But B-3 was right; it might be another year before Hygenette let him out of that antiseptic prison. He shrugged.

Bartholomew cast a wistful glance at the smiling and laughing revelers before stamping one foot. "And I plan on enjoying it." Turning on his heel, he marched over to a sword-swallower booth, leaving Gwen and Alex alone.

The two stood awkwardly facing one another. Trying to think of something to say, Alex adjusted the sword in its sheath while Gwen started to draw circles in the grass with one toe.

"So," he began. He pursed his lips into a forced smile.

"Yeah," she said. "You know, about home. I didn't mean... but it was like, you just kept. And everybody."

"Hmm?"

Nose twitching, Gwen clamped her mouth shut and stared at him, blinking.

More long silences. Great. Alex thought before crying out in exasperation. "What?"

"Why are you so friggin' stupid?" she finally blurted out.

"I don't know," Alex confessed, shrugging his shoulders. "I guess I never had a crush before.

"Yeah, a total idiot...Did you just say, crush?" Gwen stepped back.

"Gwendolyn Obranovich, if you can't tell that I like you, then you are the one who's stupid. Now come on. Bartholomew's right. We're at a castle in a painted world with magical creatures everywhere. Do you think we could have a little fun? Or would you rather just keep yelling at me?"

Gwen opened her mouth as if to retort but then, seeming to think better of it, punched Alex in the arm and scampered off toward the dancing bear.

With a tail wagging Goldie trailing behind, the three of them spent the next few hours wandering through the festival. Gwen came in second in an archery contest while Alex faced off with

419

Princess Rhea in a joust and lost. Man, that princess could wield a sword! Bartholomew used the Creation Magic to forge a new set of armor for Squire Cederic while Alex created a lighter set for the ancient Sir Donald.

"My armor shines just like when I was young knight," Sir Donald beamed raising his sword with a shaky hand.

"And I am ready for the joust in this." Cederic turned right and left admiring his reflection in front of a cobbler's booth.

Next, they spent some time with Erantha and Flynn who were taking their parenting of the baby Goldens very seriously.

"It's okay, little one," the green Erantha crooned at a sobbing hatchling that had just knocked over a pavilion in flight. "They can put that tent right back up. In fact, they already have." She wiped away its tears with her tail and caressed its cheek.

"No, you have to get a bigger breath. Like this," Flynn instructed, puffing up his ruby red chest and blowing a long flame overhead.

The circle of goldens surrounding him mimicked his fire-breathing the best they could but only two were able to produce anything but sparks.

"Where is Wade?" Bartholomew asked Rhea who was strolling up after yet another victorious sword fight.

"In the moat, teaching the babies to swim. He is a water dragon, after all," Rhea said.

Just then there was a blaring of trumpets and the heralds cried, "King Gerald requires the Deliverers! Make way! Make way!"

The murmuring crowd quieted and stared at Alex and his friends.

"Go on, Father is waiting," Rhea said as their dragon friends and the throngs of painted people parted. She reached for Bartholomew's arm and he escorted her toward the opposite end of the inner baily where the king, Prince Ulmer, and Prince Kelvin sat in high-backed chairs.

Alex held out an arm for Gwen and the two fell in line with Goldie lopping behind. When they reached the dais, they followed Rhea up the steps toward their assigned seats to the right of King Gerald while the baby dragon settled at their feet.

This was quite a different king than the one they'd met a few days before. In place of a tarnished coronet topping ratty gray hair, was a gleaming crown over a silky mane. No hunching over to cough phlegm into a napkin now. Instead, Gerald sat erect, scepter in one hand, velvet and fur mantle draped around his muscular shoulders.

"Welcome, young Alex. Greetings, Deliverer Bartholomew. Salutations, human Gwen," he said in a deep rich voice.

Alex and his friends greeted the king in turn and took their seats. Alex was about to start making polite conversation when a hush fell over the crowd.

He looked up and saw the Thinker's bronze form approaching. As always, he was stooped as if the weight of the world rested on his shoulders. He hobbled over the grassy courtyard, while every Gothian bowed reverently. When he reached the dais, he shuffled up the short stair and stepped behind King Gerald.

"It warms my heart to see you healed, dear friend," the Thinker whispered to the king squeezing his shoulders. Then he turned to the silent crowd. "Artanians, once again, that which was foretold has come to pass and our land is safe."

"The Soothsayer Stone," the crowd chanted in unison.

Gwen squeezed Alex's hand under the chair and butterflies as big as dragons fluttered in his chest.

The bronze leader continued in a gravelly voice. "But do not forget the prophecy.

Our world was born from the magic of two.
The smiling twins whose creations grew.
They painted walls with ideas anew.
Until the dark day we came to rue.
When one jealous hand used mud to undo.
And the life of many too soon was through."

"Perhaps, but once again we defeated those Swineys!" Prince Ulmer called out as the crowd cheered.

But listen to this prophecy with open ears.
To know what happens every 1,000 years.

422

The Shadow Swine will make you live in fear.
Bringing death to those whom you hold so dear."

Alex remembered the villagers running from burning buildings, the orphaned girls looking to Innkeeper Thomas for safety, and knights falling beneath Swiney battle axes. The sculpted man placed his steely hands on Alex and Bartholomew's shoulders.

"But hope will lie in the hands of twins
Born near the cusp of the second millennium."
On the eleventh year of their lives.
They will join together like single forged knives.
Their battle will be long with 7 evils to undo.
Scattered around will be 7 clues.
And many will perish before they are through.
But our world will be saved if their art is true."

"Their art was true!" Princess Rhea cried with a fist pump.

"Cha!" Gwen agreed giving Alex another electric hand squeeze.

Alex sat up straight. Having been through this twice, he had a pretty good idea about what was coming next. He elbowed Bartholomew on his other side.

But this time The Thinker did not call up friends to bestow presents upon them. Instead he whispered something to King Gerald and Rhea who nodded.

The king rose slowly from his seat and pulled a gleaming sword from its sheath. At the same time,

Princess Rhea lifted *Sightgiver* overhead. She waved the dagger to and fro as the yellow jewel in the center cast prismatic lights.

"Bartholomew Borax III, kneel," King Gerald commanded. When B-3 did so, the king tapped each shoulder in turn with the flat of his blade. "For creating a map, mirror, and dung-filled catapult; Artania thanks you. Your art was true and in the name of Gothia I do so knight thee. Rise, Sir Bartholomew and remain our honored and revered guardian for all time."

B-3 stood, his voice choked with emotion. "It's an honor, your majesty."

"Now, Alexander Devinci." As Alex knelt, the king repeated the sword taps. "Your sculpture returned the Goldens to the skies, healing all of Gothia. Healing me. In the name of true art, I knight thee. Rise, Sir Alexander and keep us safe with your creations forever more."

"Thank you, sire. I'll try my best," Alex said, shivering with pride.

Rhea waved *Sightgiver* overhead again and the topaz jewel on the handle pulsed. Soon, smog like dragon's breath began emanating from its center; pouring out until the entire congregation was so foggy Alex could barely see Prince Ulmer at the other end of the dais. Then the mist rose like a theater curtain blanketing the skies.

Princess Rhea thrust the dagger upwards as if to pierce the air and a gray shape emerged from between two cotton clouds.

424

As Rhea slowly lowered *Sightgiver,* the sculpted dragon Alex and Bartholomew had created descended. With a pulsing of great wings, it landed in front of the platform and bowed its head.

"Gwen," Rhea said as all the clouds disappeared. "During our quest, it was your strength that kept us going. From the moment you pulled me from the Blank Canvas abyss, I knew you to be true. Later, at great risk to yourself, you kept me safe from outlaws and Lucretia's flames. You acted as a knight in training should, courageously. Yet, you seemed blind to this gift." She stopped and looked to the Thinker.

"Your friends have always known your strength. And this, in turn, inspired their true art." The Thinker pointed a steely arm at the sculpted dragon.

"*Sightgiver* knew you and now know yourself," Rhea said as the Thinker placed a hand over hers. The two of them tilted the dagger toward Gwen while sun rays began to play off the blade.

Gwen shimmered in the reflected light as something like a film was projected onto her body. One moment it transformed her into the disguised page that had accompanied Rhea and Cederic and the next into the strong girl Alex and Bartholomew had painted back in Santa Barbara. From skinny sixth grader to board-shorted skater, the movie flickered, showing all the ways Alex had known her over the years. Then in a kaleidoscopic flash she was wearing the same outfit she'd had on at Lacey's party.

Gwen looked down at the white shirt that still had the mean writing on the back and made a face.

"Although others may try to convince you otherwise, you have a unique beauty which cannot be denied. Know this as you return and make it your shield and sword against the likes of Lucretia," The Thinker said.

Gwen seemed to consider this for a moment. Then she set her face in a determined expression, thrust her fists into her hips and nodded.

Alex knew that now, brats like Lacey wouldn't stand a chance against her.

"Go home and be what you were destined to be. True artists," The Thinker added.

Erantha, Wade, and Flynn strode up and bowed their great heads. Gwen bent down and whispered something into the baby dragon's ear before hugging her golden neck. When she rose, Alex saw amber tears pooling in Goldie's wide eyes. He swallowed hard and laid a hand on Gwen's shoulder.

Quietly, Alex, Bartholomew and Gwen made their way toward the three dragons. Alex didn't dare speak; long gushy goodbyes were not his thing. He glanced around at Castle Alnwick one more time before swinging a leg over Erantha's scaly neck.

"Ready for the ride of your life?" he asked Gwen who was now astride Flynn.

"You know it!" Gwen said while B-3 mounted the blue Wade.

The three leviathans unfolded their wings and a cry rose from the painted and sculpted people all around. As the dragons took to flight, the rippling breeze of their wings passed through the waving crowd; blowing back gowns, tunics, and cloaks.

"I'll never forget you!" Rhea cried running after them.

Bartholomew gave her a victorious wave. "Good-bye!"

Alex watched the castle below shrink until it was just a dot on the painted landscape. Then he glanced over at his friends. B-3 had a goofy grin straddling Wade's blue neck while Gwen, ever the daredevil, balanced between Flynn's wings as if riding her board in the X-Games.

"A worthy rider!" Flynn roared before unleashing a long flame.

"Match this, Alex. Go on, I dare you!" Gwen cried doing a handstand.

Alex gripped Erantha's spikes and crouched down, placing his front foot on her neck. He turned, and wind rushed past whipping his t-shirt against his back. Eyes narrowed, he leaned back and sprung.

His hands met only air.

Chapter 76

Gwen was in the middle of an epic hand stand when the dragon disappeared, freezing her upside down. She gaped. Everything was gone. The painted skies. The flocks of origami geese. The cotton ball clouds. It was as if time and space were suspended leaving her in a blackness darker than a Shadow Swine's heart.

A cold wasteland of nothing.

She called to Alex, but no sound escaped her mouth. Even her freezing breath was as quiet as goodbye. The silence was deafening.

Enveloped in emptiness, she shivered. Her mind raced to recall her last escape from Artania. Was this normal?

As if a freaky journey from an art-made world could be.

A metallic odor filled her nostrils and electric sparks flashed through the dark blanket. Gwen cringed, afraid of being burned. Cascading flares of red, blue, and green spat overhead. Next, a blinding explosion of fireworks erupted, and she started tumbling through space, arms and legs akimbo.

The sizzling air pulsated with a rhythmic hum Gwen would have tapped her feet to if they weren't plummeting through air. Buzzing, whirring, and vibrating; the multi-colored pulses closed in. Prickles crept over her skin, wrapping her in an electric net that slowed her descent like a spherical parachute.

She reached a tentative hand to test the boundary, and it bounced off as if hitting a static charged balloon. Colors coalesced beneath while the force field grabbed her legs and started pulling her forward.

Smiling, she bent her knees and extended her arms. With her feet going so fast she felt like a surfer chick riding a tsunami.

Vibrant lights flashed in a blur and Gwen looked back to see Bartholomew trying his best to stay upright while Alex held out an arm to steady him.

Everything suddenly stopped, and Gwen let out a long sigh. But then she was sucking water at the bottom of Lacey's swimming pool. Sputtering, she kicked to the surface next to the bobbing Alex and Bartholomew.

Even though she'd been to Artania and back nothing had changed. The kids were still pointing and jeering. But now their words rolled in one ear and out the other as swiftly as skateboard wheels over the vert.

"Dog!" Lacey taunted from the poolside.

Gwen gave her a bored look. "I'm sorry, were you, like, trying to offend me?"

"Because the only thing offensive is your face," Alex added squeezing Gwen's arm.

Pouting her blood red lips, Lacey wagged a French-manicured finger. "You just shut-up,"

"Yes, your village called, and they want you back." Bartholomew said raising his eyebrows three times as if proud of his wisecrack.

"Huh?" Lacey cocked her head.

"Their *idiot* back," Gwen corrected before adding under her breath, "Good try."

"I am not an idiot!" Lacey stomped a foot.

"No, you are wonderful and intelligent," Gwen paused and gave her an innocent look. "Oh, I'm sorry, were we having a lying competition?"

"Stop it, now!" Pivoting on her stiletto, Lacey bumped into her older brother. She staggered back and shot him a dirty look.

"They're right, I've known several asinine people, and you dear sister, happen to be all of them."

"Shut your hole, Wad!" She turned to Jose and started to slip a hand in the crook of his arm. "Come on babe, help me open presents."

"Umm, all good," Jose said stepping back.

Lacey opened and closed her mouth several times reminding Gwen of a muted SpongeBob cartoon. Wailing she shoved both Jose and her brother out of the way.

"Daddy!" Her spiked heel caught between two bricks, snapping it in two. Lacey stumbled back, halfway falling into a lavender bush.

Jose cleared his throat while Coco covered her mouth with one hand. Nobody full on laughed; they were too afraid of Lacey for that. But there were scattered sniggers around the yard when she rose slowly and smoothed the front of her skirt before limping into the house.

Jose exchanged a glance with Zach and called "Chica!" as he leapt into the pool. He gave her an apologetic splash and said, "Gwen, I knew nothing about the writing on your back. That was Lacey through and through."

"Really? Because you've been acting..."

"I know. I was like a man carried down a swollen river. I saw nothing but the rising current of fame." Jose smoothed his long black hair back.

"We're good, but in the future, check your ego at the door, 'kay?" Gwen said.

"You got it, amiga."

"Watch out, here I come!" Zach cried cannon-balling into the pool, dousing everyone in the process.

Giggling, Gwen wiped the water from her face just in time to get a hand-cannon squirt from Alex. Ducking under, she kicked her feet, splashing him back. When she surfaced, all her buds had surrounded her with makeshift squirt guns of interlocked fingers. They simultaneously unleashed jets of water tickling Gwen's face and neck. She threw her head back in laughter as kid after kid jumped into the pool.

A few minutes later when the horseplay died down, Gwen waved Alex and B-3 over to the shallow end. "Whatya say we cruise?" she suggested.

The full moon was just peeking through the clouds lighting up the September night when the three dripping kids hit the palm-tree lined street. Gwen glanced from Alex to Bartholomew and back again. Bartholomew's blonde hair still had two streaks of commando blue while Alex's was a crazy mop with spots of dayglow orange.

"You two look hot. Total Lacey bait," she teased.

"I wouldn't want to attract her, she's—" Bartholomew stuttered.

"Gwen's joking," Alex said, cutting him off.

"Oh, because Lacey is so...so..."

"Repulsive? Disgusting?" Alex gave Gwen a long look as they approached the beach. "You know, we've always seen Lacey's true face. She might be a girl you can't help looking at, but—"

"But for all her glitz, there's an emptiness. And it's as dead as the plastic plants skirting my home." Bartholomew paused and gave her a meaningful look. "She's got nothing on you."

"A strong, pain-in-the-butt girl who inspires true art," Alex added.

"And saves a world."

Gwen blushed. "You guys shut-up." Changing the subject, she pointed. "Hey, look at that swell. Who's up for some body surfing?" She shed her platforms and started running over the sand.

"Cha!" Bartholomew said.

Alex was already kicking his shoes off as he raced behind her.

Gwen arrived first, diving into the surf and gliding under the foamy crest. She swam out a few strokes and then treaded water for a moment, waiting for the next set. The silvery orb's reflection that rippled on the water lit her face in moon shadow.

Water lapping at their feet, Alex and B-3 waved from shore.

"Rip it Gwen!" Alex cried when the ocean surged for another set.

Gwen kicked and paddled catching the wave just as it crested. She felt a backward pull, then a forward thrust. Her best buds gave her a thumbs up. Arms extended, Gwen streamlined her body, arching her back with her head just under the curl.

Now she was riding a moonlit wave to shore.

And she'd never felt so beautiful.

Dear reader,

We hope you enjoyed reading *Artania - Dragon Sky*.
Please take a moment to leave a review, even if it's a
short one. Your opinion is important to us.

Discover more books by Laurie Woodward at
https://www.nextchapter.pub/authors/laurie-
woodward-childrens-fiction-author

Want to know when one of our books is free or
discounted? Join the newsletter at
http://eepurl.com/bqqB3H

Best regards,
Laurie Woodward and the Next Chapter Team

You might also like:

Darrienia by KJ Simmill

To read the first chapter for free, please head to:
https://www.nextchapter.pub/books/darrienia

About the Author

Laurie Woodward is a school teacher and the author of the fantasy books: *The Artania Chronicles*. Her *Artania: The Pharaohs' Cry* is the first children's book in the series. Laurie is also a collaborator on the award-winning Dean and JoJo anti-bullying DVD *Resolutions*. The European published version of Dean and JoJo for which she was the ghost writer was translated by Jochen Lehner who has also translated books for the Dalai Lama and Deepak Chopra, In addition to writing, Ms. Woodward is an award winning peace consultant who helps other educators teach children how to stop bullying, avoid arguments, and maintain healthy friendships. Laurie writes her novels in the coastal towns of California.

Why do I write? I get to be a kid again. And this time the bully loses while the quiet kid wins. Also, I get to have awesome battles with wings and swords, while riding a skateboard.

Why did I write Artania? Several years ago when education changed to stress test score results over everything else, I began to think of art as a living part of children that was being crushed. But I have watched children create and discover the wonder inside. To me, Shadow Swine represent bullies who subdue that most beautiful part of children.

"Our world will be saved when their art is true," the Artanian Prophecy says. Every year I tell my students how every sketch, painting, or sculpture instantaneously becomes a living being in Artania. Then I stand back as they hurriedly scribble a creature, hold it up, and ask, "Was this just born?"

"It sure was," I reply with a smile. "You just made magic."

And for that cool moment, they believe.

Artania Series

- Artania I - The Pharaohs' Cry
- Artania II - The Kidnapped Smile
- Artania II - Dragon Sky

Artania III: Dragon Sky
ISBN: 978-4-86752-498-5 (Mass Market)

Published by
Next Chapter
1-60-20 Minami-Otsuka
170-0005 Toshima-Ku, Tokyo
+818035793528
2nd August 2021